Inside the stockade, right next to the blockhouse, black smoke was pouring from a house. Skoiyasi and Smoke could now hear war cries beginning to emerge from within the fort. Skoiyasi and the other men in the creek bed began firing at the loopholes, and the men behind the portable barricade lobbed fireballs at the base of the blockhouse, and once more fire arrows soared across the clearing to the roof. Skoiyasi's spirit rose as he waited for the signal to rush the blockhouse and put an end to the hated enemy within. Surely they must soon be out of water. Surely the flames would soon drive them from their strong house like fleeing rats. . . .

SILENT DRUMS

MIKE ROARKE

ST. MARTIN'S PAPERBACKS

SILENT DRUMS

ISBN: 0-312-95224-4

Printed in the United States of America

St. Martin's Paperbacks edition / April 1994

10 9 8 7 6 5 4 3 2 1

For Gina, Alan and Rebecca

TWO SEAS MET ON THE SHORES OF LAKE ERIE. One was the blue freshwater sea that frothed white when the northern winds roared. The other, larger sea was green half the year, a forest canopy that undulated in green waves to the rhythm of the winds, for a thousand miles in three directions.

Beneath the surface of the blue liquid sea swam myriad species of fish, some the hunter, some the hunted, most a little bit of both. Beneath the surface of the waving green sea, in long easy strides, walked another species much more deadly. These were men of the Seneca nation, guardians of the Western Door of New York's great Iroquois confederacy. For several days now they had been making their way home, through the lands of the Shawnee, Delaware, Wyandot, and Mississaugi.

The leaders of this group were two Seneca chiefs, Kyashuta and Teantoriance, and they were discouraged. They had journeyed west to visit the Chippewas, Ottawas, and Hurons for the purpose of forming an alliance against the British. Their mission had failed.

Even in the midst of summer, the forest canopy offered some shelter from the heat, if not the steamy humidity. For

Kyashuta, the endless woodlands were shelter from the English and the awful changes that always seemed to arrive with them. Although the Iroquois had been allies of the English as far back as anyone could remember, there was no love lost between them.

"I never again want to see an Englishman," Kyashuta told Teantoriance, "unless it be over my rifle sights or under my tomahawk."

Teantoriance nodded his agreement. "I still do not understand how Warraghiyagey outsmarted us this time," he said. The Ottawa and Chippewa are allies of the French. Why would they refuse to join us in fighting the English?"

They had been successful in presenting the red and black wampum belts requesting war to a number of the western chiefs. They could see in the eyes of these chiefs the war lust to oust the English and bring back the French, whom the English had just defeated in a long war. And yet, when the time came for the great conference in Detroit between Warraghiyagey and the western tribes, he had somehow managed to turn those chiefs against the Senecas.

"You have watched Warraghiyagey," said Kyashuta. "How he takes the arm of a man and leads him into the shadows, and tells him what a fine man he is and what old friends they are and how good the king will treat him if he behaves and how bad it will go if he does not behave well." Teantoriance grunted assent, for he had seen Warraghiyagey work his magic many times.

Warraghiyagey was Sir William Johnson, the Irish adventurer who had come to America to manage an uncle's estates and gone on to win fortune, glory, and a baronetcy from a charmed King George. Johnson had learned the ways of his neighbors the Mohawks, their language and their dances. They in turn had adopted him into the tribe. He had mated with numerous Mohawk women to produce

a virtual tribe of his own. He had taken the part of his
Mohawk brothers in numerous disputes with whites, but
never against the crown, to whom, after himself, he owed
his first allegiance.

And as Superintendant of Indian Affairs, he had proved
adept at keeping the Iroquois peaceful when the crown
most desperately needed them to be peaceful.

"It is as Big Oak Sam once told me," Kyashuta answered.

"Ah, Big Oak Sam, the only real white brother." The two
chiefs were talking about Sam Watley, who, with his half-
Seneca son Thad, represented Wendel and Watley in trade
with the Iroquois, but was best known for his feats in battle, fighting beside the Iroquois against the French. "The
Master of Life has truly touched his brow with wisdom.
What did he say?"

"He once told me that the western tribes will never unite
with us against the white man because we laid too heavy a
hand upon their lives when we conquered them."

They were silent. For many years the Iroquois had been
masters of the red man's world from the Canadas down to
Virginia, and west even beyond Detroit. They drew tribute
from the tribes of the south and a middleman's cut from
every fur that came east down the Mohawk River. The
tribes of the west and south bitterly resented the mighty
Ganonsyoni, as the Iroquois called themselves.

"Is it possible," Kyashuta said, "that the western tribes
hate us so, they would bow down to the English even
while the English steal their land?"

"My brother," Teantoriance replied, "did not the Ganonsyoni do the same in the last war with the French?"

Kyashuta did not answer. He knew that Teantoriance
was right. The white men were a disease that the Indians
could not resist. They *had* to have the white man's guns to
hunt the deer. They *had* to have the white man's iron
tomahawks with which to slay their enemy, and the white

man's knives, with which to scalp their enemy. They needed the white man's woven blankets for warmth on a cold night in the woods. They needed the white man's kettles to cook their food. And, of course, they needed the white man's rum, because—because they needed it.

Kyashuta and Teantoriance needed rum as badly as did their braves. On days like this, journeying through the woods on their way home, they felt strong, like their fathers of old before there was rum, but when the white traders came to their villages, they would grow weak. The insides of their mouths would dry up and they would give their souls to anybody who would feed them the liquor that made them feel so very good. It was then that they loved the white man, loved his hands as he scooped the rum from his kegs into their cups, loved his face as he smiled at them and gave them more. What a fine man he was, they thought as the delicious warmth spread through their bellies, to share his beautiful drink with us, and their minds would close to tomorrow.

Their dependence upon the whites would not have been so bad, and the rum would have been wonderful, thought Kyashuta, except that, as strong as was the craving of the Indians for the white man's rum, that's how strong was the craving of the white man for the red man's land. O great Tahiawagi! Was there any end to the mobs of white men who streamed to the borders of the Longhouse? And when the borders could no longer hold them, someone would scratch some lines and loops on an animal skin, bribe some fool who they called a chief to scratch a loop or two, then a few days later tell this or that village that their land no longer belonged to them.

If the village picked up and moved, any brave returning to his old hunting ground or fishing stream would be treated like a dog by the people who stole their land.

Kyashuta shook his head. He couldn't understand how it

all worked. The English men were mostly like helpless women. How could such feeble creatures lord it over the mighty Ganonsyoni, who had driven the powerful Hurons westward and made the Delaware their children?

And so he and Teantoriance had journeyed west, to the lands of Ohio and Illinois, bringing their message of war to the Shawnees and the Delawares, the Twightwees and the Kickapoos, the Chippewa, Ottawa, and Huron nations, and many more. These tribes should have been pleased and flattered that chiefs from the great Iroquois confederacy would come to them and speak of military alliance. After all, for one hundred years the Iroquois had ruled over them. And now they were ready to deal with them as equals, if only they would do the sensible thing, unite to drive out the English whom they all hated. Surely the western tribes, most of whom had been allied with the French, would be happy to drive out the English and bring back the French, who did not eat up all the land and look down upon the Indians as if they were a low species of vermin.

Kyashuta and Teantoriance had expected to return to the council fire of the Six Nations with word of a mighty war coalition forming in the west, awaiting only the commands of their Iroquois fathers to begin the war that would at last free the Indians from the long, horrible nightmare of domination by the English. Instead, after the conference with Warraghiyagey, what they received everywhere they turned was interest and approval, followed by rejection, temporizing—disobedience, in fact—from those who for so long had feared the might of the Iroquois League.

How surprising it was, how humiliating, to present their war belts to the western tribes, only to have them run to the English war chief in Detroit and betray Kyashuta's mission. "They ate his food and drank his rum and told him about our visit. Not so long ago we would have gone home and sent out our young men to teach them a lesson,"

Kyashuta growled bitterly. "It is hard to decide who to hate more, the western tribes or the English."

The sun squatted on the western horizon as the small group wearily laid aside their weapons and packs and made ready for their final meal of the day. The two chiefs sat alone by a small fire, smoking kinnikinnick.

"I have never trusted Warraghiyagey," Kyashuta said.

"The Mohawks say he has always spoken the truth," Teantoriance replied.

"He always speaks the truth, and yet he always watches out for Warraghiyagey. There are many hills, and fields and forests that once were Mohawk land but now belong to Warraghiyagey. If he is such a friend of the Mohawks, how does he grow richer and richer while the Mohawks who bring him the furs that make him rich see their domain disappear with every year that passes?"

On this cool summer night Kyashuta reclined in the warmth of the campfire and thought about returning to his home village. They had done their very best to bring the tribes together. Like children, the western tribes had refused to think beyond today and the goods the English would soon bring. To them, except for the trading forts, the white men were far, far away. How ignorant these people are, he thought. The dangers were explained, but they did not want to hear.

"Ah well," he said to Teantoriance. "There was a time, I am sure, when our fathers heard about the white man's war with the Indians in the eastern country, when the whites wiped out the Pequots. They probably shrugged their shoulders and said, 'We didn't like the Pequots anyway. The whites just saved us the trouble of having to deal with them.'

"How foolish we were, my brother, to think that the whites would have satisfied their cravings with the land and blood of the Pequots."

Teantoriance let an inarticulate grunt escape from his throat. "And what are we to do now, Kyashuta?" he asked. "Surely we cannot fight the whites alone. Even the entire confederacy cannot fight the English without the French to help us. And believe me, the French *are* leaving."

Teantoriance had been silent throughout most of the journey from the western country. But as the party of delegates found themselves back in the familiar territory of northern Pennsylvania, he found his tongue.

"We must rest here, my brother," he told Kyashuta as he threw his pack down in a small clearing surrounded by a thick growth of elm and beech trees.

"There are still two hours of daylight," Kyashuta said.

"Ah, but three hills beyond, we will be within sight of the place the English call Fort Presque Isle. My heart is like a great rock at the bottom of a clear creek. It can see the sky but it cannot touch it. It would break to have to pass the fort by day, to have to see it, and slink by it and hope that we do not run into soldiers who would ask us what right we have to travel our own lands."

"Where is your courage, sage of the People of the Great Hill?" Kyashuta asked. "We could easily ambush a wandering party of soldiers and send them a message that the Real Adders still have poison in their fangs."

"My brother, there are times that your courage exceeds your wisdom. Now is not the time to strike the English. They would strike back without mercy."

"They have no noses in the forest, nor have they eyes that can see through the underbrush. They would never find us."

Teantoriance looked at Kyashuta through eyes filled with great sadness. "My brother, last night I dreamed this: that the English decided to punish us for our war belts, and they sent their best soldiers after us, and they hunted us down through the eyes and noses of our brothers, the Ganiengehaka."

"Mohawks—hunting us?" Kyashuta asked, emotion twisting his voice into strange shapes.

"I have dreamed it."

They drew out their parched corn and their pressed deer meat, seated themselves, legs crossed, and did not light a fire. They ate without words, then smoked until the sun was red on the horizon before either spoke again.

"Kyashuta," Teantoriance said softly. "You must hear what I say."

The war chief did not have to be told. He had felt the thoughts of Teantoriance in motion, a good man struggling to solve a problem, and he was pleased to know that he had reached a conclusion.

"If the Longhouse falls," Teantoriance said, "then we are truly lost. It is the Ganiengehaka, not the Chippewa, or the Ottawa, who are our brothers. If they are not ready to take up the tomahawk, then the warriors of the Western Door must sleep until their brothers in the east have finally seen the truth. Nothing would please the English so much as Mohawks, Senecas, and Onondagas shedding each other's blood while they look on, ready to divide up our land among themselves. In Detroit, Warraghiyagey had with him an Oneida and a Mohawk to assure the western tribes that the Iroquois did not want to make war on the British, that only a few bad birds from the land of the Genesee wanted the blood of the English."

Teantoriance paused for a moment. "You know, my brother, that when Warraghiyagey spoke of peace between us and the Ottawas, he was pretending. All the while he was telling the Ottawas things about us that would make them angry."

"This I know," Kyashuta agreed.

"We must go home and keep our braves away from the

English, and watch and wait until finally there are so many whites among the Mohawks and the Oneida that *they* will come to the council fire with a great war belt and demand war with the English. It will happen soon enough."

"What about the western tribes?" Kyashuta asked.

"That I do not yet know. Many of them are our children by conquest. It makes me feel small to ask them when we should demand of them. We should teach them a lesson. When the English traders are among them, they will learn soon enough."

"And would you help them then?"

"I would sooner see them rot like the carcass of a dead moose. But we must wait and see. Even the greatest of fools must see the light when the light shines bright enough to make the eye see what is there."

Among the warriors traveling with the two chiefs was Skoiyasi, a young man who had grown up in the village of Tonowaugh, on the Genesee River. Much of his childhood had been spent in the company of Big Oak, and Skoiyasi's closest friend had been Big Oak's half-Seneca son Thad, known as Little Oak to everyone in the village. Because of his friendships with Big Oak and Thad, he had dreamed of friendship with the English throughout his childhood, but since the beginning of the last war between the English and the French, he had realized that this was not to be.

As the two chiefs talked, Skoiyasi stared at them from under the craggy ledge that was his forehead, out of slits of eyes that looked like narrow tar pits. His face was all sharp angles, as if he had razors under his skin instead of cheekbones, a nose, and a chin. His skull was smooth and shiny with bear grease, except for the traditional Seneca-style tuft of hair on top of his crown. His body was so thin that it barely threw a shadow, and yet his arms, legs, and chest had muscular definition that promised strength and endurance.

Like the other warriors coming home from their mission west, Skoiyasi felt terribly discouraged, but unlike most of them, he was planning his own actions against the English. He did not understand how allies could be so disrespectful of the Iroquois, and so uncaring about their needs. No sooner had the French been defeated, than the English had shown they no longer needed the Iroquois. They would have to pay the price for their disrespect. The Iroquois were men. Somehow he would strike a blow against the real enemy. But at this time, his mind had not yet conceived where, or how, the blow would be struck.

That night, in the stealthy silence known only to the red lopers of the North American woodlands, the Senecas passed almost under the guns of Fort Presque Isle without the night watch being the wiser. Two days later they returned to their villages in western New York and let it be known to their associates that the tribes of the western lakes were not yet ready to take the war belts, and that the time to confront the English in battle was not yet upon them.

❦2❧

THAD WATLEY WATCHED A GOLDEN EAGLE soaring against the deep spring-blue sky and his heart leaped high to meet it.

Life on the trails of the great northeast forests always released the spirit of the young trader, but this spring was a special one. The year was 1763. The war was over. With no French left in the woods of western New York and Pennsylvania to stir up the western tribes, he and his father could breathe in the fragrances of the quiet woodlands without having to stop and hold their breaths for every sudden noise or strange shadow they met along the way.

Big Oak lived up to the name his Seneca friends had applied to him many years before. Like the tree, he yielded very slowly before the demands that age placed upon his body. Tall and lean, his face was burned red by the sun and the winds of the high ridge lines he loved to run, his long graceful muscles still rippled with each movement, and his legs still maintained their resilience as they carried him across the hills of New York. Only his weathered face showed the bare beginnings of the rounded edges of age.

His son Thad was now in his mid-twenties, and built like his father except for the dark features from his mother's side, which made his face resist the weathering process. He had been born and raised among the Senecas, as Little Oak, but he had chosen the English world. Although his hair was Indian dark and straight, he wore it in a queue tied with an eelskin, according to the white fashion, and wore no jewelry in his nose or ears.

With the coming of peace and the going of the French, Big Oak had realized that the Shawnee, Chippewa, Twightwee, Ottawa, Huron, and a dozen other tribal entities would be in desperate need of what he and Thad had to sell. The time had long passed since these people made do with deerskins and stone arrows. They could no longer survive without the cloths, kettles, beads, paints, and weapons that only the white men could provide for them.

Accordingly, Little Oak had approached his father-in-law, a merchant of the prosperous Wendel family in Albany, and had drawn from him the requisite trade goods. Big Oak was pleased to see the goods his son had acquired. Except for the beads and war paint, which they purchased from a different source, their goods were superior to those the other traders would be carrying; these goods were not the cheap, often shoddy "Indian goods" created for the trade, but goods made for whites, and therefore of higher quality.

Both father and son felt much closer ties to the tribes than most white men. But it was business that made them deal in quality. Big Oak was legendary for his fairness in dealing with men and women both red and white, and he did not wish to tarnish that reputation.

"A little less profit now will open the way to a bigger future for Wendel and Watley," he had told the tough old Dutch merchant, and Wendel had nodded his head in sage agreement. And so Thad and Sam, the Watleys of Wendel and Watley, now gently prodded seven laden horses along the trail that led southwest across New York and Pennsylvania, toward the Ohio country. It was a small trading mission compared to the boatloads of goods that would soon be plying Lake Erie to Detroit, a sort of trial run meant for the tribes beyond the reach of that trade. Big Oak knew that peace with these tribes, if it existed at all, would be fragile. And being wise in the ways of the woodland, he wanted a small mission that could travel in stealth when stealth was needed.

Topping a ridge, they found a clearing that gave them a beautiful prospect toward the west. After the long months of bare-limbed winter, the endless waves of forest that rolled across the eastern half of the American continent had the fresh look of virgin green foliage as yet untouched by summer drought or swarms of hungry summer bugs.

As they always did, father and son paused in their journey to let their eyes drink their fill. For Little Oak the pause was a fresh return to his childhood with the Senecas on the Genesee River. He was a white man now, a dweller in the small but busy city of Albany, learning account sheets and inventories in the house of his father-in-law. He could stand the smothering clutter and stress of mercantile only because his business would allow him excursions across the forests he was born to.

For Big Oak, these travels had a bittersweet quality. Well into a vigorous middle age, he had known a time when a man could travel from Canajoharie Castle to the land of the Twightwee without once encountering the log cabin of a white man. But he knew from experience that the one thing English colonists could do above all else was produce and reproduce farmers, men with a pioneering spirit, strong enough and courageous enough to carve a freehold out of virgin forest.

It wasn't that these English, Scots-Irish, and German pioneers were greedy to possess someone else's land. To them, coming from the thickly peopled towns and villages of the old world, the lands they were settling were uninhabited. The Indians, they reasoned, were unreasonable in demanding all this for themselves, and besides, Indians were not even Christians, therefore what could they know of what was reasonable or right?

As he and Thad continued on over the ridge, down into the next valley, Big Oak reflected that with the end of the war, his hunting grounds would be filling up and the game would vanish like a summer rain shower. He guessed that when it happened, both he and his Iroquois compatriots would be heading west. He would miss his son, who, in spite of his half-Seneca heritage, was settling nicely into civilized routine.

The proud Iroquois would find dispossession to be a bitter cup to drink. For many years they had been lords of the land from the Hudson to the Ohio, and even beyond. They would not give up their land without a fight, he knew, but they *would*, sooner or later, give up their land.

As if to punctuate Big Oak's reverie, a single, sharp discharge of a rifle echoed through the valley below and faded into the fragrant afternoon. Instinctively, father and son vanished behind the thick trunks of the nearest trees and waited for the return fire.

There was none. What they had heard was either a quick, clean ambush or a shot from a single hunter, a white hunter—of that Big Oak was certain, although he wouldn't be able to say why he was so sure. The thought surprised him. He hadn't expected any settlers this far west yet. To his knowledge, Wendel and Watley was the first English trading company to head out for the Ohio River valley since the end of the war. More would be following quickly. Big Oak smiled when he thought about the hot reception they'd get from Indians who had recently bought quality trade goods from him and were not about to be seduced by shoddy stuff.

Big Oak and Thad pulled the horses off the trail. While Thad stayed with them, the veteran woodsman melted into the forest, heading downhill in the direction of the gunshot. Silently, like a shadow, he flitted from tree to tree, his still sharp vision scanning the woods for signs of human movement.

Ahead of him the woods seemed to change color from deep green to a more golden hue. He knew that meant a clearing up ahead, and again he was surprised. He had walked this trail more than once before, and it had always been solid woodland here.

Now he was due another surprise.

"Get to dinner now, Jared. I'll not call you again!"

Instead of a reply, Big Oak heard a distinct growling sound emerge from the woods to his right. For just a split second he thought he had run afoul of a bear. He laughed silently as he watched a huge bearded mountain of a man plowing his way through the forest as if neither the powerful oaks or towering beeches could make him alter his direction. The man was muttering nastiness through his beard and slashing angrily at low hanging branches with the butt of his rifle.

Big Oak stifled an impulse to call out. He was certain the big man would snap off a shot at him first before indulging any curiosity. Silently, he disappeared behind a large elm and let the man pass undisturbed to his cabin, which Big Oak could now see in a clearing fifty yards from the edge of the woods.

There was nothing noble-looking about this frontier giant. He wore home-tailored britches that were more patch than pants. The soles of his boots were bound to the uppers with rawhide thongs. His gray linen shirt had not seen water since the previous summer, and neither, it would seem, had his face and hands. He was hatless, and his black curly hair swirled around his head as if it were in the grip of a tornado.

The man strode angrily through the open door of his cabin and slammed it behind him. It bounced against the door frame and opened wide. There was no further effort to close it.

The cabin, Big Oak noted, was about the sorriest-looking log hut he had ever seen. No more than twelve feet long by ten feet wide, it had a single window with a deerskin as a curtain. The hut was constructed with logs that were nowhere near uniform size or straightness, and half of the mud chinking was missing, leaving huge, gaping holes for the cold and insects. The roof was also a mess, with numerous shakes missing and a big patch of canvas weighted down by rocks to cover the many leaks that would surely flood the interior with the next strong wind. Big Oak was certain the cabin had a dirt floor, that the fireplace didn't draw, and that in wet weather a creek probably ran through the sleeping area. It was that kind of a house.

Outside, the house was surrounded by piles of garbage: rotting food scraps, the bare remains of an old wagon, rags and other less distinguishable items, radiating fragrance and crowned by an endless circle of flies.

Big Oak considered bypassing the cabin. Though he seldom judged a fellow human, these people looked like pure trouble. He had seen their kind on the frontier before. They were careless and sloppy, hated everybody, including each other, and went wherever they pleased, respecting nobody's law, only their own stubborn willfulness.

And yet if there was settlement going on in the area, these were the people to tell him about it. Unpleasant as was the prospect, he simply had to stop here long enough to talk to them. Inside the cabin he could hear clamor, as if a several-sided argument was going on. He couldn't quite make out the words, but he couldn't miss the emotion. No sir, these people were trouble, but his need to know about settlement in the area would not allow him to pass them by.

He wanted to shout, Hello the garbage heap! But he restrained himself.

"Hello the cabin!"

The clamor in the cabin immediately ceased. Big Oak could imagine the bearded bear grabbing his rifle and heading for the window, and sure enough, a barrel pointed out the corner of the square hole in the side of the house, just below the deerskin curtain. Big Oak was glad he had hollered from well behind the tree line.

"Come on out 'n' show yourself!" came the growling voice from within the cabin.

"I like it better behind a tree," Big Oak responded, "when someone's tryin' to point a weapon at me."

"A man can't be too careful out here."

"If I was after your scalp, I wouldn't have hollered at you first, now, would I?"

The barrel of the rifle disappeared inside the house, and after a minute or so the man appeared at the door. "Where are ya at?" he shouted without patience.

"Take a look to your left."

The bearded bear looked first to his right, then to his left, and spotting Big Oak standing at the edge of the forest, he grabbed the barrel of his rifle and started to raise it to his shoulder. Big Oak ducked behind the tree.

"Now why would you do such a thing? It ain't neighborly at all, and I can tell you that from where I'm standin' now, to where you're standin', I could put a ball in your ear and you'd never hear it coming. What do you say we get civilized?"

Slowly the man brought his rifle down and descended the steps into his front yard, which was a patch of scrub growth only slightly less dense than the fringe of the forest. Sam deposited the barrel of his rifle in the crook of his arm and strolled toward the frontier squatter, his face so open and friendly that the average farmer would have immediately taken his hand in friendship.

"What 'n hell are you doin' skulkin' around my cabin?" He towered a good three inches over Sam's wiry six-foot-two frame, and everything about his body, from his chest to his limbs to his neck, was *thick.*

"Nothin' that would annoy *most* men," Sam answered pointedly. "My son and I are on the trail out west, and we were just wantin' to know if many folks besides you have moved in."

The man relaxed a bit but showed no intention toward hospitality. "Maybe they have 'n' maybe they haven't. You ain't spyin' for the Injuns, are ya?"

Sam shook his head.

The man was silent for a moment, then his stupid countenance glowed with the light of confirmed suspicion. "I get it, you're spyin' for the damn king, ain't you?"

Sam started to shake his head again, but the man was no longer having a conversation, he was making a speech. Red-faced, he inclined his barrel chest toward Sam and began to yell as if Sam were still standing in the woods a hundred yards away.

"I mighta knowed you was a king's man. Or maybe a Philadelphia Quaker. There's only one thing on God's damned earth lower 'n an Injun, and that's a Philadelphia Quaker."

"Do I look like a Quaker?" Sam asked, waving his rifle in the man's face, but the latter did not seem to notice.

"I had a wife and three near-growed sons, 'n' a daughter too! Just when they growed big enough to help me on the land and give me a chance to set in the shade a bit, Injuns wiped 'em out. Three year ago, it was, 'n' only thirty mile east of here too! Me 'n' my damned neighbors, what was left of us, sent a message to Philadelphia, and you know what we get back? A Quaker man. He come out 'n' tells us we had no business out here, that it was Injun land. Like they was real *people*. We told that Quaker's man where to go with that noise, you bet. Tar 'n' feathers is how we told him.

"That tar must of been awful hot 'cuz—" He stopped for a moment and peered into Sam's eyes, then he took in the accoutrements—Sam's rifle, his beaded bullet pouch, his powder horn, and his head-to-foot buckskin. "You ain't no Philadelphia man. I knowed that all the time." Actually, he knew no such thing; he was just busting out to tell *someone* what he and his neighbors had done to the "Quaker's man."

"That tar must of been powerful hot," he went on, " 'cuz he sure started screamin' when it hit his tender parts. And while we kept pourin', he kept screamin'. But you couldn't blame us, 'cuz we was mad over them Injun raids and they weren't gonna do a thing to help us. Well, soon enough we got tired of all that screamin', and on top of that he said that when he got back to Philadelphia, why, he'd bring an army back out with him. We said how in hell did he figure on raisin' an army from amongst a bunch a Quakers, but he said they'd send an army out all right against outlaws like us. *Outlaws* like *us!* We weren't the ones who stomped all over the frontier burnin' houses 'n' killin' the womenfolk and stealin' the kids. When he said that, then we *really* got mad."

"So what'd you do then?"

"Do? Why, we figured he needed coolin' off, so we dropped him down a well. You could hear him go 'fzzzz' when he hit the water, but that was old man Fariss's well, a pretty deep 'un with a whole lot a water in it, and I reckon that gov'ment man never did come up to the top."

"Did you try to fish him out?"

"Try to *what?* Hell no. We all got shovels 'n' filled in that damn well."

"Sounds like it was an awful good well. Didn't old man Fariss object?"

"Object? I reckon not. Old man Fariss 'n' his whole family, that was nine—no, ten . . . I don't know, maybe more—them red devils hacked them all up and boiled 'em, all except the baby. We found him, what was left of him, on a stick over the ashes of a fire. Doncha talk to me about them goddamn red devils. Or them Quaker bastards in Philadelphia neither. I'd just as soon kill one as look at one, I'll tell you that."

Sam nodded his head. "Sorry about your old family," he said. "I really am. I guess you got yourself a new one?"

"Well yeah, but so far it ain't no good. First two kids sure 'nough come out girls. Now what in hell am I gonna do with girls?"

"Marry 'em off to boys and get the boys to work for you, I guess," Sam suggested, moving around enough to get upwind from the squatter.

A mean glint appeared suddenly in the eyes of the bearded bear, as he tried to decide whether he was being made fun of. The glint disappeared and the eyes widened with understanding, then narrowed with laughter. Sam stepped back, afraid the man would pound him on his back and crush his ribs. *"Haw!"* he said simply, then the laugh faded back to a smile and the smile disappeared as quickly as it had arrived.

"She's big again," he said, " 'n' this time she told me she was sure it was gonna be a boy. I just told her it better be." The smile had turned into a dark scowl. The man hawked up something and spat a long brown stream into one of the garbage heaps, and it was only then that Sam realized the man had a short plug of tobacco in his jaw. Apparently he was used to swallowing the juice when he was making speeches, instead of spitting it out.

Sam shook his head. The man was not quite human, that was for sure.

❧3❧

"**Y**OU'LL LIKE THE TWIGHTWEE," BIG OAK TOLD his son.

"What's so special about the Twightwee?"

"What's special about the Twightwee is that they ain't spent a whole lot of time around whites. That means they haven't had much chance to acquire the rum habit, like so many of our brothers."

Thad nodded. He had spent his first few days on the trail thinking about his wife, Katherine, and the child she was bearing. He hadn't wanted to leave her because he knew that trade journeys sometimes take longer than planned, but not only did *his* father insist upon his company, *her* father was anxious that the boy get some field experience in the art of long distance fur trading.

Damn Dutchman, he thought to himself again and again. His business means more to him than his daughter. But once he had grown accustomed to the trail again, his growing family had receded to a pleasant corner of his mind and he attended to the business at hand, which was keeping his senses alert and staying alive.

Staying alive was a fascinating challenge for those traders who went into the wilderness to deal with the natives of what people would soon be calling the northwest territory. These tribes were unpredictable. Although the trade goods that went west in the bottoms of canoes and batteaux or on the backs of pack animals were necessary to their survival, it did not follow that the bearers of these goods were therefore loved by their customers.

Barely tolerated might be a better description of the relationship. If a particular band included a few young men hungry for glory, the traders might wake up one morning to find that their goods had walked off in the middle of the night. That was, if they were lucky. If they were unlucky, they might not wake up at all.

Survival was a business Little Oak was familiar with, and in truth, he enjoyed it. The endless succession of hills, brooks, and clearings, the endless search for prey to hunt and enemies to avoid, all were the familiar pattern of his life since childhood, and a welcome relief from the stuffy homes and fetid streets of Albany.

The past two days, however, his mood had changed. Instead of looking forward to the pleasant task of meeting the Twightwee, which most whites knew as the Miamis, and making new friends among them, he found himself thinking about Jared Meech, for that was the name of the half-savage, all-ignorant lout who was raising his second family in his pathetic cabin by the dung heap.

Thad felt sorry for the man because he had lost his first family. He felt sorry for the man because he knew that if civilization ever caught up with him, it would roll over him like a regiment of British dragoons.

But Thad also felt instant fear and loathing for this man who hated so many so easily. During the little time Meech had spent around him and his father, he must have used the word "kill" twenty times, in connection with everything from the French, the English, the Quakers, and the Indians to his wife and his little daughters. The man's teeth were always clenched together hard, giving his jaw an ugly, stubborn, ignorant set and his face lines of stiff tension that would seldom permit a smile to bend them even a little.

The man offered them no hospitality, and scowled at the large twist of tobacco Thad's father had offered as a present. He had taken a ferocious bite out of it and tucked the rest in his belt, but offered no manner of thanks. Big Oak had taken the measure of the man quickly, squeezed as much information out of him as possible, and then at nightfall told him that they'd be staying the night in the woods, after which they'd be traveling south. No sooner had they made it back to camp than Big Oak had Thad packing the horses. Within half an hour they had left Meech's cabin a mile behind.

"You caught the way he kept looking at where he thought the camp was, didn't you?" Big Oak asked. Thad nodded. Thad had once told his father-in-law that through his brothers the Seneca, he had learned to read faces, and the face of this man Meech had the cunning look of a sneak thief. Big Oak went on. "I'd wager that by midnight that fool was runnin' around the woods with an ax in his hand, looking for a couple of folks to chop up. He saw our fine rifles and his eyes near popped out of his head. He was gonna get them, that's for sure."

They kept to the north bank of the Ohio River, which the Ottawa called the Spay-lay-wi-theepi, as it wound through the western hills of Pennsylvania and into the Ohio Territory. Little Oak had always been stirred by the silent beauty of the New York forests, but he had never seen anything to rival the Ohio River valley. Each bend in the valley yielded a fresh broad view to the next, with deer and elk grazing in herds, unafraid of the new group of travelers making their way past them.

There were swans, geese, and ducks, clouds of them,

many newly arrived from their southern migrations, and
flocks of strange, beautiful birds feathered in green and
gold. In the early evenings, while the horses grazed, Big
Oak and his son ignored the large animals and feasted on
fresh-killed duck or fresh-caught bass, huge bass, from the
river.

What they did not see was human beings. This natural
preserve, which could have effortlessly supported numerous tribesmen for the entire summer, was empty of man-
kind. It was as if the entire race of humanity had vanished
from the earth save for these two very privileged individu-
als, to whom the Lord of the earth had offered this river
paradise.

As thrilled as they were by the open green valleys that
paraded before their eyes, and their free, unthreatened
movement over them, they wondered: Where were the
Mingoes, the Delaware, and the Shawnee who called this
river valley their home and their highway?

Curious, wary, they continued west, leaving the valley
for the low hills and ridge lines that might provide them
with a better view of the surrounding country. Traveling
more slowly but feeling more secure, the river to their left,
they continued westward toward the junction of the Ohio
and Muskingum rivers. Both men had the Indian ability to
feel the nearness of other humans in the woods, but there
was nothing to feel, day after day. One cool afternoon in
late April, Little Oak looked down and nearly exclaimed
aloud to his father as he watched a herd of several hundred
large shaggy beasts such as he had never before seen.

"Buffalo," his father said, laughing silently. "The farther
west we go, the more of them we'll see, and . . ." He
paused mid-sentence. "Well, would you look at . . ." His
voice trailed off, and Thad tried to follow his father's gaze,
but all he could see was the river, with a few ducks pad-

dling back and forth on its green surface. "What do you see down there, boy?"

"The river. Is there something else?"

"See that bend down there by that stand of willows? Ever see anything like that before?"

Little Oak followed his father's pointed finger to where the river took an odd-shaped turn almost, but not quite, back on itself. Straight lines seldom exist in natural topography, but that switchback was a nearly straight line, as if in some prehistoric era a forgotten race of people had dug a straight channel and then abandoned it.

Little Oak thought and thought, and remembered. "On the map Gingego's widow gave to us five, six year back, right?"

Big Oak nodded, his mind momentarily filled with thoughts of the old Mohawk chief, his wise and treasured friend who had lost his life on Lake George fighting the French early in the late war. Gingego's widow had given Big Oak a map that had belonged to Gingego for years. But Gingego had never told his wife the purpose of the map, and Big Oak had kept it as a token of the friendship he and the old Mohawk had shared for so long.

"Come on, Pa, get the map out and let's see if this is the place."

Big Oak looked at his son with despair. "I left it up in our fur cave on the Te-non-an-at-che," he replied, using the Mohawk name for the Mohawk River.

Thad shook his head. "If this is the place, I wonder what it's the place for," Thad said.

"It's the place, all right. Look a little farther at where the river meets another. That's the Muskingum, and if you think back you might remember another river on the map."

Thad thought, but could not remember. "It's been years since I seen that map, Pa. But if you say so, that's like gold to me."

Long enough for the sun to move in the heavens they stood on the ridge and viewed the curious place. There was no doubt in either's mind that whoever had made the map had considered that valley a destination, for it was located on the extreme western edge of the map. Of all the valleys they had passed through on their journey, this one seemed the most fertile, the most teeming with game, the most beautiful. Big Oak noticed that a low ridge ran between the valley and the river, so that a river traveler might pass through without being able to observe the valley. For a long time they did not speak. They just stood there on the ridge, studying the land, each with his own thoughts, trying and failing to unravel the mystery of Gingego's map.

They found an old trail that descended from the ridge to the shore of the Ohio and followed it to the Muskingum. They then followed that river north.

"I had heard from other traders," Big Oak said, "that many years of war between the southern tribes and the northern tribes emptied this part of the valley of all those who used to live here. Still, I cannot understand why there are no signs of anybody passing through—a hunting party, a family coming home from visiting relatives, a war party returning from a revenge raid. I have walked the hills and valleys of New England, New York, Pennsylvania, and the northwest, and never have I seen such a desolate land."

"Pa!" Thad exclaimed. "You call this land desolate? Why, it overflows with game and big fish. It is the most glorious land I have ever seen. Desolate? Never."

Big Oak smiled sadly. "In the Mohawk Valley, where you and I fought the Caughnawaga, the settlers are already spilling over their frontiers into Mohawk territory, breaking up the land and wiping out the game. The Albany people will never again need to cheat the Mohawks with fake treaties. The Mohawk will feel too crowded and will either fight for their land or find new lands away from the whites.

My heart aches for them. They took our hand, but they have not the eyes to see into the future."

"Except for Red Hawk," Thad replied, remembering the renegade Mohawk who hated the English with such passion, and hated his own village for remaining loyal to the English. For his fratricidal perverseness, his brothers had tortured him to death.

"I think old Gingego had an inkling of the future, but he didn't know what to do about it. What I meant was that there are far too many people in the Mohawk Valley now for an old bush loper like me. But this land, this is something different. Strange, unnatural. Such a beautiful land, filled with everything that makes an Indian's life easy and pleasant . . . without Indians? Show me just one tiny village, with its warriors and wise men, its women and its whelps, and the valley would feel right. Show me a sign that even one man has passed before us over the past moon, and the valley would feel right. But this valley, this pathway west? No no. Without the merest handful of humanity, it is desolate as the north end of Hudson's Bay."

Overhead a strange dark cloud was approaching, but as it came closer to them, the cloud turned into an endless flock of passenger pigeons on their way from somewhere to somewhere else. The two men halted their packhorses and watched while the birds drew closer, then blotted out the sun for several minutes, and finally passed noisily, heading east. Neither drew a bead on a bird. Their packs already bulged with fresh game, and one of the horses carried corn and dried deer meat.

They had prepared for many eventualities, but not for the lonesome silence of a beautiful land emptied of its Indians. Only gradually, after many days of imagining that skillful men were watching them from distant hills, did they get used to the idea that, of the creatures that walked upright, they were alone in the valley of the Spay-lay-wi-theepi.

"I wouldn't mind," Big Oak said, "if the valley of the Ohio were peopled only by the ghosts of the struggling Shawnee and Delaware. Except that you can't trade with a ghost."

Confident and relaxed, lulled by the solitude, they were able to appreciate to the fullest the extraordinary bounty of the valleys of the Ohio and the Muskingum.

It was late the next afternoon, twenty miles up the Muskingum, when they finally spotted their first human being west of Pennsylvania. He was a lone Chippewa, clad only in a breechcloth and moccasins, carrying a bow, a quiver, a knife, and a belt of colored shells, but no firearm, racing down from the north along a bare ridge that wound parallel to the Muskingum. Once again cautious, that morning Big Oak had steered his little caravan back into the woods, but he was determined to stop the Chippewa and talk to him. As the runner approached, Big Oak appeared from the woods and begged him to stop. But the Chippewa was on a mission and would stop for nothing. Instead of pausing for a social pipeful of tobacco, he veered into the forest Big Oak had just left and disappeared. Big Oak picked up his trail and, leaving his rifle and pack with Thad, sprinted after the Chippewa with remarkable speed and agility for his age. His exertions soon put him within fifty yards of the Indian.

"Stop!" he shouted again in Delaware, but the Chippewa must have been a champion racer. When he heard Big Oak's voice, he put on an extra burst of speed that carried him away. Big Oak picked up the pace and for a while kept his quarry in sight. On and on they raced along the forest trail, swerving in and out of live trees, jumping over fallen dead ones, ducking an occasional low branch and always watching the trail for obstacles—a large rock or a half-hidden root—that might send them sprawling.

The Chippewa had some speed and determination in reserve. His moccasins bit at the forest floor as he dodged around a pair of great beech trees. Big Oak's moccasins flew across the forest path, but he could feel his man slipping away from him. It was a feeling he was not used to. His swiftness in the woods had been his extra margin of safety for more than thirty years. He was now on notice that his feet were no longer certain soldiers to carry him away from trouble.

From now on he would have to be that much more cautious and smart about avoiding peril. Just five years ago, he told himself, he would have run that Chippewa brave into the ground. Age was a terrible load for a physical man to bear. The Chippewa was now out of sight, and Big Oak had convinced himself that even his iron will was not sufficient to overcome the years that stood between himself and the young man he was pursuing. Reluctantly he quit the chase and, breathing heavily, walked back up the trail toward where his son was waiting.

"I couldn't have caught that Chippewa if I'd had wings," he told Thad, who gave his father the proper look of sympathy.

"Who do you think he is and where is he going?" Thad asked.

"He's a messenger, I'm sure," Big Oak informed his son. "With an important message."

Little Oak said nothing, but let his eyes ask the question.

"He carried a wampum belt," Big Oak continued. "All black and red."

Little Oak nodded. "Then we are at war again?"

His father shrugged his shoulders. "Somebody is at war. That is certain."

❧4❧

For THREE MORE DAYS ALONG THE MUS-
kingum they and their packhorses walked alone. The only
other two-footed beings they saw were the birds. There
were millions of them, from brown wood ducks to green
and gold parakeets, but no one to wear their feathers.

And then, on the fourth morning, just as they emerged
from an oak grove onto a stretch of bare, flat surface rock,
they heard, to the north of them, laughter. They looked at
each other as if a wood duck had spoken instead of
quacked. Indeed, it was as if one of the trees of the forest
had laughed, so long had passed without the sight of several human beings together.

It was not the laughter of happy children. It was nasty,
contentious laughter. Father and son stood stock-still and
waited for more sounds. They came, in the form of quiet
conversation, a murmur made low by distance. Big Oak
motioned to his son, who led the packhorses into a hollow
and remained with them while his father crept quietly in
the direction of the sounds.

With a stealth that any red man would have admired, he
stole closer and closer, silent because he was patient, patient because in the forests patience meant survival. The

conversation continued in a tongue that he identified as Chippewa. He was now so close that he knew fewer than a hundred yards of trees stood between him and them. In normal times he would have announced his approach with a greeting, then walked into their presence, but the events of the past few days had made him cautious.

He circled quietly, looking for a bit of cover from which he could see without being seen. Eventually he found it. There were ten of them, he thought—no, eleven, as one more appeared. He wondered uneasily if there were any others, and listened for any unusual sounds behind him. He could feel the short hairs on the back of his neck tingle in anticipation as he waited for a sound he could not identify to become a step or some other form of movement, but it did not. Gradually he allowed himself to breathe as he lay on his stomach behind some brush. Big Oak's heart sank when one of the Indians turned his head enough for him to note the white and vermilion streaks of war paint on the Chippewa's face.

They were not stripped for battle. They carried packs and rifles or muskets. Their pouches sagged with bullets. They were obviously on an extended journey. Why they had stopped, Big Oak could not guess. Almost immediately, as Big Oak watched, they were back on the trail, single file, five yards between them in the dogged trot that could take them fifty miles in a day. He watched them head off in a northwesterly direction until they were out of sight, then he returned swiftly to where he had left his son with their packhorses.

The packhorses, and Thad, had vanished.

Big Oak picked up their trail and followed them until he reached a large rock shelf. Now what? Unfailing instinct took him to the top of the shelf. Instead of crouching to peer over into the valley below, he stood full height and allowed himself to be silhouetted on the skyline. He was rewarded with a "Hssss" sound, and within a few seconds he had bounded into an area so thickly wooded in scrubby cedar as to constitute perfect cover for a caravan of packhorses.

"Good place," Big Oak observed. Thad did not respond to the praise. "Chippewa, I think. I don't know where they're goin' but they aim to kill somebody when they get there."

Thad nodded. "Look at this," he said, showing his father the recent remains of a small, discreet campfire.

"Two, three days old," observed Big Oak, who studied the ground that led away from the campfire and drew a few conclusions. "Four, maybe five braves. Long steps. In a hurry. Headed that way." He pointed in the same direction the Chippewa war party had gone.

"If they're all goin' to war," he said, "I suspect it's the English they aim to kill. The peace treaty probably came through, finally, and if the French gave the English a whole lot of Indian land that they don't own, I'll bet that the Indians are spittin' mad."

"If they're mad at us, then what in hell are we doin' tryin' to trade goods with them?" his sensible, businesslike son asked.

"Well, we don't know for sure, and anyway, they'll need what we've got. Tradin's a funny thing. When you're the only one who can get them the things they need, they'll find a way to get along with you. They're just gonna have to get used to us, because in a matter of a few moons, the king of France is gonna be gone from their lives forever. They've got no choice. Either they learn to like Englishmen or spend their winters cold and hungry."

"But Pa, suppose they haven't got used to the idea yet? Or suppose they don't know the war's over and the French are goin' home?"

"That's why we're bein' so careful. But one of these days

we're gonna have to pop out of the bushes and say howdy and find out. We can't just turn around and head on back. Your father-in-law wouldn't like it."

"He'd like it a whole hell of a lot worse if he lost his horses and all the goods we bought with his money. And his daughter would like it even less if we got lost in the bargain."

"It doesn't have to happen that way if we just be real careful about who knows we're around," Big Oak replied thoughtfully. "These Indians ain't ever yet got so united that they all managed to hate the same people at the same time."

The farther north they traveled, the more Indian sign they spotted. By the time they left the Muskingum River system and struck westward toward the Sandusky River, it seemed as if the entire Indian population of the northwest was all headed in one direction. Every trail they crossed had borne recent traffic, a lot of it. In his long career as a scout, trapper, and trader, Big Oak had associated with many tribes, including those who hated the English but liked him. He had never seen anything like this.

"Maybe we ought to turn back," Thad suggested one afternoon after watching his father's jaw work pensively throughout the day. "I don't know if we can handle this."

"Aw, we'll figure it out, somehow," Big Oak said. "We've got the goods. They need the goods."

Thad shook his head. Only in his middle twenties, he had already learned much in his years with the Seneca and his travels with his father. "We have beads," he said. "We have blankets. We have face paint. We have cooking pots. We don't have enough powder and lead. None of the English traders have powder and lead. The Indians won't like that. And if we did have more powder and lead, would we be right to sell it to them?" Thad asked.

Big Oak was the finest man Thad knew, but his heart

was still a little mixed up. His Indian sympathies made him willing to cut a few corners of the law, and if that meant a few border settlers lost their scalps, so be it. White men weren't supposed to be settled in the west anyway.

But Thad had a different attitude. Six years of living around Albany, married into a Dutch mercantile family, had changed his viewpoint. Half Seneca though he was, he had not forgotten the humiliation of being cast out of the village where he had grown up. Renegade Caughnawagas had virtually wiped out the village, which held so many friends and memories of his early years. And yet the survivors had blamed him and his father, the resident white men, for their troubles. Not much more than a boy at the time, he had cut his feelings off from those he had grown up with. Although he had the blood of Seneca chiefs flowing through his veins, and his father did not, it was his father, not he, who sympathized most with the natives who were being run off their land as fast as the English population could load a wagon, hitch up a team of oxen, and crack a whip.

April had at last turned to May. Feathery green was lacing all the hardwoods, even along windblown Lake Erie. They continued to cross the paths of numerous Indian parties, but those had passed days before, leaving the woods again empty of two-legged predators.

"The ones we saw must have been the stragglers," Big Oak said. "Wherever they were going, most of them must be there by now."

"Where do you think they are?" Thad asked.

"I don't know for sure. Big doings somewhere to the north? Detroit? I wouldn't guess."

It was as if all the paths they had seen had consolidated into a broad highway. So many moccasined feet had walked this route in the past two weeks that it would take years of solitude for the trail to return to a completely natural state. There was no attempt to hide tracks here. Men, women, and children had followed this route, leaving signs all along the way: worn moccasins and pack bags, old sacks and an occasional piece of jewelry or ragged blanket; a toy bow and a carved horse; and in one case, the freshly interred body of a baby.

The signs indicated not only many Indians, but many tribes. In addition to the Chippewas, they came upon leavings that bore the fashion of the Miamis, the Ottawas, the Potawatomies, the Hurons, and even, Big Oak was certain, Delawares. He shook his head and wondered once again what was going on.

❧5❧

THEIR JOURNEY WAS NOT GOING ACCORDING to plan. They had hoped to find Indian settlements along the Ohio River valley that had been starved for goods, people ready to conclude quick and easy deals with them. Then they could return home with new knowledge, customer lists, and better ideas of what goods would be most in demand during this new era of peace.

Instead there were signs of coming strife all over the place. Where they had hoped to find the Shawnee and Delaware, there were no Shawnee and Delaware, or anybody else except Chippewa warriors in a hurry and signs of wholesale migrations of tribal groups. Were they fleeing from someplace or going to someplace?

Thad turned to his father. "What ought we do now?" he asked. Up to now he had thought that in following the rivers, they had been searching for the most likely locations of their future trading partners. But now they were moving overland, west by northwest toward Lake Erie, and he was beginning to get that sinking feeling that comes to men who feel lost.

Although he still respected his father, many years had passed since Big Oak had lost his cloak of infallibility in the valley of the Te-non-an-at-che. Then a group of young glory-seekers led by the renegade Ganiengehaka named Red Hawk attacked them in the middle of the night, beat Big Oak senseless and nearly killed him.

During his lengthy recovery in the lodge of a Mohawk village, Big Oak was helpless as a baby. It was then that Thad began to realize that, legendary as his father was among the Iroquois and the English army, he, like anybody else, was capable of making a mistake that could cost him his life. Thad determined then to take responsibility for his life out of his father's hands and into his own.

"If we can't find them anywhere else, at least we'll find them at Fort Detroit," the older man said, checking the balance of the pack on one of the horses. "There'll be other traders there, some old friends, and they'll know what's been going on. There's a lot we don't hear about in Albany or on the eastern trail."

They followed the bed of the Huron River north until, one bright morning, they stepped to the edge of the forest and found themselves looking across the endless expanse of Lake Erie. Thad never failed to experience awe at the first sighting of one of the well-named Great Lakes. On this day the lake was so placid that he could barely make out the line on the horizon where water met sky. He tried to take in the entire wonder of these lakes, with their vast breadth and magnificent fish, their silky calm on days like this and sudden tantrums that could summon up huge waves in a few minutes' time to swamp and sink unwary sailors. Great Lakes they were, and he could not help but stand riveted, hypnotized by waters that always appeared with such stunning suddenness at the end of a long forest trek.

They did not continue north then, but turned west short of the shoreline and moved back into the woods. It was the forests that made them feel secure, the forests they could read as easily as Dieter Wendel could read his account books back in Albany. They would not leave their forest until they no longer had a choice.

For several hours they walked in silence, until they began to note some feelings of unease among their pack animals. Shortly they began to feel similar emotions themselves. To their right through the trees shined the diffuse light of sunshine on an open field. "The fort," Big Oak said in a soft voice, and the two altered the direction of their pack train.

They expected to pop through the tree line and find a stockade with blockhouse and bastions, perhaps a few huts nearby, and the noisy welcome routine of soldiers in garrison. The soldiers would be gregarious when they found that the travelers were subjects of the king of England, and they would beg for news from the east. There would be a night or two under a roof, which would be a welcome change for Thad, who longed for the trail when in town but dreamed of civilized comforts when he was on the trail. And they would finally find out where the villagers had gone and why the warriors were skulking.

What they found was a grim, gloomy, burned-out shell of a fort, a blackened, silent skeleton missing many of its bones. The two stood frozen, stricken for a moment, and then immediately melted back into the forest.

"You see how it is," said Big Oak through clenched teeth when they had led the animals out of sight of the fort. "This did not happen yesterday, or last week. The English have a line of forts, like a necklace across the northwest, from Detroit to Niagara. The Indians would not burn one if they did not intend to go to war. Not unless they were Kickapoo. Kickapoo are liable to do anything."

"Are you certain this was done by Indians?"

"We'll know for sure in about an hour. I don't believe

there's another live human being around here, but these are cunning devils and I wouldn't put it past them to lay in wait for such as us. Come down on us while we've got our minds on the death of good Christian men."

They watched and waited, saw only the wind, and finally led their packhorses across the clearing, to an opening that used to be the gate. Just outside the fort was a garden, and in the garden lay the scalped and stripped remains of a man in the early stages of decay. Within the confines of the burned-out fort they found more and more of the same, better than two dozen, all scalped, all stripped, some otherwise mutilated.

There were no signs of a struggle, no bloody weapons lying about, no pieces of cloth or deerskin in a clenched fist, no multiple bullet wounds indicating even a brief but spirited exchange of fire before defeat. Just twenty-seven men in peaceful repose, most with heads split open, their faces bearing the sad, collapsed expression that comes to men whose facial muscles have been severed at the cranium by scalping knives.

"This was a small post," Big Oak almost whispered. "I doubt that more than half of these men were soldiers. In fact"—he gazed closely at the face of one man whose lower body was nearly burned away by the embers of a building that had fallen near him shortly after his death—"this man I know. He is a trader. Was a trader. I believe they must have come up with one hell of a surprise for these folks. I *am* sorry to see this. Come on."

He tarried no longer, but guided the lead packhorse away from the rotting corpses and out the gate.

"Don't you think we ought to bury them?" Thad asked. His father said nothing, just bowed his head and shook it, which surprised Thad. His father had always been a respecter of people. "We better head back, don't you think?" the young man asked.

Big Oak merely continued to shake his head. "Detroit is not far. We have a better chance of making our way there in safety than sneaking all the way back from where we came."

"If you say so." Although the day was warm, Thad could feel cold conviction coursing down his spine in a river of sweat.

"Now," Big Oak spoke softly, once they had disappeared deep into the woods, "I want you to listen carefully." Thad peered into his father's deep blue eyes. Where he usually found profound calm, he now found a shifty nervousness like the chill he felt in his own belly.

"Bad, isn't it?" The fear like a fist squeezing his gut was unusual for Thad. For the first time in his life, danger meant losing his family as well as his life.

"We have here a—" Big Oak cleared his throat. "We're gonna have to have the devil's own good luck to make it through to Detroit. If I thought we had another choice, I'd take it, whatever it is. But there are very angry Indians all over the place, 'n' they don't know me 'n' they don't know you. Blood brothers to the Seneca don't mean nothin' to a Shawnee or a Chippewa, 'cause they hate the Iroquois about as much as they hate the English.

"Now I want you to take the horses west until I point you north. You won't see much of me over the next couple of days, but I'll be there, all around you. They may get wind of you and the horses, but they won't know I'm out there watchin' them. I believe I can get us there, son. I've got to. I'm bound to see my grandson grow up, I promise you that. Now, you've got the old eagle-bone whistle I give you way back in Tonowaugh. You give three quick toots on that thing and I'll know you're in trouble." There was something else he wanted to say. Instead he turned his head and then disappeared in a quiet pigeon-toed lope down the trail in front of Little Oak and the packhorses.

The weeks of their journey across New York, Pennsylvania, and the Ohio River valley had retuned Thad's woodland senses and retaught him the language of the forest. The birds were his guardian angels, and the trees that hissed faintly in the spring breeze were his constant background, against which any new sounds would echo in his ears like a rifle shot in an Anglican church. In his childhood he would have felt safe and secure knowing that his father was roaming the woods, watching over him. No longer. His father was a great woodsman, one of the greatest, and a great human, but human after all.

For five hours the young man and his pack train wound their way along the wooded lowland south of the Erie shore, up and down the easy swells of primeval forest, startling an occasional squirrel, his head and eyes forever in motion as he listened for changing voices in the forest chorus. The thick canopy of elm and maple could persuade a man that the sky was a deep green, but they kept down the growth of underbrush and made travel along the old trail a simple matter. About an hour short of darkness, his father reappeared and pointed to a spot off the trail. Thad followed him about a quarter of a mile into a hollow that held a lively creek with a noisy little waterfall. The waterfall, they knew, might help to mute the sounds of the horses. On the other hand, the waterfall could easily mask the sounds of any approaching enemy.

They removed the goods from the backs of the animals and piled them on the ground, unsaddled the ponies, found a bit of a clearing where grass grew, and set the picket line there, then found a comfortable piece of earth on which to rest and dine. Two courses: jerked deer meat and dried corn, plus cold, fresh creek water gathered upstream from the horses.

"Son," the older man said as they sat, quietly chewing

the tough, dried meat. "We passed a Wyandot village a while back. Old men. Women. Children. No warriors."

"None?" Thad's considerable surprise was no greater than Big Oak's had been.

"You'da thought the Great Spirit himself has demanded the presence of every warrior in the entire northwest. I can't remember when the Iroquois had *all* their men out on the warpath. Half these tribes out here don't even like each other."

"But we haven't found any of them, except a few who were in an awful big hurry to get somewhere. Where do you suppose they are?"

Big Oak shook his head. "I'll stand the first watch," he said.

All day the following day it was Thad alone, plodding west with his slow-moving packhorses while around him, unseen, unheard, glided the watchful scout, his senses acutely wedded to the rhythms, melodies, colors, and shadings of the woods.

Thad felt protected yet helpless as his horses plodded noisily along the trail. Sometimes he could sense the presence of his father, sometimes he could sense his distance, but only once did he see him, when Big Oak returned long enough to direct a turn north. Again he vanished like a flickering spirit, leaving Thad to plod along with his caravan, expecting every moment to face a howling mob of Wyandots or Chippewas.

He had proved his courage a score of times during the late war with the French, but the feeling of dread that ran up and down his backbone turned every shadow into a shaven-headed skulker aching to bury a tomahawk in his brain.

The following day the feeling of dread multiplied. There were numerous creeks and rivers to cross, courses he knew drained into the Detroit River. Like a shepherd, he herded his charges across each, talking to them softly. They were jumpy, either because of what they could feel around them or because they could sense his unease.

Late in the afternoon he saw one more shadow that did not belong, and it was then he realized, with a chill that kicked the breath from his lungs, that he had not seen his father in many hours.

He checked the priming in his pan and firmed his thumb tight against the hammer of his rifle. His head continued to swerve back and forth across his front as he continued his trek, but his glance always returned to the shadow.

It moved, and for the sparest moment a beam of sunlight through the dense green canopy revealed a nearly naked man, lithe as a weasel, in a brown breachclout, head shaved but for a lock that hung down from his crown and trailed a pair of feathers behind his left ear.

A circle of scalp in the center of Thad's head began to itch, as if it could feel the Indian coveting it. After another minute or two of seemingly unconcerned walking, he led his horses down a steep bank to a small creek and let them drink awhile. As soon as he was out of sight of his pursuer, he began removing the most valuable packs and finding little hidey-holes for them behind rocks and in the underbrush. Other, less valuable packs he let slip onto the ground. He then dispersed the horses in deeply wooded hollows, except for the two fastest and strongest. One he kept loaded with things he would need, the other he equipped with blanket and hackamore, for riding. Finally he found a hollow in the bank of the creek, obscured by brush, and there he hid himself, willing himself to patient calmness as he awaited his enemy.

❖6❖

HE STOOD STILL AS A DEAD OAK, AFRAID TO draw a breath. He stared out through his thin brush cover at the woods in front of him and wondered how well he had hidden himself. He held his rifle across his body, hammer cocked, his finger against the trigger, ready for action. A breeze blowing along the creek failed to cool the sweat that ran down the sides of his face. A mosquito buzzed around his ears and gnats tickled his eyelids, but he dared not brush them away as he strained to listen for the approach of his pursuer, or what he thought must be his pursuer. The minutes dragged by like a funeral dirge. He peered through the brush down the bank, eyes swiveling from one corner of his head to the other, searching for movement.

The birds around him had gone silent. The enemy was close by. And yet, little Oak saw nothing. He waited, unmoving, rigid, muscles tensed until they ached.

The corner of his eye caught a sudden, swift movement.

He heard the swish of a tomahawk through the air just before the brush in front of him deflected it off his left shoulder. Immediately the tomahawk was followed by the rush of a naked, painted Potawatomi warrior. Thad fired his rifle from the hip, ripping a crease in the Indian's left side but not slowing him down at all. The young trader stepped forward from behind the brush as the Indian dove toward him, knife cocked by his ear. But before the blade could descend, Little Oak drove his rifle butt forward. He felt the warrior's collarbone give and heard the crack, followed by a sharp grunt, and the Indian fell into the brush, his arm useless, the knife skittering free.

He glared at Thad through the bright stripes of white and black war paint. Fierce hatred competed with almost detached curiosity concerning his fate. Thad paused for only a moment to return his enemy's glare. He had fired his rifle. The woods would be alive with screeching warriors in a moment. Not much of a rider, he ran past his fallen and astonished enemy, struggled onto the back of his mount and urged it into motion, west, away from the shore of Lake Erie, where the Indians would most likely be camped, and then north toward Detroit.

Already he could hear the distant sounds of approaching Indians. This was their territory. They had no need for stealth, only for speed.

As he turned his mount toward the north, he saw a lone warrior tearing through the woods at an angle to cut him off. The trees slowed the horse more than it slowed the warrior, who closed the distance in a hurry. Thad was amazed. Blood was dripping down the man's left side, and his right shoulder seemed to sag. His left hand held the tomahawk he had recovered while he was scrambling to his feet.

Surely he couldn't throw with his left hand. He would have to come near enough to swing it, and Thad's rifle had a longer reach, if he could steady his horse long enough to use it. He pulled on the hackamore, brought the horse to a stumbling stop, and awaited the assault. The wounded, angry, young Potawatomi was guileless and furious as he

bounded in front of the horse and pulled back his tomahawk to strike the horse and make him buck.

Desperately, Little Oak leaned over and pulled back his
rifle to swing it, butt out, at the Indian. The horse reared as
the rifle came forward, ruining both the force and the aim,
but the animal's movement turned the Indian half around
and the rifle butt collided with the broken collarbone. The
warrior roared with pain, but Thad fell from his horse and
lost his grip on the rifle. He was up in a moment, his fingers reaching for the hatchet tucked into his belt, over his
long buckskin hunting jacket. Now he and his adversary
were on their feet, each with a weapon. The Indian was in
far worse shape, but Thad would have to finish him quickly
to survive. The other members of this Indian's band had
spotted his flight on horseback and were streaming through
the woods toward him in large numbers, screeching their
fearful war cries.

The Indian may have expected Thad to circle a bit,
looking for an opening, but he did no such thing. He had
no time. Too quickly for the warrior to react, Thad hurled
his hatchet with all his strength at the body of his foe. It
bit into the brave's ribs at an angle, then fell to the ground,
not a fatal blow, but charged with enough impact to drive
the Indian back and give Thad enough time to pick up his
rifle and chase after his horse, which had galloped a hundred yards down the trail and then halted, for no good
reason.

And now the horse wouldn't stand still to be mounted.
The war cries were getting louder. One or two rifles discharged. The horse danced around and tossed her head in
fear and vexation. Desperately, Thad jerked on the hackamore to distract the animal, and scrambled onto her back
just as the lead pursuers appeared over a rise, dodging
around trees and jumping over roots. Their whoops rose to
a devilish howl when they spotted the young white man so

close. The horse, just as determined to escape the savage screeching as his rider, found an opening in the trees and bounded through it, a scant thirty yards ahead of the swiftest pursuers.

Hatless, his eyes wide with terror, Thad hugged the back of the big animal as she responded with the hardest running she'd had to do in years. The terror faded as soon as Thad felt the distance from his would-be killers begin to increase. Several braves fired their rifles, but their bullets slammed into the tree trunks between them and their target. Thad would have liked to load his rifle, but he didn't dare release the tight hold he had on the horse's mane.

A chance bullet ripped through a fold in his sleeve. He clung even closer to the horse's back. "Come on, come *on!*" he begged the animal, desperately hoping for a little more speed.

He took a careful look back and saw a huge number of warriors in pursuit, falling farther back but by no means giving up the chase. Horse and rider had found a wide, smooth path worn by the passing of hundreds of trading parties over the years. Thad made swift work of it, outdistancing his pursuers with every jump. For the first time since he had hidden in the brush by the creek bank, Thad drew a deep, unhurried breath.

The breath was premature. He suddenly found himself bounding into a clearing, through a little village. He was no more surprised than they were as the horse leaped over a small campfire, past two startled women bearing loads of wood, past the entrance to a shabby elm-bark wigwam, and back into the woods. Women gasped and old men stared, and only one boy of about eight recovered from his surprise quickly enough to hurl a stick at the horse and rider just before they disappeared into the trees. It whirled through the space that would have been occupied by Little

Oak's head had he not still had his cheek buried in the neck of his galloping mount.

A quarter of a mile beyond the village, he allowed the animal to subside into an easier gallop while he sat up and looked around. His pursuers had vanished. The birds were singing their hearts out. He should have been reassured, but for some reason he was not. After a while he eased his horse into a brisk walk. Gradually the animal's furious breathing grew calm and steady. Evidently he had some run left in him. For the first time since he had spotted the lone pursuer Thad had time to wonder what had become of his father. He supposed that their trade goods had been lost. He looked at the meager provisions he had tied behind him on the horse's back, and hoped that he might find his way to Fort Detroit soon enough.

He crossed a stream, his senses ever wary of ambush. A map of the area lay buried in his brain where his father had placed it several nights before. He dug it up and remembered that the river took a bend east. So did he. There was another clearing up ahead. The closer he approached it, the bigger the clearing appeared to be. It must be the fort, he told himself, and soon, through the trees, he could see it, looking mighty and magnificent in the afternoon sunlight.

It was about three hundred yards from the edge of the woods to the palisades, a quick sprint on the back of his horse. And sprint they would have to do, for no sooner had they appeared at the edge of the wood line than an indignant howling assaulted his ears from the throats of first dozens, then hundreds of warriors closer to the river who, on seeing him, had grabbed their firearms and headed in his direction.

This was the largest gathering of warriors he had ever seen in one place, armed and painted and headed for him! He kicked with his heels and smacked the flank of the animal with the palm of his hand. The horse responded, lighting out for the fort like a champion racer, with at least three hundred of the huge assemblage of Indians doing their best to cut him off.

They might have done it too, but their howling woke up the fort. Thad was thrilled to see a puff of smoke, followed by the bang of one of the fort's twelve-pounders. He saw two Indians go down and the rest of them fade back away from the fort. The Indians kept up a distant fire at him as he rode around the fort, looking for the main gate, which, when he finally found it, opened to admit him. Red-coated soldiers on the parapet cheered him across the remaining space of clearing and through the gate.

Emotionally and physically depleted, he slid from his horse and, grasping his rifle in one hand at the balance, walked up to a sergeant who stood straight and tall ten yards inside the gate.

He shook the man's hand and said, "I am Thad Watley. I fought with William Johnson at Lake George."

The sergeant shook his hand but said nothing.

Thad turned around and looked through the gate at the distant hordes of Indians. "Thank you," he told the sergeant with feeling.

"What in hell were you doing out there?" the sergeant asked abruptly. "Don't you know there's a war on?" He was a grenadier type, this sergeant, tall, stubborn, and stupid.

"Well, I didn't, but I do," Thad answered with a grim smile. His close brush with the assembly of tribes was already history to the young trader. "My father and I had a load of trade goods that we were taking to the Indians down in the Ohio Valley, but we couldn't find any Indians to trade with so we followed them here, you might say."

"Where's your permission to trade?" the sergeant asked.

"Pa has it."

"Not a very likely story, and why should I believe it?"

"I guess it doesn't matter much if you do or don't believe it, seein' as I haven't got any trade goods with me, or any furs the Indians would of paid us for the trade goods."

By now a young ensign was standing next to the sergeant, saying nothing but listening carefully to the discussion.

"And where's this so-called father of yours?" the sergeant asked.

Thad shook his head. "I'm kind of worried. He was scouting for the pack train, but I haven't seen a sign of him since this morning, before we passed that Indian village south of here."

The ensign nodded. "The Potawatomi village. If they've got him, you can kiss your old man good-bye."

He ignored the snooty little ensign and glared at the sergeant. "Have you heard about Fort Sandusky?"

Both the sergeant and the ensign leaned toward Thad. "What about Fort Sandusky?" the ensign asked.

Thad sighed. "You'd better take me to your commander."

The sergeant took a step forward and seized Little Oak by his shoulders. "What about Fort Sandusky?"

Thad paused and thought for a moment. "It's been attacked. That's all I'll tell you until I see your commanding officer." In truth, he needed to see the post commander because he knew that if Big Oak was in trouble, only the commander could order a force out to help. He had dangled Sandusky as bait, and was satisfied that his information was important. The sergeant and the ensign conducted Thad to the commanding officer of Fort Detroit.

Major Henry Gladwin looked exactly like a man who had spent the past few weeks cooped up in a fort surrounded by more than a thousand hostile, angry warriors of a half-dozen mighty Indian nations. He had at his disposal fewer than two hundred soldiers, but his fort was solid, his ammunition was adequate, and Indian warriors were not disposed to sacrifice themselves in battle. Most important, Henry Gladwin was solid, and intelligent to boot.

On the other hand, the Indians were led by an Ottawa chief named Pontiac, the first chief in memory able to persuade, cajole, and browbeat tribes to forget their ancient antagonisms and jealousies in order to save themselves. Other chiefs, inspired by Pontiac but operating on their own, were gobbling up English forts all along the frontier. Pontiac's "assignment" was Detroit, and he had almost succeeded by trickery several weeks before, but his plot had been betrayed, and now he had the fort under siege, a most un-Indian way to make war, but from Gladwin's viewpoint, he was making a pretty good go of it. Food stocks were low and Pontiac knew it, thanks to intelligence gathered by local Frenchmen who were only too happy to see disaster come to the English who had just finished kicking the French king out of North America.

No wonder dire shadows chased each other across the good-natured face of the bewigged Major Gladwin.

The sergeant and the ensign introduced Thad to the grim major. To their surprise, his face creased into a smile and he leaned forward.

"Your father wouldn't happen to be Sam Watley, now, would he?"

"Yes, sir."

"Gentlemen, Lord Jeffery Amherst doesn't much care for provincials, but I will tell you that if I had just fifty men like Sam Watley, we could hold this fort against every Indian on this continent. Son, where is your father?"

"Well now, I don't exactly know. Last time I saw him, he was in the woods, just like he's been most of his life, but that's a powerful heap of Indians out there, and I have to admit I'm a bit worried about him."

Thad had a right to be worried, for at that moment his

father, arms tied behind his back by rawhide that cut deep into his wrists, was kneeling amidships in an Ottawa canoe on the way to Pontiac's war camp located on the Detroit River, east of the fort. The Ottawas didn't know of the mighty Big Oak or his reputation, and if they had, in their present mood there was not much chance that they would have cared.

❧7❧

THE CAPTURE OF BIG OAK WAS ONE OF THOSE
accidents that people who have never been victims of such
accidents call "the fortunes of war." Which is to say, a small
scouting party happened to see Big Oak before he saw
them.

Lying still in a thicket, they watched the woodsman with
admiration as he made his silent way through the forest.
Had they been more analytical, they might have wondered
just what he was doing in their woods, and then they
would have probably bagged Thad too.

Having figured out his direction, which went straight
through their location, they merely crawled behind the
nearest solid cover and waited.

There were five of them, each armed with a rifle or musket. They lay on either side of his path, so well-concealed
that the first hint he had of their presence was the sudden
appearance of all five, around him, faces painted and weapons pointed.

His heart leaped against his ribs. He took a deep breath
and willed himself back into equilibrium, sizing up his captors, then handing his rifle to the man he judged to be the
leader. His hands now free, he began to sign to them, ask-

ing why they had captured him. The leader replied by spitting on him, then signaled one of his braves to tie Big Oak's hands behind his back.

They led him a mile or two into their village to show him off to their friends and families. When they arrived, the whole village gathered around, and on the spot the warriors discussed the pros and cons of torturing and killing him then and there. During wartime such procedures were standard entertainment fare and brought plenty of prestige to the captors. Such was Pontiac's power, however, that they agreed to bring him to the great Ottawa chief unharmed, and *then* take him back to their village for the festivities.

So they kicked him through the village and threw him into their canoe. Three of them grabbed paddles and shoved off for the middle of the Detroit River. During all this time, Big Oak behaved with the etiquette required of a captured Indian. Betraying no emotion through his stolid facial mask, he held his head high and his back straight to remind them that though his body was theirs, his spirit still belonged to him. His dignity was not lost on them. They noted that he would be a worthy subject of their planned torments.

In their culture, the torture and death of an adversary was a creative endeavor. As they paddled up the river, each warrior gave considerable thought to what he might wreak with his fire and blades to draw screams from his throat and break his spirit. This was a rare white man, they thought. His ultimate surrender just before his death would be a satisfying event.

They paddled toward the opposite shore and a large Huron village, but they didn't land there. Just before the Huron village, the river made an abrupt turn to the east, which meant they glided past the village along the southern shore. They continued to paddle upstream, and now, across the river, Big Oak spotted what had to be Fort Detroit. He assumed that they were keeping to the south shore to avoid the fort's deadly artillery. There was a wooded island ahead, which the Ottawa paddlers interposed between themselves and the fort.

Once they had passed the island, they turned north and recrossed the river, landing at what was obviously a war camp. Big Oak shook his head with amazement. Throughout nearly the entire canoe journey he had seen Indians—dozens of them, scores of them, hundreds of them, none of them feeling any need to hide themselves. That meant two things: first, that they were too strong to fear the English, and second, that they were too united to fear each other. Suddenly the emptiness of the land through which they had traveled on the way to Detroit made sense to him. Of course they weren't *there*, they were *here!*

He was only half right. Many of the tribes he had expected to meet were busy attacking or preparing to attack other English outposts on the frontier. Without Big Oak's knowledge, or the knowledge of a single English-speaking white man in America, the Ottawa war chief Pontiac had assembled a coalition of tribes that would paint the valleys bloodred from New York to Illinois. Big Oak, Thad, and Herr Wendel's seven packhorses had blandly ignored all the signs and walked right into the middle of it.

With two final, powerful sweeps of their paddles, the warriors beached their canoe on a spit of land between two sycamore trees. Big Oak stood up. A warrior clapped his hands hard on his shoulders and Big Oak sat down. Then two more grabbed him by his deerskin shirt and flung him from the canoe. With his hands tied behind him, he was unable to break his fall. He landed hard on the roots of a sycamore, which punched the breath from his lungs. But he made no sound.

The one who had made him sit down in the boat now

grabbed his shirt and jerked him to his feet, then propelled him forward with a pair of stiff kicks to his rump. Still Big Oak was silent. He had been captured once by Shawnees, twenty years before, and been held prisoner for three days before he had managed to escape. He knew how to play the game. So he made no protests, gave them no petulant looks of annoyance, and above all showed no fear, either to them or to his own self.

Out of the dozens of Ottawa warriors tending to business or lounging around the camp, he picked out Pontiac immediately. The Ottawa chief was not the tallest man in camp, nor was he the strongest or handsomest. He was simply the dominant figure in the place, standing in the shade of a spreading maple, telling several men around him what he wanted done.

He was stark naked on this warm spring day, and painted from his forehead to his waist, with a silver pendant dangling from his nose. His head was shaved clean but for a short brush of hair that extended from just behind his forehead to the nape of his neck, tapering shorter down the back of his head. He was somewhere between forty and fifty years old, but the big belly often associated with older Indians was nowhere in evidence. He was trim and well-muscled, erect and haughty, every inch a forest nobleman, and a moment later, flung by his captors, Big Oak was on his belly, in the dust, in front of the forest nobleman.

This would not do for a man with the pride of Big Oak. Without haste he hoisted himself up to one knee and stared calmly, without emotion, into the eyes of Pontiac.

One of his captors spoke quickly to the chief in a dialect unintelligible to Big Oak. The trader climbed slowly to his feet and stood before Pontiac, his bright blue eyes quietly fastened upon the dark brown eyes of the Ottawa war chief.

Pontiac began to speak to him. Big Oak listened carefully. The words were vaguely familiar, but still not intelligible. Big Oak remained silent, sensing that Pontiac would not tolerate interruption. At last Pontiac's speech was concluded. With dignity Big Oak showed his bound hands, his meaning clear. "Untie me so we may talk, my brother," he said in English, just in case anybody present might be helpful.

Someone produced a knife and cut the bonds, and almost immediately Big Oak was massaging his wrists and waggling his fingers to get the blood flowing in his hands.

"Great chief," he began, trying a Delaware dialect along with his signs, "I come here to give fair trade to the tribes of the west. Why am I captive?"

The chief stood silent, arms folded, nostrils flared imperiously, somehow managing to look down upon Big Oak even though the trader was six inches taller than he was.

"He lies, Pontiac!" spat one of the warriors. "He was alone, with no packhorses."

Pontiac looked from the angry brave to Big Oak, and realizing that the white man did not understand the Ottawa tongue, he spoke a Delaware dialect, not well, but well enough. "Where are your packs?"

Big Oak did not answer, and for a moment all parties stood quietly staring at each other. Then Pontiac became angry himself.

"He does not speak because he does not wish to give anything away, fool," he snarled at the warrior. "Was he carrying a pack?"

The warriors shook their heads.

"A scout in the woods without his pack? Where was his pack? On the back of an animal, maybe? And where was the animal? Maybe with several others, loaded with trade goods, led by another white man. You missed the big prize, my brothers."

Big Oak's captors looked at each other and then began a

many-sided argument that Pontiac cut short with a sweep of his hand. "Leave me, all of you," he said. "I will talk with the trader." The Ottawas who had captured Big Oak walked away grumbling, but Pontiac was not satisfied. "*All of you,*" he hissed to the few who remained.

"Sit," he ordered.

Big Oak lowered himself into a cross-legged position easily, like an Indian, without the use of his hands. Pontiac stood over him for a moment, looking down at him, then sat in a similar fashion.

"Who are you?" he signed.

"I am Big Oak from the People of the Western Door," the trader replied.

An expression of mild surprise crossed the face of the great chief. "You are a Seneca? No, you are a fool for showing your face around Detroit. There is a war. One by one my braves are conquering the English forts. The great tribes are all joining us in this war—including your Seneca —and we will not stop until we have driven the English back across the ocean."

"And where will you get your ammunition?"

"From our brothers the French. Oh, I have heard the stories the bad birds tell that the French king has gone to sleep and that all the French will be going home to sleep with him, but we have many friends, French friends, and they will not betray us."

"That may be so. I cannot say," Big Oak responded. "But you say that my brothers, the Seneca, are fighting with you. We were not told this."

"Nevertheless it is true. Kyashuta even now is leading an attack on one of the forts back East. He is a great war chief, your Kyashuta."

"Mmm, now I see. Yes, Kyashuta tried to bring the tribes together two years back, I remember."

"Now, white man." The Ottawa chief's voice suddenly became stern. "Where are your trade goods?"

"Wandering around the woods on the backs of my horses, I hope," Big Oak said. "I was scouting for my son when I was captured, and he is worth much more to me than the trade goods, and the horses, and all else I have in this world."

If Big Oak's declaration of love melted any part of Pontiac, he did not show it. "Eh! Bright morning!" he shouted toward a neighboring wigwam. A woman appeared and walked to the chief. She was middle-aged, about thirty-five, and heavy enough that there was a bit of a waddle in her walk as she made her way over.

"Speak to the white man in your tongue," he commanded her.

"I am Bright Morning," she began. "Who are you?"

It lifted the trader's spirits to hear the sounds of the Seneca tongue.

"I am Big Oak from Tonowaugh on the Genesee River," he answered.

The woman put her hand to her mouth in surprise. "It is true," she exclaimed. "I remember you when you would come to our village to fix our guns." She turned to Pontiac. "He is a famous hunter from among the Turtle clan," she told him. "A legend among my people."

Pontiac hid any signs of veneration with ease. "I do not need you anymore," he said, and Bright Morning waddled back to her wigwam.

"So," he said. "You are truly a Seneca, though you wear the white man's clothes and a white man's skin. Did you fight in the war against the French?"

"The last *two* wars against the French," Big Oak declared.

"Then might there be some soldiers in the fort who know you?" His tone of voice was sly and confiding.

"That is possible."

"And . . . could you gain their trust?"

"I have the trust of those who know me."

"It might be possible, then, for you to gain entrance, earn yourself the free run of the fort, and then late one night find a way to unlock and open the gates for us?"

"I have no doubt that I could find a way to do this."

"My brother, if you can do this, we will *have* the English!" Pontiac exclaimed.

Big Oak looked sadly at the great war chief. "My brother," he said, "for every Indian, there are ten Englishmen. They eat up the land like grasshoppers. Where they go, they change the land to something I do not love, and then I must go west to find land that I love. If I could find a way to keep them close to the sea so that the land would remain yours, I would do it.

"But I cannot." His voice almost cracked with emotion as he spoke his deepest thoughts. "I am a Seneca by choice," he continued. "But I am an Englishman by blood. I like many of the white men I have fought beside. My brother, I cannot betray them."

Pontiac's face darkened with anger. "You cannot betray them? This is war. If you will not betray them, then you betray us. You are no Seneca. You are a white man, outside and in!" Although he did not raise his voice, his fury was so apparent to those who furtively watched them converse from a distance that they now stared openly.

"I am a warrior of the Ganonsyoni," Big Oak persisted. "The Iroquois are not at war with the English, I don't care how many braves Kyashuta claims he can get, or how many forts he conquers. The nations of the Longhouse have been one for all these many years. It will be a bitter thing when the Longhouse falls apart. But it still stands as one, and until the day that the council fire at Onondaga goes out, I remain a warrior of the Longhouse. The Ganonsyoni are at peace with the English. This I know. I have become close to the Mohawk, as to the Seneca. I will not betray the Longhouse."

"And if you were to learn that the Iroquois have come over to us?"

"Speak to me then of loyalty and betrayal. I do not deny that I am a white man. I am also an Iroquois—a Seneca. I have fought my wars, and killed many more white men than red."

This hit home with Pontiac, for he knew that in the course of his life, intertribal warfare had caused him to kill many more Indians than whites. He shrugged off the thought. All that mattered at the moment was that this stiff-necked white Seneca refused to give him an easy victory at a time when his warriors were demanding one. The thought of spending months besieging Fort Detroit while throughout the East his subordinates were winning easy conquests, infuriated him. Indians could be very fickle about what chiefs they followed. How long would they stay with him if he did not give them victory?

"You are no good to me, white man," the infuriated chief said. "In war you cannot stand in the middle and worry about both sides. You must choose your side, and give your soul to it, or you are nothing.

"Bright Morning said you were a famous hunter to the Seneca. But to my people you are just an Englishman. To my people you are just an enemy. And you do not belong to me, you belong to them.

"Hey!" he shouted to the men who claimed captor's rights. "Take him. He is yours."

❧ 8 ❧

THE FOLLOWING MORNING BIG OAK AWOKE in the dark with a sense of someone looming over him. In a split second's time he remembered where he was and therefore did not resist when he was seized roughly and jerked to his feet.

His clothes had been stripped from him the night before, from his moccasins to his cap. All he wore was a dirty old breechclout and several purple bruises on various parts of his body where he had landed after being flung by his captors.

He had to make water, badly, but the Indian who had him by a rawhide halter around his neck was not about to attend to his bodily needs. He pulled Big Oak outside the hut where he had stayed the night and led him to a level stretch of ground where about sixty Ottawa tribesman of varied ages and sexes were waiting in a double line.

Gauntlet, his mind registered, and in the ten seconds it took to position him in front of the double line, it occurred to him that he had been present at many such events, and it was often the custom to inflict a stunning blow from behind and send the prisoner on his way when he was least ready, to make him more vulnerable and less aggressive.

Big Oak was determined to get himself started at *his* discretion, if possible.

He noticed that there were only a few warriors present, lined up at the beginning of the gauntlet. The rest of the warriors must have been slothing abed, as warriors were wont to do whenever possible. Or they were out somewhere harassing the fort. The remainder of the double line was made up of women, children, and old men. While the women could be formidable, he felt that if he could make it past the first half-dozen tormentors, he might have a chance to get through without being too gravely injured.

When he was ten yards from the gauntlet, he turned his back on the warrior who was leading him and raised his bound hands. The warrior shook his head, but he did release the halter. Quickly, he raised his tomahawk to give Big Oak a sudden blow with the blunt end, but Big Oak wasn't there anymore.

The early morning sun shone red above the horizon in Big Oak's face as he raced across the open space toward the double line of Ottawas. Thrilled by his aggressive spirit, the Ottawas whooped and shrieked; Big Oak headed for the center, between the two lines. The warriors closest to him raised their clubs to strike, but at the last moment Big Oak veered toward the first one on his right, lowered his shoulder and bounced off him too quickly for the warrior to get a good swing at him with his war club. The warrior across from him struck a glancing blow across Big Oak's back, painful but not debilitating.

Big Oak bounced from one side to the other as he went down the double line, legs pumping high to prevent anyone from tripping him up with a well-aimed blow at his ankles. His stomach muscles remained taut to deflect any blows aimed at his midsection. He tried to get a shoulder into half the warriors so that they would not be able to take a full swing at him, while those close by would not be able to get at his head or face for fear of hitting the warrior Big Oak was charging at the time. To the whoops and shrieks were added cries of anger as they saw their prisoner attacking rather than fleeing in panic.

Several blows across his back and neck were so heavy and painful that he almost went down, and one clever brave dealt him a direct blow to his knee, which made him grunt and stumble. He caught his balance, barely, then almost fell from a pair of blows from heavy sticks that glanced off the top of his head. The blows made his head ache and his ears ring. He stumbled again, but by strength of will alone he did not fall.

Just when his tormentors thought they had figured out what he was doing and began to fend him off and shorten their strokes, he aimed his run dead center and sprinted hard past the last two ranks of warriors, each one of whom managed to make bruising contact but none of whom were able to strike him hard enough to cripple him or slow his progress.

He had barely taken a breath of relief after passing the last of the warriors when he was nearly brought to his knees by a blow to the face from the club of an angry female. She did not care who else she hit as long as she got a piece of Big Oak in the process. She had swung her club laterally and made solid contact with his nose and jaw. Jagged red streaks of pain shot through his head, and only his deepest reserves of determination kept his legs moving as the blood poured down his face.

She wasn't through with him yet. Raising her stick high above her head, she brought it down just as he remembered to dodge left into one of his other tormentors. The club missed his head but crashed down on his shoulder, not quite breaking it. She was following him down the line, but her next backswing nearly brained one of her Ottawa sisters, spoiling her aim, and by then three more screeching women, their faces contorted with hatred, had caught her spirit, left the line, surrounded him, and were belaboring him with their cudgels, while farther back along the gauntlet the men had forgotten their anger and were laughing at the sight.

"You've got it easy!" shouted one to Big Oak. "We have to put up with that every day!" Big Oak would have appreciated the humor had he understood the language, and were he not so busy at the time. Grunting with the effort, he lowered his body into a crouch and barreled his way through the women standing in his way. The women tumbled like ninepins and the men roared.

By this time he was supposed to have been sufficiently beaten, weakened, and fatigued that he would be reeling and practically slowed to a crawl, easy prey for the "lesser" members of the gauntlet. Many of the children had thorny branches that scratched and lacerated him as he ran past, and some of the remaining women fetched him painful strokes, but his legs, still swift and fresh, carried him past them, yard after painful yard until, finally, he came to the last ranks, made up of older men, whose strength may have diminished but who were experienced in this sort of thing.

Desperately, he ducked a shoulder into one and ran him into two others, sending them sprawling backward, while those across the line from him reached out and clubbed him, too late and not hard enough. One crafty old fellow whipped a stick across his ankles, driving him down to one knee, but before anyone could finish him off while he was off balance, he staggered to his feet and regained his forward momentum.

Suddenly he found himself in the clear. There were no more clubs in front of him, and his legs outdistanced the one diehard old man who chased him and tried to get in a few last licks. He ran thirty more yards then stopped, turned around, and stared at them defiantly, his chest heaving as he struggled for his breath, his face a mass of blood, every square inch of his body bruised and sore.

There was no escape, so he continued to stare at them, standing with feet spread apart, his lungs laboring painfully, a snarl on his lips as he glared furiously at his captors.

For a few moments they stood stunned at what this aging Englishman had accomplished. Then the warrior who had first led him to the gauntlet walked down the gauntlet slowly, approaching Big Oak, who stood silently and watched him approach, disregarding the blood that flowed from his nose. The warrior attempted to grab his tether. Big Oak shrugged him off and started to walk back to the hut. Laughing, the Ottawa stepped in front of him.

"Do not think you have done something so wonderful," he said. "Look east to the red sun now, for this is the last morning your eyes will see. By tonight your eyes will be sightless, your head scalpless, your insides delicacies for the crows." As he spoke they walked together toward the hut, joined quickly by three other braves. Once inside, surrounded by four strong men brandishing tomahawks and knives, Big Oak submitted to being bound hand and foot and tossed in a dark corner like an old sack of flour.

And there he sat, his face and chest caked with drying blood, trying to make sense of his most recent experiences. Gradually his breathing and pulse returned to normal, the blood stopped flowing, and the aching bruises merged into one unified throb. To take his mind off his pain and his situation, he attempted to imagine what was going on in the outside world.

If Detroit was being besieged by a tribal alliance, and Fort Sandusky had been destroyed, then obviously the entire northwest was about to explode in the face of General Amherst, who was in charge of all things military in North America. In spite of the jeopardy he was in, Big Oak could not help but manage a grim smile. Amherst was a competent military man, but he had no respect for the Indians and was known to fly into rages every time one of his subordinates suggested that he treat the Indians as allies rather than as dogs. To him, Indians were low-life scum with no real capacity to resist the white man if the white man made up his mind to take care of the Indian problem. When news of this uprising finally reached him, he would have an apoplectic fit.

Big Oak's thoughts of Amherst were interrupted by noises of excitement outside that grew into a chorus of whoops and cheers. Quietly he waited, with some concern, wondering if the reason for those noises would have any bearing on his future, perhaps even delaying, or hastening, his death.

As Big Oak contemplated his uncertain future, his son awoke inside the fort with a sense of foreboding so oppressive that he had no desire to eat. Only the need to keep up his strength brought him to take a few morsels from the meager store of food in his pack and chew them while he hung around the parade ground by the Rue Saint Ann and observed the interior of the fort.

Detroit was not a small post, but an entire village within a stout stockade in which lived many people in addition to the soldiers. There were a large number of buildings close together, and it seemed that if the Indians wanted to get close enough in the dark of night, they could shoot swarms of fire arrows into the fort and set it ablaze within a short time.

A private who was observing the young trader looking around walked up to him. "You're the feller that had to outrun half of Pontiac's army yesterday, ain't ya?" he asked.

Thad nodded. "I still haven't had a chance to find out what's goin' on here," he said.

"Well, you know part of it. There's at least a thousand

savages out there tryin' to get in here, and maybe two hundred of us tryin' to keep them out, and this has been goin' on for more than two weeks."

"I never saw something like this before," Thad observed. "Indians like to attack and then run. They don't like to set in one place and wait."

"That's what all the traders keep tellin' us, but nobody told Pontiac."

At the second mention of Pontiac's name, Thad's eyebrows rose. "So he's a general now, is he?"

"Must be," the private said, "if he can keep all them howlin' critters fightin' together for any amount of time."

There was a stir of footsteps along the south wall, and a cry from a sentry on the parapet.

"Convoy comin'!" he cried toward the sergeant of the guard, who took off on the double to the quarters of the post commander.

"Well now, we'll see what that devil will do now," the private said, smiling as he headed for the steps, followed by Thad. "The one thing he had goin' for him was the chance of starvin' us out. Look at them bateaux. Ain't they the sweetest sight you ever want to see? Loaded with supplies. Let them redskins come. Let 'em dance and howl and come on in twos or threes or thousands, we'll be ready for them."

The catwalk was crowded with onlookers anxious to get a glimpse of the batteaux, just beginning to round the bend, flags flying, dripping oars sparkling in the morning sun. The soldiers let out a cheer, which the civilian witnesses happily joined. For a moment they forgot that they were not witnessing a rescue, just the arrival of enough supplies to extend the days and weeks of anxious watching and waiting while at any time the Indians threatened to storm the post and dash the lives out of all its English-speaking inhabitants.

Thad did not cheer. His keen eyesight caught something wrong in the lead boat and then the one behind it. There were too many men in the bateaux. *And the morning sun was glinting off the heads of some of them.* Thad watched silently, sadly, and waited for reality to dawn on those who stood on the ramparts of the southern wall of Fort Detroit.

"Oh, my God," came the strangled voice of a lieutenant who stood only a few feet from Little Oak. The cheers died in the throats of dozens of onlookers as they watched the prisoners row, spurred on by the tender urgings of the Chippewa, Ottawa, and Mississauga conquerors who sat behind the soldiers, their weapons pointed or poking at their unhappy captives.

For the Englishmen on the shore and those on the river, it was a most depressing scene. The soldiers in the bateaux had braved a long, perilous journey across Lake Erie, only to be ambushed and captured by the remorseless Indians of the West. And now to be forced to parade past the fort was a humiliation with a pain greater than death. Nor did they doubt that more pain would follow. There was not a single, solitary optimistic soul among the whites in the bateaux that rowed past the fort on that day.

The bateaux continued up the river past the fort and came to rest at the camp of Pontiac, where Big Oak sat in the dark of a bark hut. He heard a great commotion from the direction of the river, and heard a succession of shouted Ottawa and Chippewa orders, mixed with a few English expletives. Most of those expletives, he realized, were spoken by terribly frightened men. As he sat in the dark and listened, he could pretty much tell by the sounds what was going on.

They had captives. Quite a few captives, who they kicked and bullied up the slope from the river into the camp. And there was plunder too. He could hear captives and Indians straining with their burdens up the hill. He wondered—with trade goods and cargoes moved west, he always wondered—and soon he knew. There was rum. And it wasn't long before the rum was coming out of the kegs and into the Indians. Bad news, he thought, and he began to strain at his bonds. His chances of getting loose were nearly nil. Once he showed his face outside the hut, they would surely kill him, but if he just waited, they would just as surely come for him, and then the prediction of the Ottawa whose prisoner he was would come true.

There was a large hut next to the one in which he was being kept. In fact it was so close that they could have been parts of the same building. The Indians threw several soldiers—Big Oak guessed four—into the hut and went off to join the party.

The noise in the camp rose as the Indians divided their booty and broke open the rum. They began to drink, but before the liquor had time to take much effect, the Indians who controlled the soldiers next door returned. Curious, Big Oak snaked his way to the wall facing the hut where the English prisoners were confined. There he found a crack between the sheets of elm bark siding and watched them drag a soldier outside and start beating him. The soldier was so frightened that he did not resist. One of the Indians, a Chippewa, cut the soldier's bonds, but the soldier still did not resist when the Indians continued to beat him across his back and ribs with clubs and stout sticks.

The man was short and wiry, a handsome young man not without spirit when he had fought the Indians during the late ambush, but this was more than he was prepared to handle. He grunted and groaned with each blow, and remained passive when they stripped his clothes off. Big Oak supposed that the soldier thought the Indians would beat him until they were tired of beating him, and then, if he did not anger them by trying to battle with them, they might not kill him, at least yet.

So he was more than a little surprised when one of the Indians drew a knife and cut a deep gash in the soldier's right arm and pulled out a large piece of muscle tissue. The soldier screamed, and one of his tormentors whacked him on the side of his head with the side of a tomahawk.

Now they were on top of him, carving deep gashes in his body, but not so deep as to kill him. While the others held him down, one of the Indians carved an incision around his head, neat as any surgeon, then with a great effort ripped off the soldier's scalp. The poor man was screaming constantly, an inhumanly urgent scream mixed of fright and pain.

In a small clay vessel, one of the men carried a handful of live hot coals from a nearby campfire. They held the soldier in a sitting position and poured the hot coals upon his head into the horrible, bloody wound made by the scalping. Now the man's screaming lifted into an inhuman pitch. "Ahhhhh! Ahhhhh! *Ahhhhh!*" he screamed again and again, climbing into ever higher ranges as the Indians applied new tortures. The hot coals remained on his head because the Indians had fitted a fur cap tightly over his head to contain them.

The cap was Big Oak's, taken from him two days before.

·❧9❧·

THE NEXT TWO DAYS WERE AMONG THE MOST harrowing in Big Oak's life. Bound and powerless, he lay in his hut, hungry and thirsty, while around him the camp went berserk.

First the warriors next door got tired of the scalped soldier's screams and put him out of his misery by simply hacking his head off. Next they walked over to the center of camp and joined their companions in making certain that every drop of rum in the captured convoy was drunk.

Big Oak didn't have to be there to follow the action. He had been there before, and the scenario was always the same. Indians did not drink just because they enjoyed the burn of the alcohol on their tongue. They didn't drink just because of the mild warmth that a sip or two would impart to the stomach. Indians, he had decided long ago, drank as much as they could, as fast as they could, to get as drunk as they could, as quickly as they could. They knew the consequences, and few of them cared enough to do anything about it. Their need for it was their destruction.

And mine too, he mused, as he listened.

The noise was that of a disorderly crowd, milling and grabbing but not yet hostile. Already the drums were going and several different groups were singing different songs in different rhythms, none of them exactly congruent to the beat of the drums. Next door he could hear frightened chatter in soft voices among the English prisoners. He had to concede that his own throat muscles had tightened to the point that he could barely swallow. All this time, he continued to work at the bonds around his wrists and his ankles, but to no avail. His captors knew their business, and all his efforts did was wear deep red grooves in his skin. But in Big Oak lived a will to survive so strong that it would not allow him to surrender to despair. And so he continued to work at his bonds, consider his limited options, and listen to the party as it degenerated from mild disorder to drunken chaos.

He heard soft footsteps. His stomach muscles stiffened, but the steps passed by his hut and stopped at the neighboring one. A single word emerged from the Indian. "Oh, my God!" cried one of the men. There was a short scuffle, followed by the sound of a skull being struck a glancing blow by a blunt object.

"Oh!" the victim cried, and he must have yielded, for Big Oak now heard the sounds of two pairs of footsteps, one of them shuffling. A few moments later joyous cries from the merrymakers outside told Big Oak that the English prisoner had arrived.

He waited in the dark patiently, fruitlessly, working at his bonds. From the center of camp he could hear the murmurs and shouts of the Ottawas. Once he thought he heard a groan rise above the noise. Then he heard a scream. And a few minutes later he heard an inhuman screech that repeated and repeated, louder and louder, and shouts from the aroused onlookers that nearly drowned out the tormented cries of agony that issued again and again from the tormented prisoner. Big Oak refused to imagine what, precisely, they were doing to their prisoner to extract such desperately horrible shrieks from him. Instead he thought about his bonds, and how, if only he could manage to sweat more, he might somehow slip his hands past them.

After a few moments the tumult died down. Big Oak could hear the low, incoherent moaning of the Englishman at his stake as he awaited his next torment. From next door came a soft whimper, and nobody told the whimperer to shut up. Methodically, thoughtfully, Big Oak worked at his bonds. Between the screams he could hear panicked whispering among the terrified prisoners in the hut near his.

Now came a chorus of "ahs" from the assemblage, followed by screams louder and more hideous than the ones before, cut short by a sudden silence, then followed by murmurs and grumbles. The prisoner had fainted or died, and now hung motionless by his bonds from the stake.

More footsteps, past the hut. No, they stopped, retraced their steps, then suddenly the awful bright light of day blinded Big Oak as the deerskin door lifted and the silhouette of his captor appeared in the doorway looking like death itself. Quickly he took five steps across the room, bent down and severed the thongs binding Big Oak's legs. Although he was certain that his death awaited outside, he could not cut and run. His feet were so numb he could barely stand.

With the last of his reserves of courage, he swallowed his fear and stared straight into the eyes of the Ottawa brave. The man nodded approvingly. "We will break you, you'll see," he said in his own tongue, and although Big Oak did not understand a word, he grasped the meaning.

He reached the center of camp in time to see the braves carrying the severed limbs of the freshly butchered corpse to the bank of the river, where they were having a contest to see who could toss a limb farthest out into the current. Their efforts were not impressive. Most of them were by now so drunk that their coordination was not at its best. They staggered as they took their running start toward the river. One of them was not able to stop at all after he had hurled his piece of arm into the river. He splashed head-long into the water even before the limb landed. His stumbling, drunken cohorts fished him out sputtering and angry.

Big Oak knew that if that Indian spotted him before he had cooled down, then he'd never even make it to the stake. His captor had tied a thong around his neck and led him by it, like a dog. Big Oak forced himself to stand straight and preserve his dignity. His captor began to sign to him. "You will stand and watch. You will taste what is to come for you. Then if you can still stand straight and tall, we will all admire you, even as we roast your flesh."

"Thank you," he nodded graciously. The Ottawa missed Big Oak's sarcasm.

The rest of the afternoon he stood and watched as the remaining inhabitants of the hut next door were led to the stake, bound, tortured, killed, and dismembered. As each prisoner reached the end of his usefulness or entertainment value to the warriors, he was cut apart—sometimes while still conscious—and his pieces thrown into the river. Out of control, in the grip of alcohol, the Ottawas in the war camp used up their prisoners like a spendthrift spends his cash. In fact, the surviving prisoners from the convoy had been allotted to the villages of the various tribes camped close to Detroit, and similar scenes were occurring in most of these villages.

Thad stood on the south wall catwalk with Private James Meacham, staring at the river. Meacham was one of the youngest soldiers on the post, and Thad had taken an in-stant liking to him because of his innocent good nature. Barely eighteen, he had been recruited in Philadelphia and somehow been assigned to this post in the middle of the howling American wilderness.

As they stood together watching the river swirl below them past the south wall, Thad was explaining how he and his father happened to be out in the middle of this wilderness during the worst of all possible times.

"My father-in-law," he said, "is a rich Dutch shopkeeper in Albany. Like most rich shopkeepers, his aim in life is to get richer. So one day he calls me to his desk up in the balcony of his shop and he says, 'Thad, my boy, the war is over and my gun business is down. You have talked to me many times about trading wit' der Indians out West.'

"Now James, I gotta tell you, I was raised with the Iroquois and I feel real good when I'm around them, in fact I'm one of them, but these western Indians, I don't know. The Iroquois don't like white men very much, and I don't blame them, but these Ottawa were out after my scalp and they didn't ask any questions. I believe they're out to kill every white man they can get their hands on."

"Every white man who speaks English," young Meacham responded.

"Anyway," Thad continued, "The old Dutchman says, 'If we can be the first ones to bring the goods west, we can make lots of money, you'd like that, yes?'

"I said, 'Well yes, but the risk is—' will you look at that!"

Thad's keen eyes had spotted something floating down the river surrounded by a pool of red, followed by two or three smaller somethings, and his heart sank. Over the next several hours the river carried an endless succession of body parts past the fort, including a number of heads. Inhabitants of the fort rushed to the top of the south wall to take a look, and occasionally, to their horror, one or another body part was identified as belonging to this or that obviously deceased individual. All the people who witnessed the grisly parade were moved by it, but it was almost more than Thad could bear. And yet he felt that he had to be there, watching closely, just in case any of these body parts should belong to his father.

Young Meacham, aware of Big Oak's peril, had the delicacy to keep silent.

A band of Chippewas who had been making their way south to join Pontiac's rebellion arrived in the Ottawa war camp just as the last of their prisoners from the convoy was being bound to the stake. They watched in silence as his tormentors clipped off his fingers and tried to make him eat them, then pulled out an eyeball and made him eat it.

"Where is your whiskey?" they asked the subchief who seemed to be in charge of the party. The Ottawa belched and explained that the whiskey was all gone, which put the Chippewas in a foul mood. Judging by the condition of what few warriors still stood upright, the Chippewas had missed the best part.

The torturers cut slits in the prisoner's arms and began pulling out bands of sinew, which elicited satisfying howls from him. They then pulled smoldering branches from a nearby fire and drove them into the cavities where the muscles had been. That really got him going. He was a big man. He twisted and shook so violently that the stake began to move in the loose dirt. In his torment, the prisoner felt the stake give. He leaned forward and gave a mighty pull and the stake came free of the dirt. Desperately he began to run, with the stake on his back, dragging in the dirt behind him, and the onlookers howling at the humor of it all. The stake was too big for the victim to carry, and after six or seven steps he collapsed on his belly with the stake on top of him.

The Chippewas were not amused. "Where are your other prisoners?" their leader asked. They were a fairly young band, full of themselves, and at the moment they felt supe-

rior to and contemptuous of the sloppy drunks who were
having so much fun while they, having neither rum to
drink or prisoners to torture, were feeling deprived and put
upon. The Indian way was to share, they reasoned, and
they wanted their share.

"He is the last one," the Ottawa subchief told them.

The Chippewa leader looked around the camp furiously.
This was the third village they had visited on this day, and
in each case everybody was having a good time but them.
At last his eye lit on Big Oak, who was strapped securely to
a pine tree.

"What about him?" the Chippewa asked.

"Not him," was the response. "We have special plans for
him."

The Chippewa walked to within a few feet of Big Oak.
The two stood tall and fixed their eyes on each other. Al-
though the Chippewa was four inches shorter than Big
Oak, his menacing gaze was that of a free man, while Big
Oak's was the vain one of a captive's defiance.

"We want this one," the Chippewa insisted. Those Ottawas whose senses were not completely befuddled began
to crowd around the disputants. Then there was a push,
followed by an elbow, and suddenly there was a real danger of a melee.

"Stop!" shouted a voice of confident command. Chippewas and Ottawas ceased their quarrel and turned their faces
toward Pontiac. "Why do brothers quarrel over a dead
man?"

"Obwandiyag, my brother," the Chippewa leader said,
"we have journeyed long to be with you, and we arrived
today, too late to share goods and prisoners from your victory. We know your men were very brave, and we know
they have killed many Englishmen. We wish to hear the
screams of torment of just one, but your men are very
greedy. They do not wish to give this one up."

An angry look flashed across the face of Pontiac. "Let it not be said that the Ottawa are greedy. My brothers here will be happy to present as a gift this white man. But—"

At this the Ottawas grew furious and the subchief glared drunkenly at Pontiac as he spoke. "What right have you to take our prisoner from us? He is ours. We will not let anyone take him!"

Here was a dilemma for Solomon. Pontiac, charged with the grave responsibility of keeping together the warriors from a dozen tribes, thought carefully, knowing that the wrong answer could put his two most important tribes at each other's throats.

"I will tell you," he said. "The Chippewa and the Ottawa are both renowned for their ability to bring the Englishmen to their knees. Here is a test. Tomorrow morning we will see who has the key to this white man's soul. He is a man. This I know. Your task will not be easy. As guests, the Chippewa will have him first. They may do as they wish, but they must leave enough of the white man so that the Ottawa will have a fair chance. And you must acclaim your brothers when their work is good."

The warriors from the two tribes each thought about this contest and soon their exclamations showed that they were impressed by Pontiac's solution. In fact, Pontiac was so impressed by the ease with which he had stopped a dangerous disagreement between the two tribes that he felt the need to stand before Big Oak and explain what he had just done. Big Oak rolled his eyes to the heavens and his spine turned cold. He waggled his hands, and Pontiac cut the cords that bound them. Big Oak did not want to beg for his life, but neither did he want to die.

"Obwandiyag, I am a Seneca of the Turtle clan. I know that you have allies among the Seneca and they might not be pleased to know that you have treated me like this. I am well-known among all the Six Nations. If you do not want their undying hatred, you will not allow your people to use me so."

Pontiac's nostrils flared with contempt. "My allies have no use for Englishmen," he said. "We *must* defeat the English, and we will allow no friendships with white men to come between us. As for your Iroquois?" He spat. "They are of the past. There was a time we feared them. No more." And he turned his back on Big Oak and walked away.

It was the sunset of a long day for Big Oak. Still bound tight, he sat by the door of his hut and watched the great red giver of life as it dipped toward the horizon. He remembered the many campfires on the trail after long, satisfying days of hunting the deer, or paddling a canoeload of pelts. The last years had been some of the best, for those were the years when he shared the trail with his grown son, Little Oak.

What a man his son had grown into. While Big Oak still longed for the forest canopy and grieved for the vanishing wilderness of his Iroquois comrades, Little Oak had found a home in Albany, where he had married a Dutch girl and begun a family. He no longer called himself Little Oak, the name given him by his Seneca grandfather Kendee. During the late French and Indian War he had reverted to the name his parents had given him at his birth, Thad, after his New England grandfather. As each year passed, Big Oak could see his son lose more of the Seneca warrior restlessness as he settled into the world of trade and commerce.

And yet when his business called him to the woodland, Thad eagerly responded, usually teamed with his formidable father. Thad had grown into the finest trailmate Big Oak had ever known. As Big Oak watched his final sunset, he knew that his last thoughts would be of his son and of his young grandson who would never get to know him. Toughness of mind was a critical part of Big Oak's makeup, but as the wonderful memories of the years marched before his eyes, he allowed himself a thin film of tears. Then, exhausted by the events and emotions of the past few days, his eyelids began to close. As the sun sank behind the great trees of the western forest, his chin sank to his chest and a deep, satisfying sleep took possession of this good, unhappy man.

❈10❈

LE GRAND COUREUR DID NOT LOVE WAR. That does not mean that he was a coward. Far from it. He was, in a sense, a throwback to the days of spears and stone arrowheads and war clubs, before the white man brought the magical bullets that could not be seen in flight but which allowed men weak as women to kill the mightiest warriors from great distances.

Among the Chippewas, young men who did not achieve glory on the warpath generally did not get much respect in their village, but Le Grand Coureur was an exception. The men in his village, which was located on North Bay near where lakes Huron, Superior, and Michigan meet, loved the game of baggataway, and Le Grand Coureur was the finest baggataway player in tribal memory.

By the time he was sixteen years of age, Tegwash, as he was originally called, had established himself as the fastest runner in the village. Several French traders who had won and lost wagers on footraces within the village had dubbed him "Le Grand Coureur," the Great Runner, and soon the name had stuck even among his Chippewa compatriots.

Over the next three years his body had filled out with thick, solid muscle, and he had found himself able to hold his own against the best baggataway players in his or any other village, Chippewa, Sac, or Ottawa. His stickwork was vicious, and his body collisions numbing, but what separated him most from his fellow players was his ability to pick up the ball, work his way through a crowd and into the clear without being crippled by the sticks his opponents swung at him with deadly intent. Once in the clear, he was too swift to be caught from behind and too agile to be stopped by a single warrior in his path.

Baggataway was the original form of lacrosse, but the way the Indian tribes played it, it was barely distinguishable from warfare. Broken bones and crippling knee injuries were frequent, and deaths were neither unusual or particularly shocking. The games often involved dozens of warriors on each side, on a field as big as a battlefield. Large wagers were the rule, and one game might last all day, even if the contest was to be decided by one goal.

You might say that in his day Le Grand Coureur revolutionized the game. Several times he had been known to pick up a loose ball near the beginning of the game, maneuver through an entire team of his opponents (so the legends declare), and touch the opponents' goal, thereby bringing to a speedy end a game that was supposed to provide an entire day's diversion for two Indian villages. One day it was even agreed that two games would be played, a short game that would be decided early by the superior skills of Le Grand Coureur, and a long game involving two teams very evenly matched without him.

His prowess as an athlete might have made him a powerful, happy man in other societies, but to the Chippewas battle was life, and baggataway was sport, and so when the sticks and the wooden ball were put away, and the tomahawks and guns came out, Le Grand Coureur faded into the background.

This was especially hard on his pride in time of war, and

at this time the Chippewa were up to their scalp locks in war. So when the plan for the seizure of Fort Michilimackinac was revealed, Le Grand Coureur was thrilled. At last the time had come when his baggataway skills would help to win him glory in battle, without the likelihood of his magnificent body being mangled by a rifle bullet or a cannonball.

On this day the opponent was to be an aggregation from the Sac tribe, a people Le Grand Coureur loved to hate. The game was to be played on a field a half mile long, stretching out before the gate of Fort Michilimackinac. The charade was to be planned so carefully, and carried out with such infinite attention to detail, that the surprise would be complete. To that end, the Sacs were invited for a week of festivities featuring games and trading and all the forms of socializing that made springtime on the lakes a good time for the western tribes.

The men in the fort caught the spirit too, and were out among the tribesmen watching the competitions and the horse trading and deciding that maybe these redskins were fine fellows after all.

And then the chiefs announced that the following morning there would be a baggataway match between the Sacs and the Chippewas, featuring, of course, Le Grand Coureur.

Many eyes were upon him as he, and others on his team and that of the opposition, jogged up and down the field in front of the fort in the blue half-light of predawn. Beyond the high palisades of the fort were the Straits of Mackinac, which united the seething waters of lakes Huron and Michigan. In front of the fort was the huge cleared field that was supposed to expose any and all attackers to the deadly musket and cannon fire of the fort, and east of the field were miles and miles of green wooded canopy.

The day dawned sunny and mild. Scores of Indian men intermingled with traders and soldiers of the fort, whose gates were open wide, as they had been throughout the celebration. The men were swapping good-natured insults and challenges as they made their bets on the two teams, and quite a few of the Indian women entered the fort, as they often did, to indulge their curiosity about the white folks' way of living. It seemed a fine way to open the easy living that the warm months of the year brought to this part of the country.

But if the post commander, Captain Etherington, or his second in command, Lieutenant Leslye, had been exceptionally suspicious or observant, they might have noticed that there were no children around, and they might have found that odd. The Indians, unlike the upper-class English, liked having their children with them at almost all times.

The game began, if anything, rougher than usual. Players were spending more time whacking each other than the ball, perhaps because they were determined to look authentic to the English, or perhaps because Chippewas and Sacs just didn't like each other very much. Le Grand Coureur did not pay much attention to this foolishness. His eyes, as usual, were on the ball, and on the field, measuring the openings, looking for the grand chance, retreating as the mass of Sacs drove the Chippewas back to their own goal. At last he saw the opening he had been waiting for. Swift and straight as an arrow, he flew through an open space and swung his stick at the exposed ankle of a Sac who thought he had about a hundred yards of clear field in front of him.

The sound of a bone cracking was clear enough to make Captain Etherington flinch on the sidelines. The Sac warrior sprawled and then rolled over in pain as the ball he was carrying rolled free. Quickly Le Grand Coureur scooped it up, feinted two angry Sacs out of position, and began to sprint downfield toward the Sac goal. Cheers erupted from the English, and the Chippewa contingent whooped and screeched as he darted in and out, eluding sticks and bodies with ease, pursued by many and caught by none until at last, hemmed in by four or five Sacs, with nowhere to go, he hurled the ball in the direction of one of his teammates, ducked out of the way of a stick swung like a scythe, and for good measure jammed the handle of his stick into the ribs of the nearest Sac before he broke off his charge and retreated toward midfield. The English, always appreciative of good gamesmanship, applauded his performance, while the warriors of his tribe shouted his name and urged him to do it again.

But it was his way to lurk on the fringes of the action, waiting, waiting, taking or giving no blows for the sake of combat but determined, when the moment was right, to do anything that had to be done for the sake of scoring a goal, always alert for the opportunity.

And that opportunity came, about twenty minutes later, when the ball was pitched toward the west side of the field, near the corner of the stockade. There were only three players in that area, two Sacs waiting to pick up the ball that was rolling their way, and the hard charging Le Grand Coureur. The ball, the Sacs, and the Coureur all reached the same place at the same time. In one fluid motion Le Grand Coureur rammed the handle of his stick into the teeth of one Sac, leveled the other with a swing of his stick across his head, then scooped up the ball and charged toward the center of the field so he would not be hemmed in by the wall of the fort. Some of the English were aghast. They knew the Chippewas did not love the Sacs, but they had never seen Baggataway played like this.

In the center of the field he had room to dodge around several of the enemy, who were now as determined to kill him as they were to dislodge the ball. In fact, their very fury made it that much easier for him to dodge their deadly rushes and swipes. He had a nearly clear field ahead of him now, a certain chance at scoring a goal that would add to his legendary glory. But as he drew opposite the gate, he heard a wild vibrating cry that could have only been a signal from the Chippewa chief, Minivavana.

Instead of continuing his dash toward the goal, Le Grand Coureur spotted a teammate on his wing, near the open gate of the fort, and hurled what was probably the worst pass he had ever thrown in his life. The ball cleared his teammate's head by at least ten feet and rolled through the gateway into the fort. Now in a wild, shouting, snarling, milling mob nearly obscured by a dust cloud, all the players, including Le Grand Coureur, ran through the gate chasing the ball.

Once inside, however, they ran not to the ball, but to their women, who were busily retrieving knives and tomahawks from under their blankets and handing them to the players and to Indian onlookers who had followed them into the fort. The players were suddenly warriors, attacking the nearest soldiers and braining them before their faces could even grimace in surprise.

Outnumbered, the soldiers fell quickly before the deadly onslaught. Right in the middle of the onslaught was Le Grand Coureur, scarcely aware that he had made the transition from player to warrior. He alone had eschewed the tomahawk or war club. His heavy, stout, baggataway stick was his war club. Before him was an English soldier, a musket in his hand, but not raised for defense. One downward chop of Le Grand Coureur's stick and the soldier was down forever. A Chippewa spectator, thrilled to see his sports hero in action so close to him, handed him his knife, and for the first time in his life Le Grand Coureur took a scalp.

Within two minutes' time the scene at the east wall of

Fort Michilimackinac had undergone an incredible change. Instead of the shouts and grunts of sport and fellowship, there were the howls and screeches of terror and pain as one by one the Chippewas and Sacs introduced the English soldiers and traders to swift, violent death.

There was no call to arms, no counterattack, no battle, only the frightened screams of helpless men caught in an unimaginable nightmare. Only in this case the nightmare was truth. The illusion had been the sport and fellowship in the shadow of a fort too strong to have fallen in battle.

Booted footsteps fled across the parade ground, followed by other, soft, barefoot footfalls. Then would come a brief, feeble struggle, followed by screams of pain and the laughter of satisfied victory. Another skull crushed. Another scalp ripped. Another life surrendered.

The surprise was so complete that within a very few minutes every soldier in or near the fort was dead and mutilated except for a handful who had been taken prisoner. And for the only time in his life, the glory of Le Grand Coureur was not the symbolic glory of victory on the playing field, but the real glory of the kill on the battlefield.

He found himself alone, running quickly through the alleys of the fort, looking for soldiers and English traders who were searching for a place to hide. And soon he did find one, a puny, miserable private pounding on the door of a house, pleading with its French occupants, his friends but also friends of the Chippewas, to let him in and hide him, that he might be spared.

Le Grand Coureur stalked his prey so quietly that the soldier did not feel his presence until he grabbed the soldier by the hair and pulled him off the porch of the house. The soldier tried to battle back, but Le Grand Coureur's muscles were like iron. The knife was still in his right hand, dripping blood from his first victim. He had no trouble pulling the soldier backward to him and slitting his throat, all in one fluid motion. It was a new kind of excitement and power to him, feeling the white man's body go limp as the blood rushed from his neck. Le Grand Coureur let his victim slide to the ground, lifeless. On he went in search of his next victim.

And then, all at once, it was over. There were no more white spectators standing in the field watching baggataway. Most of them had abruptly been turned into ghosts, their bloodless bodies lying in the dust of Fort Michilimackinac missing various parts of their anatomy. Others were being led away on leather leashes, their minds paralyzed by the suddenness and complete success of the attack.

There were no more privates at their post. Every single one had been killed quickly by the game players and spectators turned warriors. No doubt there were some Englishmen hiding in the houses around the fort. No matter, they'd be found.

Now even the screams of victory were dying down. The parade ground of the fort was covered with scalped and mutilated soldiers and traders, their blood still running from fresh wounds, into the dry dust of Fort Michilimackinac.

Le Grand Coureur suddenly lost all interest in the battle. Let the others look for prisoners to torture. He had done more than his share, both on the playing field and on the battlefield. His bloodlust had left him as quickly as it had come to him. He now wanted nothing but to go back to his home on North Bay.

And he did.

❧ 11 ❧

Big OAK HAD A DREAM THAT NIGHT. IT WAS A
dream he had had many times before. In the dream he and
Thad were paddling south along the Susquehanna River.
That was all there was to the dream, but it seemed to go on
forever. The river was always smooth as glass, the weather
mild, a breeze at their backs and the trees green with the
leaves of early summer. He had once told Thad that his
idea of heaven was just such an endless journey, and God
in His mercy had seen fit to grace his last night with this
dream, perhaps to give him courage in his final agonizing
moments.

He awoke in the dark, screaming. No, that wasn't right.
It wasn't him screaming at all. His Ottawa captor and another warrior were screaming at him, jerking him to his
feet, jangling his nerves before taking him outside for the
early morning torments.

As his mind cleared he realized that he still didn't have it
right. In fact, the Ottawa was having a shouting match
with the leader of the newly arrived Chippewas. It was
obvious that the Chippewa was demanding the possession
of Big Oak, and that the Ottawa was ready to go to war
against him to keep Big Oak. Both of them had a hand on

his tether and were alternately jerking him one way or the other to punctuate their arguments. The Ottawa pummeled Big Oak impersonally over his left ear to make a point, in response to which the Chippewa jerked so hard on the tether that Big Oak let out an involuntary strangling noise and lurched up against the Ottawa, who cuffed Big Oak once more.

"I owe you, you wild sonofabitch," he said evenly to the Ottawa, who was so ferociously preoccupied in his dispute with the Chippewa that he did not even notice Big Oak's attempted interruption. Big Oak curbed his tongue then, recognizing there was an even chance that the two men would compromise by dragging him to the stake and torturing him immediately for the edification of both tribes.

The Ottawa and the Chippewa continued their argument, generating more and more heat, their scalp locks shaking with barely controlled passion. Just as they seemed about to lay hands on each other, the deerskin in the doorway was lifted and the dignified figure of Pontiac made its way into the room.

The two litigants turned to him and started to make their case, but Pontiac raised a hand and the debate immediately ceased. He spoke a few words, quietly but with strong emotion. The two contentious Indians reluctantly growled their assent and left the hut. Pontiac glared at Big Oak as if he had instigated the argument, and then left the hut, leaving Big Oak wondering what Pontiac had said to stop the argument.

He did not have to wait long to find out. Within an hour he heard the sound of gunfire in the distance, steady fire directed at the fort, he was sure. Obviously the convoy they had captured had contained considerable ammunition, and Pontiac had decided to put some pressure on Detroit, if for no other reason than to keep his braves from getting restless and bored with the siege. He noted that the fort refused to reply with cannon, a sure indication that they were preserving their slender stock of ammunition.

The firing continued all day, and nobody bothered with him until early in the afternoon, when one of the Chippewa braves visited him and took him out so he could relieve himself, then gave him a little water and food. Big Oak was extraordinarily grateful for the attention and said so, his tone of voice communicating what his English could not. In return the Chippewa told him to shut up, and retied his tether a bit more tightly than before.

Early that evening the Ottawa came to visit Big Oak. He was in a foul mood, and signed that by this time Big Oak should have already been feeding the crows, as well as such Ottawas in the camp who would have liked to partake of his flesh. Big Oak recalled the Iroquois were hated by their Algonquian neighbors because they occasionally ate their enemies, but he knew that these other tribes were not totally averse to an occasional bit of cannibalism themselves.

Big Oak was a practical man, as well as a Christian. The thought of being eaten after his death held no horrors for him. Even the idea of his own death was more sad than frightening to him. It was the thought of being tortured all day by pitiless men who expected him to endure the most harrowing agonies that twisted his gut into a tight knot.

As if reading his thoughts, the Ottawa began a sequence of signs and speech explaining that the following morning he would be taken out and made to watch while his limbs were hacked off, boiled and eaten by the mighty Ottawa. There was one Ottawa brave so skilled in surgery that he could extract a liver and devour it in front of his victim while the victim not only continued to live, but remained conscious enough to be aware of what was going on in front of his eyes, though usually the pain was so great that he could not pay much attention. Big Oak missed about half of what the Ottawa was trying to tell him, but half was quite enough to remind him of what considerations they held in store for him.

Big Oak thanked the Ottawa in English, Seneca, Mohawk, and Delaware for revealing his future. When the Ottawa left, he strained at his bonds once again, but without progress. Then he maneuvered himself into a kneeling position and began to pray. Big Oak was a man who normally regarded prayer as a nagging supplication to a being who had a lot of more important things to worry about. Generally he felt that a strong man had the obligation of keeping his needs to himself and not imposing them on God unless he really had no choice. On this evening, after days of helpless fear and pressure, he finally conceded that his needs were great. He prayed for release, in whatever form God chose to provide that release. Suddenly he realized he was extremely weary. Even though he had spent the day with no activity, the tension of his confinement had taken its toll. In spite of the fact that his remaining moments on earth were precious and few, sleep again came easy to Big Oak.

When he awoke it was still pitch-black outside. Almost immediately he realized where he was and what the sunrise held in store for him. Out of habit he tried the thongs that held his legs and arms, and the tether that bound him to the wall of the hut. All were secure, and in spite of his desire to fight till the end, his spirits fell.

As his eyes became accustomed to the darkness, he saw a dark form lurking over him. He shook his head, assuming that he was still dreaming, and hoping that perhaps the entire memory of his captivity had been a dream. Then the dark form moved. The regular shape of its top indicated a shaved skull. The whites of its eyes showed clearly. An arm moved in the dark. At the end of the arm was a knife. Not yet fully awake, Big Oak braced himself for a slash across his throat or the front of his scalp. Instead the knife went against the Indian's mouth as a gesture for quiet, and now Big Oak recognized the man as the Chippewa chief who the day before had quarreled with the Ottawa for possession of him.

Big Oak nodded his understanding of the chief's gesture. The knife flashed once, twice. His legs were free, and he was no longer bound by the neck to the wall of the lodge. Behind him a brave reached underneath Big Oak's arms and pulled him to his feet. They did not untie his arms, and the chief held tight to the thong that remained knotted like a leash around his neck. Big Oak was far from pleased with the arrangement, but he had no choice but to go with them. Quietly they slipped from the hut, across the clearing, and down to the river, where three beautiful white birch-bark war canoes full of Chippewas were waiting for them. The chief pointed to a spot in the middle of one of the canoes. Big Oak began to step into it, and almost tripped and fell into the bottom, his legs still numb from many hours of being bound by the cruel thongs.

In perfect silence the Chippewas pushed off from the shore and began to paddle toward the middle of the river, eastward on a journey that he knew would soon be heading north to Lake Huron. For the next five minutes the only sounds were the quiet dipping of paddles into the river and the dripping of water from the paddles as they were lifted from the river.

Finally, the chief spoke to one of the warriors, and the warrior spoke to Big Oak, in a language he did not understand. Big Oak shook his head and the warrior tried again, in a different tongue. Big Oak again indicated that he did not understand, and the warrior spoke still one more time, this time in passable Delaware. Big Oak replied in the same tongue, relieved that for the first time in days he could communicate with someone in spoken language who didn't seem determined to cleave his skull as soon as possible.

The chief spoke, and then the warrior spoke. "We have taken you from the Ottawa," he said, "because they have no right to deny us white prisoners to torture. We want nothing to do with such stingy allies."

"I don't blame you," Big Oak replied with an irony that must have evaded the Chippewa chief, for he kept speaking, and the warrior kept translating.

"We will take you to our village to the north, and there we will treat you fine until the time has come to burn you. We hope you will be brave."

"Me too," Big Oak agreed. This time, on receiving the translation, the chief laughed. In fact, Big Oak had quickly regained his spirit. His death, instead of being hours away in a murderously hostile village, was now days away, and he was still many miles from the appointed place of execution. Optimist that he was, Big Oak's spirits were soaring. Anything could happen between now and then, he thought almost joyously.

If Big Oak had been sleeping well in the shadow of death, back in the fort, Thad was not sleeping well at all. He had spent too much time behind wooden walls worrying about his father. He was a man of action, but there were thousands of English-hating Indians camped up and down the Detroit River. His chances of leaving the fort by day and escaping the clutches of the Indians were almost nil, and if they caught him, he would probably come floating down the river past the fort piece by piece like so many before him. And what if he got out? What was he supposed to do, start asking Potawatomies if they had lately seen a tall white man in deerskins running around the woods?

He and his father had been friends and companions for a long time, and they could generally tell when the other was in trouble. It wasn't so much a mystical sixth sense as an ability to read the circumstances. Had Big Oak been free and uninjured, he would have by now found a way to make it to the fort. Big Oak was in trouble; his son was sure of that.

On the other hand, if he had been caught and killed, Thad was certain that he would have found out about it either by watching the bodies float by on the Detroit River or via the French grapevine. The Indians pretty much trusted the French and gave them free run outside the fort, but there were Frenchmen who, because of friendship or self-interest, provided Major Gladwin with information about the Indians besieging him.

There had as yet been no information concerning Big Oak. But there was no way for Thad to leave the fort. All the gates were secured during the night. At first he moped around the fort and brooded, but soon it occurred to him that if his father were in his shoes, he would use this time to gather information that might be of help to him when he finally did get out. So he began to talk to people, and he found out some interesting things—mostly about people.

The officers, he found, were not that interested in telling him anything, partly for security reasons and partly out of snobbishness—to them he was simply a young woodsman with no reputation and no financial means that they could ascertain. He wondered how they would behave if they met him on the streets of Albany dressed in the clothing of a prosperous merchant.

The privates were different. They loved to find company to swap rumors with, to relieve the boredom. The only problem was that rumors were all they knew. Their officers and noncoms did their best to keep them ignorant.

The white traders regarded him with suspicion. Their early conversations with him convinced them that he was what he said he was, a trader like themselves, and with enough resources to provide formidable competition once there was peace.

His best sources were the French traders and farmers still living within the fort. They knew the Indians best, and what they told him was not encouraging. Particularly there was Jacques Baby, who took an interest in the young man and enjoyed good company, and was glad to swap stories and information with Thad. There was a general uprising going on throughout the west, Baby explained to him, with a dozen tribes looking for English forts to burn and English men to kill.

They were angry because once the war had ended, the English refused to trade with the Indians as freely as the French had, withholding in particular guns and ammunition that the Indians had to have if they were to survive.

"Mon frere," he said genially, "the Indians are afraid that the English will not trade them ammunition because they want to make it easier to drive them away, so they can steal more land. Can you blame them?" he asked as if he expected an argument from Thad.

"Of course I don't blame them," Thad answered. "My father says that when they make somebody a general or a governor in the colonies, part of the ceremony is to remove the man's brain."

Baby laughed, hard, a laugh that resounded throughout much of the fort, a most unusual sound in these harrowing days. Then he turned serious. "Unlike most of the fools in this post, I have heard of your father. He is said to be a fine man, an honest man to the Indians. Not like most of the English traders." His face darkened. "Look at them." Thad looked around the fort and saw that there were one or two visible, but he knew that Baby was referring to the lot of them.

"I would not turn my back on one for a moment," Baby

said. "They would steal from their own mothers and then swear to God and the Virgin Mary that they did not." He shrugged his shoulders and changed the subject. "I am worried about your father. There are so many Indians out there, and most of them hate the English so, but"—he smiled encouragingly as he paused—"anybody but your father, ffffsst!" He made a slashing motion with his fingers across the top of his brow, then pulled at his forelock just in case Thad had missed the allusion. "But from what I have heard about your father? With him there is always a chance."

Thad nodded. "He has always found a way . . . up to now."

"Tell you what I will do," Baby said. "There are among us Frenchmen who are maybe more friendly with the Indians than I am." What he was saying was that some Frenchmen were still bitter at losing the war and were assisting the Indians in their uprising against the detested English.

"I understand what you mean," Thad said, realizing that he was being taken into Baby's confidence.

"I do not like these men, but I do talk to them, and from them I will find out what has happened to your father, unless he has succeeded in evading them."

"Thank you, Monsieur Baby."

"I am Jacques."

"Thank you, Jacques."

Two nights later, close to midnight, the door of the water gate to the fort opened for only a moment and Thad slipped out, into the canoe of a young Frenchman trusted by Monsieur Baby to deliver Thad across the river to a quiet landing three miles upstream from the fort.

"*Bon chance,*" were the only two words the French youth had to say as Thad disembarked with an agile leap to the shore three feet from the canoe. Thad responded with a grateful wave and the young man backed away with two quick, quiet strokes, into the darkness.

With eyes that could see through the pitch-black of a moonless night, Thad followed the river until he saw an opening in the woods. Like all good woodsmen, he found the woods to be a sheltering comfort, where his knowledge and instincts would give him the advantage over his enemies. He had rested throughout the afternoon and evening, for he desired to use this night to put as much distance as possible between himself and the Indians who swarmed around the fort.

Quietly yet rapidly he found his way between trees, through thickets, up and down rises, around swamp holes, unerringly heading east around what would come to be called Lake St. Clair. If Baby's information was correct, his father was alive and captive somewhere along the eastern shore of Lake Huron. Thad had no idea how he would find him, or, once he did, how he would rescue him, but the idea of not trying had never occurred to him. The news that his father lived, and the feeling of stretching his legs in the cool night air, away from that accursed fort, made him feel better than at any time since his recent narrow escape. The miles flew by beneath his moccasins and his rifle felt light as a feather in his hands.

As the first rays of dawn filtered through the forest canopy, Thad found that his instincts had set his feet on a clear trail. Immediately his pace picked up, into a relaxed, loping run that ate up the miles. He could see the lake through the trees on his left, the choppy water afire with the sunlight of a new day.

❧12❧

THE MOHAWK INDIANS CALLED THEIR RIVER the Te-non-an-at-che, the River that Flows Through Mountains. In the hills beyond the river, surrounded by their own fields of beans and corn, stood the Mohawk village of Louis, son of Gingego, village chief and seeker of peace.

His father had been a mighty warrior and a comrade-in-arms of Big Oak. Gingego had fought loyally for the English and perished in battle fighting for the English. Louis's loyalty toward the English was not as strong as his father's, but he had seen their might and knew that there was no way to turn the world upside down and spill the English into the ocean.

But Louis was also determined to keep the six nations of the Iroquois confederacy together, and so when the Seneca band of Skoiyasi entered through the gate of the palisaded village, Louis and his braves smoked the pipe with them and listened to all they had to say. And they said a lot.

"My brother," Skoiyasi began. "Many moons have passed since the day we met, after the Caughnawagas destroyed our village. They were once Ganiengehaka like yourselves, until the French came among them and their priests taught them to worship the man at the stake. At the Lac St. Sacrement they fought against you. They killed your father.

"Is it true that they are now, suddenly, your allies, my brother? I know this could not be so, for the Ganiengehaka have long memories, and do not let a mild breeze blow their enemies close enough to them to make them friends."

Not so long ago Louis had been a warrior bound for glory on the warpath. He had been chosen to succeed his father as the village chief, and in the few short years since he had taken up the deer horns that went with the office, he had learned much. He knew why the Senecas were in his village, and he knew how to throw Skoiyasi's rhetoric back in his face.

"My brother from the Western Door," he responded. "We are six in the Longhouse. Five of us hold fast to the Covenant chain the English offered to us so many years ago. Only one lets slip the Covenant chain, then picks it up, then lets it loose again, like a woman who can't make up her mind. I know of the war out west. The Ganiengehaka can see far. We can even see all the way into the hearts of our Seneca brothers."

Skoiyasi smiled. "That is good, my brother. Then we need waste no words between us. It is clear to every tribe along the lakes that the English mean to cast us aside. They trade us no goods, especially no guns and ammunition. We dread the coming of winter without weapons to hunt the deer."

"I have heard about your newfound brothers on the lakes." Louis half smiled, half sneered. "All French allies, were they not? No wonder the English will sell them no guns. They were just lately their enemies. The English are wise, with longer memories than my brothers the Seneca. The English remember who their enemies were. Have the Seneca forgotten that the Ottawa and the Chippewa are our enemies, outsiders who have seduced our children, the

Delaware? Now they are your great friends, these French Indians. Why have you forgotten our friends the English, who have served us so well these years, especially our friend, Warraghiyagey."

"Warraghiyagey serves himself," Skoiyasi answered, remembering Big Oak's skeptical appraisal of the great English landowner and trader who had become rich championing Iroquois causes over the years. "Under the English, your land vanishes before your eyes, to reappear magically under the plows of English farmers. Under the English, the number of your people grows less and less, while the English grow and grow in strength and numbers. Will you hold tight to the Covenant chain until they finally wind it around your throat and choke you with it? Why can you not see the truth, my brother?"

Now the dialogue stopped and the antagonists looked at each other through thick clouds of tobacco smoke. Skoiyasi stared sadly through the smoke at Louis, whom he liked and respected. It was obvious to Skoiyasi that Louis would go to his grave loving the English. All that was left was for Skoiyasi's band to leave the village without letting the Mohawks know that their next stop would be Fort Venango, to do their part in Pontiac's war on the English, the war they had to win if they were to retain their freedom.

"We will be leaving for Tonowaugh tomorrow," Skoiyasi said.

"Tonowaugh," Louis responded skeptically. He thought for a moment. "I wish you a safe journey back to . . . Tonowaugh, my brother."

A few more moments passed in silence, then Skoiyasi spoke. "I must tell you this. The western tribes are fighting a brave struggle against the English. If the Ganonsyoni entered the fight, we could push the English into the great sea."

Louis shook his head. "You forget, my brother, we rely on the English for our blankets, our cooking pots, and our guns. How will we get these things when the English are gone? We, the Mohawks, are the flint people, but I tell you, we will never go back to flint arrows. And what will you do—you, like us, who conquered our enemies with English guns, supplied with an open hand by English traders?"

"Open hand, you say? We trapped every beaver in the valley of the Te-non-an-at-che to pay for those guns, and then we traded with our enemies out west for more beaver to pay for those guns. What you call the English open hand is the clenched fist of a miser. Louis, my brother, the English give nothing and take all.

"And when the English are gone, we will bring back the French. The French do not steal our land. They do not treat us like fools. They are white men we can trust."

Louis smiled. "My brother," he said, "living close by the English, I have learned much, these years. Some of what they tell us is lies, and some of what they tell us is truth. They have always told us that if we help the French defeat the English, then when the war is over, the French will help their Indians to wipe out the Six Nations. But I see now that you and the French Indians have buried that hatchet so deep that you will never again find it. The English lied about that, I see.

"But, my brother, even if we drive the English off our land, they will not leave the shores, and they will never let the French come back. The big canoes of the English are much more powerful than those of the French. They hate the French like we hate the Cherokee, and on the other side of the water they defeat the French. It is not that I love the English more than I love the French. White is white. Who can love a white man? But the English are the most powerful white men, no matter how weak they sometimes seem to us."

Skoiyasi stared back at Louis through the smoke. "Who can argue with such a stubborn Mohawk? If you are a man, you strike your enemies so they can no longer torment you and make your life miserable. If they are more powerful than you, they defeat you. That is the way of the world but, aigh, if you are a man, you must fight for your freedom.

"Tomorrow we go," Skoiyasi repeated. "My brother, do not wait too long. We need the strong arms and keen eyes of the Ganiengehaka."

The pipes were smoked out. The words were all said. Skoiyasi and his men stood up and left the fire, and Louis's spirit left with him. How could he explain to the Seneca that the Ganiengehaka, the fiercest of all the Iroquois nations, had spent their strength and manhood in warfare and no longer could summon enough braves to be a powerful force in any great war? Perhaps if they could endure ten years of peace, then when the youngsters were grown, and more outsiders had been adopted into the Longhouse, maybe they would be powerful enough to resist the English.

But no, even then it would be impossible, for the whites would increase by five for every one new Mohawk warrior. There was no end to the supply of English people. They must live horrible lives across the big lake that so many of them would want to come west and fight for more land, especially considering what bad fighters they were, and how easy most of them were to kill.

Louis sighed, and wished that his wise father were here to counsel him. But no, his father must not have been so wise, else why would he have thrown his life away in the service of the English? He thought about his mother, old but still wise, but no, maybe not so wise, else why would she have put so much faith in the words of the English trader, Big Oak? He wondered about Big Oak. He knew that Big Oak told the truth, as he knew the truth, but maybe Big Oak was not so wise either. Besides, he was an Englishman. Louis thought of Red Hawk, the renegade Ganiengehaka who had preached that all their English friends would desert the Longhouse when the time seemed right to them. Louis and his men had tortured Red Hawk to death on the high trail after they had wiped out the Caughnawagas that Red Hawk had been running with.

Louis sat back for a moment and savored the greatest victory the Mohawks had ever won over their Canadian brothers. Already it was a legend to be told and retold around the campfires in all the Mohawk villages, and he, Louis, had led the Mohawks in that battle. Big Oak and his half-Seneca son had been their comrades in arms in those days, but where had they been since that time? The boy had married a white girl in Albany and now wore white man clothes, while Big Oak plied the rivers and streams of New York with canoes full of furs and trade goods, taking his profits back with him to Albany.

Of course Red Hawk had been right. So why, Louis wondered, had he and his braves hated Red Hawk so? Because Red Hawk had joined with the enemies of the Ganiengehaka, and it was an evil thing to betray the Longhouse to the enemy.

In the morning, Skoiyasi and his men departed from the village along the high trail. Two of the young Mohawk braves wanted to go with them, but both Louis and Skoiyasi had talked them out of it, Louis because he knew these Senecas were going up against the English and he did not want the Mohawks being blamed; and Skoiyasi because he did not completely trust the Mohawks not to betray their Seneca brothers to the whites. Most of the villagers were out at the main gate of the castle to see the Senecas off. Outside the gate Louis put a hand on Skoiyasi's shoulder.

"On the way back to your village," he smiled, "should you find yourself midst hungry wolves, kill them all, and remember, we are still your brothers."

Skoiyasi nodded, and recalled Big Oak's story of how Louis had gotten his name. His father, the village chief Gingego, had once had a quarrel with the English governor, who had developed a bad habit of taking the friendship of the Mohawks for granted. At the birth of his son, Gingego had invited Warraghiyagey, Superintendent of Indian Affairs, to the village for a feast, and there announced that the name of his son would be Louis, after the fine French king across the water. William Johnson—for that was Warraghiyagey's white name—was happy to take that piece of information back to the governor, and for years thereafter the governor treated Gingego with much more respect. Those were the days, Skoiyasi thought, when the feelings of the Longhouse counted for something with the English. But now that the French were gone, the English cared nothing for Iroquois feelings, and did as they pleased.

As they swung down the high trail, into the woods, and disappeared from the view of the villagers, Skoiyasi smiled a secret smile. The Englishmen in the cities will be soiling their breechcloths, he thought, or whatever it is that they wear, when they find out what has happened to their forts from Detroit to Niagara.

From the hills the Seneca band dropped down into the valley trails parallel to the Mohawk River, heading west toward the Finger Lakes. The men in Skoiyasi's band were a varied lot. Some of them, he would never have shared a trail with in former days. None of them were from his village. Two were Senecas from the shores of Lake Erie, two were Mingoes, a people who had split themselves off from the Longhouse years before, and two were Hurons, who spoke an Iroquoian language but who had been deadly enemies of the Iroquois for many years. These were leaderless men frustrated by the loss of the French to the disrespectful English.

Tonowaugh, the tiny village where Skoiyasi lived, had been a prosperous and peaceful trading town on the Genesee River until the massacre. Devastated but still a beautiful town site, over the years it had become a magnet for lost Indians from a number of Iroquois-speaking tribes. Skoiyasi was the one local warrior left in Tonowaugh with fire in his belly. And so he had emerged as a war chief in the making, but he was careful not to indulge himself in the ancient war lust of the young brave to pick a fight, any fight.

When word had reached his village that several western tribes were planning to follow Pontiac against the English, and that Kyashuta and his Senecas were planning to join the conspiracy, Skoiyasi decided that here at last was a fight worth fighting.

To the north of the Finger Lakes region the land flattened out a bit. Their third morning on the trail, making good time in their loping run, they turned a bend in the trail and found a cleared field where there had never been a field before. In the distance they could see two log cabins plus the beginnings of a third.

They came to a halt and melted into the woods. A normally quiet young Mingo the whites called Open Hand walked up to Skoiyasi, his eyes bright with excitement.

"Now," he said, "is a chance to strike a first blow. Let us destroy these people and burn their houses to the ground. Look at them. They will never see us before their scalps are on our belts."

They looked out at the new little settlement. The men were sweating over the huge logs they were raising onto the walls of the third house. If they had guns with them, they were certainly out of reach. There were only three of them, and all the children in sight were small and helpless.

Another of the braves agreed. "They are ours to pluck like the wild plum. Skoiyasi, let us do this."

Five years of authority and responsibility had pushed him into the habit of silence before making any important decision. He looked from one face to another until he had read the eagerness on all six faces.

"No, we will not do this," he said. "This is Oneida country. If we attack these people, the whites will punish the Oneidas. Louis will know we were the ones who did it, and neither the Oneidas nor the Mohawks will ever forgive us."

A Mingo warrior named Oossas then spoke up. "Why should we care what the Oneidas and the Mohawks think? Where it concerns the English, they have no spine."

"You are a Huron, Oossas. You do not understand. The power of the Longhouse comes from its unity. We do not take the Iroquois League lightly, and neither should you. If we can get the other five nations to join us, we can push the English across the big river forever. If the other five nations stay neutral, we still have a chance. But if we make them angry, they may fight on the side of the English, against us."

"What, then, do you think they are so powerful that the mighty Seneca shake before them?"

Skoiyasi squelched a desire to reach out and strike the big-mouthed Huron with the barrel of his gun. Wisely he said this: "We cannot go to war against our brothers in the Longhouse just because it would be fun to show them how strong and mighty we are. There is a war to fight, and that war we must win or we will lose all of our land. *All* of it!"

"If there is a war to fight, then when are we going to fight it?" The questioner was a young Seneca named Rabbit Shakes.

"In less than three suns the scalps of English soldiers will be hanging from our belts," Skoiyasi said.

"Look there," Oossas said, pointing to a white boy of about nine or ten years, who was prowling through the woods in search of berries and hadn't heard the Indians' quiet speech above the sound of the wind in the trees. Oossas was reaching for his scalping knife, but Skoiyasi gripped his wrist.

"No, my brother. We will take no scalps here," he insisted. "The child will take us to the men, and they will give us food. They will know that Skoiyasi's band of Senecas is returning to their village on the Genesee. They will not know that once we are west of the Genesee we will run south to the Allegheny River and then on to Fort Venango, where Kyashuta will be waiting for us. It is there that we will have our blood."

Oossas fixed Skoiyasi in an angry gaze. "I mean to have the scalp of that white boy," he said. "You Genesee Senecas are still too close to the English, that you would wish to spare even one." He threw off Skoiyasi's grip and began to creep toward the boy, who was still unaware that the fate of his hair was being debated one hundred yards away by a pair of passionate Indians. For a moment Skoiyasi paused in confusion. He looked at the rest of his men and saw in their eyes no feelings one way or another. Good, it was just he and Oossas. Oossas was a troublemaker. Time to put him in line. Only room for one boss. He took five quick steps forward and barred Oossas's way to the boy.

"We want no trouble with these people," Skoiyasi said softly. "Not now." His words were gentle but his look was deadly. Oossas tried his will against Skoiyasi's and failed. His gaze dropped.

"Come, my brother. We will let the boy lead us to his family, and we will collect what they owe us for the use of our land, although I hope"—his dark eyes twinkled—"they will not be using it for too long."

The two Indians, with smiles on their faces, walked toward the white boy, who saw the smiles and was too young to know that on another day these smiles might have meant mortal danger to him.

Skoiyasi held up his right hand, then took the boy's hand in a firm grasp. "Father," he said clearly, that word being one of twenty or thirty English words Skoiyasi had picked up and remembered during his years of friendship with Big Oak and Thad. He pointed toward the clearing, where the men were working on the cabin, and repeated, "Father."

The boy understood. He began to walk from the woods, into the large clearing and toward the houses, followed by the seven Indians in single file. One of the men looking up from his work noticed the parade, tapped his neighbor on the shoulder, and the looks of alarm turned to smiles of pleasure as they saw the apparent peaceful dispositions of the Indians.

"And a child shall lead them," said the largest of the three men. The boy and his Indians crossed the clearing and approached the three men, all of whom had climbed down from their work stations. One picked up an old musket and handled it casually, not wanting to display hostile intent but not completely trusting the Indians. Skoiyasi chose to assume that the biggest one was the leader. He drew near the man, rubbed his own stomach and pointed to his mouth.

"Martha!" shouted the man, who understood instantly. A face appeared in the doorway of the nearest cabin. "We've got some guests. Would you bring out some corn cakes and springwater for them?"

A few moments later the door opened and out walked a stout woman with a platter full of corn cakes and a pitcher with water sloshing over the sides, her hand shook so. She did not bring any cups out, but the Indians didn't seem to mind. One after another took a corn cake, and they took turns drinking from the pitcher, each one in turn feeling disappointed that water was all the pitcher contained.

Oossas fingered the handle of his tomahawk. "What is the matter with these people that they offer us water?" he asked.

"Some of them do not have rum," Skoiyasi replied. "And keep your hand away from your tomahawk or I will slit your throat and cut out your heart, right in front of these white men."

Oossas did as he was told, but Skoiyasi laughed inside as he watched his warrior's hand again and again unconsciously slide down to the handle of the weapon. How badly he wanted to kill something white. Well, he would get his chance soon.

The Indians finished the food they had been given and passed the pitcher around again. Skoiyasi walked up to the woman to thank her. Her eyes wide with fright, she nodded, and tried to curtsy and back away all at once. "Stupid woman," he muttered and turned to the big man. He grabbed one of the man's huge hands and shook it, then from a little bag he carried he took a carved bird's head and gave it to the boy. The boy looked at it with wonder, then impulsively threw his arms around Skoiyasi and hugged him in gratitude. Skoiyasi put a hand on his head, swallowed a lump in his throat and said, in a language understandable only to his fellow Iroquoians, "The next time I find you in the woods, I will chop you into tiny pieces." He patted the boy's head while his trailmates laughed. The white men also laughed, thinking that Skoiyasi must have said something witty and congenial.

Then the Indians began to shake hands with each of the white men. Those who knew a bit of the white man's language said "Thank you" to each of the white men in turn. Once more Skoiyasi saw Oossas's hand slipping down toward his tomahawk.

"The corn food did not appease my brother's hunger?" Skoiyasi asked Oossas. "You are bound to drink some blood, now?"

The Mingo nodded his head.

"In a short time we will be feasting on redcoat blood. Have faith, my brother."

Oossas nodded. "I wish I could have the hair of just this one," he murmured to Skoiyasi as he took the hand of one of the white men and shook it, the last handshake of the day.

"I am pleased that you are so keen to kill white men, my brother. In two dawns you will have your chance." With that, he and his braves disappeared into the forest.

"Nice Injuns," one of the white men commented after the Indians had vanished.

"Yuh," replied the large one of the three. "Keep your eyes open and your priming fresh."

❖13❖

HAVING ESTABLISHED THEIR ALIBI, JUST IN case anything should go wrong with the rebellion, Skoiyasi and his little group turned south and headed for the Allegheny River. They trotted along their woodland trails with purpose and anticipation. They were warriors. This was what they were trained for; the years they had spent raiding Mingo or Shawnee or Huron villages had merely been exercises, to earn their reputation and gain experience.

But now they felt they were fighting the war that would determine the survival of their people for many years to come, and honors gained in this war would be legendary honors. It hurt Skoiyasi that he could not make the rest of the Longhouse, even many from his own tribe, from his own *village*, understand that the Iroquois stood at the edge of disaster if they did not back the western tribes in their rebellion against the English. But Skoiyasi was not politically naive. He knew that if only the coalition could win enough battles against the English, then the Longhouse would be forced to join the rebellion. So far the Ottawa, Chippewa, and their allies had been successful nearly everywhere. Runners from the west had spread the news like a summer forest fire. It pleased Skoiyasi that he and his men would now play a role in the enterprise, and he was determined that they be as victorious as their new brothers of the West.

They followed the valley of the Allegheny River west and then south. Once they were within two miles of the fort, Skoiyasi had his men camp while Oossas went out in search of Kyashuta and the main body of Seneca warriors. Oossas found Kyashuta, then returned to the camp and led the little band to him.

"You are just in time," Kyashuta told Skoiyasi. "I thought we might have to begin without you."

"I am honored to be here with you," said the young leader from Tonowaugh. "Tell me what we have to do and when we must do it."

"We will attack tomorrow morning," Kyashuta confided as he led Skoiyasi to where a group of Seneca and Shawnee chiefs sat in council.

The "attack" was in fact a procession. With dignity, Kyashuta and two Shawnee chiefs walked slowly toward the gate of Fort Venango, followed by a half-dozen subchiefs more or less in formation, then perhaps forty warriors. They all wore their best feathers, beads, and blankets. "Makes the English think we have something important to tell them," Kyashuta explained to Skoiyasi before the procession began, and he put the young man in with the second rank, even though he had no official standing, because he and Skoiyasi saw eye to eye on many things and he wanted to raise the status of the brave among the Seneca.

The post commander was a Lieutenant Gordon. He had heard rumors about hostilities out West, but like many of the English commanders, he fancied that he and *his* Indians got along well. Maybe Kyashuta might have an idea of what was going on up on the Great Lakes, he thought, putting on his best friendly but dignified meet-with-the-Indians face.

He met them at the gate, shook hands with the chiefs and escorted them into the fort. The rest of the Indians casually followed the party through the open gate, and, while most of the chiefs joined the lieutenant in the council room, Skoiyasi and the braves scattered around the post to socialize with the soldiers. There were only fifteen soldiers on the post. Two or three Indians moved in on each one to shake hands, slap them on their backs, smile and speak in tones of enduring friendship.

Most of the soldiers welcomed the attention of the primitives. Life in the wilderness was deadly dull, and they were pleased to have other faces to look at besides each other's. Languidly they went through the usual rituals of overcoming the language barrier with signs and fragmented phrases. There was even time for several of them to begin to exchange little gifts. Skoiyasi and Oossas were laying on the charm thick as molasses with a sergeant of such long experience on the frontier that he should have known better. While Oossas stood beside the sergeant patting him on his shoulder, Skoiyasi was showing him his beautifully beaded bullet pouch. The sergeant smiled, showing them a mouthful of bad teeth, and with his right hand reached under his tunic for something.

And then a shrill cry issued from the council room. A tomahawk appeared from underneath Skoiyasi's blanket. There was no threatening gesture, no warning war cry. Oossas had grabbed the soldier's arms from behind and there was only a flutter of resistance as Skoiyasi quickly raised his tomahawk high above his head and with horrible force sank it deep into the soldier's skull. He died instantly, painlessly, and so did fourteen other soldiers at almost the same moment.

Skoiyasi's companion admired his dexterity as he

whipped out his knife, made the quick, circular incision, and ripped the scalp from the soldier's head. Oossas released the sergeant from his grasp and let his body fall to the ground.

The door to the council room opened and out walked Lieutenant Gordon, stripped naked, his hands tied behind his back, a look of wide-eyed shock upon his face. Scattered around the parade ground, in varied sprawled postures of death, were all the men who but a moment before had received their orders from him. They tied him to a post near the wall by the gate, and while two Indians stood by him to watch that he didn't harm himself, the rest began to loot the fort.

Lieutenant Gordon had a fine view of the end of his military career. Before him were the bloody, mutilated remains of every man His Majesty had entrusted to his care. Sometimes the Indians had to step over them as they carried from the fort all the guns, ammunition, lanterns, mirrors, light furniture, food supplies, and other goods they thought would be useful to them. Illogically, as the worst of the shock wore off, he wondered how he would ever pay for the supplies he had signed for, and how he would ever explain to Colonel Bouquet why he had survived while the rest of his command had perished.

Then the full dimension of his tragedy dawned on him and, quietly, he began to weep.

Seeing his tears, one of the Shawnee chiefs approached Lieutenant Gordon with a knife, cut a deep incision in his thigh, and ripped a long strip of flesh from his leg. Suddenly it no longer mattered what His Majesty or Colonel Bouquet thought about his military abilities or anything else.

Along with the rest of the Senecas and Shawnees, Skoiyasi whooped and shouted with every agonized screech. Each participant had his own pet torture that he was sure would outdo the other tortures in extracting screams of pain from the prisoner. Not being an Indian trained to resist such displays, Lieutenant Gordon was no challenge, but they made do with what they had. Soon he was a mass of blood and exposed interior from top to bottom, but they still left him with enough life to feel every bit of pain they meant for him to feel. When they gave him a few minutes to rest, he watched wide-eyed as a dozen Indians danced before him smeared head to toe with blood, *his* blood.

Then came the fire.

The three canoes skimmed over the water along the north shore of Lake Huron. Fourteen Chippewas were heading for home under the high, almost-summer sun glinting dazzling yellow off the choppy waters of the mighty lake, which for today, at least, was conceding them a safe passage west. Tirelessly, four paddles to a canoe, the men stroked and the canoes leaped eagerly forward, drawn to the Chippewa village that stood north of where lakes Huron, Michigan, and Superior all but came together.

In the second of the three canoes, in the bow, muscles rippling with explosive power, was a man less bronzed than the rest, rather too red of body, in fact. Only his hair was bronze, where it was not already gray.

Behind him sat Owl in the Dark, the chief of the Chippewa band that now, for all intents and purposes, owned Big Oak. Owl in the Dark and Big Oak had discovered over the past two days that they could converse somewhat, in a Delaware dialect that both found awkward but serviceable.

"I have never seen anyone so eager to meet his death," said the Indian as he watched Big Oak's mighty arms move the water swiftly past the side of the canoe.

Big Oak laughed. "Paddling a canoe is one of the great

joys of my life," he replied. "Should a man not enjoy his last days of life?"

"Your joy is at my pleasure, Red Shoulders," the Chippewa said. "One knock from this tomahawk and there is no more joy for you."

Big Oak dug his blade deeper into the lake and stroked harder than ever. "You have complete power over me," he agreed, "perhaps until the moment of my death. Are you certain it is as you wish it? You do not know me."

"What? Do you beg for your life? I would not have thought you a coward."

Big Oak shook his head and continued his powerful stroke. "Not beg," he said. "But the waters of life flow strong inside me, and I would not give them up until your knives and hatchets drain them from me. It is hard to die at the hands of men who are not my enemies."

The Chippewa snickered. "You are an Englishman. You would starve our children this winter. You would spread your foul diseases among us until there are none of us left. Oh yes, I have heard about the English, and I would give thanks to the Manitou to wake up one morning and find that the English were just a bad dream sent to test my courage."

Big Oak said nothing as his paddle bit deep into the water and swept back among the waters that boiled past the speeding canoe.

"Ah, you have no answer?" The chief poked Big Oak sharply in the back with the handle of his tomahawk.

"I have spent my years as an adult in the woods with my brothers, the Seneca, and their brothers, the Mohawk. I have fought beside them in war and never in my life lifted a hand against them. Since the Seneca now fight alongside the Chippewa, the Ottawa, and the Lenni Lenape, I am no longer your enemy. And yet, I was born an Englishman and would not take up arms against the English, so I would understand why you consider me your enemy. There is nothing I can do about that."

"Good. You are a real man. It will be an honor to torture you."

Big Oak did not reply. For a while he contemplated the possibilities of escape. His neck tether was tied to a strut in the framework of the canoe, and so were the bonds that were knotted around his ankles. They were more than a mile from shore, and the only weapon within reach was the tomahawk Owl in the Dark held tightly in his fist. There was no escape, so Big Oak let go of the future and thought only of the fresh smell of the hissing water and the cadence of the canoe. In matching the rhythm of the paddle strokes, he was, for a while, at one with his tormentors of tomorrow, and the perfection of that rhythm gave him satisfaction.

But the following afternoon, when they pulled their canoes out of the water and butt-stroked him into the village with their rifles, the choking fear of the trapped animal returned to him. Like a trapped animal he looked around, desperately, the moment he found himself standing among the bark-covered wigwams surrounded by curious women and children as well as warriors of all ages. With great effort he forced himself to stand straight and tall and scan the members of the village, hoping against hope to find an old acquaintance, or at least a potential ally.

What he saw was a broad sea of hostile faces, the faces of a proud, powerful people worried about the changes that threatened them, worried about the peace and what peace might bring, worried about the war and what war might bring. At least, he thought, they weren't lined up and driving him through another gauntlet.

He was sweaty and filthy from his matted hair to the soles of his bare feet. His normally slender frame was now gaunt; he had been given little to eat over the past week.

His sunburned shoulders ached and his body itched from lice and chiggers. He looked out at the lake and for a moment thought it might be worth dying to take a last cool dip, but the end of his tether was wound three or four times around the right hand of Owl in the Dark, and Owl in the Dark did not look as if he wished to go bathing, not at this time.

Owl in the Dark brought him to his wigwam and told his wife, "Feed him." His wife took one look at Big Oak and told her husband that this man was not coming into her house until he got cleaned up. Big Oak would have been surprised if he had understood the exchange, for the village was none too clean itself.

Nevertheless, he was pleased when Owl in the Dark led him to the edge of the lake and pointed at the water. Half the village stood at the edge of the water and watched Big Oak as he waded chest-deep into the lake, then splashed around until his body felt reasonably clean. Children and women poked each other and laughed at the pale chest with the reddish-blond hair across it, and the red, sunburned shoulders. Then Big Oak asked Owl in the Dark if he could borrow a mirror and the sharpest knife in the village. To the surprise of both Big Oak and many of the villagers, Owl in the Dark granted the request.

"He wishes to look his best when we are roasting him," Owl in the Dark told them, and they responded with a chorus of "ahs" in admiration of his poise and pride. In fact, as he stood in the water with the mirror in one hand and the knife in the other, shaving his beard as close as the knife allowed, he cast a few quick side glances to judge his chances of escape.

Seeing none, he finished shaving with perfect dignity, scanned the faces on the shore with a long searching look, and walked to the shore, where he handed the mirror and the knife to Owl in the Dark. In turn he received a clean breechcloth, which made him feel considerably more comfortable than he had with the miserable stiff piece of canvas he had been issued by the Ottawas.

Owl in the Dark's wife brought him back to the wigwam and handed him a steaming bowl of boiled fish and wild rice, undoubtedly the most savory food he had eaten since he and Thad had left Albany a month ago. She brought him some tea too, and a young woman. He raised his eyebrows at this. She had a little wooden vessel filled with an oil that smelled like pine. She said nothing to him, but began rubbing the oil gently on his sunburned shoulders. The pain receded and the tense muscles in his upper back relaxed. The good food and warm tea filled him with a sense of well-being.

There is always hope, he thought, even though he knew that some tribes treated their prisoners as honored guests the day before they took them to the stake and inflicted unimaginable suffering upon them.

Owl in the Dark sat down across from the fire and began to work on his own bowl of fish and wild rice. For a while both men ate in silence. Then Big Oak spoke, in the Delaware tongue.

"Your hospitality makes my heart feel warm, my brother. Do I die tomorrow?" He asked his question matter-of-factly.

"Not tomorrow. Maybe day after," responded Owl in the Dark, as if Big Oak had asked him when he intended to go fishing. Nevertheless, living one day at a time as he had been for a week now, the thought of a single day when he might live as a human being instead of a slaughter animal filled his heart with hope and gladness.

"I thank you for one more day of life."

He said it so simply and honestly, that it touched something inside of Owl in the Dark. "You are a most unusual Englishman," Owl in the Dark said. "You have a soul. I did not believe that Englishmen have souls. I am certain you will bear your sufferings well, and when they become too much for even you to bear, I will be there to end them."

"I am grateful," Big Oak said. "In truth, if I had my choice, I would choose not to suffer, but since I have no choice, I will do my best not to disappoint you."

"I am certain that you will prove brave to your dying breath," Owl in the Dark answered, then rose to his feet and left Big Oak alone by the fire with his thoughts.

❧14❧

THE FOLLOWING DAY WAS ONE OF BIG OAK'S
most pleasant days in months. From the time he awoke,
various members of the village visited with him, and chat-
ted with him in their way. Big Oak had always been a
sociable man when he trusted the people around him. Now
he found himself learning about the lives of a complete
group of strangers, and they learned about his.

They brought him food, asked about his health, and several even gave him little presents. They assured him that at
another time they would be thrilled to adopt him into the
tribe, but that there was war between them and the English
and they were sure he understood that they liked him very
much but that they were going to burn him the following
day.

Yes, he said, as nobly as he could. He understood that
there was war and that he was their enemy and assured
them that he would not hold it against them personally
when they stuck pine splints under his skin and lit them, or
cut him slowly into little pieces. But throughout all the
pleasantries he was aware of the sun rising over the pines in
the east, sailing serenely overhead throughout the day from
horizon to horizon, then plunging its way down beneath

the waters of Lake Superior. He ate his final meal of the day and thanked the visitors who had provided it. He was beginning to prepare himself to resist the panic of still another final night on earth when a shout from one of the children announced the appearance of a small convoy of canoes on the horizon.

The entire village, including Big Oak on a leash, streamed down to the shore and watched as a party of Hurons hove into view paddling five canoes loaded with goods.

The goods, they said, were weapons that they had received from the capture of one of the lower forts. Most of the goods were going to their home village, but they had heard that this particular band of Chippewas was low on ammunition and they had come to trade some to them.

"My brothers," Owl in the Dark said, "I am moved by your care for our welfare. With such allies we may truly be able to defeat the English and chase them back across the water. For many years we have trapped the furs and traded them to you, and you have always provided us white man's goods at a fair price. We had a fine winter trapping beaver," he continued, "but as you know, the English have been stingy with their trade goods. So we will go and fetch our finest quality furs to trade for ammunition.

The Huron chief smiled.

"My brother of the puckered moccasins," he signed, referring to the seams peculiar to Chippewa footwear, "furs are fine, and I suppose we can take some, but we have nowhere to trade them yet, as you know. The French will soon be gone, and the English are being stingy. What else do you have besides furs?"

"We would trade our rice, and yet this we cannot do, for our stocks are low, and in time of war our needs are great."

"This is as it should be," the Huron replied. "You must carefully watch your food in time of war. Happily for us, we have great stores of dried fish and deer meat, and even much of last year's corn, so we do not need your wild rice."

It was evident that the Chippewas did not possess anything that the Hurons truly coveted. The Hurons wanted the Chippewas to have their ammunition, so that they might be active in the struggle against the English. But they wanted to get something in return that they could use. The Chippewas desperately needed the ammunition, but they could not think of anything with which they could tempt the Huron. The Huron chief let his eyes wander around camp, hoping to find something worth having. He spotted the tall, blond, slender but well-muscled man with sunburnt shoulders, his hands again bound, standing among the villagers.

"That man is not a Chippewa," he surmised, pointing to Big Oak. "Is he a slave?"

"He is a slave," Owl in the Dark said. "He is also a magician."

The villagers close enough to read the signs snickered to themselves, knowing that Big Oak claimed no magical qualities, but anxious for ammunition, they kept their faces solemn and noncommittal.

The Huron walked over to Big Oak. "Are you a magician?" he asked.

To the surprise of everyone, Big Oak responded in an Iroquoian dialect close enough to be understood by the Huron: "I am no magician, but I promise you I am useful."

"How?" the Huron asked, shrewdly.

"Do not ask me now," Big Oak responded, conveying his fear that among the Chippewa might be someone who understood the conversation.

"I do not believe that a white man can be a magician," the Huron signed to Owl in the Dark. "But he looks strong and I believe he might be of use to us. You may have your ammunition. We will take this white man. And a canoeload of furs."

In the deepening twilight Owl in the Dark looked at the Huron, then at Big Oak, pretending to ponder a deal that was already made. It was a good deal: furs they could not use, a small share of a large stockpile, plus a prisoner they were planning to execute the following day anyway, for ammunition they desperately needed. But when he signed that the deal was done, there arose a chorus of objections, especially among the women and children.

"We want him here. He is ours, we love him," was the sense of the uproar. There were some tears, and one older boy grabbed Big Oak's tether and held tight to it.

"Bring out the furs," Owl in the Dark ordered one of his braves. To the Huron he signed, "The prisoner is yours. The furs are yours. Please bring the ammunition and place it here." Several old blankets had been stretched out on the ground. The young men of the village were pleased to see the quantity of lead and powder brought up and placed upon the blankets. To this the Hurons added three muskets, not of the latest pattern, but clean and well-oiled. The Chippewa warriors were delighted by this unrequested acquisition, but still the caterwauling continued.

"Stop this noise!" Owl in the Dark demanded sternly. He turned to the Huron. "Down the shore, on the next point," he pointed northward, "is a fine place to have your camp. When you have made camp. Come back here. We will have a feast."

Once the Hurons had taken their prisoner, returned to their canoe, and pushed off for a point a quarter of a mile up the shore, the women and the children gathered around Owl in the Dark and demanded that he bring Big Oak back. He let the uproar rush up against him like storm waves on Lake Superior, then raised his hands for silence. The hands made no difference, but the angry sparks in his eyes finally quieted the crowd. The newly kindled campfire threw a sinister shadow on his face.

"Hold your tongues," he said. "Have the French finally brought you to the Cross, that you love your enemy so?" Owl in the Dark asked.

"He is a good man, that white man," came an answer from one of the old men of the village.

"Do you not know that he was to be burned to death by us tomorrow?" Owl in the Dark asked. The murmuring response told him that they did know. "You love him so much that you want to have the honor of torturing him to death?"

"Better that we should torture him to death than those miserable Hurons!" one of his braves interjected.

"We would give his death honor," another added.

"You fools," Owl in the Dark responded. "We need this lead and powder, these weapons. War is too close for us to think first about things like keeping the white man for torture. Be glad he was here to give us something we could trade for all this wonderful ammunition."

In the mist of the cool early morning, Thad was determined to eat a hot breakfast. Accordingly, he made a tiny fire of very dry wood, placed his skillet on top, seared a slice of fresh meat from a deer he had killed the day before, added a few dried vegetables he had left soaking all night, and dined.

As he sat cross-legged eating in contentment, he remembered something Big Oak had told him when they had first begun sharing the joys and hardships of the trail. "It's wonderful," Big Oak had said, "how good a bad situation can feel when it's better than what you had before."

Thad was in a bad situation. He had lost the entire pack train his father-in-law had entrusted to him. His father was prisoner to a band of Chippewas who were taking him

Lord knew where to do Lord knew what to him. And now Thad was attempting to follow them through unfamiliar country without even having found their trail, knowing that their route was water, but not knowing where they were heading. He was attempting to follow them only because he had to do something.

And yet, because he *was* doing something, his spirit was strong as, day after day, he loped through the strange woods hoping to find a band of hostile Chippewas without them finding him.

His eyes caught a sudden movement off to his left and his instincts told him he had to react to that movement. A moment later his ear caught a sound that did not quite fit in. Though his heart quickened, he did not betray any concern. Instead he continued to nibble at his deer meat and wash it down with water. He reached over the fire and grabbed the skillet. The sound came again. Right behind him. There was where the danger was.

In one motion he sprang to his feet, pivoted on his toes, began to swing the skillet, and when he saw his target, altered the path of the skillet mid-swing just enough to catch the stranger across the side of his head. The woods rang with the clang of cast iron on bone. Before him a man went down, conscious but stunned. His rifle and tomahawk flew in two different directions. He stumbled to his feet satisfied that he did not want any more of Thad. Moaning, he fled through the woods and quickly disappeared.

Then Thad did two things in quick succession that saved his life and forever stamped into him the confidence that he could handle himself in the woods alone against almost anybody. Again he saw a moving flash between the trunks of some trees, but his mind also registered, "Behind!" At that moment he ducked his body and a figure in buckskin went hurtling over his shoulder.

He now distinguished the motion in the woods to his

front as a lone rifleman with a clear field of fire and a rifle that he was resting on a branch in front of him, preparing for the killing shot.

Quickly, Thad dove to the earth, grabbed his rifle, brought it into position, pulled the hammer back and fired.

The primer flashed, then the rifle bucked against his shoulder. A thick cloud of gray smoke prevented him from checking on the state of the rifleman, but he could hear moaning, two or three French curses, and thrashing in the underbrush. That meant he could turn to the sprawled figure who had regained his feet and was now rushing at him with a large knife raised above his head.

"Come on, monsieur." He smiled quietly. The tone of his voice had stopped the *coureur de bois* in mid-step. "Your knife against my rifle," Thad said softly, almost soothingly.

Now the Canadian smiled. *"Mais mon frere,"* he replied, "you have fired your rifle." As if to prove his statement, both heard a piteous moan from some bushes less than a hundred feet away.

"All right, then, your knife against my club," Thad said, holding his rifle before him. "I don't have anything worth stealing, except my rifle and maybe my scalp, and there's nobody left to pay you a bounty for that. Are you sure you want to take the risk?"

Then the Canadian made a mistake. He was watching Thad's eyes carefully. Thad knew what the Canadian was doing, so he let his eyes wander for just a moment to give his adversary a false sense of security. When the Canadian sprang, Thad stepped forward to meet him with a solid rap from the butt of his rifle on the point of his chin. Big Oak had often told Thad that when Friedrich Deutschmann down in Pennsylvania had made these rifles, he had brought the craftsman several rounds of fine, close-grained walnut for stock parts, because a rifle with a broken stock was nearly useless and he did not want his stock broken on

the hard head of some Indian or Frenchman in the middle
of a fight.

Thad looked closely at the prostrate *coureur de bois* to
make sure he was unconscious, took the man's knife and
tucked it in his belt, then reloaded his rifle and reprimed
the pan. Quickly he approached the bush where the
wounded Canadian lay moaning. He studied the wound
carefully, and noted that the ball had entered and exited
the shoulder.

"You'll be all right if you wash that wound out, but you
probably won't," Thad said, noting the filthy, greasy buckskin shirt the man wore. He picked up the man's rifle and
his knife, and went off in search of the third attacker.
Something was gnawing at his brain, but he couldn't make
sense of it until he picked up the trail of the third man,
who had fled headlong through the brush. They were
wearing no packs. Either they had dumped their packs before they had attacked, or . . . or what? Or they had left
their packs in a canoe. It was just a hunch, but the third
man's trail led toward the lake, and now he heard a grunt
and a splash. A quick run to the tree line and two jumps
down the bank brought him to the edge of the water,
thirty feet away, where the third attacker was struggling in
panic with his paddle, trying to get the canoe pointed out
toward the middle of the lake.

"*Arrêt!*" Thad cried. He dropped the Canadian's rifle,
raised his own rifle and pointed it at the back of the paddler. The man turned around and stared into the steady,
unwavering muzzle of Thad's long rifle. He considered taking a quick stroke or two and dropping to the floor of the
canoe, then thought better of it and raised his hands.

Thad motioned with his rifle for the man, who wore a
dirty white linen shirt and shaved his head like a Huron
warrior, to turn the canoe around and bring it back to
shore. The paddler did as he was told. Thad was surprised

to find two rifles lying on the floor of the canoe. He assumed that the three Canadians had spotted him through the trees from their canoe and decided to stalk him for sport, two of them opting for tomahawks and knives, and only one taking his firearm with him.

Coaxing his prisoner up the side of the bank to where the fight had occurred, Thad found the wounded man kneeling beside the unconscious one, slapping his face. He watched while the man slowly returned to this world, groaning a bit, but soon regaining his senses.

"Look at what you did to him," the unwounded one said once he recalled the sequence of events that had given him an atrocious headache. He appeared to be the only one of the three who could speak and understand English.

Thad sneered. "I apologize. And what was it that you were trying to do to me?"

"We saw you from the canoe. You had a fine rifle. My rifle is broken, and so is Henri's." He pointed to the man who had tried to make his escape in the canoe.

"And you were going to kiss me with your tomahawk, eh?" Thad grinned, thinking that if he had not ducked in time, the bugs would now be crawling all over his scalpless skull.

The Canadian laughed. "With my tomahawk I was going to crush your head, but it was your rifle we wanted, not you."

"I feel much better about that. I'll tell you what I will give you. I will give you your lives, if you will give me some information."

"We are at your service."

"Which direction have you come from?" Thad asked.

"Why do you need to know?"

"I am looking for my father. And it is not me, but my rifle that needs to know." His gaze was steely cold and the muzzle of his rifle loomed large and deadly in the eye of the Canadian.

"We have come down the eastern shore of Lake Huron," he said.

"Good, did you see any Chippewa along the way?"

This seemed in the nature of war intelligence, and the Canadian did not want to answer.

"I am not hunting Chippewa. I just want my father. Even you had a father!"

The Canadian sighed. "We saw two bands. One of them had a man who could have been your father. They were traveling north along the shore toward their village. Their village is near where the three lakes meet."

"Thank you. I will give you more than your lives. I will give you back your weapons. You, in return, will give me your canoe."

"But that is not right," the English-speaking Canadian complained indignantly.

The one who had tried to escape must have understood more English than he let on, for he now tried to grab Thad's rifle. Thad jerked the rifle out of his grasp and planted the weapon firmly against the man's mouth. Two teeth tumbled to the ground, and the would-be hero fell backward, his hands covering his mouth too late to save his teeth.

He gave the Canadians a deadly look that froze them into silence. "I have a loaded rifle in my hands. I also have your rifles and tomahawks. You can choose life, or you can choose death. When people give me that choice, I choose life. Do not follow until your canoe—my canoe—is out of sight." Abruptly, Thad was on his feet, running the hundred yards to the canoe, taking the Canadians by surprise, so that for ten seconds they did not follow, and then, when they did, it was slowly, all of them being the worse for wear at Thad's hands.

At the shore, Thad threw the Canadians' packs and rifles out of the canoe and was about to jump in. Then, at the last moment, he picked up their one good rifle and stuffed mud into the barrel. He tossed all his things into the canoe, pushed off, and leaped in just as the Canadians appeared at the top of the bank. Five quick strokes took the canoe fifty yards offshore.

"Ho, you left us our good rifle, English fool. Henri will put a hole in your cowardly back from half a mile. I think you had better come back and maybe *we* will let *you* live, eh?"

Thad took another pair of leisurely strokes and let himself drift more than a hundred yards from the Canadians.

"I wouldn't try to shoot that thing if I were you," he laughed, then resumed paddling. It wasn't until a few seconds later, when he heard loud French curses being hurled at him from the shore, that he knew for certain they had investigated his warning and were not going to blow themselves up.

❧15❧

THE DAY DAWNED ON A LAKE SMOOTH AS glass. A mile out on the lake Thad felt his muscles warm to the task of finding and dealing with the Chippewas who had taken his father.

Wise to the ways of survival in the wilderness, he focused most of his attention on the dark shoreline, but not a minute went by without a look to his front, his back, and his left. He would not be taken by surprise.

And yet he nearly was. Daybreak light is no light at all for men who know the shadows. Out of the dark background, visible only to an eye keen as an osprey, flew a white canoe paddled by two strong Chippewa braves. Thad had no doubt that they had spotted him long before, and were trying to close on him fast enough to catch him unawares.

They were still half a mile away. Thad stopped his canoe and lay prone in the stern, his rifle pointed straight back at the Chippewa canoe. Five hundred yards away the Chippewas stopped their forward charge and began moving broadside to Thad, hoping to draw his fire, then charge forward close enough to get a good shot at him.

Thad resumed paddling. He turned his canoe toward

them, took two quick strokes, then dropped to the bottom again and raised his rifle to his shoulder while the canoe drifted closer to the Chippewas. Estimating range on the water was difficult, but he believed he was pretty close to a sure shot. He would fire low; a low shot might skip off the surface of the water and hit something, at least intimidate his foe, but a high shot might fly by without even disturbing the air around them.

And then, which of the two should he try to hit? It didn't matter he told himself. Just hit something.

He fired. His bullet hit the water a good fifty yards short, and if it skipped, no one knew it. He had severely misjudged the range, but at least he now knew what it was. The Indian in the rear was paddling like a fiend, coming full-tilt toward him, hoping to reach him before he could reload. Quickly, confidently, without panic, he reloaded. Powder, patch, ball, primer, faster than the two Chippewas had ever seen it done, and yet so smoothly that they didn't realize their jeopardy until he was priming the pan. The one in front dropped his paddle, picked up his rifle, aimed and fired—too rapidly, and Thad presented a poor target, with only the top third of his face exposed above the bow.

The paddling Chippewa abruptly swerved his canoe sideways and began paddling as hard as he could, trying to move away from the deadly muzzle. They were within fifty yards of each other when the Chippewa canoe swerved, and Thad could not miss at that range. He had the back of the paddler in his sights and nearly pulled the trigger when he realized he needed them to tell him the whereabouts of his father. At this close distance he could choose what part of whom he wanted to hit. But if he missed, the Indians would be so close they would surely have him. In a life or death situation, he decided, you shoot to kill. Thad aimed for a killing shot and began to pull the trigger.

That's when the Chippewa broke his paddle. Right in

mid-stroke it snapped in the middle, and the canoe drifted in an arc less than fifty yards off Thad's bow. The Indian tossed the handle away and reached for his rifle. What Thad did next was not a judgment, but a reaction. He fired his rifle, picked up his paddle and began to backwater. The paddler was hit and down, and now the Chippewa who was busy reloading his rifle had a decision to make. He could finish reloading and try to get off a shot before Thad paddled out of range, or he could grab a paddle and charge after him. He chose to reload, but then he put his rifle down, crawled over to his partner and began to fuss with him. Calmly Thad reloaded his weapon; then put down his rifle and paddled toward the canoe. The Indian spotted Thad approaching and dove for his rifle, but Thad picked his back up, and the barrel looked mighty big and the Indian didn't dare reach for his weapon for fear of getting shot.

"Did I kill him?" Thad asked in his fragmented French.

"No you come close!" the Indian said in French that was little better than Thad's, ignoring the question.

"Is he dead?" Thad demanded to know.

"No, but he is hurt."

"Why did you attack me?" he asked the Chippewa. The Chippewa looked back at Thad as if he were seven kinds of a fool. Thad shook his head and looked down at the Indian he had shot. The wound was a bloody crease in the side of his chest; the bullet might have struck a rib, knocking him down. A bruise on his forehead suggested that when he fell, his head had struck a part of the canoe frame, knocking him out.

The other Indian picked up his paddle and began to stroke toward shore, followed by Thad. Without any further conversation they had come to a tacit agreement ceasing hostilities. Thad peeled some bark and moss and brought it back to the Chippewa, who had revived his cohort and now proceeded to apply the substances to the wound, which was painful but not too severe.

"I'm sorry," Thad said. "I had no desire to injure you. I was only defending myself."

Both Indians nodded. Thad drew from his pack a bit of tobacco and gave it to them. They accepted it.

"I am looking for my father," he said, and the wounded one smiled.

"Ah, big man, like you," he said, raising his hand up to indicate impressive height. "We burn him by now."

The other one shook his head. "People in village like your father. He will live another two suns at least."

"That is my father. Where is he?"

"In the village of Owl in the Dark. He is a good man. He will give you the bones of your father to take home with you," said the standing Chippewa, slapping moss fragments off his hands.

The wounded Chippewa laughed, and grimaced. "If he doesn't burn you too," he said.

"Will you take me to the village of Owl in the Dark?" Thad asked.

"There is war. It is dangerous for you," said the wounded Chippewa, who had struggled to a sitting position and was pleased to be feeling fairly normal, other than the headache, and the ache in the side of his chest where Thad's bullet had creased him.

"He is my father," Thad repeated.

His father was actually in considerably better shape than Thad had a right to expect. When the Hurons had left the Chippewa village, they headed straight for their own village about fifty miles to the east. To their surprise, the tall thin white man they had acquired kept up easily as they paddled along the lakeshore toward their village. The kindly treatment he had received in the Chippewa village had done much to restore his energy. Within two days he was an object of curiosity in another Indian village, still a slave, but no longer in daily fear of his life. Now it was time to pay the Hurons back for their rescue.

"You have guns that need repair?" he asked the Huron chief, who was called Wahkee.

"You know how to do such things?"

Big Oak nodded. "I lack the right tools, of course, but if you can provide certain things, I'm sure I can help you."

"I had thought from what the Chippewa told me that you were a *coureur de bois*. I do not understand how you can be a hunter, a trapper, a trader, and a repairer of guns."

"I cannot do what a gunsmith can do," he tried to explain, "but there are some things I can do." The Huron did not understand but he dropped the discussion, reminding himself that white men, especially the English, are odd people.

"What do you need?"

"First, I do not have your tough skin. The sun burns my hide, so if any of you have any white man's clothing, I would feel much better than I do walking around in this." He motioned to his breechclout, the deluxe one the Chippewas had given him.

The Huron chief nodded. "I have such things to wear myself but do not use them. Everybody else, when they get such clothes they cut out this part." He patted his bottom.

"Makes good sense," Big Oak said diplomatically. "If I wasn't a white man, I'd do the same thing myself."

"What else do you need?"

"Have the people bring out all their tools and knives of different sizes. I will figure out what I can use. And I need ramrods, and cloth patches, and . . ." He explained oil successfully to the Huron, who brought out a gunky substance Big Oak thought might do.

The chief provided him with a pair of serviceable buckskin breeches and a gray linen hunting shirt, a slouch hat, and an old pair of moccasins. Big Oak felt more the master of himself now that he had the right kind of clothes on his back. He had Wahkee's woman spread a blanket in front of his hut, and as he had done so many times in so many villages, he went to work with the whole village gathered around to watch.

"Why are you not at Detroit?" Big Oak asked as he picked up Wahkee's rifle and let the sunlight show him the inside of the barrel.

"We are not about to follow that miserable Ottawa Pontiac. Some of his own Ottawas will not follow him against the English. Why should we? He believes the French will return. We believe that he is a fool."

Big Oak understood. Wahkee gave ammunition to the Chippewas, goodwill for the rebellion just in case Pontiac won, but he demanded Big Oak in return, good will for the English just in case the English won. Big Oak felt a great burden leave his shoulders. Unless rebels attacked the camp and took him away from the Hurons, he was safe.

"Wahkee, my friend, I will never forget what you have done for me. When this war is over and the soldiers come to punish the rebellious tribes, I will stand before General Amherst and proclaim your loyalty to His Majesty."

The chief said nothing, but he seemed pleased.

"Now I have some bad news for you. Your rifle is old and the barrel is worn-out. We must find you a new barrel or a new rifle, for this one will not kill a deer at two hundred yards." The chief's face dropped.

"But let me show you something." He picked up a small mold good for making buckshot and pointed to it. "If you load your rifle with a bunch of these things, then you can knock down small animals, or, at close range you could kill two or three men with one shot." The chief brightened. "But get a new rifle as soon as you have the furs to trade for them. In fact, after this war is over, I will go back to Pennsylvania and find you a special rifle, one that cannot miss."

He spent the morning and the afternoon working on rifles and muskets, doing more cleaning than anything else. These Hurons, like most Indians, were hopeless when it came to maintaining their firearms. He was able to improve the performance of nearly all the weapons that could still fire, and Big Oak fixed one musket that had not fired in nearly a year by making an adjustment to the hammer function, to the wonder and delight of the village.

Among the villagers was a young woman who was an outsider. As a girl she had come west with a raiding party of Tuscaroras and been captured in the midst of a skirmish. She had been first enslaved, then adopted into the tribe, then married to a Huron brave and almost immediately widowed.

Although she was attractive, the other braves in the village had refused to look at her, considering her bad luck. Now she looked upon Big Oak with great interest as he made his way through one weapon and into the next. He studied each carefully before he made an attempt to fix one. He felt that they could accept him if he said, "This one is no good," or, "That one is more dangerous to the shooter than the target," but he was determined not to lose credibility by failing to fix one that he worked on.

"Would you like some water?" she asked him in Tuscarora dialect, and he was pleased to answer in the affirmative in the Tuscarora tongue. He had already noticed her attention, as she had intended him to, and he was glad to have an Iroquois daughter with whom he might pass some pleasant time once he had taken care of his gun-repairing chores.

"Yes," he replied, pulling a hammer back and snapping off a shower of sparks from the new flint he had clamped onto an old French trade rifle. Piece of junk, he thought.

The trade rifles were often pieces of junk. If the rifles were good, they were probably stolen. The girl returned with a clay pot filled with cool water. Big Oak suddenly realized he was very thirsty. And tired. And hungry.

"Wahkee," he said. "It takes a good eye to see all that must be seen on a rifle. Where the sun is now," he pointed to where the sun lay balanced on a red horizon, "I cannot see like I should. You see, my eyes are not what they once were."

The chief understood. His eyes were no longer what they once were either. Silently, Big Oak gathered his tools and rolled them up in the blanket. Those who were still gathered around watching the entertainment began to drift away.

"I have food if you would visit my fire," said the young woman. He looked at her dark skin, her long dark eyelashes, her dark eyes, so much like his long dead Seneca wife, Willow, who had given him Thad.

"I would like that," he said. "What is your name?"

"I do not know anymore," she replied.

For two nights he visited the fire in front of her hut and ate her food. They talked very little, but he enjoyed sitting with her and believed that she enjoyed his company, although she didn't say so. By day he continued to work on the rifles and muskets, until he had done his best with all of them, then he tried to repair their broken tomahawks and kettles. The Tuscarora woman usually spent some time close by, watching him.

After dining with her each of those nights, he went back to the hut of Wahkee, as he knew was expected of him. On each of those nights he lay awake on his back for many minutes, thinking nighttime thoughts about the woman before sleep finally came.

On the third night he sat by her fire, letting the dancing

flames warm his chest in the early cool of the late spring evening. Over the fire sat a cast-iron pot filled with savory fish and vegetables. His shirt lay in the corner of the hut, and behind him sat the Tuscarora girl, gently but firmly rubbing his shoulders with her strong hands.

She had twenty-four summers and no children, she told him. She did not know her Tuscarora name anymore, but the Hurons called her Touches the Sky With a Soft Hand. After her husband had been killed in a raid on a Sac village, his mother had thrown her out of her lodge to fend for herself. That was exactly what she had done over the past four years.

He turned to face her and asked her to sit next to him by the fire. Instead she took his hand and led him inside her hut. In the dark within the hut they sat close together speaking softly to each other. She told him that she had built the hut herself and that she took care of herself fishing, gathering nuts and wild berries, and occasionally inheriting somebody's cast-off clothes. What she could not do, she said, was find her way back to her people through these woods. For four summers she had been waiting for someone to come who could take her back to New York. Could he do that?

He could, he said, once he was reunited with his son.

The darkness within was not total. He looked at her fine bronze face. She was in the prime of her beauty, slim, her small breasts still firm and young, her eyes dancing bright in the firelight, her hair dark and shiny and hanging long and unbraided.

She stirred a part of him that had been untouched since Willow had died fifteen years before. He was not certain that he wanted to be stirred. Many times over these years he had missed the warmth and the laughter of his own woman, but having risked his life so many times, he found it hard to risk his heart again. Life was too uncertain on the frontier. He was unsure if he could bear another loss like his loss of Willow.

He continued to stare at the young woman, no longer a child, and chuckled at the thought of her loving him. She was younger than his son. The thought nearly made him dizzy. No. He would drive such feelings away. The young are for the young. He would bring her back East and find a young man for her.

And yet the thing in him that stirred would not go away, perhaps because she had placed her hand on his. "You look so sad," she said. "Your eyes have seen too many bad things." Her own eyes mirrored the feelings she saw in his. In fact, the sadness she saw was a longing for a time in his life that was past.

"I was looking at you, and listening to you, and wishing that I had known you before."

"Before what?"

"Before I had lived so many summers."

She looked alarmed. "Are you not feeling well?"

He thought for a moment. Considering what he had been through over the past month, he felt fine. "I feel fine," he said.

"You are a great man." She smiled. "I know who you are. All children of the Longhouse know who you are. I would be honored to take you into my house."

He laughed. Among the Iroquois it was the women who owned the houses. They were the boss. And yet they were not the boss. Nobody was the boss of an Iroquois man. He looked around the hut. Small and humble it may have been, but it looked like home to him. Suddenly he longed to try it out. Suddenly he realized that she had invited him to do just that.

He felt her arms around him then, her hands exploring his back, her warm body close against his, her mouth against his, taking his breath away.

"Stop," he said.

She stopped. "Have I done something wrong?" she asked.

"No," he replied. "You've done something right. I just have to get used to the idea."

"Will that be soon?"

He thought for a moment. Then came silence as he sought to put what he felt into words. He felt the sweetness of the twilight hour and the soft breeze that pierced the stillness, and drifted through the doorway of the hut. Back, back in time went his soul, to things that he had all but forgotten, sweet things, contentment things, unrestless things. "That will be now," he said. He trembled inside as she spread a blanket away from the fire and let her skirt drop to the floor.

She fell to her knees and beckoned him to do the same. She reached for him and pulled him down. "You do not know. You could not know," she whispered. "When you came into camp, I asked myself, 'Could I even dream of having that man with me?' Then, when I saw you with the braves, I said, 'no, he is too good a man. There must be a woman for him already.' Now I know there is not, or you would not be with me tonight."

She was small but built firm, with limbs brown and warm from her days on the lake. He kissed her slowly and she twined around him as if he were something great and precious. He felt her small feet against the sides of his legs. She loved him slowly, watching him beneath happy, sleepy eyes. "I know you," she said, exultantly. "You are a good man."

"Shhh," he said softly.

She smiled. Then all he could hear was her breathing, gentle in his ear, then a soft cry, thin, high-pitched, and delicious, followed by another. Her ankles trembled against him. Her arms squeezed him against her, and then there was another soft cry, longer this time, very long, like a sweet musical sigh, the sweetest his ears had heard in many years. She whispered something to him in the Tuscarora dialect, words that came so fast he could not understand them, and yet they too were music to him.

Her cries, her whispered affections, were so sweet that they were more wonderful to him than his own satisfaction. With a long, low sigh he found peace.

For a while longer they lay close together, savoring something neither could have imagined as a reality before this day.

"Do not leave me, ever," she said.

"Why would I?" he responded, and then, to himself, Why would I?

⋇16⋇

SKOIYASI STOOD ON THE SHORE OF LAKE ERIE, looking west across the glimmering ripples. Inside of him was an abundant feeling of satisfaction. With their strong arms and stout hearts, his Senecas and their new allies were righting seven generations of wrongs, putting things as they should be.

The English were being exposed for the hollow shell they were, odious creatures who could buy victories with their purses but could not win them with their courage.

Such a stupid, stubborn, cowardly people had never walked this land before the English came. Fort Venango had fallen so willingly. Never had he seen so many men at one time die so easily. It was as if their sense of their own evil were so great that they had chosen to close their eyes to the Seneca trick and bare their heads to the Seneca tomahawks.

"Here is my scalp, take it," they might have said. "Wear it on your belts with pride and dance around the campfire with it before your women and your gods. You deserve to have our scalps. We give them to you, with pleasure, along with our useless lives."

And that fool at the stake, screeching like a woman every time one of them showed a knife. Begging, begging, begging. First begging for life then begging for death, with no pride in his heart to help him take courage during his tribulations. And he was their leader!

Skoiyasi stared out toward the western horizon. Even when the water was choppy from an east wind, where the sky met the water, the horizon always looked perfectly straight. But his keen eyes caught tiny breaks in that straight line. He leaned forward as if to get a little closer to the horizon, and squinted to cut the bright yellow reflection of the sun off the choppy water. Patient, motionless, he stood, resting against his rifle, minute after minute, watching the breaks turn into canoes.

No tiny party of warriors looking for a fight, this was an Indian armada: Huron, Mississauga, Chippewa, Ottawa, Potawatomi, hundreds of them. They could only have been sent east by Pontiac to conquer Presque Isle.

Skoiyasi was impressed. He knew that Kyashuta had gone west not long ago to bring the Indians together against the English, and that he had failed to get the western tribes to agree to anything. And yet here they were, like the deer and the wolves together, old foes united to kill Englishmen and drive them from the land. Skoiyasi's spirit soared out to meet them, and on they came, painted and dressed to kill.

Skoiyasi turned his back on the shore and ran through the woods toward Fort Presque Isle. In very little time he had found Kyashuta among the Delawares, Shawnees, and Senecas who were watching the fort. Kyashuta and two others ran back with Skoiyasi to the shore just in time to be there as more than two hundred braves disembarked, pulled their canoes from the water and carefully hid them in the forest.

Kyashuta stepped forward to greet the Mississauga chief,

Sekahos. "You are like the sun," he said, "rising from the lake when you are most eagerly expected."

Sekahos did not smile. "Do they suspect an attack?" he asked.

"It may be so," Kyashuta answered, "but you will see when you get there that when we attack, we will not fail. Has Pontiac taken Fort Detroit?"

"The English are shut up tight in their fort," Sekahos said. "But we ambushed their supply boats and captured many men. We had bodies, and parts of bodies, floating down the river past the fort for days." Both chiefs laughed at the thought of the English watching the parade of floating corpses.

Now Sekahos cast a serious look at Kyashuta. "My brother, what of the Iroquois? Will they join us?"

"My brothers of the Longhouse are very stubborn. The Mohawks have lived too long too close to the English. Sometimes I think they are more like the English than they are like the Seneca. And even though their numbers are no longer so great, they have great power inside the Longhouse. The other tribes will not oppose their will."

"But the Seneca, the Guardians of the Western Door, do you not also have great power in the Longhouse? Do you not have more warriors than all the rest? Why do your people not come?"

"Our sachems still believe it is more important that the Longhouse stay together than that they join with their brothers of the western lakes," Kyashuta said. "But if we keep winning victories, the rest of my people will join you. If they join you, the other nations will not be long in coming, except perhaps for the Mohawks. And if the Mohawks do not come, we will consider them English, and treat them that way."

Sekahos shook his head. "Not the Mohawks," he said.

"They are still powerful. We do not want to fight against them if we can avoid it."

"Ah, my brother. It was so when we were both very young. But we are no longer very young, and the Mohawks are no longer very powerful. If the other nations of the Longhouse join us, then it does not matter if the Mohawks join us or not. The Senecas do not fear the Mohawks. With our warriors, the Shawnees, the Delawares, and all the tribes of the West fighting together, we can push the English back across the ocean and they will leave so much of their blood in our forests that they will not return until their children's children have forgotten where that blood flowed from. Then they will try again, for they are very stubborn, but this time we will be waiting for them, united, on the shore, our guns loaded, and they will never again set their foot upon our land."

In the murky blue-gray of early dawn, a sizable handful of Senecas and Shawnees found their way through the woods to a creek bank that shielded them from the gunfire of the fort. They had to cross open ground to get there, but no shots were fired at them.

The wind was still. The fort was silent. A few birds were saluting the dawn. That was all.

"We have caught them sleeping," the youngest of the Seneca warriors, called Smoke, told Skoiyasi confidently.

"Maybe," Skoiyasi replied tersely. They crawled along in the cover of the creek bed until they were so close to the fort's blockhouse that they could not miss the loopholes with their fire. Carefully they checked their weapons to see that they were loaded, primed, and ready. They all took aim, and at Kyashuta's signal sent a terrifying fusillade through the loopholes into the blockhouse.

There was a brief pause while the Indians reloaded and the suddenly shaken soldiers scurried around inside the sturdy log building. Then they began to return the fire and the warriors hunkered down, well-covered by the bank of the creek.

For a while the men in the creek bed exchanged fire with the soldiers, while on the other side of the fort the Chippewas and their western allies scaled the wall without trouble and hid among some of the buildings.

"They're all in the blockhouse," Skoiyasi told Smoke. "Fools."

"Why is that foolish?" the young warrior asked.

Skoiyasi smiled. "You will see."

To save ammunition, the Indians in the creek bed began to throw rocks through the loopholes, whooping and hollering and making enough noise for five times their number. The soldiers responded to the racket and the activity with heavy fire that took little toll on the invaders on that side of the blockhouse. In the meantime, more and more of the western Indians continued to invade the interior of the fort over the walls farthest from the blockhouse.

Now the Indians inside the fort began firing at the other side of the blockhouse, screeching their war cries. The short hairs stood up on the necks of every defender in the blockhouse. They knew they were in for it now. The group in the creek bed resumed their fire. It was a desperate time for the blockhouse defenders, crouched beneath their loopholes listening to bullets thudding into the logs inside the building and praying that the next one might not find its way through the chinking and into one of them.

Once the Indians determined that they had the soldiers cooped up in one place, they attempted to roast them where they were. They made portable barricades to get closer to the blockhouse without exposing themselves. They shot fire arrows into the walls and on the roof, but time and the white man may have deprived them of the art of fire arrows, because they could not seem to ignite the building that way. The arrows fell short, or bounced off, or burned themselves out before they could do any harm. The morning was passing fast, with no further progress on the part of the attackers, but then, they had plenty of time to figure out a way to destroy the fort, and the soldiers.

Skoiyasi watched with approval while several fire arrows landed on the roof and the flames started to spread quickly. Just as quickly the fires went out and water began dripping down the walls.

The sight of the dripping water made his mind itch, as if there were something it was trying to tell him, but he couldn't figure out just what. He pulled back the hammer of his rifle, aimed it at a loophole in the blockhouse, and waited for a gun barrel to appear. When one did, he fired at the face he imagined to be just behind the rifle. Through the smoke he saw the rifle disappear inside, and he knew that he had failed to hit anything soft and fleshy. For all the fire they had directed into that building, the defenders all ought to have been dead, and yet somehow he doubted that any of them were. For one thing, he could hear no moaning or screaming wounded inside.

"It might be good if we could find out what is happening on the other side of the fort," Skoiyasi told Smoke, and Smoke was off, down the creek bed, into the forest, and around the perimeter of the fort. He found his way over the wall to a group of Chippewas and Ottawas who were standing around something of great interest to them. Smoke approached and saw what they were staring at and immediately understood. One of the older men said a few words to him, and off he went, back over the wall, into the forest, back around to the creek bed, then along the bed to Skoiyasi.

"They found the well," he told the young Seneca leader breathlessly.

"Where?" Skoiyasi asked. "Not in the strong house?"

"Outside the strong house."

Skoiyasi slapped the stock of his rifle with his right hand. "We have them!" he said. And he ran to every brave in the ditch who had a bow with him, or a pile of pitch balls in front of him.

"If we can set enough fires," he told them, "they will run out of water and then we will burn them where they roost."

Then he turned back to Smoke. "What else did you see inside the fort?"

"Our braves have begun a tunnel to get us under the strong house."

Skoiyasi smiled to himself. The English were so easy. Braves around him were firing more fire arrows on top of the blockhouse. The roof was beginning to burn furiously, until a brave soul made his way out on the roof and started ripping off burning shingles and throwing them down. Skoiyasi took dead aim on what little part of his person was exposed, and he fired. The soldier continued ripping off shingles, apparently unharmed. Skoiyasi loaded his rifle and again fired it at the man on the roof, muttering to himself when the shot went wide without even attracting the man's attention. The Seneca reloaded as fast as he could, hoping to snap off another quick shot at the brave man on the roof of the blockhouse, but by the time he'd finished the process and raised the weapon to his shoulder, the soldier had disappeared.

Several braves had constructed a large movable shield of planks and logs. Grunting, they pushed it forward until it was close enough to the blockhouse walls for them to lob fireballs against the base of the walls, where they ignited the blockhouse. The soldiers inside, always aware of the danger, managed to put out every fire, but their supply of water was dwindling, and the Indians outside knew it. As the night quietly closed in on the scene, the attack had settled down to a deadly chess game that the English could win only if they could get relief from the outside.

Aware of their isolation, none of the defenders really thought that rescue was a possibility. They could only hope that if they held out long enough, and picked off enough careless Indians, then the attackers would get bored and weary of the exercise and go home. But there were also those who thought, in their heart of hearts, that it would be better to surrender now, before any more Indians got hurt. There were Delawares and Iroquois out there, old allies who might let them live.

On the other hand, the way the red devils were whooping and screeching, and hollering their challenges and insults at them, most of them had a strong feeling that there was not a trace of friendship for them left among the old allies. Surely surrender would bring with it the risk of treachery, followed by torture and massacre.

In the meantime Ensign Christie, the commander of the fort, had his men desperately digging a tunnel to the well, knowing that if they did not get more water, their goose would be cooked.

If the soldiers had an ever diminishing stock of water, the Indians seemed to have an infinite supply of fire arrows and fireballs, which they let fly through the night, arching from their hidden positions onto the roof and against the sides of the blockhouse. From his snug place in the creek bed, Skoiyasi admired the pyrotechnics as he chewed his jerked venison. And he felt that he had been born to do this, make war on the English and reclaim the land for his people. He imagined what it would be like to walk the trail again without worry that the next bend would bring him to a new patch of cleared land with a log cabin and a nasty white family full of nasty white children who would catch a nasty white disease and kill a whole Seneca village with it.

What a pleasure it would be to run the northern trails like his grandfather did, making war on the Hurons and the People of the Panther without having to worry that the French might send their Indians down on them. Unlike the western Indians, Skoiyasi did not esteem the French above the English. White men were white men, and he wanted them out, so that things could be as they were before, or as he imagined they were before. It felt strange for him to claim Hurons as his allies. He was glad they were on the other side of the blockhouse. Not that Hurons were strange people to him—his village had adopted several Hurons over the years—but still, he would rather have Hurons as his enemy than his ally. It was just the way things were supposed to be.

He looked at Smoke, curled up in his blanket, sleeping easily through the occasional gunfire and the fire arrows. The white men were getting no sleep tonight, that was certain. We'll see how long they can keep going, Skoiyasi thought. For a moment he pictured how satisfying it would be to sink his tomahawk into the skull of an English soldier as he rushed from the burning blockhouse. Then he wrapped his blanket around him, wedged his body up against the bank of the creek bed, and let his eyelids sag shut, naturally, peacefully.

His hands grasped the polished maple railing of the balcony as Dieter Wendel looked down upon the noisy floor of his prosperous mercantile establishment. It was a busy midweek day, but not as busy as it would be when the English finally took care of their problems with the French Indians and the fur trade really began to move again.

There was something going on out there. Many people had an inkling of it but nobody seemed to have any really solid information. Close to Albany, the Mohawks were quiet, but there were some who worried that they were a bit too tight-lipped, even for Indians, as if they were hiding something. There was a rumor that the Indians were acting up around Detroit. There were always rumors. Wendel could not understand. He had thought the end of the war meant peace, and yet his son-in-law and Big Oak were now gone many weeks without a word.

Wendel's daughter Katherine appeared on the floor of the store and looked up at him. Her eyes asked for a letter from Thad, or at least some news. His eyes answered no. She turned and slowly walked from the store, and he regretted once again that he had ever financed their trade mission. Thad was a capable boy, he had to admit, and he knew that Big Oak was one of the wisest of the white woodsmen, and one of the most formidable fighters the colony of New York had ever produced.

But he was worried. He should have heard from them by now. For the first time in the history of Albany, the menace of hostile French and Indians was gone from the lives of the townspeople. But without having to worry about his own security, Dieter Wendel found himself feeling very concerned about the fate of his son-in-law. It was as if removal of danger from himself only magnified the danger faced by those out West.

He thought of the goods he had sent, and the horses, but it wasn't the goods he was worried about. It wasn't really Thad either. It was Katherine, who had begged Thad to delay the trip awhile longer. "Let someone else cut the trails," she had told him.

Wisely, Thad had replied that it was the people who cut the trails who would earn the trust of the Indians, and for them there would be good trading for years to come. A wise boy, Wendel thought, observing that character in the parents nearly always gets passed down to the children.

Children. Children should grow up with a mother and a father. His grandson, though not yet six years old, was spending too many days without his father. When Thad got back, he would keep the boy around Albany if he had to chain him behind the counter of the store to do it.

Skoiyasi and Smoke had nothing to do but wait and watch the blockhouse. All morning long the Indians on the other side had been digging a tunnel. It would be only a matter of time before the blockhouse went up in flames and the soldiers came boiling out like bees from a smoked-up honey tree.

Skoiyasi took from his pack a small whetstone and began to stroke his tomahawk blade against it. The metallic scraping sounded good to him. It was something for his hands to do while he waited. The stone took the dirt and the old blood off the blade and made it shine like silver. There was a little nicked part near the top of the blade. He worked hard on that, then went back to the rest of the blade until it was keen enough to suit him. He raised his head, looked through a screen of brush at the blockhouse and saw nothing out of order. There was almost complete silence throughout the area, save for the chirping of birds, the buzzing of insects, and, maybe, the faint scraping of tools against dirt under the ground.

He fired his rifle now, into the nearest porthole in the blockhouse, and was pleased to see a little movement inside, as if he had interrupted somebody's noontime snooze. But there was no return fire, and the afternoon heat seemed to have slowed the whole world down to a crawl. He ate a few mouthfuls of corn, washed them down with a bit of creek water, and, seeing that everybody around him was more or less awake and alert, took a few winks himself.

His hooded eyes opened a short time later. It was the scent of smoke in his nose that did the trick, plus maybe the sharp poke in the ribs from Smoke, the warrior, who knelt by his side, pointing toward the fort.

Inside the stockade, right next to the blockhouse, black smoke was pouring from a house. Skoiyasi and Smoke could now hear war cries beginning to emerge from within the fort. Skoiyasi and the other men in the creek bed began firing at the loopholes, and the men behind the portable barricade lobbed fireballs at the base of the blockhouse, and once more fire arrows soared across the clearing to the roof. Skoiyasi's spirit rose as he waited for the signal to rush the blockhouse and put an end to the hated enemy within. Surely they must soon be out of water. Surely the flames would soon drive them from their strong house like fleeing rats.

But somehow the handful of men inside the blockhouse endured. Though smoke from the fire next door poured into the blockhouse, they managed to put out all the fires and fire a few rounds back at their attackers to boot. Gradually the black smoke turned gray and then died as the afternoon slid into evening and then night. And Skoiyasi chewed on his corn and dried deer meat and sat back and once again awaited the inevitable.

He might have even admired the men in the fort if he had room in his heart for anything but anger and hatred toward most Englishmen. But this was not like war with the Abnaki or Hurons. This was the future of all Indians, and he realized that this may have been the first time he had ever thought in terms of the good of Indians rather than the good of the Longhouse, or the good of the Seneca, Guardians of the Western Door of the Longhouse.

Late into the night, he caught another catnap. Which was more, he figured, than the men inside the blockhouse would be able to do.

He awoke to the sound of French being hollered toward the blockhouse from inside the fort. He had never learned any of that language and did not know what was being shouted, though he could guess.

For a few minutes there was no response from the block-house, but eventually a weary voice wafted across the night air asking for the message to be repeated in English. There was more silence. The smell of wet smoke hung in the cool of the night. Skoiyasi sat up, alert, and listened. Soon a voice came from outside the blockhouse, English, spoken not by an Indian, but by a colonial; Skoiyasi could tell that much, and he could tell that the voice was demanding surrender. That was strange. He did not know there were any Englishmen fighting on the Indian side. Somebody who had been adopted into one of the western lake tribes, probably.

In a little hollow of the creek bed a hundred yards down the creek, someone had made a little campfire. Skoiyasi walked down to the creek and rubbed some water on his face. He directed a brief prayer to the Holder of the Heavens, took a mirror from his pack and in the light of the campfire began to apply fresh war paint, black, white and vermilion, with lots of slanted lines that accentuated the severe angles of his lean face, the face of a predatory warrior.

But the fort was not yet ready to surrender. Ensign Christie asked for, and received, more time. Now the guns were silent, and the fire arrows stayed in their quivers. Everyone, the two-dozen brave soldiers cooped up in the blockhouse, and the hundreds of determined Indians camped around them, knew where matters stood. Tomorrow would surely be the day of triumph. One last time Skoiyasi found a safe niche beneath the creek bank and slept.

❧17❧

THAD GROUNDED HIS CANOE IN AN OLD
wreck of a forest, where a big wind had at one time torn
trees from the ground like so many twigs and laid them
helter-skelter. It was the place he'd been told about two
days before by a pair of wandering Menominees. The Menominees had refused to take part in the uprising, but the
fighting tribes, not wishing to make more enemies at this
time, had not declared themselves hostile toward that powerful rice-gathering people and their great chief, Oshkosh.

The two Menominees, with ears like the fox, had heard
of the Chippewa prisoner, and that they had traded him to
a Huron chief for ammunition.

"Was that good?" Thad had asked them.

It was better for the prisoner, the Menominees told him,
because the Chippewas were certain to have killed him
sooner or later. But Big Oak was not free to leave the
Hurons, they said, and the Hurons were not fond of the
English, and if they were to get more heavily involved in
the rebellion, Big Oak's safety was not assured.

Thad thanked the Menominees humbly and promised
them that when the rebellion was over, he and his father

would launch a special trade mission that would bring them the finest trade goods for the best prices.

Thad hid the canoe carefully, in a hollow between two large uprooted trees, and draped a mess of long, running vines over it. He headed due north until he struck the trail the Menominees had told him he would strike, then followed it west.

It might have been better for Big Oak if Thad had found his Menominees a day earlier. The wise old woodsman had been determined to stay on good terms with the village until the time came when he might escape with Cilla, as he had taken to calling his new friend, but yesterday had not been his lucky day. A hunter named Black Fox had stumbled into camp with a large buck on his back after having been gone for half a moon. Black Fox was one of those men any community dreads having in their midst, a big, strong, stupid bully with a bad temper.

When he saw Big Oak sitting in a clearing in the middle of the village reshaping a flint, he flung the deer down in ferocious anger, kicking up a huge dust cloud.

He directed a storm of Huron invective at Big Oak until Wahkee, disturbed by the one-man riot that had walked in on his peaceful village, took leave of his hut to find the cause of the commotion and squelch it.

"Who is this Englishman and why is he sitting in the middle of our village?" Black Fox asked.

"He is our prisoner and he knows how to repair rifles," Wahkee answered. "Where should he be if not in the middle of our village?"

"Crackling at the stake," Black Fox snarled. "I have spoken to Chippewas and Potawatomis. The English are losing their forts all around the lakes. If we do not take the warpath with our brothers, they will remember after they drive the English away, and then they will come down on us."

His words were reasoned but his voice was furious. He

did not wait for the patient Wahkee to respond. Instead he turned to Big Oak, who was now busy with a rifle, clamping the flint tight and checking the primer hole.

"Fix my rifle, English dog!" he sneered, throwing the piece down in the dust in front of Big Oak.

"It's a holy miracle your weapon works at all if you treat it that way, fool," Big Oak responded testily in English. Unfortunately, the temperamental Huron had been around the English just enough in his life to pick up the word "fool," and his dark skin darkened further, with rage. He kicked at Big Oak, suddenly but not quite unexpectedly. Big Oak's quick hands grabbed Black Fox's foot and twisted it, bringing him down into a sitting position beside him.

Big Oak would have been happy to see the struggle end there. But Black Fox reached for his tomahawk.

Wahkee grabbed his wrist. "My brother," he said, "stay your hand until he fixes your weapon. His work is nearly done here and soon we will hold council to decide what to do with him."

The angry Huron dropped his arms, and Big Oak noticed a smug smile flicker across his face for just a moment before he turned to the white man and signed that if he didn't make his rifle like brand new, then he, Black Fox, would cut his hands off and Big Oak would no longer be able to hold a rifle, much less fix one.

"You are wise, my brother," Black Fox told the chief, "more deserving of my name than I." And with one final glare at Big Oak, he stalked off, leaving Big Oak staring at the rifle. He shook his head, understanding now why the Huron had flung the rifle down so angrily and carelessly. He didn't have to disassemble anything to figure out that the weapon had a broken hammer spring. In a factory, or a gun repair shop, it would have been a snap to fix, and the rifle was otherwise well-cared for. But Big Oak had no way to fix this weapon, and Black Fox would have his scalp, or at least his hands, when he found that his weapon was useless.

Big Oak turned to Wahkee. "It is that time, now, when the shadows are too deep for me to see what I must see. This rifle is a difficult one to repair, and I must have the full morning light if I am to make it shoot the way it should."

The chief nodded coldly. To Big Oak that was a bad sign.

"Sssst," he whispered very softly in her ear as they lay close together in her hut. "Do not answer me yet. Listen closely. Black Fox wants me killed, and I believe that Wahkee will give in to him. Tonight must be the night that I go. Will you go too?"

She squeezed his hand. "More than anything I have wanted to go to be back with my people. Now it is different. I want to go with you, to be with you." Her lips touched his ear as she whispered so softly that a spy outside would not be able to hear a sound. He kissed her cheek.

"I have the knives they have given me for tools," he whispered.

"I have blankets, food, and a canoe," she responded. "But they are watching you, even tonight."

"I know. We must wait for them to stop watching."

With one of the knives that he had sharpened to a point, he drilled tiny holes in each wall and stared through them in turn. His eyes were still keen enough to make out two shadowy figures near the north and south corners of the hut. Both were seated, and both faced toward the front of the building. But he was certain that if they tried to leave through the back of the hut, the guards would hear. He had to wait until the two either moved away or went to sleep.

The presence of the guards also showed him that if he

stayed, he would not have long to live. Until tonight there had been no guards. Black Fox must have believed that Big Oak had sensed his danger, and insisted that guards be posted. Big Oak had been surprised by Wahkee's sudden coldness toward him. Perhaps the chief feared Black Fox, or perhaps Black Fox had served as a reminder to Wahkee that he really didn't like Englishmen. Whatever the reasons for Wahkee's changing feelings, Big Oak was certain that this night he had to find a way to escape.

Characteristically, he decided to take a short nap. Once the action began, the night would be a long one.

When he awoke, he found Cilla asleep. There were food bundles made up, but stowed in such a way that anybody walking in would not suspect flight. He looked through his peepholes. One of the guards was gone, the other one was seated in the light of a dying campfire leaning against a nearby tree, facing the door of the hut but sound asleep. Big Oak moved to the other side of the hut, and softly, as he had planned, slashed the bindings that held a sheet of bark to the frame of the hut. Then he awakened Cilla and noiselessly they crawled beneath the frame with their blankets and their small bundles.

Silent in their soft moccasins, they crept through the village in the direction of the small creek that led to the lake, and walked the remaining distance to the place where she kept her canoe. Big Oak wanted to slit the bottoms of the other canoes, but not all of them were hidden there, and time was crucial. Carefully they turned the canoe right side up and slid it into the water, then began to place their bundles into the bottom of the vessel. Big Oak was pleasantly surprised at how strong Cilla was, how easily she did her part in spite of being only about five feet tall and less than a hundred pounds.

He felt the cold steel of a rifle barrel against the back of his neck.

"I have another rifle, one that works, eh?" said the voice behind the weapon, Black Fox speaking understandable French.

Big Oak's heart turned as cold as the steel of Black Fox's rifle.

"I thought you might leave," Black Fox said. "I did not know you would take the Tuscarora with you."

Cilla immediately lunged at Black Fox, but the Huron caught her mid-jump with the barrel of his rifle, a swipe across her right shoulder that knocked her back into the canoe. Big Oak, forced into action to protect her, jumped from the canoe and grabbed the rifle barrel just as Black Fox pulled the trigger. With a roar the barrel fired a sheet of flame just over Big Oak's head. Big Oak slipped on the muddy shore and went to his knees, his left hand still clutching the barrel of Black Fox's rifle, his right hand reaching for the Indian's leg, to pull him down to him.

Black Fox reached into his belt, pulled out his tomahawk and raised it over his head, but before he could bring it down upon the fallen trader, Big Oak heard a solid *thock* sound and looked up in time to see the Huron's eyes go glassy. The blade of an English hatchet had split his forehead halfway to the bridge of his nose, and blood was pouring down toward his chin. The Huron pitched forward headlong, then lay still.

Behind him stood Thad, clutching his rifle. "Come on, Pa, get that stuff into my canoe," he said, pointing a few yards downstream, where a beautiful white craft lay waiting.

Big Oak gave directions to Cilla, who had quickly regained her feet. It was but a moment before Thad's canoe was loaded. Big Oak had relieved the dead Huron of his rifle, powder, ball, knife, and tomahawk, laid it on the canoe bottom, picked up a paddle and moved to the front of the canoe. The three could hear a commotion in the village in response to the shot. Several of the braves had naturally headed for the creek. The three could hear their footsteps on the path. Cilla had grabbed her paddle and taken her position in the middle of the canoe, while Thad gave the canoe a powerful push and leaped into the stern. They managed a half-dozen quick, powerful strokes and shot off into the darkness. By the time the braves had made it to the shore, where they had to pull their canoes from cover onto the creek, the fugitives had their craft well downstream and close to the St. Joseph Channel that would eventually take them out onto the waters of Lake Huron.

In later years the legends told of how quickly Big Oak and Thad managed to get their canoe out onto the broad expanse of Lake Huron. But in truth there were not two paddlers on that night, there were three, and in the blue light of the half-moon, Thad admired the young Tuscarora woman in front of him as the muscles in her shoulders bent to the task of moving her share of the creek past their canoe.

Most of the time she paddled on the same side as Thad, to neutralize the furious strokes of Big Oak in the bow. For several weeks now he had known the torment of slavery, with torture and death hanging over his head, forced labor, constant humiliation, and worst of all, suffocating confinement. All his life he had been a man accustomed to going where he wanted to go and doing what he wanted to do when he wanted to do it. Even in warfare, when his scouting abilities, calm courage, and deadly shooting eye were in such great demand, he refused to serve in the ranks, where his freedom of movement and his life would be subject to the whims of officers whose judgment he did not respect.

For a time, prisoner to three different bands of Indians, he had wondered if he would ever again be a free man. And now, a free man again, his powerful will pushed his muscles far beyond their reasonable limits, restrained only by the lurking fear that too powerful a stroke might break the paddle. But his determination overcame his caution. Power surged from his back, through his shoulders and arms, into his paddle, and the water boiled its way back past the canoe in mighty swirling eddies, so that Thad and Cilla had to work hard on their side of the canoe to keep it moving in a straight line. Their canoe knifed through the water, which seethed past the bow in a high wave and gurgled in a turbulent wake.

Behind them they could hear the whoops and cries of angry Hurons responding to the challenge, men accustomed to the cadence of rapid canoeing. A creek is a one-way street, unprotected by the night. With three or four strong men powering each canoe, the lead craft was bound to overtake them in the channel unless they could figure out a way to slow them down.

"Pa!" Thad shouted above the hissing water and the screeching Hurons, who were closing in. "I'm going to stop paddling to get a shot at the lead canoe."

"Don't miss, boy, or we're finished," Big Oak shouted back, and let up just a bit on his stroke to allow the Hurons within range.

This part of the creek wound a little. There would be no shooting yet. Thad put down his rifle, grabbed the paddle and resumed his strokes until they found another straight stretch, then quickly he snatched up his weapon, checked the priming with his finger, and lay down on his stomach, bracing the rifle as best he could.

Through the night they came, eyes gleaming in the moonlight, knowing the creek bed so well that the lead paddler of the lead canoe had his head down as he bent his back in time with the other paddlers in a mighty stroke that took six feet off the gap between the canoes. Only fifty feet in front of them, Thad could not miss, even in the dim moonlight that filtered through the overhanging branches.

The sudden explosion in the night startled even those who knew it was coming. Thad's ball pierced the breastbone of the first Huron and lodged in the belly of the second. The lead paddler slumped to the side, tipping the canoe over, into the path of the following canoe, piling up the next three canoes behind them.

The noise and confusion behind him told Thad everything his eyes could not. Several shots were fired in his direction without effect. He snatched up his paddle and the three of them began to put some real distance between their canoe and the angry shouts behind them. It would take time for the canoes to get untangled, and then they would be far more cautious in their pursuit, perhaps even keeping one warrior in the bow holding a rifle at the ready instead of paddling.

Eventually the creek poured them into the St. Joseph channel, a much wider body of water with less current. They continued to paddle hard for several minutes, and then Thad looked back and saw nothing. Now they paddled less urgently, more silently. Pursuers might use their ears in the night where their eyes failed them, and Big Oak was determined to be a difficult quarry. For several more hours they paddled, strong but silent, Cilla matching the men stroke for stroke. They were on what seemed to be a large body of water, and with clouds beginning to obscure the stars, it would be easy for them to lose their direction. But Big Oak had been here before, and kept the land visible to his right until at last they glided through a narrow passageway onto a huge expanse of water that he knew was Lake Huron. He headed the canoe southeast, and the three paddlers kept up a steady stroke. There was land to their left now, and they kept it in sight. The moon was of little help, but the water was calm.

Big Oak told Cilla to get some sleep, which she did. He and Thad stroked on silently, both exhausted, both knowing that now was not the time to talk, but both glad to be together again, regardless of the peril. Thad wondered about the young Tuscarora woman for a while, then all thoughts left him as he went into his paddler's trance, stroke after stroke. No signals were necessary. They'd done this often before, switching sides when their arms wearied of stroking, Thad to the left, Big Oak to the right, now Thad to the right, Big Oak to the left.

After a couple of hours Big Oak moved to the stern, Thad lay down in the middle for some rest, and Cilla moved to the bow. Firm and wiry, used to hardship and hungry for freedom, she picked up her paddle and with Big Oak continued their strong pace. Thad quickly found sleep, and did not awaken until the very first light of dawn. Before the sleep had left his eyes he was repriming his rifle. Only then did he look behind Big Oak.

"What do you see?" his father asked.

"I'd say we've got the whole Huron nation behind us," Thad said. Spread out, more than two miles to their rear, set against the blue-black horizon of the still dark western sky, revealed only by the feeble light of dawn, were two dozen white canoes, breasting white-frothed through the blue-green waters of Lake Huron, each one filled with dark, painted men whose bare scalps glistened in the early morning sun.

In spite of their long experience, Big Oak and Thad stared in awe at the overwhelming force that pursued them in powerful surges, one stroke at a time. Thad had no idea how they could fight off so many enemy.

"They must have signed up some of their Chippewa neighbors along the way," Big Oak declared. "I think I need to grab a little sleep. Wake me up when you need me."

Thad knew what his father meant. Their pursuers would

gain on them, that was certain. But it would take them some time to do it. In the meantime, Big Oak had to rest if he was to be of much use. Slowly Thad's heart, which with his first glimpse of the dawn armada had leaped into his throat and clung there like a child clinging to its mother, made its way back to its usual place. The calmer he became, the more he realized that on an open inland sea, against Indian marksmen, there was a chance for all of them to survive.

They were not going to outrun this armada. It was more a question of outgunning them. But he did want to give his father an opportunity to rest, so he and Cilla bent their backs and kept up a strong, persistent stroke that would make the chase a long one. The young Tuscarora had taken a cloth from her pack, dipped it in the lake and fastened it around the top of her head as protection from the merciless sun that would soon be beating down upon them like a sledgehammer.

That was her only indulgence. For an hour the two of them paddled silently, working hard, their faces and arms glistening with sweat. Thad stripped off his soaked shirt and resumed his stroke, and Cilla continued hers, without complaint, shoulders flexing, breathing easily, tireless in her toil.

The pursuing armada drew closer. Thad could see the white froth as their bows bit into the waters of Lake Huron. He and Cilla picked up their stroke a little, to give Big Oak more rest. Fifteen minutes later he awoke on his own and took the stern position.

When Thad moved toward the middle and dipped his paddle into the lake, Big Oak told him, "Don't work too hard. I want your hands steady when they draw within range." The mighty old trader's shoulders heaved and the canoe surged forward with new energy.

"I'll give them another hour, not much more, before they draw within range of your rifle," he said.

"*My* hands! You are the steadiest shooter in all North America," Thad replied, astonished.

"And you, my son, are living in the past. My hand is still steady, but long distances take young eyes. They will be in your range before we are in range of their rifles." He raised his paddle high and dug it hard into the water. "I will tell you when you are close enough. Meanwhile, do not work too hard."

Abruptly they grew silent and listened to the dissonant chorus of whoops and cries to their rear, gradually growing louder and more distinct. A mild breeze blew cool spray in their faces as they breasted a swell.

The screeching warriors drew closer. Two or three optimistic braves fired their rifles, but their rounds landed well short of their targets, so their cohorts held their fire and waited for the distance between them and their prey to close.

A gentle headwind cooled the sweat on the refugees' brows. In unison, like one six-armed creature, they pulled at a controlled tempo. Thad and Cilla had faith in Big Oak's confident judgment. They were determined not to wear themselves out in a race they could not win.

Shortly after noon, shooters in the five or six leading canoes began to pour a steady fire toward the enemy they were pursuing. The rest of the canoes fanned out farther and caught up to the leaders, then their riflemen swung into action. At first the range was too far to menace Thad and Big Oak, but after another fifteen minutes, Big Oak could see the rounds splashing, in some cases skipping across the water, though still well short.

"Pick up your rifle, son. It's time for you to show them a little Watley shootin'."

Taking directions from his father, who was paddling on

the starboard side, Thad lay across his father's left leg and took aim at the lead paddler of the closest canoe. By now the enemy's shots were beginning to find the range, although their windage was still off.

With bullets splashing the water all around him, Thad fired, but the lead canoe kept coming, apparently untouched.

"I must have missed," Thad growled, dismayed, and reached for Black Fox's rifle. But even as he checked the priming, he looked up and saw his target drop his paddle, lurch forward, then roll sideways, nearly swamping the canoe. The other three Indians in the canoe had their hands full keeping the canoe upright and preventing their badly injured mate from falling overboard. Several more shots came from angered warriors in other canoes, one of them close enough to splash water on Big Oak.

"All that shootin' they're doing, I'm surprised they haven't come closer," Thad said through clenched teeth as he took careful aim at the canoe with the best marksman. "I thought surely they would shoot better than that."

His father smiled. "Maybe the sights on those weapons aren't what they should be."

"Did you—of course you did." Thad chuckled. Big Oak switched his paddle to the port side, and Thad lay across his father's right side. "Would you bear a little right so I can draw a bead on 'em?"

Big Oak pulled a little more easily, allowing Cilla's powerful sweeps to turn the canoe enough to bring his rifle to bear on the closest canoe to their right rear.

"Did you mess up this rifle too?"

"No, never had a chance. Give it a try, see how good it is."

Thad fired, catching his target in the shoulder and spinning him around so he landed bloodily on the lap of the man behind him. Like the first, the second canoe withdrew from the pursuit. Now the war cries of the Hurons and Chippewas turned even bloodier.

"They sound angry," Big Oak noted.

"But they're all fallin' back," Thad said, dropping to the floor of the canoe and pouring powder into the barrel of his rifle.

"No, here they come again," Big Oak declared. "They must have seen you reloading. "Pull, Cilla!" he shouted, and the canoe shot forward as the two paddlers pulled with everything they had. Now the pursuing canoes spread out even more, with all of them keeping their distance but several canoes pulling even with Big Oak and Cilla on their flanks. They fired as quickly as they could, but stern shot or broadside, they could not seem to find a target. Two or three rounds landed short, found water and skipped over their targets. Thad loaded both rifles as quickly as he could, but carefully. Finding his next target could save their lives, and might depend on him loading the rifle with the precise amount of gunpowder.

"How's your supply of powder and ball?" Big Oak asked.

"Between mine and what we took from that Indian, I've got plenty."

"Well, sooner or later they're bound to catch up, so let Cilla reload for you and I think you'll surprise 'em pretty good. They think they're outside your range, but fact is, they're a good hundred yards too close for their own good. Go get 'em, boy." He sank his paddle into the water and took a bite out of the lake.

Thad fired off to his right flank and picked off an Indian in the center of a Chippewa canoe. The force of the bullet striking the Chippewa tumbled him sideways and swamped the canoe. The wounded Chippewa struggled for a moment then slipped beneath the surface of the lake, while his cohorts wrestled with the canoe, righted it, and bailed it out enough to accommodate them. But with their weap-

ons lost, that canoe was out of the fight. Thad took aim
with his own rifle and tried for a more distant canoe, which
held a rifleman who had fired too close to them several
times. The round missed flesh but tore a hole in the birch-
bark shell and made the paddlers veer away from the long
reach of Thad's rifle.

Cilla handed Thad Black Fox's weapon. He turned to his
left flank, resting his arm against the frame for steadiness.
He squeezed the trigger and caught a Huron in the thigh.
The Indian hollered with pain, dropped his paddle and began to writhe around in the canoe. Several Indians fired
their rifles, with little effect until one shot pierced the canoe amidships just above the waterline.

"A little lower and we'd have been in real trouble," Big
Oak observed as Thad took his freshly loaded rifle and
pointed it at one of the more distant canoes. He fired and
sent another Huron tumbling, and only then did their pursuers realize the full extent of their jeopardy. They slowed
their stroke, trying to get Big Oak to put some distance
between them and Thad's deadly shooting eye, but Big
Oak slowed his paddling too, and Thad carved some flesh
from another Huron. Now the Indians actually retreated,
and fanned out farther along their flanks, till they looked
more like an escort than an adversary.

Cilla picked up her paddle and she and Big Oak did
some serious stroking to put more water between themselves and their pursuers.

"What's their next move?" Thad asked.

"I believe they're gonna try to wear us down," Big Oak
answered. "But we're about to run into a piece of luck."

Big Oak's piece of luck was a cloud front coming at them
from the east. He was counting on a moonless night to lose
the attackers.

"I sure hope you're right, Pa."

"I better be right, son. After what you did to their little

navy, I don't think they'd be kind to us if they caught us."
Thad knelt on the bottom of the canoe and raised his rifle
toward a canoe on the right flank. The canoe veered and
added an extra fifty yards of range plus a stern rather than a
broadside profile. Thad held his fire and waited for another
target to come closer, but the enemy had had enough for
the time being.

"No sir," Thad agreed. "I don't think they'd be a bit kind
to us if they caught us."

❧18❧

LAKE HURON IS REALLY TWO LAKES, A MAIN body, known, appropriately enough, as Lake Huron, and an upper body called Georgian Bay. The two bodies of water are connected by a wide stretch of water known as Lucas Channel. It was this channel that Big Oak meant to run for when the night descended upon them.

As he had hoped, a heavy cloud cover darkened the night, shrouding their movements from the enemy. But the same cloud cover made it necessary to head north for the shore so they would not miss the opening that was Lucas Channel.

"What we need to do," Big Oak whispered to his son, "is to take the most direct route back to friendly territory. Georgian Bay is the way to go, and we might lose the Huron-Chippewa navy in the bargain."

Slowly, quietly, Cilla and Big Oak paddled through the blackness. How his father could keep a north course without the stars was a mystery to Thad, who knelt behind Cilla in the bow of the canoe, rifle at the ready, just in case a Chippewa canoe suddenly emerged from the darkness. How many were still following them, they could only guess. Perhaps by now some were ahead of them. Only constant alertness, they knew, would give them a chance to survive this deadly game of blind man's bluff.

Soon they could hear the water rolling against the shore, but they could not see the shoreline until they were less than one hundred yards away. Now they ran east, parallel to the shore, while Thad kept a sharp eye astern, where their pursuers stood nearby, somewhere in the dark. Ever so slowly, ever so silently, the old trader and the young Tuscarora woman pulled the canoe forward through the night.

At one point Thad thought he heard the sound of paddles dipping through the water. Then all three of them heard it. Big Oak and Cilla shipped their paddles and waited. They heard two voices, so softly there was no way to make out the words in any language. Then the voices stopped and the sounds of the paddles grew more and more faint, until they faded into silence. Now all that could be heard was the lapping of water against the land. Big Oak and Cilla resumed their paddling, slowly at first, and then, as Big Oak gained confidence in their isolation, more rapidly. He was keeping a sharp eye toward shore, waiting to see the land begin to swing away, which would tell them that they were entering the channel to Georgian Bay.

When they saw the shore start to recede, Thad scooped up a handful of water to drink and lay down for a nap. Big Oak piloted the canoe along the bending shoreline for a while, then past the headland of a large island and a smaller island, before they came to a sort of land's end. Here he continued on a more or less easterly course to take them through the channel and into Georgian Bay. Tired as he was, of the three, only he had the instincts and knowledge that could navigate their craft into safe waters. He would continue on until dawn. He would then hand the job over to Thad and get some sleep himself.

On and on they paddled, Big Oak and Cilla, like two

people chained together in a hypnotic trance, focused only on their clean, methodic strokes and their changes from one side to the other. But they had no thoughts, and only the barest hold on consciousness. They were up in the bay now, and the land was on their right. Big Oak ran the canoe through the thick night until the dim outlines of the land appeared in the gloom, then he maintained a course parallel to shore, as he had in the lower body of water.

By the time Big Oak noticed the early light, the sky had a hue more medium-blue than dark purple. His head jerked into full wakefulness and he wondered what it was that had seized him and jerked him so, a bad dream perhaps, or maybe—the maybes vanished. Not fifty yards off their port bow was a Chippewa canoe with two men stroking ghost-like through the murk of early dawn. Gently Big Oak nudged Thad's foot with the toe of his moccasin. The young man turned and stared at his father through weary slits of eyes. His father looked toward the other canoe. Thad followed his gaze and his eyes widened to full awake.

Big Oak stopped paddling and took a quick look around. There were no other canoes in sight. He let their canoe drift to a stop. The Indians were not keeping up much of a pace, but their canoe continued its forward motion, with neither warrior raising his head to look left or right. Their chins were nearly on their chests. Only instinct and will-power, not sinew, drove them on.

Big Oak turned the canoe toward shore, praying that the Indians nearby would not suddenly become alert as he did, and that more canoes would not appear over the horizon. Once close to shore, he paddled along the shoreline until he spotted an entrance to a creek so small as to be nearly invisible to anyone more than a quarter of a mile out on the bay. He turned into it and forced the canoe around a bend about a hundred yards up from the mouth, which was as far as the creek would permit before it became too shallow.

"Cilla," Big Oak said softly. "This is my son, Thad."

The young Tuscarora looked at the tall, dark young man from beneath heavy-lidded eyes. "Hello," she said in English. Then without another word, she wrapped a blanket around herself, lay down, and immediately went to sleep.

Only then did the two men permit themselves a mighty bear hug. They laughed, softly, and pounded each other on the back. "How did you ever figure out where we were?" Big Oak asked.

"Just a whole lot of luck. A few questions in the right places. Who's the girl?"

"I'm not sure yet, but I think she might be my new wife."

Thad raised an eyebrow but didn't comment further. Life on the frontier was full of surprises, and over the years his father had provided quite a few of them. The two men walked downstream until they reached the tree line.

There they knelt, concealed by tree trunks and brush, and stared out at the water. To their right, more than a mile out on the water, they could see the lone Chippewa canoe making its way southeast, casting a stronger wake than when they had been so close. Apparently the crew of that boat had come back to full consciousness, or perhaps a third member, who had been sleeping, had awakened and relieved his cohorts.

Big Oak pointed toward the horizon on their left. Five more canoes were approaching. Reenforced by each other's presence, the paddlers were working hard, closing the distance between themselves and the canoe in front of them. Big Oak and Thad watched them as the canoes came abreast of them, graceful as a gaggle of white swans as they knifed their way through the waters of the bay and then continued their way east, chasing a phantom.

They watched the bay for more than an hour, saying

virtually nothing but enjoying each other's company never-theless. No more canoes crossed over the horizon. "We've cut down the enemy a good bit," said a satisfied Big Oak quietly. "Let's eat."

Cilla's nap must have been a short one. Thad and Big Oak returned to their camp to find a meal of fish arranged before them on leaves, fish she had caught in the stream and somehow cooked without sight nor smell of smoke, along with mushrooms she had found, and some wild rice she had taken with her from the village.

Thad looked at Big Oak. "How long were we watching the canoe races?"

Big Oak shrugged. "An hour, maybe more."

"How'd she do all this?"

Big Oak shook his head. "She's still new to me. All I know is she can pull a canoe as hard as we can, and then cook up a meal in secret that's better 'n anything we can get in Albany." He and Thad had seated themselves cross-legged before their meal. Big Oak looked up to show his appreciation, but she was gone. He looked down the creek and saw her, through the foliage, peering out at the bay, on guard for the return of their pursuers.

They both sat in silence, filling their empty stomachs with food so good they longed for more even before it was gone. And they both stared at her as she stood, lithe as a child, motionless, watching the water.

Big Oak put his hand on his son's. "No more," he said. "I'll bet she hasn't eaten any herself." Thad watched his father stand up and walk quietly along the creek until he was standing by the Tuscarora girl, one hand lightly on her shoulder. He heard his father's voice, soft and gentle. He saw the girl nod.

She turned, walked back to the camp, and sat on the blanket across from Thad. She picked up a piece of fish and began to eat. She pointed to another piece, then pointed to Thad and said, "You." Her manner toward Thad was courteous but distant.

Thad patted his belly as if to show he was full, and drank some water from the military-issue canteen he carried with him. She ate another piece of fish, and some mushroom, chewing slowly, as if each morsel of food were something very special to her. Then she picked up a piece of fish, stood up, and carried it to where Big Oak was standing, rifle in hand, watching the horizon. Thad observed as she handed his father the fish, watched as he tore it in half and handed one of the halves to her, watched as they both chewed for a while.

She stood up on the tips of her moccasins, her hands gripping his arm for balance. He stooped down just a bit. And she kissed him on the cheek. Thad saw his big hand grip her small one and squeeze.

"It may be faster to canoe on down to the end of the bay," Big Oak argued, "but it will be safer to go by land."

Thad did not want to hear his father talk about the safer way, but then he had not spent two weeks enduring the tender mercies of Chippewas and Hurons who wanted above all else to cook Englishmen.

"There were a score of Indians still on our tail," Big Oak warned his son. "We watched them pass. They'll be coming back."

"When they come back, they'll be hugging the shore just like they did, and we did, on our way here, right?" Thad said. "If we go on farther out on the bay, we'll be over the horizon and they'll never see us."

"Son, you never spent much time with me up on these lakes. A storm can come up faster than I can tell you about it, and if we're not close enough to shore to run on home, prayers won't do us a bit of good. Now this is still your wise old pa talkin' that's got us out of a few scrapes before, and in this case the slow way is much the better way. And I want to know why you're in such an all-fired hurry to get on home anyway. We were supposed to be spendin' a lot of the summer going from tribe to tribe trading a little and showing off our goods, remember? Me, if we get home in one piece, I don't care to face your father-in-law without the goods or the furs. We're better off taking our time and making sure we get home with our hair."

"Yeah, well, I miss my wife, and I miss my child, and I'll tell you, suddenly I'm damn sick of being in these woods."

"Well, son, I can sure understand missin' your family and your home." He looked through the trees out over the bay. "Having a family and a home is a fine thing. It's a mighty fine thing. And you'll never get to see it again if we get careless." He was almost absentminded as he spoke. "No, boy, we don't want to get careless now. We want to get home."

Thad looked into his father's face and saw a man exhausted from his ordeal. Although Big Oak was in fine shape for a man his age, and could still keep up with most men in the woods, he was at this moment worn down to his limits.

"Pa, why don't you go back to Cilla and get some rest. We don't need to get started right away, and I'll watch out for us the rest of the day."

Big Oak looked away from the bay, into his son's Seneca-dark eyes.

"You're right. I'd better turn in if I'm gonna be good for anything come tomorrow morning."

Thad watched his father walk back to Cilla, who was puttering around in camp. She had pulled the canoe from the creek and carefully camouflaged it, then gathered some very dry twigs for their next meal. No doubt more fresh fish would come later.

The old trader said a few quiet words to her. Then he laid his body down on the blanket she had spread, curled up and went to sleep. Thad thought that the Tuscarora woman must be exhausted herself, but she did not lay down with Big Oak. Not yet. Not until the sun finished its long journey and hid itself in the dark. Mostly she sat beside him, looking down at his sleeping form as if she were afraid he would disappear if she left his side for a moment.

As the light faded from the woods, she laid herself down next to Big Oak and allowed herself some badly needed sleep.

In the dirty gray light of a weary dawn, Skoiyasi opened his eyes and started to stand up. Then he remembered where he was, and that rising to his feet might invite an English bullet into his brain. He looked around at the other men in the creek bed, all awake, all ready for the good things they were certain were about to happen.

He motioned to Smoke to follow him, and together they ran up the creek bed until they were in the woods, then they circled around to the front of the fort and dashed to the gate, which was open. They arrived just in time to see two soldiers walk from the blockhouse to the center of the parade ground, where two Indians Skoiyasi did not know waited to meet them.

Although only the four of them were visible, the two soldiers acted as if any moment they expected a score of enemy to jump out of the shadows and hack them to pieces. Skoiyasi watched them as they stared at the blockhouse. The Indians inside the walls of the fort had spent the night quietly piling incendiary materials against the walls of the blockhouse. It was obvious from the look on their faces that the soldiers expected to be cooked if they went back into the blockhouse.

So they signaled the people in the blockhouse—cleverly, they thought, though every Indian watching them caught on. The door to the blockhouse opened and out walked a lone English officer in a stylish uniform. While the officer and the two Indian negotiators found a way to communicate, a few soldiers began to emerge from the blockhouse. Mississaugas began to creep out of the woodwork, determined to be on hand for the finish. Skoiyasi and Smoke joined them as they and dozens of others dashed through the door of the blockhouse and emerged, dragging the soldiers within, one by one, out into the sunshine.

How easy this all is, thought Skoiyasi. Why, why have we waited so long to get together and rid ourselves of these feeble people? And why can we not pursuade our brothers the Mohawks to join us? Is it possible that the Ganiengehaka have become too white for their own good?

Skoiyasi found Kyashuta as the chief entered the fort. "Let us get rid of them all now," he told the chief. "They are such miserable men that they are not even worth torturing."

"No," Kyashuta answered. "We have made agreements with the other nations. They are our prisoners. The Chippewa will get some, the Mississauga will get some, the Ottawa will get some. And so will we. But hurry now. There are goods to be taken."

Skoiyasi saw that those Indians not guarding the prisoners were busy ransacking the fort. Skoiyasi wanted something he could take back to his woman, Kawia. Quickly he made his way through the door to the commander's house, where he found a spare officer's uniform and a number of other items, including a pair of gold earrings, which he knew would be perfect for himself. He also found a dress, made for a much larger woman than Kawia, but she would trim it down to size.

It occurred to him that he had had his fill of fighting for a while. Without another word, he slung his pack on his shoulder and headed north for the country of the Senecas, on the Genesee River.

❊19❊

BIG OAK WAS OVERJOYED TO BE BACK ON the New York side of Lake Ontario. The past two weeks had been a nightmare of nighttime marches through swamps and forests, stratagems to obliterate signs of their presence or mislead would-be pursuers concerning who they were and where they were going, and occasional near-scrapes with small groups of Chippewas and Hurons who weren't looking for them in particular but nevertheless seemed keen on finding Englishmen to kill.

There were also hostile French Canadians prowling the woods, bitter-enders refusing to acknowledge the defeat of their side by the English, and determined to carry on their hostilities no matter what. Big Oak managed to avoid everybody except one party of Ottawas, and then he got lucky.

This group happened upon the three of them as they made their way out of a creek bed just when the Indians were emerging from some dense underbrush. For both parties the encounter was totally unexpected. Fortunately, these braves were from a large Ottawa faction that had refused to follow their own war chief, Pontiac. They gave Big Oak a haunch of venison and invited them to their village farther north, but Big Oak told the Ottawas that he was determined to make it back to New York as soon as possible.

With the woods full of enemies, they could not use their rifles to hunt for food, and they might have stayed hungry had it not been for the gift from the Ottawas, and Cilla's superior ability to find edible wild vegetables, berries, and mushrooms. Slowly, carefully, they skirted the south shore of Lake Ontario, crossed the Niagara River, and finally made it into Fort Niagara.

For the first time in months Big Oak found himself among people who knew him, including the commander, Major John Wilkins. Like many officers, Major Wilkins did not go out of his way to take regular exercise, and he looked it. But once in a while he forced himself to take a sluggish stroll around the parade grounds, and on this evening of Big Oak's first day back in civilization, Wilkins asked the veteran frontiersman to accompany him on his stroll.

"Sam," he said, "when we were together during the last war, I told you we had paid for this land with our blood. And when the war was over, I thought so was the blood. But this beats all. Have you any idea what's going on out there?"

Big Oak laughed, not the hearty laugh that turned his lanky body to rubber, but a mirthless, three-syllable chuckle. "I been out there for two months," he answered, "and I've told you what we've been through."

"I don't mean just Detroit and the woods, Sam. Those redskins have taken every fort between Detroit and here except Fort Pitt. They attack a place, and we don't hear from it for weeks until somebody stumbles over the ashes, and then suddenly there's prisoners turning up outside the walls of Detroit. Those devils'll drive a prisoner five hundred miles just so they can torture him within a scream's distance of Detroit, and then once they've got 'em there, they burn 'em some and chop 'em up and make sure the fort gets to see 'em in that shape. Now that's an awful long way to drive a prisoner just to cut 'im into pieces."

"That's Indians for you, Major. They've got a lot of faith in taking away the enemy's spirit, gettin' him real down so he can't fight so good anymore."

"They've been raising Cain around here too, I'll tell you. If I were you, I'd stay with us for a while. We can use good men like you and your son to keep the Senecas off our back."

"Eh?" a surprised Big Oak said. "Are you sayin' the Senecas are a part of this?" Big Oak's surprise was so genuine that Wilkins could not hold back his laughter.

"I forgot, you're brother to them devils, aren't you? I'll tell you what—blood brother or not, you'd better stay with us for a while. You're still a white man to them, I don't care who you're related to."

"I understand. But are all the Senecas supposed to be out there on the warpath?"

"I'll be honest and tell you that I haven't been in the woods taking census on the creatures. There's some still come by the fort to trade with us. Then there's them that's out there lookin' for scalps. Our scalps. But I have to tell you, my friend, if Lord Jeffery Amherst decides to send a big army thisaway, his orders will be to kill every redskin they find, and don't give any passes for good conduct."

"Sorry to say this, Major, but if his army does the way a lot of the English armies do, they'll never catch the ones that do the real mischief, and the ones they do capture and punish, they'll be the ones that have been on our side all along."

The major nodded his agreement. "Will you stay here for a spell, Sam? We can use you."

"I would if I could, sir, but we've got some vital business to take care of, I'm afraid."

"What's more vital than the king's business, Sam?" The major had suddenly become a bit testy.

The truth was, Sam did not want to stay cooped up behind the walls of Fort Niagara, because he liked the major a good deal more than he respected the major's military judgment. Big Oak was as brave as they come, but he had been around Indians most of his adult life, and even the bravest of braves did not choose to put himself under the command of a chief who he believed did not have good medicine. Sam thought he saw more than concern in the commander's eyes, something more like fear. He could understand the major's apprehension. As strong as Fort Niagara was, it was still surrounded by wilderness, and the wilderness belonged to the Indians.

"You'll do all right without me, John," Sam said, with special emphasis on the man's familiar first name. He knew the major could detain him if he desired, and so Sam turned on the charm. "On my way to Albany I will stop at Warraghiyagey's, and I will tell him all I have seen and all you have told me. If anyone can persuade General Amherst to take this uprising seriously without trying to wipe out every Indian on the continent, he can."

The major looked at Sam's bright blue eyes from behind his rough desk, as if measuring the sincerity of his declaration. "Well," he said, "you just be very careful, because I'll tell you, the woods are swarming with Iroquois."

"Iroquois?" Now Big Oak was more than astonished. "Don't tell me that Pontiac has managed to rope some Mohawks into his rebellion."

"If he has, I wouldn't be surprised. Anyway, Mohawk, Seneca, they're all Indians. They all stink and they'll all steal you blind."

This time Big Oak's laugh had a little more joy in it.

"Ain't that somethin', John, that's what they say about us. And you know what I think? I think we're both right."

Major Wilkins had opened his mouth to say something more about the savages with whom his friend across the desk romped around the wilderness, but Big Oak's comment shut his mouth quick as a mousetrap. Then the corners of his mouth turned up and he began to laugh until his false teeth dropped onto his tongue.

"Well—as usual, you have got right to the truth of it, Sam. Be gone from this fort tomorrow, then, with that accursed long rifle of yours that can shave the hairs off a gnat's arse at a hundred yards."

"Major, Major, haven't you noticed?" Sam asked, holding up his rifle for the commander's inspection. There's a Potawatomi out in the western woods somewhere that's outshootin' all his associates because he's got *my* rifle. This one here is about half as good. Hellfire, Major, without old Thunder, I'm not any good to you on the rampart anyway, right?"

"Truth is, you old woods rat, I'd trust you more with a sling in your hand than most of my men with rifles. But I suppose I'd better let you get to Albany and rearm yourself. I expect at the least you'll soon be back in the woods makin' it hot for the heathens, and you were always one to do it your own way."

They stayed an extra day at Niagara. Sam Watley, the Big Oak, never sick a day in his life, had eaten something, or drunk something, or caught something in the fort that laid him low for a day. The major tried to throw his aide out of his quarters to give Big Oak a roof and some quiet, but Sam just found himself space in a quiet corner of a storeroom, wrapped his blanket around himself and shivered away the next twenty-four hours. Cilla begged some venison from a trader and a few vegetables from a company garden and made a broth for her stricken beau. The night found Big Oak awash in perspiration, but the following morning he stood on his feet, pronounced himself good as new, and within an hour the little party was on the trail east.

They didn't stay on the trail for long. As soon as Fort Niagara was out of sight, they left it for the depths of the forest. This was home territory for Big Oak. He could navigate these seas by feel alone. He knew where the ambushes were and where few feet ever trod. And he was heading for his old home on the Genesee River, near the Seneca village of Tonowaugh.

From Fort Niagara to the house on the Genesee was normally two days' journey. Traversing the difficult routes where they were least likely to encounter marauding Mingoes, or Senecas for that matter, it took them a full three days of wandering through the thick primary-growth forests of hardwoods and hemlocks before they finally found themselves on the banks of the Genesee, perhaps ten miles north of the village. Thad and Big Oak both remembered the last time they had returned to Tonowaugh.

They had approached the village from the east in a rainstorm so heavy that they found it nearly impossible to maintain their footing on the hillside trails. Dripping wet, peering out from beneath their heavy, wet blankets, they had caught the strong scent of wet ashes while still a mile away from the village. Horrified by fears of catastrophe, they ran the remaining mile through the rain, to find that their worst fears were as nothing compared to the reality. The village had not only been burned, but most of the villagers massacred. Five of the warriors had been bound and forced to witness the massacre before the invading French-led Caughnawagas tortured them to death.

All this was easily read in the grisly remains of the village, but what nobody could have read was the reaction of the returning villagers to the massacre. They had blamed their adopted brother Big Oak, and his half-Seneca son, Little Oak, for provoking the attack by the mere fact of their living in the village. Having made that determination, what was left of the village leadership demanded that Thad and Big Oak leave. Since so many of the people they had loved were dead anyway, they did not contest the expulsion. Within two days they were gone, and they had never returned. Not until now.

Coming down toward the village, Thad felt a few powerful tugs at his heartstrings. These were the scenes of his childhood: the grassy hillside that he and his friends used to race down full-tilt, usually falling and tumbling half the distance; the fields where he used to watch his mother and the other women weeding around the corn and beans; the Genesee River, where he and his friends, Kawia, Skoiyasi, and John Thompson, used to swim together.

John Thompson, a full-blooded Seneca who had been named for the Scotsman who saved his father's life, was tortured to death during the massacre. Kawia, the girl Thad had dreamed of taking for a wife when he was still called Little Oak, had turned against him, and instead became wife to Skoiyasi, who was now a leading warrior among the Senecas of the Genesee Valley.

Silently, carefully, Big Oak, Thad, and Cilla crept through the woods along the river. The soft June sun still stood well above the horizon, big and orange and casting cool shadows everywhere a tree stood. His mother slept now so many years. Thad looked at his father and tried to read his thoughts as he brought his new woman into the land of his old. Thad's mother had not been that much older than Cilla when she had died, and thinking about that made him feel odd. Time was like a handful of water; no matter how tight you held your fingers together, it soon slipped through and left you dry. These days it was hard for him to remember just what his mother looked like.

Eventually they came to a thicket across the river from their house. Through the bushes and oak trees on the other side they could see the ivy-covered pile of stones that had for years been home to himself and his father. Hidden deep in the thicket, protected by a large sheet of canvas, was an old canoe they had used strictly as a ferry from one side of the river to the other. The elm-bark sheeting was in bad need of repair, but the framework was sound. They set to work fastening the canvas to the hull well enough to get them across the river in dry condition. For the three of them it was the work of only a few minutes.

Having crossed the river, they paused a moment to assure themselves that the stone house still had a roof over it. Neither Big Oak or Thad voiced any desire to enter their old home. They continued on south, determined to make it to the village while it was still daylight. First they passed over the old village, the site of the massacre. Nature had done its job with great compassion. The brush and the small trees that grew where ten generations of hill people had raised their young had hidden the burnt timbers and the shards of clay pots, broken amidst the terrified screams of the victims.

The new village was little more than a mile south of the old. There was no talking among the three as they neared the clearing. It was understood that they must walk into the village and be among the people, not be spotted along the trail by some hotheaded, glory-seeking, white-hating young warrior.

At last, with the sun balanced on the horizon like a wagon wheel on a rutted road, they came to a tree line beyond which spread the village with its score of lodges. Two of them were built in the old longhouse form, with the clan emblem above the door on the end of the house.

They could see the normal acts of daily living going on in the village: women stirring pots over outdoor fires, men working on their equipment or talking animatedly with each other, children running a race down a path between houses. The sights and smells of the village stirred the memories of all three of them, but especially Thad, who had passed his childhood with many of these people, within a couple of miles of this spot.

At a signal from Big Oak, the three walked out of the woods, single file, first Big Oak, then Thad, with their rifles resting on their left forearms, then Cilla in the rear. For a few seconds nobody in the village looked up to notice them, but just as they got to the foot of one of the paths of the village, an older woman raised her eyes from her kettle and almost dropped her spoon. Her left hand went up to her mouth and she uttered a muffled sound that attracted the attention of her husband, who had been lying on a blanket in the doorway of their lodge, eyes half closed, mind half dreaming.

He climbed to his feet and let out a few words that brought to life most of the people in the lodges around him. But they didn't rush toward the intruders, hollering either welcome or nastiness. They stood in front of their lodges and stared.

The three walked up the street until they came to the first lodge. Big Oak stopped and looked carefully at the man and woman who stood before them along with two scruffy, growling dogs.

His jaw worked as if it were a pump for his brain, which was trying hard to place these familiar faces. They were not originally from Tonowaugh, but had lived in one of the villages farther down the Genesee. Tall Hat was the man's name, after a headgear he had once purchased from a trader many years before. There was no such hat on him today.

"Brother Tall Hat," he said to the man in good Seneca dialect. "I did not know you lived in Tonowaugh."

The Seneca would have been no more amazed had one of his dogs spoken those words to him. He leaned toward Big Oak and studied him through cataract-glazed eyes. "Ah," he said. "The face has changed but I know the voice. Woman, this is Big Oak, do you remember?"

The woman snorted contemptuously. "Do I remember? Women remember. It is the men who forget." Now four or five other people were gathered around, including a woman Thad recognized.

"You are Blue Star," he said. "I remember you."

She studied him for a while. "I do not know you, Englishman. Why are you here?"

"Englishman? I am your cousin. I am Little Oak."

She looked up at Big Oak before looking back at Thad, and then, suddenly, she began to cry, great big generous tears. She stood up and hugged Thad against her large breasts and she said some words to several of her friends who had come running down the street to see what was going on. Then they began to cry too, and tried to explain what was happening to several of the men who had joined them. One of the older men began weeping, but most of them stood aloof, arms folded, waiting for the emotions to calm down.

A younger man joined the group and gripped Thad by the shoulder so Thad would turn toward him. "Runs from Himself," Thad said softly, recognizing the brave as the small child he had befriended when the children his own age teased him for being so shy.

The young man stepped back from Thad. "I am called by another name now, my brother," he said. "How I wish you had not come."

And then, suddenly, above the tumult of crying women and chatting men, there came the loud voice of authority.

"Who are these people?" cried the voice.

The Senecas who had gathered around now parted so that the voice of authority faced Big Oak and Thad.

"Ah, Skoiyasi," Big Oak purred. "So you are the chief in this village?" Thad, who had been fooling with one of the children for a moment, heard Big Oak and turned around to look.

"Skoiyasi, my brother!" Thad said, his voice nearly choked up.

The Seneca brave put a hand on Thad's shoulder. "I never thought I would see you again, Little Oak." He looked from the son to the father and back again. "You both look well." There was silence for a moment. The moment stretched out. Skoiyasi was considering his next words. "Kawia would like to see you both, I am sure," he said at last. "She still speaks of you." There was a silence among them, each thinking his own thoughts about times past.

Trailed by half the village, Thad, Big Oak, and Cilla followed Skoiyasi to his lodge on the south side of the village. Two young boys were wrestling in front of the lodge, too close to the fire where a woman was stirring a large pot in which boiled a savory mix of meat and vegetables.

"We have just eaten," Skoiyasi said, "but you must be hungry and we have plenty of food to share."

Thad did not hear Skoiyasi's last words. Before him stood Kawia, the young girl who had once followed him around like one of the village pups, who had long ago dreamed that Little Oak would be her husband. Still beautiful, but more full-figured and mature, she smiled quickly at Big Oak, stared for a few moments at Thad, then fastened her gaze upon Cilla and left it there.

"This is Cilla," Big Oak announced. "She is a Tuscarora. She is with me." If Kawia was surprised, she hid it well. Cilla was close to Kawia's age, but not having borne children or settled into a home routine, she was still as slender as Kawia had been when she was seventeen.

"You look well," Kawia said to Thad. "Why are you here?"

The suddenness of her question surprised Big Oak and Thad, and appeared to irritate Skoiyasi.

"We were out west to trade, and we ran into a war between the English and the western tribes," Thad explained. "And now we're on our way back to Albany. We both"—Thad gestured toward his father—"we both wanted to see our village again."

Skoiyasi sneered. "Do you still think of Tonowaugh as *your village*?"

"I was born here," Thad responded simply. "My happiest and my saddest memories are here. Before we leave we will visit the grave of my mother. And I will think of John Thompson and Long Racer and Kendee my grandfather. I miss them all. And I miss you too, my old friend."

Kawia passed around bowls well-filled with the stew she had been cooking. Big Oak and Thad began eating with gusto, but Cilla ate carefully and quietly, missing not a word or a nuance. "Do you live in Albany?" Kawia asked.

Years of tender memories bubbled to the surface as he answered her. "I live in Albany. I have a wife in Albany, and a child."

"You are a white man," Skoiyasi spat. The sneer threatened to become a snarl. With great effort he managed to twist it into a smile. An angry smile, upturned corners on lips set rigidly beneath furious dark eyes.

Thad was not intimidated by Skoiyasi. He glared at his old friend. "I am Little Oak, the son of Big Oak and Willow, from a village that cast us out," he said. "What would you have me be, a wanderer in the forest with no one to call kin but my father?"

Skoiyasi ignored the argument. "I always knew that be-

neath your skin you were a white man like your father."
Then the hard lines on his face softened. "But we grew up
together. You were my brother."

"We loved the same girl," Thad said. "She chose you."

"She chose a Seneca warrior over a white trader, of
course."

Thad nodded solemnly. Skoiyasi now turned to Big Oak.
"You look thin, my father," he said. "Have you not been
well?"

"The Ottawa and the Chippewa were poor hosts," Thad
explained.

"We are good hosts," Skoiyasi declared. "Our home is
your home for tonight."

"We are grateful," Big Oak replied. "We wish we could
tarry with you longer, but in the morning we must be on
our way. I hope you will understand."

Skoiyasi missed the irony in Big Oak's words. "We understand."

"When we come back this way," Big Oak continued,
"would you like to trade with us? You must remember that
when I trade, I always give good value."

"Of course, my father. I remember well the fine gunpowder you always brought, and the good cooking pots. I hope
you can return to us soon with the goods, but"—he stared
at Big Oak through narrowed lids—"do not bring whiskey."

Big Oak did not try to keep the annoyance from his
voice. "I *never* trade whiskey!" he growled.

"All English traders trade whiskey," Skoiyasi insisted. "It
makes the trading 'easier.' "

"I do not! And nobody *forces* you to drink it. Nobody
pours it down your throats." Thad poked his father. He was
not happy with the direction of this discussion.

Neither was Skoiyasi. He arose suddenly and walked off
toward the woods. Thad was not surprised by his old

friend's abrupt action. It had always been Skoiyasi's way of ending an unpleasant discussion.

Kawia looked at Thad. Her face held no expression, but he assumed that she was feeling apologetic for her husband's rude behavior.

"So you have a wife," she said. He nodded. "And children."

"One child."

"Oh yes."

He looked into her hazel eyes, so un-Senecalike in their brightness. "Is it well with you, my little sister?"

"Am I, still?" she asked.

He smiled. "Always."

She thought for a moment, absently stirring her kettle. "That is good," she said.

He looked at her more closely than he had before. Her hands, he noticed, were dirty, and her fingernails worn. Her hair was carefully arranged, but greased in the Indian fashion, a way he was no longer used to. There was a small scar on her chin. Her breasts, of course, were those of a mother, not of a child, as he had remembered her.

She sat quietly, staring back at him, looking serene, not sad. This was the life for which she had been raised. That he had gone off to Albany and become a white man was merely further proof to her that she had made the right choice. Hai! She could no more imagine herself married to a white man than to a squirrel. She could remember her childhood, and all the things they did together. Sometimes it was as though they were the same family, so often did one appear at the other's fire.

But she could not feel the emotions that went with all those shared moments. She knew that she had once cared for him, but she no longer remembered what it felt like. She knew that once long ago he had held her, but she could not picture the moment. She remembered that he had been a kind boy. She even thought that she *should* have feelings toward him. Tender feelings. But she didn't. And she was glad. It was much better this way.

Thad did have those feelings, but they were not for the woman who sat in front of him with no window on her heart. His feelings were for a child who had died long ago at the hands of a lustful enemy.

Cilla watched the faces of these two people with the acute senses of a born survivor. She did not know their history, but she could read emotions even where faces betrayed none.

The evening was growing cool, but Cilla moved away from the fire, closer to Big Oak. She could draw warmth from that white man. She had known it the first day she had seen him. She knew that with every step east, he led her farther and farther away from the world in which she had lived her life. She was a little afraid, but not much. She had known too many changes to fear change. Already she knew: her world would not be Tuscarora. Neither would it be English. Her world would be Big Oak.

Three small children emerged from inside the lodge, where they had been playing games underneath layers of blankets and deerskins, their muffled squeals barely audible to the adults seated by the fire outside the lodge.

Automatically Kawia began spooning food into their bowls and they began eating, fiercely. Skoiyasi returned, as abruptly as he had departed. "You must stay with us tonight," he said again to Big Oak. "You are always welcome in our house," he added. The words were friendly, but the tone of his voice was neither friendly or hostile.

"We would be honored, my son," Big Oak said. There was something about the invitation that made him feel they would be safe for the night. The morning, he thought, might hold a different fate.

❊20❊

THERE WAS NO LOOKING BACK ON TONO-
waugh. Once they made their way into the thick dark canopy of forest, Tonowaugh vanished as if it had never been.
Before they left the village, Thad and his father had visited
the grave of Willow, briefly. They could barely find it in
the undergrowth. Big Oak stood there for only a moment,
staring at the small patch of weeds, then looked up toward
the figure of Cilla standing patiently at the head of the
trail.

The early morning breeze blew a few dark strands of
hair across her cheek, but she paid no attention.

"Let's go," he said.

Big Oak and Thad were quiet as they headed east. They
had agreed to let Willow's spirit sleep, but both knew it
was not *Willow's* spirit they were trying to keep quiet. It
was their own. For the same reason, they decided that they
had too much to do to stop and visit their old stone house
on the east bank of the Genesee River.

Finally, after a ten-minute dogtrot that took them a mile
east of the village, Thad broke the silence.

"It was good to see them again. Sad, but good too. And
they were kind."

Cilla had not spoken at all. Big Oak had introduced her to Skoiyasi and Kawia, but they had barely acknowledged her. And when Big Oak told them she was a Tuscarora, they exuded the strange muffled hostility that continued to creep through Skoiyasi's facade throughout their visit.

Up to this time Cilla had said nothing on the trail either. But now she spoke up, coolly, almost in a whisper.

"He hates you both," she said. "And the woman is not much better."

"We grew up like brothers," Thad protested.

"I do not trust him," she persisted. "Much time has passed since you and he were like brothers. That time has been good time for the English, bad time for the Iroquois."

"Why has it been bad time for the Iroquois?" Thad asked. "They fought on the winning side. They gained many scalps. They are friends to the English."

"Ah, but are the English friends to them? I fear, Little Oak, that you have been a white man for too long. We Tuscarora once lived in the south country, near the land of the Cherokee. Our enemies respected us and feared us and kept their distance from us—until the English. The English kept moving into us, closer and closer, always taking our best land, until we could not stand it anymore. So we fought them, again and again, and even when we beat them they always came back and took more. There never seemed to be any end to them, and they were all so hungry hungry hungry. This my father told us.

"There were always more English and fewer Tuscarora until finally our chiefs knew that if we stayed any longer there would be many English and no Tuscarora. We journeyed through the land of the Lenni Lenape, far to the north of our homes, and moved into the Longhouse to get away from the English. But there is no way to get away from the English. They are everywhere, always more and more of them, until it feels like there is no place to lay your blanket where an Englishman will not come up to you and say, 'Why do you lay your blanket on my land? Get off my land.'

" 'This is *Tuscarora* land,' you say to the English.

" 'Oh no!' the English answer. 'This is my land.'

" 'But we are brothers,' you say.

" 'Brothers? You are just an Indian. You can be no more a brother to me than a swamp mosquito.'

" 'But where do we go? You have taken all our land.'

" 'We don't care. Take somebody else's land. Just get off mine, or I will shoot you. And I have the right. See? Here is the writing that says I have the right.'

"We moved into the Longhouse, but not far enough away from the English. I can see why that Seneca warrior hates you. He can see the English coming. When he was young, he thought you were just one man. But now he sees that you were just the first one of many, that they will soon take all he has that he holds dear in this world. Watch out for that one. He will kill you if he can."

Big Oak did not intervene in the argument. He had seen what Cilla had seen in the eyes of the man who as a child he had taught to shoot.

"Shhh," he told them both. "Spread out behind me and keep quiet, both of you."

They hoped to make Canandaigua Lake before the end of the day, but Big Oak took a few diversions from the usual trail routes. He trusted Cilla's instincts, and shared her caution, if not her fears, about Skoiyasi. He gave her the tomahawk they had taken from the Huron Black Fox and told her how much he needed her sharp eyes on the trails. It was a day of large cumulus clouds that sometimes plunged the sparse woodland into gray darkness and other times bathed them in bright sunlight that made them squint. Most of the time, however, they loped beneath such a dense woodland canopy that gloom was their constant companion.

Big Oak reasoned that any ambush would be set up where the ambushers could get a good look at their quarry. Every time the woods thinned enough to allow the light in, he drew on extra reserves of caution. The woods were hot and humid, and the bare ridge lines hot and dry. Thad felt released to be out of the country of the angry Chippewas and Hurons, but Big Oak and Cilla knew that this rebellion was more than a western uprising by a former French ally. They knew that every tribe that had to live side by side with the English had cause to hate or suspect them.

Thad was still puzzling over his old friends Skoiyasi and Kawia, wondering how he and they could have so little left in common, when Big Oak motioned him to get down. They had just emerged from the woods into a meadow, a former cornfield now overgrown with blackberry. Automatically he faded down into the brush and squatted there motionless until he felt his father's breath close to his ear.

"They're out there," Big Oak whispered. "There will be a fight, and it will be your friend."

Thad nodded. "How soon?" he asked.

"When we reach a place of their choosing. We will try to avoid that. Follow me."

They ran through the thorny brambles parallel to the tree line, up a slope until they reached a large rock shelf in the center of a clearing on a hillside that commanded the surrounding area.

"From the bottom of the hill, where they are now," Big Oak told his companions, "we are sheltered from their fire. They will try to work their way around to the hill behind us, but they have to go through the woods or the bushes to do that, and when they get there, we'll be gone. Let's move."

Crouched low, they ran along the rock shelf until the

clearing ended and the woods began. Then they straightened up and broke into a sprint. Thad had just begun to be amazed at the speed and stamina of the Tuscarora girl on the trail when he heard the war whoop sound from half a dozen mouths, and through the trees he saw motion. His father had been right about the Indians' tactics, except that they had worked their way the hard way, around their front rather than their rear, and now there was indeed going to be a fight. The three fled from their attackers.

The trick was to find a clearing with cover and fields of fire for them, where they could bring their deadly rifles to bear on their adversaries. The Senecas would not charge into the mouths of rifles. Big Oak allowed Thad and Cilla to run ahead of him while he kept watch on the rear and tried to guess how many were pursuing them.

He watched, and he smiled. Not more than five, spread out and vulnerable. Suppose, just suppose . . . he turned to Thad as they ran. "Did you make them out?" he asked.

"Four or five," Thad replied.

"What I thought. Wanna take a run at them?"

"Why not?" came the answer.

Abruptly the two men changed course and ran directly toward the small party that pursued them. Cilla immediately perceived what was happening and followed, about fifty yards behind.

This was what war was about! Big Oak thought as he and Thad picked up the pace, weaving through the trees, eyes bright and searching. With excitement mounting in his throat, Big Oak saw and heard the movement that told him they and the Senecas were closing in on each other. As the combatants spotted each other, the Senecas, Thad, and Big Oak screamed their war cries and raised their weapons. Two of Skoiyasi's men fired from fairly close range but missed, and then they found themselves short of tree cover. Big Oak and Thad were nearly upon them with loaded rifles. The two Indians turned and fled, pursued closely by the two frontiersmen.

Suddenly from their flanks two other Senecas attacked. Thad and Big Oak had run themselves into a trap. One of them dropped to one knee and fired, and Thad felt hot lead buzz past his ear like an angry hornet. He turned toward the sound and fired quickly just before the fleeing figure vanished, limping, behind a clump of maples. Then he dropped to the ground and began to reload while he waited for more gunfire.

Instead, what he heard was an inhuman screech, followed by a triumphant whoop, and the light thudding sounds of Indians retreating.

"Are you all right?" Big Oak asked, staring at the hole in Thad's buckskin shirt.

"You tell me," Thad answered. "Where's Cilla?"

"She'll be along," Big Oak said, and then Thad knew. The war whoop had been hers. Slowly, Thad rose to his knees, in time to see the woman walking toward them slip a bloody knife into her waistband and shake a few drops of blood out of the scalp she had just taken.

An angry Skoiyasi ran limping down the back trail to a previously designated rendezvous point. He was angry at the braves in his village, most of whom had declined to follow him on this raid. Some of them respected Big Oak too much, and the rest of them feared him, except for three young braves who thirsted for glory and blood.

One of them, Smoke, had paid for his bloodthirst with his life. When they prepared their trap, they had forgotten about the woman, who had lain lurking in the brush until Smoke had stopped to brace his rifle against a tree, but before he could put a bullet into Big Oak, this she-demon had emerged and buried a tomahawk in the skull of the young brave.

And now the three of them sat in camp examining Skoiyasi's wound, which turned out to be superficial, but felt bad nevertheless. It was his old boyhood friend Thad who had done this to him, and his anger toward Thad surpassed all the other hatreds on his list, which included hatred toward the western tribes who had rejected the initial Seneca attempts to start a rebellion many months before, hatred toward the Mohawks who still refused to join the rebellion and kept most of their Iroquois brothers out of it, hatred toward Smoke's mother, who would make life miserable for Skoiyasi when he returned home without her son, and of course hatred for the English, whom he deemed responsible for everything that had ever gone wrong in his life.

Also, there was a special hatred reserved for Big Oak, who was the Englishman incarnate, the gentle, kind man with the never-miss rifle who always seemed to bring disaster upon his village—first the massacre and now this.

His logic may have been flawed, but his hatred was consistent and relentless. He would rise from this failed mission and cat the hearts of both father and son the next time they appeared in his forests.

"You were very lucky," Cilla explained to Thad as she ripped off a long strip of her blanket and used it to bind the wound.

"Lucky that it was only Skoiyasi I had to deal with and not you." He smiled, staring at the loathsome trophy that hung from her belt.

"I wanted to have something to take back to my village," she said. "They will have thought me long dead. To see me returned with . . . this . . ." She started to lift it from her belt, but Thad raised his hand.

"No no," he said. "I can see it from right where I sit. Yeah, that will get their attention."

Big Oak stared at his son and remembered a battle in the last war between the French and the English, when Thad had cut his hand trying to scalp a dead enemy. He had chastised Thad for his behavior, and Thad had reminded his father that *he* had taken a few scalps during his career in the woods. Skoiyasi had been right about Thad becoming a white man. Big Oak realized that it was what he had wanted for his son. Big Oak loved the Indian way of life. When he had begun his own career in the woods, there was no way of knowing that that way of life would be going so soon. He was glad that his son had broken free of it. But he, Big Oak, had not, and neither had most of the men of the Longhouse. Their hardest years were yet to come.

Thad looked across the fire at his father, who was cleaning his rifle. "Will they be coming back?" he asked.

"There were four of them," Big Oak said. "Three of them were very young, including . . ." He nodded toward the scalp that rode on Cilla's belt. The fourth was Skoiyasi. "We weren't too popular with him when we left the village. I'd say we've slowed his rise as a war chief among his people. Hope you're not expecting any dinner invitations from him and Kawia, not soon."

"No, and I don't think they'll be back either, but I don't want to take any chances. Let's put the fire out and move to where we're not so easily found, before we sleep for the night."

The following morning they turned southeast. Cilla had declared her desire to visit her village, which was at the eastern edge of the Onondaga domain, and after she had saved Big Oak's life with a well-timed blow of her tomahawk, neither of them felt that they could refuse her anything for any reason.

Much of their travel occurred along the shores of the

beautiful long lakes of central New York that spread like the fingers of the hand from north to south. And it was on the south end of one of these lakes that they expected to find the Tuscarora village, but what they found when they emerged from the woods were several large farms with plowed fields that seemed to flow like green and brown water from the tops of the first row of hills, nearly down to the shore.

Big Oak saw the look of loss and horror on Cilla's face. "Are you sure this is the place? A long time has passed," he said.

She was sure, and if she was sure, Big Oak was sure, because this woman knew where she was *all* the time.

For the first time, he saw a look of self-doubt cross her face. She walked across one of the fields, ignoring the two men who followed her, peering at the plowed rows of corn as if they could give her a clue as to where her people had gone.

Big Oak caught up with her. "Only way to find out anything is just leave this to me," he insisted. "And that means walk behind me so whoever lives on this land won't think they're bein' attacked by a whole tribe of wild savages and try to put a bullet through you—and us too."

Through the rows of cornstalks they could see what looked like a well-made log house with windowpanes in it, which meant that this farm was past its hardscrabble start. There were no stumps in this field. The soil had been turned many times before. The Tuscaroras were long gone and the white men were here to stay.

By now they could see two tall, thin men struggling with a heavy fence log, attempting to lay it in position between two log forks. Although they appeared very strong, the log was getting the best of them.

"Need a bit of help?" Big Oak asked.

"Just that much," grunted the older of the two, who

seemed to be stuck with the heavy end. Big Oak moved to help him, and Thad took hold of the middle, and with the four of them straining, the log moved easily into position.

"I'm obliged," said the older one, whose coarse, gray work clothes were soaked solid with sweat.

"Sam Watley," Big Oak said, holding out his hand. "We were on our way to Albany when we decided to make a side trip to find this lady's village. Seems like you're it."

The man took off his hat and ran his fingers through wet, gray, thinning hair while he decided whether or not to take the conversation beyond where the stranger had begun it. He gauged the honesty of Sam's face and decided to invest the time and effort.

"There was a Tuscarora village here," he began. "A politician from Albany bought the land from the Tuscarora and we bought part of it from him."

Big Oak signed a translation to Cilla, who became so agitated that for a moment Thad thought she was going to leap on the farmer's back like a cougar on a fawn. Instead she began to shake her head violently.

"My village could not have sold the land," she said. "This was Onondaga land. It was not Tuscarora land to sell." Big Oak explained Cilla's words to the farmer.

The farmer gave Cilla a look that was filled with sympathy.

"Howmsoever," he added, "he did buy the land from Tuscaroras and he has the paper to prove it." He looked at Big Oak. "Tell her that when a powerful politician wants to do something, he does it. Tell her that twenty year ago I squatted on some land west of the Hudson when some politician turned up with a land title that was phony as a four-penny gold piece and everybody in the neighborhood knew it. So he went down to New York City and got them to put a seal on the title that he said made it authentic. The local law believed him and threw me off the land at the point of a gun.

"The day I left the farm with my family, I promised them that next time I'd be on the winnin' side of the law. Kin you blame me?"

Big Oak and Thad shook their heads.

" 'Bout ten year back I was back in that districk and I went by the farm. They had built a plantation there and slaves was workin' the land I cleared with my hands. So I headed down to New York and got to know people and kept my ears peeled for new land grants to someone who was willin' to take me on. I just missed a couple of them that belonged to William Johnson, but then I heard about this one, and I bought my way onto it."

"And what happened to the Tuscaroras who lived here?" Thad inquired.

The older man scratched his head. "Well now, I don't really know. I suppose they went west. Isn't that what they always do?"

If the man hadn't told them about the Tuscaroras, Big Oak might have wondered if Cilla had been wrong about the location of the village. Any evidence that the Tuscaroras had ever been there had been plowed under.

He turned to look at Cilla, who had regained her composure, her face an inscrutable mask that could be hiding anything from indifference to a thirst for vengeance.

"I am like you," she told Big Oak. "My village has also been wiped out, and my people gone."

"Not like me, Cilla. Yours are alive somewhere. Mine sleep forever. We will not linger here. We have friends among the Mohawks who might know where your people have gone."

"Would you like a bit a whiskey before you get back on your trail?" the farmer asked.

"Thank you, no," Big Oak responded. "We have a long way to go. Thank you for your help."

The man nodded. "Tell the lady I hope she finds her people," he said. Then he and the younger man went back to mending their fence.

They found a crude wagon road that headed east between two cornfields. They walked down the road between the cornstalks and did not look back until the road petered out into a path that headed up a nearby hillside. The three of them toiled up the steep hill until they had made it to the top, from which they could get a very good view of the valley.

Below they could identify three farmhouses, all made of logs, but neat and comfortable-looking. There were also several rough outbuildings and acre after acre of cultivated fields, planted in corn and beans, plus some fenced grassy fields where horses and cows grazed.

"Look!" Cilla cried, pointing across one field that stretched far to the south. At the southern end of the field was a large group of trees planted in rows. "Our apple trees. Those are our apple trees." For a moment she smiled. "We made cider every year when the leaves turned."

Then she turned her back and began to walk east. "Come on," Big Oak said to Thad. "We must visit the Mohawks."

❖21❖

IN THE GATHERING COOL OF THE SUMMER
evening they sat quietly around a small fire. The Mohawks
smoked their pipes. Big Oak and Thad did not.

"Big Oak, I do not wish to offend you. You are brother
to our Seneca brothers, our Guardians of the Western
Door. You lived in their lodges for so many years. You
knew their women and you knew their warriors, and their
war chiefs and their sachems. How is it that you did not
know that they were wild like the ones that couple with
horses west of the Lacota?"

The angry words came from the chief of the Mohawk
village, Louis, son of Gingego.

"The Ganiengehaka have held tight to the Covenant
chain for all these many years," he said. And so have the
keepers of the council fire, the Onondagas. So have our
little brothers the Oneidas and the Cayugas, and our new
little brothers, the Tuscaroras. When our brothers the
Caughnawagas began to worship the man tied to the stake,
they moved their lodges to Canada and left the Longhouse.

"Senecas, they are different. They pretend to be a part of
the Longhouse, but they have always had one ear for the

French. And yet, my brother, never did I believe they would join their enemies the Hurons, and their enemies the Chippewas, against their ancient allies, the English. My heart is heavy that they should do this."

"But Louis, is it not true that most of the Seneca people have refused to join the rebellion? Kyashuta, is he not a rebel from his own people?" Big Oak replied.

"What has happened to the people of the Western Door that they cannot remain united among themselves?" Louis asked. "We are not so many as the Chippewa and the Ottawa, or the Huron before we crushed them. But we are feared from the deep snow country all the way to the land of the big mountains because the Six Nations can come together in council and all agree on a thing to do. That is our secret. Without it we could not keep our enemies off our land."

"We cannot keep our enemies off our land," spoke a quiet voice from across the campfire. "My brother, why did our father name you Louis and me George? You, the older, he named Louis to tell the English that they must not take our friendship lightly. Then, years later, when French traders treated us bad, he named me George to let them know that he had powerful English friends. The English are our ancient allies, yes, but they cared about us only as long as the French forts rose high above the rivers. Pontiac will bring the French back. And then the arrogant English will not treat their allies so lightly."

Big Oak stood up, so tall and straight that the campfire scarcely lit up his face from below. "If I were a man of the mighty Ganiengehaka," he said, "I would speak as you just did, George. But because I am an Englishman, I can go places where you cannot, and hear things that you do not. Because my son Little Oak is a trader in Albany, and is married to the daughter of a Dutch trader, he hears things that I cannot.

"The French will not be back. They have not the—" He stumbled for the word that the Mohawks might understand. "Wampum" was not the right word. "Money" was an English word. Wampum would have to do. "To fight a war across a great ocean takes more wampum than you could dream of. The French do not have enough wampum to do this."

"We could get them more wampum. Some tribes pay us with wampum just so they can use the land we took from them when we defeated them," said a young warrior whose face Big Oak had seen but whose name he did not know.

"Across the ocean, little seashells are not wampum. Gold is wampum," Big Oak explained. He took out of his pack a small gold coin to show the Mohawks, many of whom had heard of such a thing but few of whom had seen it, gold being a scarce commodity on the frontier.

"George, my brother. You know my tongue is straight," Big Oak said. "I tell you now that I believe the French will never be back. The English king you are named for has a long memory. He will reward the nations that fight on his side, and he will punish those who oppose him.

"And Louis, I must tell you this because you are wise and will understand. General Amherst is a man who angers easily, especially when it is Indians who anger him. He does not like Indians and he does not respect them. But if we do not anger him, he will go home soon, and the next general in charge will probably be General Gage. He respects the Ganonsyoni, and will do the right thing."

"And then he will go home, and who will they have after him?" Thad spoke now, and his words struck his father with surprise. "And Warraghiyagey, the man who is always there for the Mohawks, what happens when he is no longer there? Suppose he dies? Or suppose he gets so rich selling off Iroquois lands that he can go back to Ireland and live like a duke? Oh yes, on the streets of Albany I hear other things too."

With grave dignity Louis held up a hand that stopped Thad's garulous monologue between breaths.

"We too hear bad birds whispering in our ears. You told us about your friend Skoiyasi feeding you like a king and then ambushing you like a dog. My brother, I hope you do not think that Skoiyasi has been sitting at Tonowaugh under his blanket over the past two moons. You talk about the long memory of our father King George, and about the bad temper of Amherst, now I must tell you of the bad fighting of the English. They have lost nearly every fort between Detroit and Niagara. And your brothers the Senecas have played their part at two forts in Pennsylvania, maybe more. And your brother Skoiyasi?" Louis leaned toward Thad and whispered, like one of his "bad birds," "Your brother Skoiyasi was with them."

"Do not tell us what the English will do to their enemies after they win," George said. "Tell us how much they need us if they are going to win."

"I can tell you nothing about that," Big Oak replied. "But I know the English, and so do you. There are many of them, and because their ships rule the big sea, the French will *never* be back. We have seen the English lose many battles, but we have never seen them lose a war in this land."

"My brother George is angry with the English, and so am I," Louis said. "They do not treat us well, this you know, Big Oak. Even now they do not furnish us with the goods the way they used to, when they still needed us against the French. But we will not fight them, because we will choose our own allies, we will not have them forced upon us by our brothers, the Seneca. This we have also heard from the little birds, that the black smoke of English lodges has been seen rising in the west, where your friend

Skoiyasi roamed. We do not like such things to go on in the Longhouse. We will not give your Amherst an excuse to send his soldiers down upon us. Can you get us trade goods, Big Oak?"

Big Oak was not caught by Louis's sudden request. He knew Louis, and knew that he had not called this council out of hospitality or a desire to swap old war stories.

"Can you still get furs, in the middle of this war?" he asked the village chief.

"The Ottawas will trade furs as long as there are furs to trade. We will have your furs for you by the end of the summer, but we need ammunition. We must think about our brothers in the west, who might take it as an insult that we do not join them. And we are also concerned about winter. Better that we have our ammunition now, for you might not be able to get it to us when the leaves have fallen."

Big Oak could not challenge the good sense of the eldest son of Gingego. But neither could he guarantee him the goods. He decided to explain the situation.

"Our partner," he began, "is the father of Little Oak's wife. Two moons ago we started on a trade mission along the valley of the Spay-lay-wi-theepi. We found nobody to trade with and so we continued on to Detroit. We were attacked by Potawatomies. We lost all our goods and our horses, and we were fortunate to escape with our lives. We are on our way back to Albany. All this time I have been thinking that when Herr Wendel hears of the war he will be so worried about the husband of his daughter that he will hold a joyous feast for us when he finds that we have returned with our scalps.

"But then, when he sees what we have lost, he may decide that the fur trade is too risky. You see, he has a shop in Albany that brings him much good trade, and it is only the longing for still greater wealth that has made him our partner. I believe we can talk him into providing goods for you on a promise, but I am not certain. I will try, and I will return to you to give you an answer, whichever it is."

"Your word is as good as your aim from one end of the Longhouse to the other, my brother," said the older son of Gingego.

The following morning they prepared to leave for Albany, but before they left, Big Oak stopped by the longhouse of Gingego's widow, White Bird, who was the mother of Louis and George.

As the whites closed in on the land of the Mohawks, many had turned their backs on the traditional clan longhouse, to live in individual family dwellings. Some were even beginning to consider white-style houses with windowpanes to let in the light and keep out the wind. Gingego's widow, however, still preferred the longhouse, where she was the matriarch and she could hear the laughter of her grandchildren one fire over.

He found White Bird sitting outside by the doorway of the longhouse, mending a small legging.

"I knew that whenever I found you, you would be hard at work, Grandmother," Big Oak said. She looked up and laughed at the old joke between them, for she was not much older than he, yet to her he never seemed to lose his youth and vigor, and so it seemed appropriate that he call her Grandmother.

But the hardships of her life, the child-bearings, the long winters deprived of food and warmth, the death of the husband she loved, had taken their toll without depriving her of the will to continue. "I have seen so many changes," White Bird had once said. "Many have not been good, and yet I wish to live to see my grandchildren doing well."

Now, she asked him with feeling, "Big Oak, my friend, why have you been gone for so long?" He was one man whose face she longed to see, to remind her that there *were*, after all, good white men in the world, and that therefore there was hope for her grandchildren.

"I promise you, Grandmother, that thoughts of you and Gingego are never far from me," he replied, and he told the truth.

Gingego was an old, venerated sachem, and sachems were not expected to go to war, but he was determined to fight one last battle for the sake of his friend Warraghiyagey, the (Man who Undertakes Great Things). Thanks in part to the Mohawks who came to fight with Gingego, the English had won a great battle on Lake George. Gingego had died with his rifle and tomahawk in his hands at an age when most Mohawk men slept with their fathers or dreamed by the fire of better days.

His sons had grieved over his body, decapitated and otherwise horribly mutilated by his lifelong enemies, the Abnakis, but when the war party had returned home with news of the great victory and the death of several of their comrades, Gingego's widow had refused to indulge in the keening and wailing that struck so many of the lodges in her village, although she would miss her man more keenly than any of the other women in the village would miss theirs. With magnificent dignity she had prepared the village for the long ordeal she knew the war would bring.

"So we have war again, so soon," White Bird said to Big Oak as he sat across the fire from her. "I have heard that the men who fight for the crazy Ottawa chief have won many victories over the English."

"I have heard the same," Big Oak answered, "and I hope that we can prevent General Amherst from trying to punish the Iroquois for the behavior of the western tribes."

"I have heard that some of your Seneca brothers are on the warpath."

"My Seneca brothers ambushed us a few days ago."

"I have heard this too." She paused thoughtfully for a moment. "Do you remember the animal skin I gave you?"

Of course Big Oak remembered. It was the map he and Thad had discussed during their journey, a memento of Gingego that she had given to him after Gingego had been killed. "We thought we might have found the place shown on the map when we were in the valley of the Spay-lay-wi-theepi, but now we think that it was not the place."

"Do you have the skin with you?"

"I do not carry it with me. It is too precious to me. I was captured by the Potawatomi and would surely have lost the map if I had been carrying it. Do you need it?"

"No," she said. "I wanted to see it one more time. Last year we had a visit from some of the braves from Caniengo. With them was a friend of Gingego's, an old man you would know as Three Fingers. Big Oak, he knew about the map. Gingego told him that the white officer who made the map said it was a hidden valley that many people could live in, safe from the people on the outside."

"Did he say where it was?"

"I asked him, and he pointed to the setting sun. That was all he knew. He said that Gingego had asked about such a place during a time when the French were very powerful and their Indians, like the Caughnawaga and the Chippewa, were growing stronger day by day. And yet, he said, Gingego told him, 'We can beat the Caughnawaga and the Chippewa whenever we fight them. I do not fear them. It is our friends, the English, that I fear.'"

Big Oak nodded. "And now you fear the English."

"Some men came to Louis and tried to buy our village. Louis told them it was not in his power or the power of any other chief to sell the land. The men told Louis that they would have the land and that if he would not sign a deed, they would find a person who would. Big Oak, I am frightened for the future of our people. Louis laughs at me when I say this. But I am."

"I do not know how I can find this place," Big Oak said. "I must have more information."

"I will talk to more of the old people. Maybe somebody else knows something," White Bird said.

Big Oak took her hands in his. "I must leave now, Grandmother. If I can get them, I will be back before long with supplies for the village."

"That is good," she said simply, and he left.

When Thad spent a couple of months in the woods, he always forgot about just how filthy and muddy Albany was. The woods are carpeted, with moss, or pine needles or old leaves, sometimes with grass, when the trees are far enough apart to let in the light, often with varieties of weeds that thrive in the shade.

But the streets of Albany were one of two extremes. In dry weather they were hard-packed paths with dust clouds clogging the nostrils and the stench of rotting horse manure first lacerating then numbing the senses. In wet weather they were rivers of mud, mingled with the ubiquitous horse manure; people would take their shoes off to walk through this sea, lest the mud suck the shoes from their feet, and of course they watched every step with care. At least, Thad thought, a wildland marsh did not pretend to be civilized, and in the woods, when you wanted to lay your body down after a long muddy day, there was no one to tell you not to track mud into your house.

It was early summer, following a dry spring, and so the dust was thick, especially where the wagons and carriages rolled and clattered through the rutted streets. Thad loved to run, he loved to walk, but he could not abide the un- sprung freight wagons that shook the teeth out of a man's head. A canoe in a rapid rode smoother than a wagon on an Albany street.

Dieter Wendel was not fastidious about the floor of his store during the day. He could not afford to be or he would have no customers. At the end of the day he saw to it that it was swept out so thoroughly that "you coot eat off da floor."

But during business hours an endless stream of customers from far and near left a wide variety of topsoils, pebbles, and crumbled plant residue on the floor of Herr Wendel's store.

So he didn't notice their feet when Thad and Big Oak clumped in with dried clay falling off their worn moccasins. He was so pleased to see them after two months without word, fearing the worst for his business associates, one of them the father of his grandson. With ponderous grace his massive body bounded down the stairs of the balcony that overlooked the store's huge floor space. Behind him, dress hem gathered in one hand, a tiny baby on the other arm, hustled Thad's wife Katherine. While she tearfully hugged her long-vanished husband, Herr Wendel was not ashamed to clamp the big old woodsman in a bearlike embrace.

The four—or five, actually, for the baby took that moment to let out a squall—made such a racket that business stopped for a moment while everybody stared at the scene. The group stomped up the stairs to the balcony while various customers remarked to each other that they had never before seen such tender emotion from the sour old Dutch shopkeeper.

"Everyone who passed through here we asked if they had word of you, but we got no word. We were very worried," Wendel said again and again to Big Oak. Katherine clung tightly to Thad's arm, her sweet face smiling wordlessly up at him, her other arm gently jiggling the baby up and down, trying unsuccessfully to quiet her. Behind them, unnoticed, walked Cilla, who had stayed outside the store until she saw the group start to climb the stairs.

Only then, when she was afraid of being left alone on the street, did she follow them to the top of the stairs. One of the clerks crossed the floor to intercept her, but his instincts told him there was a legitimate connection between the leather-clad woodsmen and the beaded little woman who followed them, and he had heard stories about the price a white man could pay for wounding the dignity of an Indian.

Wendel's balcony was furnished with an accounting desk for himself, another for Katherine, and a number of chairs, tables, and other furniture arranged in the form of a sitting room. As they walked toward the arrangement of chairs, Katherine noticed the young Tuscarora woman following them and cast a quick anxious glance at Thad, who gave her a wink. Wendel also noticed, and interrupted his chatter with an astonished, "And who is dis?"

"That is Cilla. She is a Tuscarora woman. I owe my life to her." Big Oak's tone of voice told Katherine and her father that he intended to pay that debt for a long time to come.

Wendel nodded. "It is good. You have been alone in the woods for too long."

"You might send me back to the woods when you find out what happened to your trade goods."

Wendel nodded his head again. "I know there is a war. We have heard all about it. Maybe I was a little worried before I sent you off, and that is why I had two of my trading partners in New York underwrite your mission."

Herr Wendel looked extremely proud of himself, but Katherine's eyes flashed with fury. Coldly she turned to her father.

"Let me see if I understand you," she said. "You found

this mission too dangerous to risk more than a third of your own capital, but you were willing to risk the father of your grandchildren!"

Cilla, who had never in her life sat in a chair, had been standing in the shadows, but now she stepped forward to where the sunlight shined through the windows, where the white people sat. In her village, although the clans ran through the female line, and although women chose the village chief, in the home daughters did not debate the decisions of their fathers. Cilla knew just enough English to know that Katherine dared to question her father's business. And she respected Katherine for having the spirit to fight for her family.

"Now, daughter," Wendel said placatingly, "a trade mission poses greater risk to the goods than to the men who transport them. One can abandon one's goods to the savages and they will be satisfied. Isn't that what happened to you, gentlemen?"

Big Oak was inclined to go along with the merchant for the sake of his goodwill, but Thad laughed, almost snickered, in fact. "Dieter," he said, "if the Potawatomi that got your goods had been a bear, my britches would have had a big bite taken out of the seat. If his aim had been this much better, and his tomahawk this much longer"—he held his hands about two inches apart—"my scalp would be on his belt this day." Katherine's hand was over her mouth.

"Surely you exaggerate, young man," the merchant responded with alarm.

"Then speak to my father. My *father* does not exaggerate. When he speaks, only the truth passes his lips. In the light of evening campfires he has told me of the weeks he passed in the camps of three nations, each of which wanted to cook him and serve him up in a different recipe."

The father of his wife began to look very uncomfortable.

"Katherine, dearest," Thad said, turning to his wife. "See

the look on your father's face and tell me if that is the look of a man who knew the danger we would have to face. He didn't know. We didn't know."

"Nobody knew," Big Oak added. "The English gave those people no respect, and many good men have died. It was not your father's fault."

They took a few moments of silence to recover from the unpleasant words. Cilla stepped back into the shadows.

"We shall not go back to the freshwater seas until the war is over," Big Oak said, and there were nods all around. "But there is still trading to do closer to home. Herr Wendel, our Mohawk allies need ammunition. They have refused to join the rebellion and they are concerned that their enemies to the west may try to punish them for their loyalty to the English."

"But I thought all tribes feared the mighty Mohawks."

"That has been so," Big Oak said with feeling. "But no more. Only the unity of the Ganonsyoni—the Iroquois confederacy—gives them power. But now some of the Seneca—Thad's mother's people—some of them have joined the rebellion, and there is fear that they may pull more Seneca and the Cayuga in with them. We must keep our Mohawk allies armed."

"General Amherst has said that we must not trade ammunition to the Indians, any Indians."

"Other generals are wiser. General Gage, for example, has seen to it that the tribes he trusts get powder and bullets. We must do the same."

The merchant thought for a minute. "A bit of smuggling then, eh? What do they have to give us for taking this risk?"

"Their word that come fall and winter they will go west to receive furs promised by those Ottawas who would rather trade than fight."

"They tell me that Pontiac is an Ottawa," Wendel grouched.

"He is a war chief of the Ottawas. Many Ottawas do not follow him. They will trade with the Mohawks, and the Mohawks will trade with us."

"I do not wish to risk such trade."

"I'll tell you what I'll do. You give me the ammunition and I will be responsible. If I lose this load, then I will pay you back."

Wendel was impressed by Big Oak's persistence, and the deal was struck then and there. Business having been concluded, Thad and Katherine brought the baby back to their home down the street from the store, but Big Oak and Cilla decided to make camp in the woods outside of Albany.

Once in the house, Katherine immediately set to boiling water for her husband's bath. "The scent of the wild is heavy upon you," she told him.

"I don't smell a thing," he answered.

"You have been living with it for too long."

He soaked in the hot water and felt his weary, tense muscles loosen and relax. After a while she removed some of the tepid water and replaced it with hot, boiling water. He sighed his appreciation. "Thank you, sweet," he said.

"Thad, is your father not taking a big risk?" she asked him, rubbing his shoulders as he soaked.

"Why, would your father send mine to debtor's prison?"

"He would not, but he might insist upon a working arrangement until the debt is discharged. Your father loves his freedom better than he loves anything else. He would not be happy unloading supplies down at the docks day after day, when his body longed to be free ranging the woods."

Thad laughed. "You know my father well. What you do not know is that my father has gold and furs cached in three different places within a hundred miles of this spot. The cost of the ammunition is not so much that he could not easily make it up."

What Thad did not tell Katherine was that once their Mohawk friends were properly armed, he and Big Oak would be heading west for a showdown with the mischievous Seneca renegades who had attempted to kill them just a few days before.

⊰22⊱

SKOIYASI'S ABORTED AMBUSH HAD BEEN A DI-
saster for his prestige among his fellow villagers in Tonowaugh. The death of Smoke, and his failure to bring
back even one scalp, along with the respect many still felt
for Big Oak, convinced most of the villagers that he had
neither the judgment nor the military skill to lead men into
battle.

So when word came to the village from the Shawnees
that they would be attacking Fort Pitt, no warriors would
consent to follow him, or even go with him. He har-
rangued the experienced braves first, then turned to some
of the younger ones. Furious, their mothers chased him
from their lodges and made certain that their boys were
watched carefully by their fathers, who were equally dis-
pleased by the idea of their children going off to fight the
English, especially with that miserable failure, Skoiyasi.

They needn't have bothered. Nobody in the village
wanted to follow Skoiyasi into battle. His bitterness toward
Big Oak and Thad was now greater than his friendship
toward them had ever been. But vengeance was out of the
question. There was no way for him to get at them unless
they returned to western New York.

In the meantime, Skoiyasi thought, there was a war to be fought. True, it would have been far more glorious to fight as a warrior of the Iroquois confederacy, but it had been a long time since the Longhouse had united against a common enemy. The Shawnees and the Delawares were certainly no Iroquois, but at least they had the courage to fight the English, who were the real enemy.

At the last moment he had almost decided to stay home. A Seneca family that had gone to visit relatives near Fort Niagara had come home feeling sick and feverish, and now the village was worried that they had the pimple sickness, which might mean that everyone could come down with it. Skoiyasi looked at his children as they played around the lodge, and told Kawia that he would not leave them alone to the pimple sickness. Kawia hooted at his obsession with smallpox, and her wisdom was confirmed within the next two days when the sick family recovered.

Nevertheless, she pointed out, it would be a good thing if he stayed home to help his children grow up instead of going off to fight the English with a pack of mangy Shawnees and Delawares.

He had no desire to explain to her that the pimple sickness had everything to do with fighting the English. A Delaware chief named Buckangehela had told him that the English had presented one large band of Indians with some blankets to help them through the winter. The blankets had the disease in them. Why, Skoiyasi asked Taounyawatha, the God of the Waters, were the whites sent to plague them?

He paddled up the Genesee to where the oaks and sycamores grew close to the river's edge and formed a dark, brooding canopy over the water, matching his mood. He thought about his childhood years spent with Big Oak, Little Oak, and Little Oak's grandfather, Kendee. The memories made him angry. They were lies. They taught him that the English were his brothers, when they were his murderers. He remembered a time before he was angry, before he had understood the truth.

That time had been a lie, but a pleasant lie. It would have been nice to have been able to live that lie for a while longer, but that was impossible. The horrible truth was too clear, too close. The English were too close.

He pulled the canoe from the water and hid it in some tall grass. Then he struck out southwest for the valley of the Allegheny River. His pack felt light on his back, his rifle like nothing in his strong arms as he loped the trails that would take him to Fort Pitt. How strange, he thought, that he should feel so happy on the trail to do deadly battle. He imagined that his ancestors had felt the same way on the trail to the glorious wars against the Wendat, the Tionontat, and the Attiwandaronk in the olden days. Too bad he could not be part of another glorious moment in the history of the Ganonsyoni. Perhaps, he thought, when his people realized their mistake, they would remember him as one of those who kept the fires burning when most of the longhouses had gone dark.

While the Ganonsyoni had decided to sit and wait for their doom, something wonderful had happened to the Lenni Lenape, which was what the Delawares called themselves. Once they had been a mighty nation; but many years ago, when the Iroquois were wiping out all the tribes around them, the Delaware decided to make peace. With deliciously sadistic intent, the Iroquois had demanded, as the price of peace, that the Delaware take on the status of women. They could not arm themselves, they could not make their own treaties without Iroquois approval, they could do virtually nothing without first acknowledging that the Iroquois were their masters.

But now it was the Delaware, not the Iroquois, who had finally taken the warpath against the English. Chiefs like

Buckangehela had more heart and courage than the mighty Senecas and Mohawks, and Skoiyasi found that he liked fighting side by side with them, at Venango and Presque Isle. And now it was the turn of Fort Pitt to submit to the fire and fury of the tribes. Naturally the Iroquois were furious that their children should dare to fight the English without first asking permission.

Thanks to the English, Skoiyasi realized for the first time that he had a kinship to the Shawnee and the Delaware, as well as the Ottawa and Huron. He did not doubt that in time he could even get to tolerate Chippewas, though that would take some doing.

After three days' travel, ten miles northeast of his goal, he ran into a small party of Shawnees who explained to him that there had been a change in plans. The attack on the fort had been delayed. The English, with the stubborn stupidity that made them such a reliable, predictable foe, had sent a large force of soldiers and militia from the east to relieve the fort, and they were taking the same route that had led them into a deadly ambush a few years before. Once again there would be soldiers, on their knees, begging Indians to unburden them of their scalps before another day had passed.

Skoiyasi and the Shawnees made for a steep valley along a creek called Bushy Run, where they found hundreds of warriors whose homelands stretched from the Delaware River to the north shore of Lake Huron. Every hour or two a runner would come from the east to announce that the English army was making splendid time, wearing themselves out in what was for them a swift march over the long succession of heavily forested hills and ravines.

In short order the troops could be heard tramping noisily through the woods, their rifles, canteens, and powder horns clinking and clacking, their high leather boots and pack straps squeaking, their officers chattering like birds to each other while telling the men in the ranks to keep their mouths shut and their ears open.

As usual, the Indians found cover behind trees and concealment in the heavy brush that grew where the tree lines ended. They watched and waited, and it wasn't hard at all for them to see the advance guard as they approached. Hot, tired, and weary in their pretty red coats, they made wonderful targets against the green forest.

In total silence, and stillness, the ambushers waited until this first group was completely blanketed on both flanks by the lines of concealed warriors. Skoiyasi was a part of the line on the right flank, his finger light upon the trigger, as Big Oak had taught him so long ago.

He watched, amazed, as the soldiers toiled forward. They looked so dog-tired that they seemed not to notice how vulnerable they were, even though so much English blood had been shed so close to this spot not so long ago. They dragged themselves forward, eyes on the ground, heads hanging like the heads of weary old plow horses. Skoiyasi recalled the women of Tonowaugh harvesting corn, how easily they plucked the ears from the tall plants and placed them on old bearskins, then hauled them home to the longhouses. Often as a child he had helped his mother harvest corn. It was not hard work. Nor would harvesting the English on this day be hard work.

A single shot echoed through the hills, followed immediately by dozens of others. Gray smoke rose high in the woods and sifted through the tree canopy, toward the blue heavens. Fingers of fire spurted from the hills all around the falling soldiers. More redcoats arrived at the scene on the run, expecting to chase away the small ambush. Instead, the fire thickened and more soldiers went down. Now the rest of the army flooded into the battle area, charging up the hills after the smoke, muskets with bayonets thrust forward.

Skoiyasi and the rest whooped and hollered and fled. Heedlessly the soldiers used up their last reserves of energy, and then they ran into the real ambush set up some distance into the woods. Skoiyasi knew that whites thought Indians couldn't shoot. Calmly he reloaded his rifle and watched the English approach through the trees. A furious barrage of fire from all sides warned the English that they were just about surrounded and cut off. As quickly as they had advanced, now they turned to retreat, but not before Skoiyasi sighted down his barrel at the white cross belts of an English foot trooper and pulled the trigger. The pan flashed, his rifle kicked hard, and through the smoke he saw the Englishman, like a number of his barracks mates around him, crumple and lay still. Can't shoot, eh? Skoiyasi thought as he reloaded, then followed his companions in the chase. He leaped over the body of the soldier he had gunned down. The scalp could wait.

There were whoops and shrieks echoing through the woods, as if all the fiends from Hell itself had assembled against the English. There was no avenue of retreat for them. The convoy in the rear was an especially juicy target to Shawnees hungry for supplies. The English were returning a heavy fire, but as in previous ambushes, they had few real targets and their bullets found mostly trees, rocks, and the earth itself. Maddened packhorses ran screaming wildly through the thick smoke as once again red-coated soldiers scrambled desperately for a safe place to fire from.

Like his cohorts, Skoiyasi spent the entire afternoon charging from tree to tree till he found a target to shoot at; then, having fired his rifle, he slipped back into the impenetrable cover to load, size up the situation, and hunt up another target. For him this game was second nature. His experience and instincts grasped the nuances of cover and concealment. He knew where to find the enemy. He knew how to keep the enemy from finding him. He was free to roam the forest. The soldiers were pinned down to a spot. Their fate was sealed. Time and patience would finish them off, and then the real fun would begin. He could have pitied them for their feckless, blundering stupidity had he not known how dangerous they were. These were not like wars between Indians. You couldn't adopt a bunch of soldiers into your tribe, and they certainly weren't about to adopt you. They came to kill you, and you had better do the same. There were no choices here.

From behind a large oak he leaped to the shelter of a huge hollowed-out beech, but saw no enemy, then to a clump of birch, but saw only a plunging horse with its pack hanging clumsily off one side. There was some thick brush below, and these were his next shelter, then on to another oak . . . and a redcoat facing an imagined enemy in another direction. He was just thirty yards away. A dozen running jumps, Skoiyasi calculated, and he could open this fool's skull with his tomahawk. That was real warrior warfare. But no, these were not warrior games. He raised his rifle to his shoulder and fired.

The redcoat sprawled across the roots of a sugar maple, blood spilling from his mouth in a mighty gush. Skoiyasi did not see, but rather felt, pressure from the right in what he knew was English gunfire. Quickly he pulled back, into a defile, before he was spotted. From there he watched, reloaded, and waited until he saw a pair of advancing English soldiers. He fired quickly at one of them and drove them back into the trees from which they had first appeared.

As darkness fell over the battlefield, amidst the moans and screams of the wounded, Skoiyasi and the rest of the attackers could feel the exhaustion and despair of the English troops. About half of the attackers pulled back to get some rest, while the other half remained to keep up a steady gunfire and add a few savage noises to the sounds of the night. At around midnight they would change shifts, and in the misty dawn the fresh, tough, nearly unbloodied Indians would face a sleepless, worn-out, worn-down, depleted and frightened army. There was nobody to help them but the men in the fort, and the Shawnees and Delawares had them penned up like cattle.

Another victory seemed certain. Skoiyasi could not understand how, in the face of this unbroken string of triumphs over the English, his own people could remain so passive and detached from this war. It wasn't as if they were Mohawks, so historically linked to the English, so reduced in numbers that they could not imagine themselves without the English. No, the Seneca had for many years been close to the French too, and they knew that without the French, life would be harder. And now the western tribes had shown themselves ready to do the toughest part. Why, then, would not the Seneca, at least, and the Cayuga, join in rising up against the greedy English?

His people were foolish. Skoiyasi did not wish to think beyond that.

The word had come down from the chiefs, but the warriors in the woods didn't have to get it to know what they needed to do. Deep in the dark, wooded hills of Pennsylvania, another English army was about to be wiped out. There was no need to make a furious, tomahawk-waving charge into the gaping muzzles and shining bayonets of the English ranks, which was something the Indians did not love doing anyway. They just needed to wear the soldiers down until they collapsed and turned into a mob. Then numbers of them would attempt to flee, every man for himself, and the Indians could collect them as if they were so many pumpkins. Of course, if it looked as if the soldiers were on the verge of collapse, a well-timed charge could force a quick and bloody end to the battle.

Skoiyasi had taken a new, advanced position while it was still dark. When the first rays of daylight filtered through to leafy cover, he was not surprised to see a number of English soldiers exposed and bleary-eyed. He took careful aim and squeezed his trigger. His bullet sped so true that a soldier tumbled noiselessly to the ground, instantly dead, while his companions around him quickly dropped back out of sight. Around the perimeter of the English position came the popping of gunfire that told him other Indians had made the same discovery as he, and had taken advantage.

Skoiyasi darted forward and took a position behind a tall old pine tree. On his flanks he saw several of his comrades also press forward. This was still not a headlong attack, just the aggressive instincts of born hunters and warriors.

They had settled down once again to the routine of move and fire, move and fire, when one of the chiefs noticed what he took to be a weak spot along the enemy's perimeter, just in front of a treeless rise. It was so quiet down there, with no return fire, and no movement. Somebody had left the door wide open.

After a few more minutes of careful observation, he and others suddenly charged forward shrieking, into the English lines, followed by their allies up and down the line, all converging upon this one vulnerable place. Skoiyasi ran forward until he saw a target, then fired his rifle, dropped it, whooped, and dashed headlong into the enemy, his tomahawk swinging in a deadly arc.

Tired as they were, the retreating soldiers they were facing did not break into headlong flight. Instead, they faced their enemy and fired back. The Indians had come down a rise to make their attack, and now, abruptly, from both sides of the rise, hundreds of rifle barrels appeared from behind trees, pouring a deadly fire into the flanks of the attacking Indians.

Around Skoiyasi, unbelievably, a dozen Indians fell, killed or badly wounded. For the first time since the battle began he felt fear, and when another deadly volley brought down more of his comrades, he needed no chief to tell him to turn around and head back up the rise for the safety of the thick, wooded area he had just left. Behind him most of his cohorts held fast for a few moments, but the English were coming on, in a murderous bayonet charge. The Indians fled, but more English had circled around them, and now, as the retreating Indians approached them, the English fired another murderous volley. Swift as was his flight, Skoiyasi had not forgotten his cover, and only the trees saved him.

He had broken through the English circle and was heading back toward where he had dropped his rifle early in the charge, when suddenly, before him, loomed a lone English infantryman, with a gleaming bayonet at the end of his musket, which he held before him. There was blood dripping from the bayonet.

"Come on!" the soldier shouted. "C'mon, damn you!" Skoiyasi cocked his tomahawk and flung it at the Englishman, who ducked and listened to it whirl past his ear. Nearly unarmed now, Skoiyasi fled past the soldier, who knew better than to pursue him toward where there might be a whole lot more like him.

Away from the action, Skoiyasi found a rifle next to a dead Shawnee. He grabbed the Shawnee's powder horn, bullet pouch, and the tomahawk in his waistband, took a quick look around for any dead or dying enemy to scalp, found none, and moved on.

Fleeing Shawnees and Delawares were overtaking him.

Somehow the stupid, stubborn English had turned defeat into victory, and Skoiyasi had lost any desire to stay around. He made a beeline for a wooded hill to the north. Once there, he would not stop to see what the chiefs would do next. The sounds behind them indicated that his cohorts had had enough. The gunfire was slackening, the war whoops were no longer to be heard. Here and there he could see men creeping through the woods, making their escape from the battlefield, perhaps to fight another day, perhaps to return forever to their home villages.

That's what happens, he thought, when you ally yourself with Delawares and Shawnees. But he too had had enough fighting this time around. Victory was one thing, but to be beaten by this loathsome enemy was more than he could bear.

When Skoiyasi picked up the trail north along the Allegheny River, he found that he was not alone. Three Seneca braves from a different village were there waiting on the trail for two others. Like him, their spirits were very low, and they were concerned that their tardy friends might have fallen during the English counterattack.

As they waited, they talked about the battle. The three had left the battlefield after Skoiyasi, but had taken a shorter route back to the trail. As Skoiyasi had thought, the counterattack by the English had driven the Indians off the battlefield and discouraged their desire to return. Several of the chiefs had tried to regroup their forces. "We have them!" they shouted at their men. "They are so tired they can no longer stand on their feet. If we hit them again, they will fall into our hands."

But the chiefs had lost their men. Unlike English officers, they could not order their men back to battle. They could not threaten to shoot them, or warn them that they would be brought up on charges of cowardice in the face of the enemy. These men were their own men, and for many of them, the time of fighting was over.

The Senecas Skoiyasi met on the trail were all very young. As they talked about the battle, he could see how bitter they were that none of the older warriors in their village had agreed to fight. "The People of the Great Hill would not have accepted defeat like this," cried one of them, a youth named Degata. "Even now we would be brought together in another place, attacking where they least expect."

Skoiyasi looked at them, listened to their fire, and his face creased into a grim smile.

"I have been fighting this war for three moons," he said. "I have seen three forts go up in smoke, seen English soldiers fall beneath this tomahawk"—for emphasis he pulled from his waistband the weapon he'd taken from the Shawnee—"heard the screams of English soldiers at the stake. We have not lost this war. And we have taken so many forts that we need not take more. If the soldiers in the forts cannot get out to fight us, then they are useless."

He was the scarred veteran. He had their attention.

"The great war chief Kyashuta has gone to the chiefs of the Longhouse and tried to stir them to rise against the English. But the chiefs are afraid of the English. It is the young warriors like you who are not afraid of the English. In Pennsylvania the Shawnees have been attacking the whites who come into their country and plow up the soil. If we do the same in New York, the English general Big Nose will send his soldiers to attack our villages, and then our chiefs will have to fight. If the Ganonsyoni join the western tribes against the English, we will push them back against the ocean, and then maybe they will have to swim home."

The young braves laughed and their spirits rose. Although in the end their side had met defeat, none of them had been wounded and all of them had killed, or at least thought they had killed, for the first time. For them that was heady stuff, and although they did not understand much of what Skoiyasi was telling them, the idea of swooping down on farms, killing, burning, and carrying off booty sounded wonderful. It was, after all, part of their tradition, the way to fame and fortune among their people from time immemorial.

This man had led Senecas at Fort Venango and Presque Isle. He was older than they, and yet he spoke of fighting the whites, not like the old sachems who were always telling them they must learn to live with the English.

Degata was the dominant of the three. "We must wait for our brothers," he said.

"If they do not come by morning," Skoiyasi answered, "then they will not come at all."

"We will wait till morning," Degata agreed.

Skoiyasi stepped off the trail and walked down to the bank above the Allegheny River. There he sat, picked up a small twig and tossed it. The river breeze took it and carried it into the current. He watched it as it began its journey downriver toward Fort Pitt. The rivers were his highways. He knew that the waters of the Allegheny became one with those of the Spay-lay-wi-theepi, and that the Spay-lay-wi-theepi wandered west to meet up with the Mississippi. The Mississippi flowed south into the great salt sea.

How did he know this? Kendee, grandfather of Little Oak, had taught him this when he was a child. Kendee had taught him many things. He was a wise man of great experience.

And yet Kendee's grandson Little Oak, Skoiyasi's friend, his brother, had decided to become a white man. The thought that his friend had had such a choice seemed so strange to him, as if Little Oak had successfully chosen to be an eagle, or perhaps the monstrous, legendary two-headed serpent of Genundewah, who with his deadly breath had wiped out so many Senecas.

At that moment Skoiyasi did not feel great hatred for his old friend. But deep within him remained the iron conviction that Little Oak must be destroyed, and that he, Skoiyasi, must be the destroyer.

❧23❧

For Katherine, Cilla was a brand-new experience. While her husband, father, and Big Oak made their rounds of suppliers, gathering small supplies of ammunition here and there to avoid suspicion that they were preparing to smuggle weapons to the Indians, she and Cilla sat in her sunny sitting room, attempting to communicate without benefit of an interpreter.

Cilla refused a chair, preferring to sit cross-legged on the floor. Katherine, forever polite, refused to talk down to the young Tuscarora woman, and sat on the floor herself, holding the baby. Cilla had learned a smattering of English as a child living close to the English, then relearned it in her days with Big Oak, so the two of them spent an hour or so exchanging small talk and drinking tea that Katherine had prepared after Cilla had arrived at the frightful hour of six in the morning.

Katherine was astonished to learn that Big Oak intended to marry the Tuscarora in a church service. She was further amazed to learn that Big Oak was not particular about the denomination, knowing little of such things, as long as it was not the Romish Church. Katherine suggested that they marry in the large Dutch Reformed church, which they could see from the window of the sitting room. Frightened by the thought of entering such a huge building, Cilla shook her head, and Katherine dropped the subject. It was a bad idea anyway, she thought, a product of her mischievous mind that the Dutch patricians of Albany would be thrilled by the idea of a wedding in their big, beautiful church between a rude woodsman and a heathen Iroquois savage.

Cilla watched the play of emotions on Katherine's face and more or less read her thoughts without difficulty. They talked some more about how delicious the tea was, how the big windows let so much sun in that it was like being outside, and how noisy were the streets below, heard through the open windows.

Katherine noticed that during most of this conversation Cilla was staring at the girl-child she held in her arms. But when Cilla beckoned that she wanted to hold the child, Katherine had to catch her breath, and she hesitated for a moment. A look of hurt passed across Cilla's face, then disappeared behind a blank mask. Katherine did not miss the pain, however, and she blushed with embarrassment. They stared at each other for a moment, Katherine with embarrassment and fear, Cilla from her shell.

They were interrupted by Thad and Katherine's oldest son, David. The six year old had just eaten breakfast. In a few minutes, Thad would be walking him down the street to his tutor. There was just time for a curious glance at Cilla, and a hug and kiss from his mother. Then the boy was gone.

Cilla and Katherine both watched the boy leave in silence, both aware of how much the boy resembled his woodsman grandfather.

"I'm sorry," Katherine said finally. "She is so precious to me, I hate to let anybody else hold her." She passed the baby to Cilla and watched her as she held her so sweetly and gently that she decided then and there to close her eyes and go to sleep.

Cilla smiled for the first time. "You know," she said, "your husband a Iroquois also. Like me. You no be afraid a me."

Katherine understood what Cilla was saying, and she decided to be as honest as she could. "But Thad lives like a white man. His ways are not strange to me." She decided not to talk about the stories she had heard since she was a child, about white babies being kidnapped by Indians, sometimes being raised as Indians, and other times being brutally murdered. "I am used to Thad. I only met you yesterday."

Cilla laughed a soft, musical laugh that sounded good to Katherine's ears. "White man, red man—no. Only 'man.' All man strange to woman. Man go out. Woman stay home."

Now Katherine laughed. "I heard that you paddle a canoe like a man, roam the woods like a man. Fish like a man. Fight like a man."

Cilla shook her head. "Any woman can do anything when she must. Woman do what she has to do. Man do what he wants to do. That is what I see."

Katherine understood the wisdom of the Tuscarora. Having been raised by her father, she thought she understood men, but her father was a part-time parent at best. Life with Thad had turned out to be a complete surprise to her; his moods, his needs, his silences, his restlessness were things to which she was still unaccustomed. It was his kind heart and his willingness to learn her ways that helped make their marriage a loving one, but in return she had to trust that his fierce streak of independence would not stand between them.

She watched the young Tuscarora woman as she rocked the baby. "You be nice to me," Cilla said. "I marry Big Oak,

I be baby's grandmother." And she laughed once more, softly, while the baby slept on.

Louis's Mohawk village was not a very big village. The amount of ammunition they needed was not all that great. But the day Big Oak, Thad, and Cilla pulled their short train of packhorses through the gate of the palisade, you would have thought heaven itself had descended upon the village with enough munitions to wipe out every Algonquin on the face of the earth.

It was not just that they were getting the ammunition they so desperately needed, though that surely was a part of it. It was also that a pair of white men had made them a promise, and had kept it.

Not that Ganonsyoni always kept the promises they made. In warfare, if you could lie your way into the confidence of the enemy, and then use that confidence to defeat him, that was considered clever tactics worthy of admiration. But in the father-son relationship that both the Iroquois and the English had tacitly agreed upon over the years, the Iroquois had expected their English father to keep his word, and were always bitterly disappointed when he failed to do so.

Big Oak and Thad had also scrounged up a set of tools and some spare parts for rifles. This was a special gift to the Mohawks. There were no new rifles in the packs of Wendel and Watley, and Indians were notoriously hard on their weapons. When they made treaties with the whites, these treaties often included the services of gunsmiths. The Indians, with their cultural character carved in stone, could not seem to raise among them a caste of artisans who truly understood how to repair a firearm.

Of the eleven weapons submitted to him by hopeful warriors, Big Oak managed to get nine back into working order. The other two were sorry old specimens of muskets that belonged to sorry old specimens of warriors who were as likely to overcharge their weapons as they were to blame their failure on the hatred of some malevolent god.

"If I fix this weapon so that it will shoot, the third or fourth time you shoot it, it will more likely kill you than your enemy," he would tell its owner. "If you wait till you get a new rifle, you will live a long life," he would add confidentially, softly, just in case he was wrong. "Next time I come, maybe times will be better, and then I will come with a new rifle for you." And the old Mohawk would walk away feeling pleased with himself that he had consulted with a wise man and thereby saved his life.

On the third day they were in the village, a runner came in from the west, a Cayuga with strong clan ties to the Mohawk village. His breathless news was not welcome. The men of the village held council that night to discuss it.

It was a warm night under a quarter moon, a night so clear that the stars looked close enough to touch. Thad looked around the circle at the stalwart warriors who listened with much dignity as each man rose to speak in accordance with his rank. They all smoked, and none talked out of turn. This was an important night for all of them.

The news, said Louis, who had spoken at length with the Cayuga runner, was of the worst kind. Western New York was aflame. The victims were the newly arrived farmers whose clearings dotted the fertile valleys from the long lakes to the Genesee River. The marauders were a small group of renegade Senecas who must be stopped. It was Louis's feeling that he and his warriors would have to be the ones to stop them.

"They are sowing the seeds of a war that will be death to the Iroquois confederacy," Louis concluded gravely, before he sat down.

His brother George arose, looked around the circle, and then straight into Louis's dark eyes. "My brother," he began, "since ancient times the Ganonsyoni have been the mightiest of all the nations. We are not the biggest. We are not the richest. But we are the mightiest. We have been the mightiest only because we have always buried our differences for the sake of unity. The Hurons had a 'confederacy.' The Eries had a 'confederacy.' Both those unions fell apart when we blew on them. But the Longhouse stayed secure. We guarded the Eastern Door. The Senecas guarded the Western Door. From the snow country of the north to the big mountains of the south, we were feared and respected.

"If we take up the tomahawk against our brothers the Seneca, even though they are renegades, we will anger the Seneca nation, which has many more warriors than we. If they are renegades, then why do the chiefs not punish them? And if this is not a Seneca problem, then it is an English problem. Let them punish the renegades, and then the Seneca chiefs will not blame us." The cries of approval from around the circle showed appreciation for George's wisdom. None of the warriors really wished to take up arms against their Seneca brothers, renegades or not.

Louis stood up and spoke. "Among us tonight is our brother Big Oak, who has gladdened our hearts with powder and lead at his own risk when the English have denied us. He has made many of our guns that were broken shoot again. I don't know how he does this. He is a man of many gifts. He is also brother to the Senecas. He knows their hearts. Tonight I ask him to speak, and I hope you will open your ears and let his words into them, because he is a man who will tell you the truth."

Big Oak stood up and waited nearly a minute before he began to speak. The braves who sat around the fire were not impatient. The long silence added to the feeling that this speech would be important for their future. They looked forward to such a speech. In their minds the Ganonsyoni had been drifting, while in the West their long-time enemies were deciding their destiny by acting with courage.

"You are my brothers," he began simply. "You see around you things happening that you do not like to see. Your allies the English do not do for you as they did in the days when they needed your strong arms to be raised against the French. You fear that they no longer are your friends.

"In the West they have lost battles against your enemies, the Chippewas, the Hurons, and the other western tribes. So you have been watching your enemy fight your enemy. If the western tribes win, then your day as their masters is over. If the English win, then they will have no use for you at all and can treat you as badly as they wish. And so you do not know who you want to win."

The warriors voiced their approval because he had put their thoughts into his words. Most of them did not want to voice the thought that the English were their enemy because the English had been their allies for so long. They were pleased that Big Oak understood their feelings.

"Most of the time it is good to stand by while your enemy fights your enemy, to watch them both grow weaker while you keep the peace, and your children all grow up to become strong warriors."

Again the warriors voiced their agreement.

"Most of your brothers of the great hill feel as you do, but there are a few who want to bring you into war against the English. They are out now, burning down the cabins of English farmers, taking the scalps of mothers and fathers and kidnapping children."

He paused again to gauge their reaction, but there was none. They had heard about the raids. Now an older brave, without rank but still respected in council, rose.

"May I speak but few words?" he asked Big Oak politely.

Big Oak bowed his head in assent and the old Indian spoke.

"I am sorry," he said, "to hear that the white people are losing their lives and their children are losing their mothers and fathers. It is a sad thing, a thing that we have all seen happen to our people during our lives. But it is not our place to defend the white people. If they are so powerful, let them defend themselves." He sat down, to a chorus of cynical assent from his comrades.

Big Oak continued. "I know that you believe the English are very weak. My son sat in a fort for many days while the western tribes kept the English locked up behind wooden walls. And they are still locked up in Detroit. It is also true that the western tribes have taken many small forts from the English.

"But you have short memories. Not long ago, the English defeated the powerful French, along with all the western tribes. And except for you, the Ganiengehaka, they did not get much help from their allies in the Longhouse. After the English win a war, it is their way to go to sleep for a while so they will not spend as much gold paying soldiers.

"The battles in the West have awakened General Amherst, the one you call Big Nose. He has a bad temper. He is not a good Englishman like General Gage. He wants to punish all the Indians for what the western tribes have done. But there are good English generals too, and King George, who loves the Iroquois. And they will not let this happen."

Again he paused, looking out with pleasure over the silent, serious warriors who were listening so carefully to his words.

"If the bad Senecas continue to attack the white settlements, even though those Englishmen should not be there, then General Big Nose will assemble a big army to attack your villages. Some of you may think that you can beat the

English, but if they truly wake up, then they will put ten soldiers in the field for every warrior, or twenty soldiers in the field for every warrior, or whatever it takes to do the job. You know how they are. I do not have to tell you. They lose and lose and lose and then, suddenly, the war is over and they have won. That is how the English are."

The warriors knew that this was true and they said so.

"I know it is true," said Big Oak, "because I am one of them, and that is how I am. And so I must ask some of you, not many, just a few, to come with us and help us stop these bad Senecas from bringing war down upon our heads. If you can do this, you will be heroes to your people, for you would have kept them out of war, and come winter, your children will have food to eat and you will still be free."

Now the old warrior arose again. Once again, humbly, he asked permission to speak. Once again, he received permission.

"Why," he asked, "should we defend those farmers who come upon our land without our permission? You know, Big Oak, that every year there are more of them, nibbling here, nibbling there, sometimes grabbing a big slice like they did years back to the Delaware, mostly taking such a small bite at a time that we don't even know they have taken it until the following spring when we go out to hunt and we see a new field, with a cabin, where the woods used to be. Every time I see that happen, my heart falls down and I want to weep. I know that I can't go there anymore, because the English now think that that land is theirs. Would it not be better to let the raids go on and meanwhile get ready to fight the English if the general with the big nose attacks us?"

The old one sat down.

"You can attack a settlement and then vanish into the woods so that they could never find you," Big Oak said.

"But they could find your village, and wipe it out, and you would have no home, or wife, or children to return to. Think of how needy you might have been during the coming winter had I not brought you ammunition for the hunt. If war comes between you and Big Nose, nobody will be able to bring you ammunition. *The French are gone from here, I promise you!* And so are their trade goods, forever. You may think that your tomahawks and courage are mighty enough to defeat English guns, but that is not so."

One more time, the old one stood up. He looked toward Louis, and Louis nodded.

"If the English attacked, Big Oak, would you not be here to furnish us with ammunition and weapons, knowing that we are in the right, knowing that we have the right to defend ourselves against General Big Nose?"

He sat down.

Big Oak looked around at the faces of men he had come to love as dearly as he had loved the men of the old village of Tonowaugh. The truth was that his conscience would not let him smuggle arms to the Ganiengehaka for them to use against the English. No matter how unjust was the English cause and how just was the Mohawk, he could not side with his new brothers against his old ones; rather weep for slaughtered Mohawks than massacred Englishmen.

But Big Oak knew he could not tell that to these people. They would not understand. Why should they? For them the Longhouse was all they had. Their families were all they had. Their lives were all they had. Why should they care about his conscience?

Well, his life and family was all he had. And so, when it came to this, he had to say the words that would be best for him.

"My brothers," he said, "if by bringing you weapons to fight the English I would bring you hope of victory, then I could not bring you weapons and ammunition. Against the English there is no hope. If I could bring you ammunition and weapons to last you a thousand summers, along with a place that would take you far away from the English, then I would gladly do so, that is how much I love you.

"But I do not know such a place. Not yet. So, my brothers, I beg you, do not think thoughts of fighting the English. Such thoughts will only destroy your people."

He paused again, and tasted the silence. Before he could continue, Louis spoke.

"My brother Big Oak. How can we survive if the English take all our land? For a long time the Lenni Lenape lived as women to us. But we are *men*. We cannot live as women to the English."

Both men were standing. Big Oak faced Louis and framed his words for him alone. "There are good Englishmen, like Warraghiyagey, and bad Englishmen, like Big Nose. The good Englishmen will help you to keep your land. But you must do your part. You must help us stop the bad Senecas."

Big Oak sat down and let the braves chew on the silence that followed. He was glad that his thoughts were not an open book to the Mohawks, because he feared for their future no matter what they did. Big Oak was a reluctant realist. In his travels west, his heart leaped at the sight of the beautiful valley of the Spay-lay-wi-theepi. He was afraid that New York was already lost, but there was so much land to the west, and he was certain that if he were wrong, and Sir William Johnson could not protect the future of his Iroquois, then they would thrive in that valley.

As for the Shawnees, the Delawares, and the Mingoes who might feel crowded by having to share that valley, it was too much for him to worry about. He was, after all, a fur trader, not a missionary.

They smoked in silence, pondering what had been said.

For five minutes not a word was spoken, and Thad began to wonder if any of them had been listening to his father's last words. Finally Louis climbed to his feet.

"My brother Big Oak," he said. "You are wise. We are fortunate to have you among us." He looked around the circle, at the dozen Mohawk men whose dark faces flickered in the light of the council fire.

"I want our three mightiest warriors to go with me, and Big Oak and Little Oak. I believe there are only a few bad Senecas doing this mischief. It will not take many Ganiengehaka to handle them."

Big Oak smiled inside himself. Had Louis asked for all of them, he might have gotten none. By asking for a small party, he left the village defended and made a place in this party a place of honor that few of them could resist. And as Big Oak looked around the fire, he could tell that not a single one of the young braves cared to be left out of this challenge.

❊24❊

THE THREE MOHAWKS WHO JOINED LOUIS, Big Oak, and Thad were a particularly tough lot. Two of them were brothers known to Big Oak as Three Bears and Jack, men in their late twenties who had terrorized the French and the Abnakis during the last war.

Traditionalists both, they hated to use their rifles unless they absolutely had to. They were adept at spotting a column of the enemy loping through the woods, then sneaking up on the last one or two and dispatching them so quietly that the column might not notice their absence for another mile or two. Jack in particular found pleasure in the feel of the kill—the quick, fruitless struggle of the foe as he felt a hand clamp over his mouth from behind, the warm spurt of blood on Jack's hand as he drew his sharp knife across the throat, the feel of his enemy's body yielding to death and sliding gently to the forest floor.

But they were as stalwart in hand-to-hand combat as they were in mayhem by stealth. Three Bears reveled in the shock that traveled up the length of his arm when he brought his war club down on the skull of his adversary. Jack, on the other hand, was partial to the sweet, clean crunching sound he heard when his keen-bladed tomahawk bit deep through the skull into his opponent's brain. Sometimes they would argue with each other over which was the more manly way to dispatch an enemy.

They were thick-armed and brawny-chested yet amazingly light on their feet, both for silent loping and agile legwork in individual fighting. Both were completely dependable when it came to the Indian style of making war.

The third warrior Louis had selected was a prodigious youngster of nineteen who had seen his first action three years before in Canada. His name was Tagaowatha. For sixteen years he had lived quietly close to home, such an obedient son of his mother that his family had been terribly worried about him.

Their worries came to an abrupt end one morning near Quebec, when a small band of Mohawks on their way to a big fight caught a group of French Canadians sleeping off a previous night's carouse. The Canadians barely had time to reach for their knives and hatchets before the Mohawks were upon them, and Tagaowatha, using the butt of his rifle like the scythe of the Grim Reaper, laid low several of the Canadians by himself, but did not hang around long enough to watch his cohorts finish the job.

Noting that one of the Canadians had vaulted into a thicket to make his escape, the youngster took off after him. Moments later the Mohawks in the Canadian camp heard a short series of agonized screams. When Tagaowatha returned to the camp, his left hand clutched a hank of the Canadian's hair. Hanging from the hair, swinging in the morning breeze, was the rest of the Canadian's head.

Louis knew then and there that he had something special. Back home in the village, Tagaowatha still spoke seldom, still obeyed his mother, still kept pretty much to himself. In battle, however, he was a killing machine.

All these things Louis told Big Oak and Thad as the six men headed west to take on the Seneca renegades.

They loped through the woods along the trails west, through the heat of the peak of the summer. The forest canopy seemed to collect the humidity without shutting out any of the sun's radiant energy. There had been plenty of thunder showers around the Finger Lakes, with the resulting bumper crop of mosquitoes and other annoying bugs.

The Mohawk war party did not feel the heat, they did not feel the humidity, and the rancid bear grease made them too gamy for even the mosquitoes to feast on. Single file they put mile after mile of trail behind them in their relaxed, long-legged jog up and down the hills of central New York, occasionally breaking out of the thick green canopy into the sunlight of a bare rocky ridge, where the high country breezes cooled their sweaty bodies. They would run the ridge for a mile or so, until the trail plunged them back into the primeval darkness of the dense forests. When, as happened occasionally, the trail passed by a new farm clearing, the war party gave a quick look for signs of marauding, and if no such signs were forthcoming, they swept by the farm and continued west.

Finding an enemy in such a vast stretch of woodland was a nearly impossible job. Their intent was to journey all the way to Tonowaugh, and lurk in the vicinity until they caught the renegades in a forest ambush. Instead they got lucky. Toward the end of the third day, as they skirted the northern edge of Cayuga Lake, they emerged from the forest and saw a black smudge on the horizon. They knew what it was. They had been watching for it over the past twenty miles, not really expecting to see it, but not surprised when they did. They were loping along the upslope, and now, as the slope leveled off, the smudge turned into a more distinct column of black smoke. They ran awhile longer, and now they could smell the smoke, and see a second column, fainter, smaller, so close to the first that the smoke columns merged as they spread out.

The strongest emotion was one of satisfaction at having found their enemy so quickly without having to hunt for their trail all over the lake country. None of the Mohawks felt any particular dread at what they might find. They were all seasoned warriors without emotions to spare for white people they did not know and who probably would not like them anyway.

When their efforts had brought them within two or three miles of the smoke, they slowed to a walk and increased the distance between them. Their nostrils flared, and their ears probed through the silence in search of sounds beyond the usual forest chorus. The closer they came to the desolation they knew they would find, the more carefully they walked, watching, listening, sniffing, staying alive.

They crossed a small, quiet stream, slipped down a short, steep hill, and suddenly the forest opened up into a field of tall grass and tree stumps. A few cows were grazing without concern, their heads turned away from the smoke that rose up behind them.

The six spread out along the tree line and for several minutes watched the house and barn finish burning to the ground. There was no movement that they could see, and so half their number left the woods and began to walk toward the house. Big Oak and Thad remained concealed at the tree line, their rifles covering the movements of their cohorts, their eyes scanning the field for any unexpected movements.

There was no breeze to stir a single leaf or blade of grass on this late afternoon. To Thad, the world felt hot and dead. Like the Mohawks, he had experienced the horrors of war, but he was weary of it. He had thought that peace between the French and the English meant the killing might stop. The past two months had shown him that this was not so, and that the civilization of Albany was an illusion that ended nearly at the city's gates.

Louis waved to them. Big Oak and Thad moved forward across the field to a skeleton of blackened timbers where a house had stood. Within the remnants of the house lay the scalped, charred body of a man. Louis and the two brothers were paying no attention to either the house or the body. They had located the direction of the marauders after they had done their deed. The trail signs, he told Big Oak, showed that they had taken prisoners, at least some of them children. That made the Mohawks ecstatic because it meant that they would travel slowly, and that they were confident no one was out in the woods hunting for them.

Furthermore, even if they kept their mouths shut, prisoners moved noisily. There would be no ambushes sprung on the Mohawks this day, for the Mohawks could move silently, carefully, knowing that they would still catch up to their prey in a short time.

About fifteen minutes later they changed their minds and decided to pick up the pace. What changed their mind was their finding the blood-covered body of a woman sprawled on her back. She had only one visible wound, a yawning bloody crack in the top of her head. There was no discussion necessary. Either her wails of mourning had disturbed her captors or she had not moved fast enough for them. Now they found that the men they were pursuing had struck a well-traveled trail west; following them would be even easier. What puzzled Big Oak was why they had bothered to take captives. Surely they couldn't bring them back to their villages, because their villages were not at war with the English.

Suddenly all six of their party froze mid-step. They had heard it, distant and faint, but distinct, and they would not move until they had heard it again. And a minute later again it came, the long, keening cry of a child, abruptly cut short. With unerring instincts, they gauged the distance, ran about a quarter of a mile, then slowed to a crouching walk until Louis, in the lead, began to hear sounds up ahead.

It occurred to Big Oak and Thad that seven years before, they, Louis, and more than a dozen Mohawks had wiped out twice their number of French and Caughnawagas in an ambush that instantly had become a part of Mohawk folklore. Here they were again, but this time the target came from within the Longhouse, a moment perhaps signaling the end of the great Iroquois union that had dominated a huge territory for centuries with their energy, savagery, and politics.

Would the Senecas, mightiest, most populous nation of the Longhouse, stand silent when the bodies of some of their fiercest warriors were returned to their villages by their allies and rivals, and killers, the Mohawks?

Now Louis caught his first glimpse of them, through the maze of tree trunks that stood between them. He stopped and crouched, and the other Mohawks did the same. Big Oak crept beside him and saw, ahead, one lone Seneca warrior, painted like a demonic nightmare.

They heard voices too, indistinct mutterings muffled by the stirring of the trees. The two crept closer, until they could hear Skoiyasi telling someone that here would be a good place to make camp. He was talking to a small, wiry, tough-looking young man with prominent scars on several places of his body. Skoiyasi went on, telling the warrior it would take several days to make contact with the Twightwees, that the Twightwees had plenty of goods taken from the English at Fort Miamis, and they might be willing to trade some for a trio of white children. Going west would give them a chance to find out for themselves how much of the news of the rebellion was true and how much rumor.

"Young Eagle, tell the warriors not to hurt the prisoners or I'll cut their ears off," they heard him say. "We need the things we can get in exchange for them."

The Mohawks began to fan out, to surround the Seneca camp. Respecting the keen senses of their brothers, they drew back a distance before they began to encircle them. The Senecas, who felt that they were in home territory and need fear no man, took no precautions.

There was to be no stealthy, silent tomahawk attack; they were to wait till the camp settled down, then get close enough for each to draw a bead on a Seneca and pick him off.

Thad had the easiest job. He was to wait for his cohorts to surround the camp, then creep straight in and pick off Skoiyasi, who was already in plain sight. Thad believed that Louis had chosen Skoiyasi as his target with malicious intent, knowing that Skoiyasi had been his friend, that Skoiyasi had tried to kill him, and that it was time for him to repay his friend in kind.

Perhaps Thad had by now too much white nature in him, for this was the folly of a white man thinking he could think like an Indian. In fact, Louis had chosen him because Skoiyasi was the leader of the Senecas and Thad was the best shot; Louis had seen that time and again in the late war with the French.

The air was again still, and the forest so heavy with heat that it felt lifeless. The very birds and squirrels all seemed to hold their breaths. The conversation of the Senecas and the whimpering of the two smallest captives was all there was to hear, as the Indians, and Big Oak, circled left and right.

Thad couldn't see them, but he could sense them, closing the loop around the unsuspecting Senecas. Their ability to creep noiselessly and invisibly through the woods was magical. Thad crept forward over the sparse forest floor ground cover until he spotted three Senecas talking. One of them was Skoiyasi. He had the Indian in his sights and his finger tightened on the trigger.

He never heard the noise that Skoiyasi heard that suddenly made all three of the Senecas move out of sight. As Tagaowatha moved into position, his rifle made contact with the root of a big beech tree in front of him. The contact was not much, the sound was not great, but the finely tuned senses of Skoiyasi heard a man-made sound where there should not have been men. Suddenly they leaped to where the three children were bound not hand and foot, but only by fear, and crouched beside them, tomahawks raised.

"No move!" he cried out in English to his unseen enemy in the forest. "We kill!"

From fifty feet away Skoiyasi heard a laugh. The voice was Mohawk speaking Seneca. "Their lives mean nothing to us, my brother!"

There was silence for a moment as Skoiyasi searched his brain for a clue to the familiar voice. "Ah," he finally said in Seneca. "Louis, the Mohawk named for the French father. We kill the children first, then we kill you." And he raised his tomahawk to strike the first, a sandy haired boy of about seven, whom fright had frozen into silence.

During the dialogue, Big Oak had continued to creep closer, until he saw Skoiyasi, raising his weapon. Big Oak had no doubt the Seneca intended to use it. He stood up and walked forward. "No!" he shouted with such force that Skoiyasi flinched before he spotted the veteran trader and smiled.

"My father Big Oak," he said. "But your heart is not of oak, it is soft. You have spent too much time in the English cities."

There was no question of Big Oak squeezing off a shot. The Seneca had the boy held in front of him. Big Oak stopped walking forward and ducked behind a tree. He could not see all of the Senecas, and had no desire to present himself as a target.

Once again the gloomy forest was plunged into silence, as each side pondered its choices. Big Oak spoke.

"Let the children go," Big Oak said. "They won't hurt you."

"Their father had no business on Iroquois land," Skoiyasi replied.

"And he paid the price with his life, you saw to that. Why must the children pay too?"

"English talk, Big Oak. You are not in the English world now, my father. Don't you remember? The children are ours. We do as we please with them."

Big Oak did not respond immediately. As long as they had not known they were being followed, the Senecas had been at a disadvantage. Now that they knew, and by whom, the advantage was theirs.

"Skoiyasi, if you will give us the children, we will let you and your men go back to your villages. If you will not . . ." He did not finish his sentence, for he knew Skoiyasi would take it as a challenge, and then the children would be doomed. Big Oak could see all three children now, stunned by the killing of their father, then the sudden murder of their mother before their eyes, and finally the fear that their own lives were about to be ended. There was a younger boy, slender, thin-faced, with a massive shock of blond hair atop his head that a hostile Indian might find irresistible; and a girl of eight or nine, plump, with happy features that were now ghastly and pathetic with grief and fright. The oldest, a year older than the girl, stood pale, still, and numb, his entire being a complete blank.

"Where are you taking them?" Big Oak asked.

"They are ours. We need not tell you."

"Will you kill them if we return east?"

"They would make fine Indian children, don't you think?" Skoiyasi asked. "You once thought well of Indian children, old father. You raised your son to be one."

"We will turn back," Big Oak said.

"I want to see you all on the trail behind us."

"I must talk with Louis about this," Big Oak responded. Thad had moved well off to the side, beyond the view of his father, the captives, or any of the Indians. Meanwhile Big Oak withdrew to talk with Louis. He knew Skoiyasi, he told the Mohawk. Skoiyasi did not care, he would kill the children, and causing the death of children in order to kill five Senecas was not justice.

Louis agreed, not because he loved English children, but because his war spirit had cooled as he reflected that any blood drawn would cause a crack in the Longhouse. There was still time. Let Pontiac lose a few battles, and the rebellion would wither away. The Longhouse must remain strong and united, no matter what.

Five pitiful Seneca rebels out of hundreds, he thought. Why bother with them?

The other three did not see it that way. They had no great love for the English either, nor did they harbor great hatred for the Senecas. They had put on their war paint, however, and they were anxious to contest this little piece of forest with their Seneca brothers.

But they had great respect for Louis. They had seen him become a leader in battle, a worthy successor to his father as a Mohawk leader. He looked at each of them in turn and said, firmly, "We're going back," and none of them considered arguing the matter with him.

Louis appeared on the trail, within sight of Skoiyasi.

"We are going back," he told the Seneca. "Brothers of the Longhouse should not fight over the fate of white children.

But I warn you. If you continue to raid the English settlements, you will bring the English army down on all of us.

Skoiyasi sneered. "You Mohawks are turning into women. That will not happen to the Guardians of the Western Door. I mourn for the passing of the great warriors of the Te-non-an-at-che. We will not give up the children. Go."

Louis turned to Big Oak. "We will do as they say. I do not see how any good can come if we have a fight now. They will kill the children and we will kill each other and the Longhouse will suffer."

"I understand," Big Oak replied. "But we are not Mohawks. Thad and I will follow them and decide what to do with them at the right time."

"You linger like women washing clothes at the river," Skoiyasi shouted from the Seneca camp. "I am waiting for you to disappear, my Mohawk brother, and my once white father."

By that time Louis's three warriors had joined them, and together the five men returned up the trail leading east. The trail led up a rise, out of the woods onto a ridge, and then down into a valley where lay a rocky old dry creek bed. It was here, where trail signs cannot be traced, that Big Oak shook hands with Louis and vanished in the woods. He then did a wide sweep that took him well south of the Seneca camp.

When Thad had failed to return, Big Oak knew what the young man had done. They had loped down too many trails together not to know each other's minds. Boldly he leaped across a dry creek bed and stomped through the dark forest, which was growing darker now as the sun found the horizon and began to sink into it. He did his dove call, rapped on trees with the butt of his rifle, and crackled every dry leaf in his path until he was certain they must have passed each other in the dank half-light. Finally, just when he thought he'd have to camp alone for the night, he caught a glimpse of his son, dove-calling and stomping and leaf-crackling from the opposite direction.

Big Oak walked to where Thad stood and clamped a firm grip on his shoulder. "Tomorrow," he said, "we will follow your old friend. When our chance comes, we will free the children, and we will kill Skoiyasi."

❧25❧

NOW CAME A GAME THAT COULD ONLY BE played by the greatest of woodsmen. Big Oak and Thad would have to follow Skoiyasi and his band closely enough so as not to lose them, but not so close as to be discovered.

The Senecas would be on their guard. On the other hand, they did not know that Thad had been part of the Mohawk party pursuing them. "They will be setting ambushes for us," Big Oak whispered to Thad as they lay wrapped in their blankets that night. They will be scouting their back trail to see if me and Louis and the braves have gone home. I think I know where they're going." Big Oak proceeded to explain his strategy to his son, and Thad said he agreed that it was their only choice.

"Our advantage, you see," Big Oak added, "is that they can travel no faster than the children."

The normal mode of travel for Big Oak and Thad was a long-legged, loping run that ate up the miles without consuming their energy. But now they had to travel slowly. They had no problem keeping contact with the Senecas. The children were noisy. Even their fear of their Seneca captives could not keep them from whimpering or crying. And the Senecas were so cocky, after having talked their pursuers out of contesting with them, that they were having a great old time kidding each other and talking about how Louis and Big Oak feared them, or how easy it had been to kill the whites and take their children.

Instead of following them from the rear, Big Oak and Thad kept on the left flank of the Senecas. Hour after hour they kept a careful watch with their ears, searching for an opportunity to strike a blow and free the children. Maybe Skoiyasi's young followers would quarrel with him. Maybe they would split up for some reason, maybe they would get careless. Big Oak was willing to pursue his quarry with the patience of a hunter on the trail of a deer. There were no guarantees that the deer would stop long enough to be caught, but that was just part of the hunt.

Although Big Oak and Thad could still hear the children, there was no evidence that they were being mistreated. Big Oak was not surprised. Generally Indians had a special love for children, even white children, and often adopted them into their tribe. The children, given time, often came to feel a part of the tribe that adopted them. It was amazing how often white children could forsake their roots and settle down into Indian routine so that wooing them back from the blanket became impossible.

Another night came and the Senecas made camp. Big Oak and Thad moved a little closer, to make sure that their quarry would not sneak off in the middle of the night down some trailless creek bed. Big Oak had no desire to have to hunt from scratch again.

Silently, speaking only in signs, the two traders made their beds of pine needles, wrapped themselves in blankets and slept.

Such was their vigilance that they awoke before dawn. They crept close enough to the Seneca camp to make out that their quarry was still sleeping. Patiently they watched and waited, and they were rewarded.

When the Senecas woke up with the first blue-graying of the dark horizon, Skoiyasi told his men that he intended to go hunting for something fresh to eat. Big Oak chuckled to himself, remembering that Skoiyasi would do anything to get into the woods alone with his rifle and take a shot at an animal. For all their warlike ardor, Skoiyasi's young braves were a lazy bunch who welcomed Skoiyasi's decision. While he was gone, they could lay around camp, occasionally putting a scare into one of their captives, until Skoiyasi came back with something more succulent than the monotonous diet of parched corn they had been nibbling throughout their little campaign.

Big Oak and Thad observed their old friend preparing to leave camp, and withdrew to make their own plans.

"I've been watching these boys," Big Oak told him when they'd put the proper distance of forest between themselves and their foes. "I think I know how to take them, but you need to take care of Skoiyasi. Are you up to it?"

There it was again. It was his job to kill his oldest friend. Thad nodded, but Big Oak, watching his son's face, was unconvinced.

"I'm about ready to turn around and go home," he said. "If it weren't for them kids, I would. Now let me tell you something, son. I've known that boy all his life, and you may think of him as your old trail buddy, but he'd slit your throat with pleasure. And I'll tell you something else. When we were back in Tonowaugh talking to Kawia, I was watchin' Skoiyasi and he couldn't stand for you to even look at her. There's *nothin'* he'd rather do than take your scalp home to his lodge and hand it to Kawia and say, 'This is the hair of that dog you thought was so wonderful. Now you can finally stop thinkin' about him because you're *never* gonna get a chance to lay down with him.'"

Thad looked at his father, wide-eyed. "What are you—"

"You can be pretty dense about some things, boy, and you're lucky, because that way things usually come out right for you and you spare yourself plenty of frettin'."

"But she had her choice and she made it, Pa. She treated me like I was some sort of low critter, and then I turned around and there they was, her and Skoiyasi, together like they'd always been lovers, and it broke my heart."

"Well now, son, look back and try to remember that her family had got massacred just a little while before. She wasn't in her right mind or she wouldn't a made such a choice."

Thad shook his head. "Can you beat that?" he said.

"How does that make you feel?" Big Oak asked.

Thad thought about it for a very few seconds, then shrugged. "It's like another life," he said. "I could no more live my life in a Seneca village now than I could live at the bottom of Lake Ontario. I belong in Albany with Katherine and the kids, and come to think of it, I wish I was there right now, and I'm goin' back as soon as this bit of business gets cleared up."

"Then you clear it up right," Big Oak insisted. "You can handle Skoiyasi. I know you can. You know you can. But only if you remember that he is your enemy. He is not the boy you grew up with and hunted with and played war games with. He's the man that loves raiding English settlements and wearing in his belt the scalps of Englishwomen.

"That's who he is now, and there are right now harmless folks sleepin' in their beds who'll be dead if you give him another chance on the warpath against the settlements."

"But Pa, you said it yourself, those folks got no right to be in those settlements. The King says they're not supposed to be there. They just up 'n' came, roosting on crooked claims and not caring a bit for anyone else's rights."

Big Oak sighed. "My son, I am proud of you. You have a love for justice. But you have to see things as they really are. What do you see?"

Thad knew what his father was getting at. "I see Albany bustin' at the seams," he said. "When Dieter and I went down to New York, I saw a big harbor full of ships, and then when we went all the way to Philadelphia was when I saw a real city."

"Do you think the Indians can stop the English from coming?"

Thad shook his head.

"The only hope our Iroquois brothers have is to get so far away from the whites that it'd be too much trouble for them to come and take the land away from the Iroquois."

Thad laughed. "Pa, we just got back from the valley of the Ohio River. We saw nobody. There it was, empty land full of birds and fish and deer, prettiest land I ever saw. Take forever to fill up that land. All they gotta do is put a few mountains between them and the English, they'll be all right."

Big Oak leveled a dark gaze at Thad. "You really think so?"

"I hope so."

"Good, then go on out there and get rid of Skoiyasi and make it quick. He's tough and he's clever, and he could slit your throat with a goose quill if you give him a chance. Don't give him a chance and you'll be fine."

Thad nodded. "Well," he said, "you be careful with these boys. You make a mistake, and the only grandpa my boy'll have is that penny-pinchin' Dutchman in Albany."

"Don't worry about me," Big Oak said. "I can still take care of myself."

By this time Skoiyasi had completed his preparations, and Big Oak could hear him through the trees giving his last orders, and the barely audible sound of his moccasins as he began his morning hunt. Thad cocked an ear until he figured out Skoiyasi's direction, then headed out after him, leaving Big Oak to ponder his plans for eliminating four active young Seneca braves without giving them a chance to kill the children.

The older Watley moved in close to their camp to observe them, and for a half hour he pondered his problem. Four braves, as young and careless as these, were a tall order even for a master killer like Big Oak. And then, suddenly, his task was reduced to simplicity itself. His Mohawk allies turned up.

He saw them before they saw him, slipping through the woods, watching their enemy on the south flank just as he and Thad had done a few minutes before. He hid in a hollow behind a clump of young oak trees and waited for them to pass by him, then in the gentlest of whispers murmured, "Louis," and was rewarded by nearly having his skull caved in.

"I thought you were going home," he said softly, once Louis had collected his dignity and slipped his tomahawk back in his belt.

"The others," Louis said, gesturing to the three men around him, "had a hunger to speak with their brothers." He left no doubt that the conversation would be a bloody affair.

"Are you not worried that such a fight might shake the confederacy apart?" Big Oak replied.

"My brother, there have been such fights in the past between the Senecas and the Ganiengehaka. The confederacy has always survived. Besides, these are renegades."

"I don't want to spoil your party," Big Oak said. Louis smiled inside at the figure of speech which was not part of the Mohawk world, but whose meaning he understood nevertheless. "Where do you wish to attack?"

"From this side," Louis explained simply.

"The children are being held on the west side of the clearing. I'll come in from there to protect them."

Louis nodded. "You love the white children, eh?" he asked.

"I have two young grandchildren. I love children."

Big Oak traveled in a wide arc that took him west of the camp, and found a place that was close to the children and provided a good view of the clearing. He lay down behind a tree, his rifle pointed toward the open space between the children and the closest of their captors.

There were four Senecas in the clearing, and four Mohawks ready to attack from the woods. Had the children not been there, Big Oak might have viewed the coming contest more with interest than with trepidation, as if the two groups were baggataway teams rather than warriors determined to fight to the death.

Thad had a problem. He wanted to attack Skoiyasi far enough away from the camp that the noise of the attack would not be heard by Skoiyasi's men, but he also knew that the longer he waited to attack, the greater the chances of the Indian's finely attuned senses picking up something amiss in the forest. The dilemma made him cautious, and consequently it was nearly an hour before he found a place he considered perfect for the ambush. The Indian was crouched by a stream bed, on one knee, examining a deer track, when Thad brought his rifle to bear and his finger tightened on the trigger.

For the rest of his life Thad would wonder what made Skoiyasi sense his presence, whirl and fire a bullet into the underbrush right by him. The movement caught Thad by surprise and his own shot went wide. Scarcely had the bullet left Skoiyasi's rifle when he dropped it and, quick as a panther, sprinted toward Thad, his tomahawk raised for action.

A mighty whoop escaped his lips, matched by a horrible screech from Thad as he stepped away from the tree to meet Skoiyasi's charge.

As the Seneca launched himself at Thad, Thad checked him by hurling his rifle broadside into his face. Skoiyasi knocked it aside with his forearm, but the force of the thrown weapon staggered him and gave Thad time to draw his hatchet.

"Come on, you big ugly moose," Thad growled at his old friend. "I used to lick you every day before breakfast when we were boys. I aim to do it for good right now."

Thad tested the balance of the hatchet he held in his right hand, and he felt great confidence. Had he not fought many battles in the last war, and done more than his share of killing without ever being overwhelmed? This was just one man, a man he had bested many times during their childhood. He would do it again, of that he was certain.

In a little clearing overlaid with the lush green canopy of a western New York midsummer, the two circled, each watching the other, both taking note of the treacherous footing on the forest floor.

Each had great respect for the other's abilities, so neither one expected to be able to take the other by surprise with a quick rush. They circled several times, waiting for a slip or an opening, something to give them an advantage. Thad noted a confidence in his old friend beyond that of the years they had been together. Skoiyasi must have been very successful on the warpath, he reflected.

Each had his eyes locked on the eyes of the other. Each waggled his weapon, adjusting his grip for comfort as they circled, right, always to their right, always looking for the offensive.

Strangely enough, there were no words between them. Neither told the other that he ought to quit now and go back to his family. After Thad's opening challenge, neither told the other that certain death was about to descend on him. There were no mind games going on. It seemed the entire purpose of their lives led up to this moment, when they would meet and one would destroy the other. There were no words necessary.

Skoiyasi charged forward suddenly. Thad stepped backward, then shifted his weight forward and brought his hatchet back, timed perfectly to split his Seneca brother in two. Skoiyasi stopped so suddenly that Thad realized it had been a bluff, meant to probe for a weakness.

What he didn't know was that Skoiyasi had already found one. As they circled, there was one moment when a shaft of sunlight through the canopy caught Thad's left eye, a distraction Skoiyasi was determined to use. They circled again, but this time Thad's path had changed, so that the shaft missed his eye. Two more times they circled, then Skoiyasi feinted forward again, drawing a response from Thad. Then the circling resumed.

This time the shaft of light hit just right.

Skoiyasi feinted left and struck to his right so swiftly that Thad had barely moved when the Indian's tomahawk glanced off his left collarbone and knocked him to his knees. Thad grunted with pain, and only his formidable courage and instincts allowed him to swing his hatchet as he went down, catching the Seneca on the back side of his lower left leg.

A strangled groan escaped from Skoiyasi's mouth. He tried to step forward and finish Thad with a mighty swipe of his tomahawk, but his wound made his left leg useless, and he sank to one knee.

Neither uttered a sound, although each gasped with pain. They swung their bloody weapons, and when the weapons met, Thad's flew away like a wounded duck and bounced in the dust, thirty feet away. Sensing the kill,

Skoiyasi brought his tomahawk back, and then, with all the force he could muster, swung it down toward Thad's skull.

Nothing in Big Oak's long experience as a woods warrior had prepared him for what he had just seen. When the warriors of the Ganiengehaka attacked, he had rushed toward the children to protect them from any last minute Seneca vengeance.

He needn't have bothered. The young, cocky, unseasoned Senecas were no match for the formidable Mohawk veterans. Disdaining the white man's rifle, the stealthy Mohawks sneaked nearly into the camp before they were detected, and with a wild fearsome whoop and a quick furious rush, were on the young Senecas before they could reach for their own weapons. Within a minute's time the four Senecas lay quivering scalpless in the dust of the clearing, and the Mohawks were busily shaking the blood out of the scalps before tucking them in their belts.

Big Oak stood aghast at the savage efficiency of Tagaowatha, who had run head-on into his quarry and dispatched him with one chop that had bitten through the young Seneca brave's upraised forearm and into the side of his neck. An artery had let loose a geyser of blood, and the Seneca had slid softly to the ground, but Tagaowatha did not witness his final death throes. In two steps he was on the back of the largest and strongest of Senecas, who had been getting the best of the portly Three Bears. Tagaowatha's forearm locked across the head of Three Bears's would-be conqueror and with a mighty twitch broke his neck just before Three Bears freed his knife hand and sank his blade deep into the Seneca's chest.

Louis and Jack each finished an opponent after brief, fruitless opposition. The children, watching the struggle from the tree trunks to which they were bound, cried out in terror. To them one set of devils had been traded for another. Painted Mohawks and painted Senecas were indistinguishable in their world full of ghastly horrors. The first set of devils had at least kept them alive. This new group was so ferocious, and had so easily killed the killers of their parents, that the children would feel fortunate if they weren't eaten on the spot.

Big Oak signaled for Louis and his men to vanish, while he cut the bonds of the children and tried to soothe them. "Don't be afraid. They're all—asleep now." He found himself hugging the girl and the younger boy, both of whom were hysterical, while the older boy clung to his hand so tightly his arthritic finger began to ache.

"It's all right. It's all right," Big Oak said over and over again. "Nobody is going to hurt you," he said, feeling like a cheat, knowing that they were already hurt far beyond the ability of his puny words to take the pain away.

Thad's life depended on the quickness and strength of his right hand. It had never failed him before and it would not fail him now. He grasped Skoiyasi's wrist and turned the tomahawk aside. The struggle turned his back to Skoiyasi for a moment. Skoiyasi reached around Thad's head with his left hand to gouge his eyes, but Thad tilted his head up, caught Skoiyasi's little finger in his teeth and bit down to the bone. The Indian roared with pain and tried to free his left hand.

Meanwhile, Thad continued to squeeze and twist Skoiyasi's right hand until the tomahawk dropped to the floor of the forest. Thad kicked it away just as Skoiyasi managed to free his painfully mangled finger from his mouth. Skoiyasi knew that Thad's left arm was useless. With his left hand Skoiyasi now reached into his waistband for his knife, but Thad could feel that move coming. He let go of Skoiyasi's right hand and battered the Seneca with a backhand blow as he brought his arm across his body.

Skoiyasi had slid the knife out and was shifting his grip so he could bring the knife up into Thad's belly. With his forearm across Skoiyasi's neck, Thad pushed hard with his legs. Skoiyasi's left leg was so badly injured that he had no balance. He fell over on his back with Thad on top of him, reaching for his left arm and finding it just before the Seneca could plant the blade underneath Thad's ribs.

Long minutes elapsed while they grappled. The great strength of Thad's right arm and the crippling of Skoiyasi's left leg neutralized any advantage the Seneca may have had with his two good arms. Skoiyasi tried pounding the back of Thad's neck and head with his right fist, but Thad shifted his body so that it pinned part of Skoiyasi's right arm beneath him, and he managed to put the weight of his legs on the Indian's wounded calf muscle, which made him cry out in pain and distracted him from his purpose.

The men grew weaker from the exertion, the pain, and the loss of blood, but they still had plenty of hatred and fight left in them when Big Oak found them. He wasted no time in kicking the knife out of Skoiyasi's hand. Skoiyasi continued to pummel Thad on the back of his neck and head, but he had no leverage. Thad let go of the Indian's left arm and set his ears ringing with a blow to the side of his head. Both were losing strength fast, and were continuing the fight on heart and hatred only.

"Get off him, Thad," Big Oak said calmly, but Thad did not hear him. "Thad, it's over!" Big Oak said firmly. For good measure, he clubbed Skoiyasi on the head with the butt of his rifle, not viciously, but hard enough to take the fight out of him.

Thad rolled off Skoiyasi, grunting with the pain. "Pa, I think—I think he near cut me in half."

Skoiyasi rolled over and struggled to his feet, but when he tried to run to where his tomahawk lay, his left leg caved in and down he went.

"Skoiyasi, my son." Big Oak said mildly as he picked up the tomahawk and the knife and slid them into his belt. "Sit still while I take care of Thad, or I'll blow your head off." Thad sat on a fallen tree trunk. Big Oak handed him his rifle, and Thad kept it trained on the Seneca while Big Oak ministered to the wound. "I know it hurts," he said, "but it's not as bad as it feels . . . I hope."

Skoiyasi said nothing, just sat on the ground giving his two adversaries poisonous looks through fierce, narrowed slits of eyes.

Now Big Oak turned his attention to Skoiyasi, taking care not to let himself come between the Seneca and the muzzle of his rifle, which Thad continued to train on Skoiyasi with his one good arm.

"Lay down on your belly," he said to Skoiyasi, but the young man refused to budge from his half-sitting, half-kneeling position. Big Oak grabbed him by the back of his neck and pushed him face forward to the ground. Skoiyasi resisted feebly. "Lost some blood, eh?" Big Oak observed. "If you weren't so light-headed, you'd a taken a poke at me, that's for sure."

He looked at the nasty gash in the Indian's calf, the muscle tissue awash in blood, and he shook his head. "I can clean it out. I can sew it up, but there's things in there might not heal like you want it to heal."

Skoiyasi growled and tried to push himself up, but Big Oak was sitting on his back and he was too weak to make much of an effort.

Big Oak washed out the wound as best he could, and stitched it shut with a needle and some black thread he used for repairing his clothes. Then he stood up and looked down at Skoiyasi, who was regaining his senses. The Indian rolled over and sat up, refusing to grimace, his lean face devoid of emotion.

Thad stood up, his arm in a sling that Big Oak had fashioned for him, his lips compressed with the pain of his wound. He walked toward Skoiyasi until he was within five feet of him. Then he looked down at him and spoke to him for the first time since the beginning of the fight.

"I'm sorry I did not kill you, my brother who is no longer my brother, murderer of women, kidnapper of children. I am surprised you took them with you instead of just roasting them and eating them. I loved you like only one brother can love another. My heart is broken to find out that my brother is a snake."

Skoiyasi gave Thad a look of pure hate, but his dignity did not leave him. He thought in silence for a few moments, and then he began to speak. "I was not mistaken about you, Little Oak," he said. "In the years since you left Tonowaugh, you have become a white man. You forget how the English have made us suffer, not just the warriors, but our women and children. Come to the village when the English have denied us trade goods and we have not gone out to get them ourselves. You will see hunger. You will see suffering. Your darling Kawia, desperate to feed her children, who could have been your children. Oh yes, I know how it was with you and Kawia. Do you think she has been silent about you all these years? She is a good woman, our Kawia, but once every few moons she will think of you, and ask me what I think about you. And when I tell her that you are nothing but a white man, she nods and she falls silent. Then she says, 'But he is a *good* white man.' And then I say, 'But still a white man,' and she nods.

"Those could have been your children starving because there were no trade goods. Would you then go out and look for English to kill yourself?"

"Not women and children."

"Your soldiers do not come out to fight us. They stay behind walls and think us stupid enough to charge against the big guns like they do. That leaves the farmers who cut down our woods and plant their crops, and then every year they cut down more woods and make their farms bigger and bigger and chase the game away. They are men, even if they are farmers. If they want to take our land, they will have to fight us for it, as we fought the other tribes to take it.

"You talk about women and children. Your silly white-man rules that you make up to suit yourselves. When you deny us the guns to hunt with, are you not making war on our women and children?" Skoiyasi snorted with disgust. "I do not know why I bother to say these things to you. For a moment I forgot, you are just a white man. You never understand, and you never learn anything except how to take what does not belong to you."

Abruptly, Skoiyasi stood up and began to walk toward him, but his left leg collapsed and dumped him to his knees. Big Oak walked over to him. "You will never make it back to Tonowaugh alone," he said.

Skoiyasi snarled. "I am not alone. My men will take me back."

Big Oak shook his head. "Your men all sleep."

Skoiyasi dropped his eyes and wondered if he had heard right. For a moment he thought his own thoughts, then his fierce eyes once again met those of Big Oak. "You did this?" he asked.

"Not I," Big Oak responded. "Although I would have."

"Who then, the filthy Mohawks?"

"It does not matter. They are dead and you will never make it home alone. We must take you."

"I'd rather crawl," he said. "And if you take me into the village, and I tell the people that four young warriors are dead, then you will never leave Tonowaugh alive."

"I have thought about that," Big Oak agreed. "Still, we are taking you back to Tonowaugh."

First, though, there was the matter of the children, who

were waiting with Louis in the camp of the dead Senecas. When the son of Gingego saw Thad in his bloody hunting shirt, his arm in a sling, and Skoiyasi hobbling in on the shoulder of Big Oak, he showed that sportsmanship was strictly an English virtue.

"Ah, the Seneca with big dreams," he said. "I'm afraid your band has deserted you. Deserted this world. I can't understand it. We came into camp and put out our hands and they handed us their scalps and fell over dead."

Skoiyasi's face did not betray him, but the sight of the four dead young men, lying still with the tops of their heads a mass of bloody gore, was hard to bear. The fresh bloody scalps, hanging from the Mohawks' belts, nearly unnerved him. But silence, he was certain, was the right thing at this time.

"Louis," Big Oak said. "I have never seen warriors like yours. The Ganiengehaka are a great nation, and your warriors are the mightiest of the Ganiengehaka. Now we must bring this—my Seneca son—back to his village. I do not think he will ever again lope down the warpath. It will be a long trip, as you can see. So we'd better get started right away."

Louis nodded. "Would you like us to care for the children?" He turned to the three still-shaking bundles of fear huddled together in the middle of the clearing.

"My brother, I do not think they wish to be around red men any more than they must. I have a friend who farms among the long lakes who could take care of them until we bring Skoiyasi home. I think we will have no problem," Big Oak explained.

"That is good, my brother," Louis replied. "Come back to the village and visit us soon. And be careful with this one. He may not be much of a leader"—cruelly, he turned to look at the four still bodies, with flies already infesting their bloody crowns—"but he is sly and he will try to kill you if you let your attention stray." He thought for a moment. "I would just kill him now and be done with it."

He turned to his warriors and spoke quietly to them. Within two minutes they had vanished from the clearing, heading east and leaving Big Oak and Thad with three terror-filled children and a bitter, crippled, would-be Seneca war chief.

❈26❈

THEY TOOK TURNS HELPING SKOIYASI ALONG the trail. For a few miles he walked, leaning on one, and then, for the next few miles, he leaned on the other. Whoever he leaned on carried an empty rifle, while the other kept a fully loaded rifle aimed at the heart of the Seneca rebel.

Thad was surprised to find that his shoulder injury was more painful than serious. Apparently the blade had deflected from his collarbone, bruising it, then hacking through some flesh. The wound had been bloody but it was healing nicely.

As they struggled onward, Thad found himself wishing that this adventure were ended, and that he was at home in Albany with his family. Between Skoiyasi's inflamed, painful leg, and the three children, progress was painfully slow. Big Oak and Thad regarded Skoiyasi as so bitter and dangerous that they dared not give much of their attention to the children, who certainly needed it.

Their names were William, Barbara, and Richard, and their ages were seven, eight, and ten. The first night, after he had bound Skoiyasi to the trunk of a small beech tree, Big Oak sat with Richard and explained how, as the oldest, he had to take care of his brother and sister. Pale and freckled, skinny and frightened, Richard did not want to take care of anybody, including himself, so it was up to Barbara.

"We have a good place to take you," Big Oak told her, "but you must help us get there. If your mother were here, I'm sure she would tell you to be strong. You must. If we take our eyes off that Indian for a moment, he will kill us all. Please help us."

She was nearly as tall as Richard, tanned and dark-haired, used to helping her mother around the house, and better able than her brothers to understand that they would never see their parents again. She took charge of the two boys and like a sheepdog herded them along the trail, so Big Oak and Thad could pay their full attention to Skoiyasi, who, not being in a cooperative mood, leaned a little more on his white father and half-white brother than he had to.

It took them several days before they struggled over the last hill into the familiar valley that George Hayes and his eight sons had turned into the finest farm in western New York. As they descended the hillside through a ripening cornfield into the valley, Big Oak found the road that led down to the plain, massive stone home where George and his late wife Ida had brought up eleven children. In front of the house stood a stout, stooped old man with a red face, waving his arms and berating three younger men in a voice that drifted up the hill to Big Oak and Thad.

"That there George?" Thad asked in amazement. "Looks like he aged quite a bit in the seven years since you brought me here."

"It's George all right, screamin' his fool head off about something probably no more important than a wormy apple."

In the midst of one particularly violent gesticulation, the

arm-waving suddenly stopped and his gaze froze on the six figures coming down along the road through the tall rows of pale green stalks, into the valley.

"Where in hell did you come from and what in hell do you want?" he hollered.

"Maybe his eyes ain't so good, Pa," Thad said. "Don't you know who we are, Mr. Hayes?" he hollered back as they came closer.

George took a few waddling steps up the road toward them. "I know who you are all right, you half-red miscreant," he snarled. "And it figures that do-gooder father of yourn 'd be a-carryin' in a Injun like he was a real person. And then them kids draggin' along behind ya. Look like the devil's leavin's, they do."

"Take him from me, will ya, Thad," Big Oak said, "and let me talk to George before he runs his mouth off one too many times. Jughead, will you take this rifle and keep it aimed at my friend here?" He handed his weapon to the tall man who he recognized as George Hayes's oldest son.

"Yeah, your friend," George interrupted. "Everybody's your friend. I don't know why—"

"George, will you walk with me for a minute?" Big Oak requested, locking arms with the old land baron and walking him toward the house.

"Let go of my arm, you're like one of those old political fools from New York."

"Okay, now listen to me, George. These children are all that's left of a family that got massacred a few days ago."

"Yeah, and I suppose that Seneca over there is the one that did the massacrin'?" George asked facetiously.

"Actually, George . . . he is. One of 'em anyway. The others are dead."

"Well then, let's make it unanimous," George muttered through clenched jaws.

"Well, I can't, George. I sorta helped to raise him. He's

like a son. We're taking him back to his village. After the way Thad chopped his leg up, I don't think he'll ever take the warpath again."

"Uh, well, then . . . chmmmm!" He hawked up some heavy gunk from his lungs and spat it into the cornfield. "I can shackle that buck in the barn while you and the rest come on in. You don't mind if I don't invite the Seneca in, do you?"

When Skoiyasi saw one of George's other sons walking toward him with a set of shackles, he tore himself free from Thad's grip and attempted to run. But before anybody could react and give chase, his injured left leg gave way and he collapsed.

Jughead and still another of George's sons started to run toward him, but Big Oak stopped them. Instead he walked up to Skoiyasi, who was on his knees in the dust, trying to crawl into the cornfield.

"No irons for you, Skoiyasi," he said, taking his arm and lifting him to his feet. "We will stop here only long enough to leave the children, then we will take you home."

If the Seneca felt any gratitude for Big Oak's intervention, he hid it well. The fear in his dark hooded eyes quickly turned back to black hatred. "Oh yes," he said. "You English believe you have conquered us, but there is war in the West, and there will come a time when you will come to me and beg me to spare your children."

"Thad," Big Oak said, "take care of your brother here. I will talk briefly with George, then we'd better be going."

A look of surprise came across the face of Big Oak's comrade-in-arms from another war more than fifteen years ago. "Sam!" he exclaimed. Big Oak's Christian name sounded strange to his ears, so seldom was it used. "You must stay for a while. Old friends cannot just pass through."

"We'll stop on the way back, perhaps a week or so from now. But now I need a favor from you."

The angry red color had faded from George's face. The bombast was mainly a pose. Folks who knew George Hayes were devoted to him, including the Onondagas in the village to the north, to whom he was related by his second marriage.

"I can deny you nothing, you old Injun lover."

"George, I know it's hard for you to understand, but this murderous Seneca really is like a son to me, and a brother to Thad, even though the two recently chopped each other up pretty good. The children saw their parents butchered before their eyes by the Seneca and his band. And yet I cannot say the wrong is all on one side, for the children's parents had no business being on that land, and there's no reason to believe the governor would push them off. Thad did a pretty good job on Skoiyasi's leg. He doesn't know it, but he'll be draggin' that leg around like a chain for the rest of his life.

"Will you take care of the children for us until we get back?"

The short, round farmer looked at the three children, who, out of the woods, surrounded by farmland, had recovered some of their composure.

"Well, you know, Rachel has only dropped one calf in the eight years we been together. We can use a few more around here. I'm tired a kissin' my grandkids good-bye before dark so they can head back up the valley. Let's see how they work out. I might like to keep 'em if they like stayin' here."

The two boys were still too demoralized to even bother listening to the conversation, but Barbara's eyes were alive as she picked up on the exchange between George and Big Oak. She was looking around the valley at the broad, cultivated fields that made her family's farm look like a weed patch, and the well-kept houses scattered along the lower hillsides above the valley. This little girl was a survivor, Big Oak thought. Already her mind was racing toward the future.

"Don't go just yet," George said, and turned toward the house. Rachel must have been watching from inside, because at that moment she opened the front door and walked out toward him, then toward the children. Tall and graceful in a light blue cotton dress, she looked down at the two boys, then at Barbara. The two boys looked away, as if the sight of any Indian were still too much for them to bear, but the girl looked her straight in the eye. She must have seen something there that she liked. She stretched out her hand, and Rachel took it and led her toward the house. The two boys followed, confused, sorry to leave the two men who had saved their lives, but pleased to be far away from the man who had led the raid on their home that had killed their parents.

George watched his Onondaga wife and the children enter his house, then turned to Big Oak.

"Hell of a thing, ain't it?" he said. "Damned Injuns."

Big Oak shook his head in wonder, a gesture George took as a sign of agreement. But it was George he wondered at; George, the man who hated all Indians like poison, all except the woman he married, and all except the people of the Onondaga village to the north, and all except any Indian that George managed to get to know. Well, Big Oak thought, considering the differences in the way the two races thought, maybe George had the right idea. Between the red and the white there was going to be a fight to the finish, and maybe there was no room for conscience when it came to people you didn't know.

By the time he and Thad had slung their packs over their shoulders and picked up their weapons, Big Oak had worked himself into a state of melancholy that did not begin to lift until they had put three hills between themselves and George Hayes's valley. He was miffed with George, and men like him, but he was also annoyed with Skoiyasi, who was putting so much weight on him and Thad that he was driving them to exhaustion. Finally, at the top of one ridge line, he gave Skoiyasi a push that sent him tumbling into the dust.

"I know what you're doing," he growled at the Seneca. "Think of this, my son," he said, putting an ironic twist on the word "son." "If we leave you here, you will never see your family again. You have no rifle. You have no weapons. You have only one leg that works. You will die in the forest."

"What good am I to my family with one leg?"

"You'll have two if you take care of that wound. Meantime, I want you to stop leanin' all over me or I'll shove you down some mountainside and let the buzzards find you."

Skoiyasi showed his stone face, the one most Indians showed most whites most of the time. He had to remember that Big Oak was just another white man and that Thad had chosen to be Thad, not Little Oak.

And he had to get home, and get better, so he could fight again. To do that, he would have to lean on his onetime father and his one-time brother, but not too hard, or it might make them angry. His helplessness filled him with fury, made him want to die with his hands locked around Big Oak's throat. But now was a time to live, not to die, so step after painful step he made his way, on Big Oak's and Thad's shoulders, across the country of the Finger Lakes. He was so dependent upon them, he realized, that he could not even bother to watch for an opportunity to grab a rifle and kill one of them. What was the use, if he could not get home? He burned with anger, and sought a way to avenge himself on these arrogant men.

And then, two days journey from the Genesee River, it

came to him. There were still people in Tonowaugh who considered him an important man, and many of the people in Tonowaugh still blamed Big Oak and Thad for the French/Caughnawaga raid on the village and the massacre of most of its inhabitants. Nearly everyone living there today had lost relatives in that massacre seven years ago.

He would behave better to Big Oak and Thad these next two days, make them think he still saw them as family. When they arrived in Tonowaugh, he would invite them to his home for dinner. And while Kawia was feeding them, he would gather his allies outside, and they would kill the white man and the half-white man.

The next morning the lines of angry strain had disappeared from Skoiyasi's mouth. He did not say much, but he leaned lightly on Big Oak as they made their way along the final low ridge lines that led to the Genesee River, and Tonowaugh.

"Your leg seems to be hurting you less," Big Oak said.

Skoiyasi gave Big Oak a mild glance but said nothing. At the midday meal and rest, he ate what they gave him without comment but did not grab angrily. Both Thad and Big Oak were aware of the change but they said nothing to him. They came down from the final ridge and found themselves in the familiar dense lowland forest close to the village.

"Do you think you can make it in from here, Skoiyasi?" he asked.

The question caught the Seneca by surprise. At first he decided upon silence, but when he realized Big Oak was ready to leave him there, he decided to speak.

"Why would you leave me here? Tonowaugh was your home. Kawia would wish to see you."

"I don't think so," Big Oak answered.

"It is wrong for you to leave me here. It is a long way to the village on one good leg."

Big Oak flashed a knowing smile. "You could make it to the village without any legs, Skoiyasi. I know you," he said.

Thad walked close to Skoiyasi. "I will always carry the memory of when we were brothers. I would give almost anything to have us still be brothers."

It was a moment of weakness Skoiyasi had been waiting for, but he did not have the words to take advantage.

"You must not leave me here like this," he said in a soft voice. But Big Oak and Thad had turned and were already into their long-legged lope, down the trail headed east.

Skoiyasi looked around and found a long thick stick to use as a crutch. Now why hadn't they given me a stick to use? he wondered. Then they wouldn't have had me leaning on them all the way home. But of course, they had feared that a stout stick could prove a fierce weapon in the hands of a Seneca warrior.

There would be no great honors for him when he reached his village. The people would want to know what happened. How could he boast of the farm he destroyed and the children he captured, when he had lost all his braves to the brothers they sometimes hated, the Mohawks. The old ones would criticize him for fighting with the English, especially outside Seneca country, and trying to break up the Iroquois union. His braves had not been from his village, so at least he would not have keening, wailing mothers screaming at him. Still, it would be a bad night for him in Tonowaugh. Some of the villagers might even accuse him of lying. "Mohawks attacking our braves? Never!" they would say.

Better not to tell them anything now. Tell them his braves decided to go home and await word on the next great battle against the English.

That's what he would tell them.

Slowly, his left leg hurting like fire on the inside and itching on the outside, he started for home.

❊27❊

On THE WAY BACK EAST BIG OAK AND THAD stopped overnight at the Hayes house, just long enough to determine that the three children were settled in. In a few days' time they had recovered considerably from their ordeal. The night before, neither of the boys had awakened screaming in the middle of the night, and their sister had taken over the chicken coop with plans for doubling the egg output of the chickens by getting rid of all the roosters but one. Their ordeal was not over, not by a long shot, but at least the healing process may have begun.

In some ways things were better for them, and they knew it. The presence of a huge family of confident sons, daughters, and inlaws, the golden sweep of the fertile valley, and the calm assurance of their new Onondaga "mother" made them feel a security they had never felt when they lived on a tiny farm with dark, sinister forests closing in on them from all sides.

The children were obviously glad to see their two rescuers when they arrived for the evening. But the next morning, when it was time to go, the two boys wept so bitterly that Big Oak had to promise he would be back first chance he had. Barbara looked at him sadly, as if she knew he didn't mean it. Big Oak was forced to promise that indeed he would be back to visit them, and that when he returned, he would bring presents. She nodded and looked relieved, as if the promise of presents proved his sincerity.

He and Thad then continued on their way east to Albany. This time they did not stop at the village of Louis and George and their mother. Thad had made it clear to his father that he wanted to get home to his family, and Big Oak was anxious to see Cilla.

As they loped down the trails that were so familiar to them, it occurred to Big Oak that Thad was unusually silent and serious, despite the prospect of going home. Although it was still summer, there was that touch of something in the air that central New York feels when the first fingers of autumn reach around summer's corners. Maybe Thad had felt those fingers. The last night out from Albany, sitting on opposite sides of a campfire munching on some early apples the Hayeses had given them as part of their trail provisions, Big Oak asked Thad what was on his mind.

Thad leaned back and looked up through a hole in the oak canopy at the stars, so crisp and clear to a young man with keen eyesight. He flexed his arm and felt fortunate. The wound he had received from Skoiyasi had proved to be little more than an inconvenience, though the painful collarbone bruise would serve for another week or two as a reminder of the struggle.

"Next to my family, there is nothing I love so much as the trail," he said. "But tomorrow is the end of it, Pa. I have no right to run around the woods fighting Indians and gettin' involved in things that are not my business when I have a family to take care of."

"We're in the middle of an Indian rebellion, son. Somebody has got to fight it or we'll be manning the walls of Albany again like they used to way back when."

Thad smiled then, because he knew his father was tweaking his tail. "I fought the last war, Pa. You fought the last two wars. Let the army fight this one without us. It's too deadly out there. I like the fireplace in a brick home near the Hudson River. It's not smoky like the longhouse. The wind doesn't howl through the cracks like the longhouse. The Indians don't come roarin' down from Canada in the middle of the night to whet their tomahawks on your family's skulls. And there are no Jared Meaches lurking behind some tree looking to even old scores.

"I like eating with a fork off china. I guess when you sent me to that reverend in Oquaga to school me, you kinda spoiled me."

Big Oak didn't reply. At least not right away. Instead he pulled his pipe from his pack, filled it with tobacco, lit it, and drew on it in silence. They stared at each other for a while across the flickering fire.

Then he smiled. "You know," he said, "when a man starts gettin' old, he kinda likes knowing that his offspring are gonna be close by."

"Which means what?"

"Which means that maybe there's two of us won't be travelin' so much as we used to be."

"But what about that Indian rebellion you're so all-fired worried about?"

"I'm not as good as I used to be, so maybe they don't need me."

Thad laughed. "Sometimes, Pa, when I hear the things they say about you, and then I remember some of the mistakes you made on the trail, I get the feelin' that you were never as good as you used to be."

Now Big Oak laughed, silently, as if there might be Chippewas hanging out in the nearby woods. "Son, the things they've said about me, nobody was ever that good."

"Then why'd they say 'em?"

"Well," Big Oak said, pulling on an earlobe, "they had to believe that someone besides the Indians knew what the hell they were doin' out in the woods. They knew I lived with the Indians. They knew there were Indians out there who were my brothers, so they figured I knew what I was doin'. And sometimes they were right."

"And most of the time?"

"Most of the time I just made it up as I went along, and usually it come out all right. You oughta know that. I seen you do a lot of the same thing. Pretty good at it too. If you were to stay out there in the woods long enough, they'd start sayin' the same things about you. 'Chip off the old block,' they'd say. 'Only better,' they'd say, 'cause he's got Injun blood in him.' What do you think of that?"

"I'd rather they say, 'Hey, you remember that half-breed get of Sam Watley? Can you believe that boy had the nerve to marry a girl in Albany and settle down in trade like a reg'lar white man? And would ya believe he done pretty good at it? Hear he had a pretty big family too. And they all look white, so now there's injuns all over Albany and you can't even tell the heathens from the Christians no more.'"

In the village of Tonowaugh, the waters of the Genesee River brought news with the coming of the frosts. The news did not announce more great victories of the Ottawas and the Chippewas over the English. Nor did news of defeats at the hands of the English come to the ears of the waiting Senecas.

What they heard, if they listened correctly to the visitors who came down from Lake Ontario, was a quiet petering out of the siege at Detroit. And Detroit, after all, was the heart of this war. Like canoes set free on a gently rolling river, Pontiac's men drifted away from him: Hurons, Potawatomies, Chippewas, and even some of his own remaining Ottawas. One sad day in the middle of autumn, the great chief sent a message to Major Gladwin in Detroit, announcing his intention to lift the siege.

Alone in his lodge on the Genesee, Skoiyasi tried to understand what it meant for his people, for his family, for himself. The day he had dragged himself out of the forest into his village, he was surprised to find that his people did not scorn him for his failure.

And they knew he had failed. By the fire that night, he spared himself not at all, nor did he glorify his accomplishments. They had raided in the east, he said, burned a farm in the lake country, he said, and then a small Mohawk force had wiped out his band. Little Oak, he told them, had fought against him and delivered this wound. He had wounded Little Oak too, but not as badly.

He did not speak about his treatment at the Hayes farm or his attempt to entice Big Oak and Thad into the village for their capture and death. He said only that for now he had fought all he could and that he was going to rest and try to get better. He asked for no medical help, saying that his wife, Kawia, would take care of him.

Inside the lodge, he and Kawia spoke. The young woman worried that the village did not have enough supplies for the winter.

"We need to trap beaver and trade," she told him. "We need for the men to hunt the deer, for we did not harvest enough corn, beans, and squash to see us through the winter." Skoiyasi looked around the lodge, at the various vegetables hanging down from the rafters, and he knew that what she said was true.

"Big Oak and Little Oak wanted to trade with us. Why did you make them our enemy?"

"They *are* our enemy," he insisted.

"How can they be our enemy when they would give us fair trade for our goods?" she asked.

In spite of the pain from his healing wound, he explained patiently. "We must have our land. Without our land we will have nothing to trade. Little beaver remains where we are. We get our goods by trading Huron skins, Ottawa skins, Miami skins, Chippewa skins. The whites have too much power over us. There is much that I do not yet understand. We need them to live, but they are deadly to us. There was a time when we did not need them to live."

"Is there a place we can go that is close enough to them to trade for their goods, yet far enough away that we will not lose our land to them?"

Skoiyasi did not answer. He was surprised to hear her talk about leaving the land of their fathers. And yet on the long way home, even while he snarled at his captors, he had wondered about that very thing. He was confused. Time after time through the summer he had seen the English defeated and humbled by their clever Indian foe. And now with winter coming on, the English were still strong enough to hold Detroit. Rumors were beginning to spread about a force as big as some of the armies that fought in the last war being raised to go out and punish the warriors that had fought the English during the summer. If the rumors were true, then the English were, as Big Oak had insisted, too powerful for them.

And so, as his wound healed, Skoiyasi felt the winter chill coming on through the cracks in the elm-bark covering of his lodge. His eyes focused on the fire for hour after hour, and his mind wrestled with questions: How to defeat them, or, how not to need them as much, or, how far did he have to go to get away from them? And as he thought, his anger faded.

He remembered a story told to him by Little Oak's grandfather, Kendee. One time, he and some other warriors went on a raid deep into the land of the Abnakis. Although the Ganonsyoni considered themselves far superior to the Algonquian Abnakis, this time everything went wrong on the raid. The Abnakis were ready for the Senecas when they arrived at the village, and met them in the middle of the night with a hail of bright gunfire. Miraculously, nobody was hurt on either side, but the Seneca raiding party fled in disgrace before the pursuing, shrieking Abnakis.

All the Senecas fled, that is, except for Kendee, who slipped in the slime of a mudhole. He struggled to his feet and scrambled desperately for his rifle, then slipped down again and found himself staring up at the muzzles of five Abnaki rifles.

"Another Seneca," Kendee told Skoiyasi, "might have called the Abnakis a pack of lowly dogs and lamented that he would have to end his life at the stake of such an unworthy enemy." But Kendee decided at that moment that he wanted to live. Rising to his feet, he began to walk toward the Abnaki village with such determination that the Abnakis saw no need to bind him or kick him or cuff him. They had a warrior of the Longhouse to torture. "Let's see how mighty he is when we drive splints of pine into his belly and set them afire," they said.

When he entered the village, they began to prepare for a good old, Iroquois-style prisoner burning. Except for a handful of braves who intended to chase the Senecas all the way back to the Genesee, the entire village was out to take part in the torment. Particularly, Kendee said, the women were out for his blood.

He asked them if he could speak before the torture began, and when they said yes, he began to tell them how clever they had been to be so prepared for the raid. He had been on many raids with his fellow Seneca braves.

Never had they failed to raise havoc in the unfortunate village they attacked. Never had they taken a backward step before an enemy. The Abnaki had taught the Seneca a lesson they would never forget. They had earned the respect of the entire Longhouse. It would be a privilege, he declared, to test his courage against their torments.

On and on he went in this vein, for nearly an hour. By the time he was through speaking, there was not a man or woman there who wanted to see him die. His earnest admiration for his enemy had won their hearts.

"They tied me up and threw me in a lodge and spent a long time deciding what they wanted to do to me," Kendee said. "All that time, I was hoping the braves who were out trailing the Senecas would not find them. They had sent too few to do the job. I was sure that if they ever caught up with them, the Guardians of the Western Door would have cut them all to pieces, and then my life would not have been worth a single mussel shell.

"Fortunately, their braves came back empty-handed, pleased with themselves for having driven off the Seneca raiders, who haunted the dreams of all the tribes of the East. So when one woman from a high-ranking family reminded the village that she needed a new husband to replace the one who had lost a fight with a bear, the village agreed. For three months I was an Abnaki. In fact, I was the happiest Abnaki in the village. When they began to trust me, I began to hoard little bits of things I would need later on, and when I had saved enough, I awaited a certain opportunity, and one morning, when I was supposed to be out fishing, I lit out for home.

"I don't think I stopped running from the shores of Lake Champlain to the banks of the Genesee River. When I arrived at the village, my wife thought I was a roaming spirit and she nearly went mad.

"My son," he told Skoiyasi, "I never again fought the Abnakis."

"Because you were afraid of what they'd do to you if they caught you?"

Kendee shook his head. "Because I truly did admire them. I would have never told the people in Tonowaugh. They would have thought I'd gone mad.

"There is no shame in survival," Kendee had told Skoiyasi. "Life is to be lived, not to be thrown away for glory. Live in dignity, yes, but above all, live.

"Don't worry," he said. "Those who know how to live, when the time comes, also know how to die."

Kendee was the wisest man Skoiyasi had ever known. He was no war chief. He was no sachem. He did not quest for power. But around the council fire, when he spoke, the other men leaned forward a little more to hear what he had to say. When he did not speak, which was often, the leaders of the community often asked him for his thoughts.

Long after the pain of the Tonowaugh massacre had faded from Skoiyasi's dreams, he continued to miss Thad's grandfather. And now, faced with the need to make decisions, he summoned Kendee's ghost and asked for its thoughts.

As the fire danced before his eyes throughout the autumn, Skoiyasi thought less about the honor of the Seneca nation and more about the future of his children. There was no room for anger when it came to saving his family. Anger clouds judgment. Anger makes wrong moves. He had to make the right moves. In the bitter winter that followed, Skoiyasi made his passage from war to wisdom.

In Albany, Thad was drawing his own conclusions about life. On a clear, crisp November morning he walked into his father-in-law's mercantile establishment and saw that, once again, the store was one clerk short. Their best clerk when the store was crowded and the customers were clamoring was also their hardest-drinking clerk, and prone to miss about one out of every four Monday mornings. Thad had won the heart of his father-in-law by making it his business to come in every Monday morning. If Wendel's prize clerk was absent, and the day looked like it would be a busy one, Thad would don an apron, take his place behind the counter and sell goods.

On this day, Thad was about to remove his coat when he heard a "Psssst!" from the balcony loud enough to make the few customers in the store jump. "Thad, I need for you to come up here . . . please." The please was always an afterthought with Wendel, more like the completion of a command than a polite request.

Thad took the stairs two at a time and confronted Wendel, who was sitting at his accounts desk in his open balcony office. Thad did not sit down. Using a trick that he had learned from the aggressive and domineering Dutchman, Thad stood over him so that Wendel would have to look up at him when he spoke.

"The West has quieted down a lot, yah?" he asked, and Thad knew that a moment he had dreaded was upon him. "It is time that you and your father went trading with the savages again, I think."

Thad looked down at his father-in-law and took a moment to respond, not because he didn't know what to say, but to let the older man know he had been thinking carefully about it. "Not yet, Dieter," he answered.

Long ago he had decided that he would work with his father-in-law only as a partner, not as an employee, and that therefore it would not do to address the man with formal titles of respect. The merchant, on his part, viewed the accomplishments of Thad and his father with awe, so he did not demand rank.

"Pontiac may have given up. His warriors may have gone

home, but there are Senecas and Shawnees and Delawares that haven't quit yet. I'm afraid that two traders with a string of canoes wouldn't have much of a chance if they ran into a flock of angry Lenni Lenape starved for trade goods."

"That's just it, my boy. Now is the time to go, when they *need* things that nobody else is bringing to them."

"They need 'em all right. Need 'em so bad that they won't bother to trade for them, they'll just take 'em, along with our hair."

"What does your father say?" The astute Dutch merchant had noticed that the elder Watley was more likely to crave a risky adventure than his son. Wendel could not understand it. The boy was half Indian. What was the good of being half Indian if you didn't long for woodland adventures?

"What does my father say?" Thad laughed. "I haven't seen my father in two weeks, since he and Cilla got married by that Congregationalist preacher. They up and headed for the woods, and I haven't seen them since."

"Do you think something bad has happened?" asked the Dutchman, who was extremely fond of Big Oak.

"To be honest, I'm not sure I expected them back before spring. They went west to visit her people. He feels like I do. With or without Pontiac, there's still a war goin' on."

Wendel shrugged his shoulders. He was annoyed. To him, traders were people who should go out and trade, otherwise they were useless. But since Thad and Big Oak were not his employees, and since they did not take orders from anyone, not chiefs, not generals, not governors, he knew better than to expect them to take orders from him.

Big Oak woke up long after the sun. He had gotten home very late after having walked a long trail in search of game. Only on the way home, in the last light, had he finally stalked and bagged his deer. It was a big one. He had field-dressed it, rigged a sledge, and pulled it home over the snow-covered trail.

Cilla had been thrilled by the appearance of fresh game. In a short while she had a savory mixture of venison and vegetables boiling in the kettle, filling their lodge with a delicious fragrance. But Big Oak was so exhausted from pulling the sledge up and down hills in the dark that he had immediately fallen asleep.

When he awoke, he was pleased to see Cilla bustling around, stirring the warm coals into flame and piling on more wood to heat up the stew that had been simmering overnight. The smell of good food was like a potion to his famished soul. She saw him move and leaned over to touch his face.

Big Oak sat up and silently held her hand. How had he survived all these years with that empty place in his chest? The answer was that only when Cilla filled it had he noticed how empty it had been, and how good it felt now that it was filled. He was taking no chances with this one. No doubt Thad's father-in-law would soon be badgering him and Thad to head for the frontier to open trade negotiations with the Ottawas. No thanks. He had had enough of the Ottawas to last him seven lifetimes. He and Thad would wait for the spring, and only then, *if* the forests were quiet, would they do some trading in the West.

Before they had begun their journey to Cilla's Tuscarora village, Big Oak scouted out a place well north of Albany, which he had first noticed during the last war on the march up to Lake George, when it was still called Lac St. Sacrement.

It was a hillside clearing with a long view of a wooded valley, a home for a woodsman if ever there was one. Winter or no winter, he was ready to start building as soon as they returned to Albany. When he had told his idea to Cilla, she had simply replied, "I will help," and after what they had been through together, he had no doubt that she would do more than her share.

❧28❧

HE HAD LOST, BUT HE HAD GAINED. NEVER again would he be a mighty Seneca warrior who could run fifty miles in a day, then fight a battle at sunset. His leg injury had seen to that.

Now healed, it would support him all day in long walks through the woods. But his running gait was a lagging limp. Deprived of his warrior ambitions, he devoted his thoughts to more practical concerns, like survival for his family.

It was spring. The dust in his nostrils told him that the trails were at last drying out from the snow that had covered them all winter.

A week ago he had made his final transaction with the whites in the crown colony of New York. He had traveled east alone until he had found a fine log cabin. He had lain in the woods almost two days before he judged the right moment had come, meaning that all adults and children were out of the house and out of sight.

What he found in the house was the finest, most beautiful rifle he had ever seen. He had taken it, a powder horn, a couple of bars of lead, a bullet mold, and all the powder he could carry, but he took nothing else.

And now he and his family had traveled south until they had found the Allegheny River. Avoiding Fort Pitt, they would travel the valley until it became the valley of the Spay-lay-wi-theepi. Somewhere along the way he would find the Mingoes, a mixed people made up of emigrants from several tribes but led largely by Senecas. Among them, he knew, he would find a home, far from the white men, yet close enough to trade, when and if peace should finally come.

The winter had not been a hard one, in spite of the absence of trade with the English. Skoiyasi had had little activity while his leg healed, and little activity after, while he brooded and ate huge quantities of food. Consequently he had put on enough weight that his painfully angular cheekbones had smoothed out into a rounder, softer configuration. He had a bit of a gut too, not like the big-bellies, as some tribes called their older, stouter ex-warriors, but like a powerful bear about to go into hibernation.

During this long winter, Kawia grew up. Her family having been wiped out in the massacre seven years before, and Skoiyasi a silent, brooding hulk by the fire, she found herself making more and more decisions. It was she who had at last decided it might be a good idea if the family moved west. Skoiyasi talked about getting away from the whites, but she didn't believe he would move without prodding. Hating the English had become so much a part of his life that he wanted to live close by them so he could strike a blow every now and then. She did not want to raise her children in a lodge full of bad feelings. She waited until she thought he was ready, and then one night she struck.

"You would not really consider moving us into Mingo country, would you?" she asked as if it were an absurd idea.

"Why not?" he responded indignantly, and suddenly the absurd idea had become reality.

During the last weeks of winter, Skoiyasi began to spend

much of his time in the woods, hunting game for Kawia to fashion into food and clothing for the trail. By the time spring had come, the family was ready to travel. Skoiyasi was not surprised that nobody wished to join them in their journey west. The village seemed to have sunk into a morass of apathy as they waited for something to happen that might tell them what they should do.

Maybe the king would hold back the frontier farmers like he said he'd do. Maybe a new chief would arise in the Longhouse who would drive the English back to the shores of the eastern river. Maybe the spirits would sicken the whites with their own disease. Or maybe the whites would just go away. The old men smoked and dreamed. The young men waited. Skoiyasi and Kawia made ready to depart.

The day came to take leave of their home. In the gray mist of a cloudy spring morning, they said good-bye quickly to their friends, packed their goods and children in their canoe, and stroked it gently out to the middle of the Genesee River.

"It is sad to leave our home," Kawia said.

"That is not our home," her husband replied. "We lost our home long ago. This Tonowaugh is a village of strangers. Our Tonowaugh is a village of ghosts. We cannot live with ghosts, and these strangers have forgotten how to live, or they would be with us."

Kawia knew he was right. They did not speak another word until mealtime.

Two days later they shifted their burden from the canoe bottom to their backs and set their feet on the trail west. He was proud of his two older children. Aged six and five, they were tireless on the trail, carrying their packs without complaint. As for his wife, small as she was, she was capable of carrying great burdens in addition to the baby girl.

Nevertheless, somewhere along the western bank of the Allegheny he stopped his family and told them that he needed to get something for them to speed their progress.

"I will be back by morning," he told them. And he retraced his steps about seven miles to a farm they had passed in the first hours of the day. He'd seen several horses grazing, and he was determined to extract one last penalty from the English for the sake of his family.

In the light of a half-moon he saw them. The lights were out in the cabin, which was not necessarily good. A man may be more wary lying in bed in the still of the night than awake with a mug of toddy, talking to his wife. He ignored the one that looked swiftest for the one that looked strongest and gentlest, tied a makeshift leather thong bridle on him, and led him into the woods.

Two hours later, around dawn, he found his family where he left them, put the two boys and some of their baggage on the horse, and started them off immediately. He wanted no fight with white men now if he could help it. He wanted nothing at all to do with them, ever again. Except for a little trade now and then. Damn them. Two of the very few English words he knew and understood. Damn them.

Tired as he was, they made good time that day, and the next, giving Fort Pitt a wide berth and then moving along the flood plain of the Spay-lay-wi-theepi, heading west, almost a year after Big Oak and Thad had made their fateful western trek.

But Skoiyasi had a better idea than the two traders of where he would find red men; and he knew they would be Mingoes. There would be kinsmen among them, men from among the Guardians of the Western Door, guarding the door no more. He would make a new life among them, one without the English constantly pressing down around them. He had done the right thing by not waiting, as his

Mohawk brothers had done, until white farmers, traders, and soldiers were all around him, killing him with their pimple sickness and their rum.

The morning of the second day after he had stolen the horse, he sent his family on their way and backtracked to see if they were being followed. There was no sign of pursuers. The farmer either thought his horse had gone off by itself or was afraid to take to the woods in pursuit. Skoiyasi turned around and walked as fast as he could, back up the trail to his family. At times like this he hated Thad for having taken his speed away from him. But that was past. He would never see Thad or Big Oak again, and that was good.

As he turned a bend in the river, three days later, he emerged from the woods to one of those beautiful long prospects to be found up and down the Ohio River valley. Silhouetted against the new spring green hills were his two boys, seated erect on the fine plow horse they rode, being led by Kawia, the proud wife of a Seneca warrior. His heart swelled, and he saw for him and them a future wide open and free.

For a moment he stopped and fixed his eyes on the woman who had chosen him over the rich half-white boy. He was proud of himself for having won a woman smart enough to make such a fine choice. The older of the boys looked down at his father from atop the horse. "Look at me," the proud look said. And the father looked. Two big strong boys. Leaving their village brought no tears from them. This was an adventure. He had told them to keep an eagle eye out for their ancient enemies, the Eries, and they did, with all the joy a warrior feels when he is on the warpath.

Fine boys, he thought. Maybe they would grow to ride horses the way the men did on the other side of the big river. Maybe he, Skoiyasi, would ride. Astride a horse, an injured leg no longer mattered, he thought. Perhaps the warpath still lay in his future.

Kawia touched his hand as if she could read his thoughts. In fact Skoiyasi had no doubt that at times she could. No, said the touch, the time has come to use your thoughts, and not your strong arm, to take care of your family.

In Albany, Thad stood at the head of his father-in-law's massive dining room table. Seated around that table were a garrulous, malodorous, leather-clad group of men with mugs of beer in their hands, their eyes on the only young merchant in all of Albany that they respected. He knew the dangers, he knew the rewards, and he was ready to gamble on them.

"My father and I," he explained to them, "know who needs what. And we have purchased goods that will satisfy your customers. You will see that we give you a little rum, but not enough to drive them as crazy as they would like. The rum is not for trade, more like a gift to them for doing business with us. But we will treat them fair and we will not get them very drunk. We will guard our good reputation. Everybody thinks that traders are all a bunch of scum."

"They're right, of course!" shouted one burly adventurer with a scar on the side of his nose where he had once cut himself trying to shave with a dull bayonet after a long, bad night. The men roared at his remark.

"For the most part," Thad jabbed back. "But we know about you men and we're betting on you to do the job. The time is right. They need our goods. They will have the beaver to pay us with. You will do your trading as quickly as possible, come on back to Albany as quickly as possible. Beaver will be high, we will get good prices for them, you'll get a good commission, and only then will we know our strategy for the rest of the year. You will tell us what they

need and when they need it. We will furnish you the goods
and turn you back out on the trail before you have had
time to drink and whore all your money away."

"Don't bet on it!" shouted a stumpy runt with only half
an ear on the left side of his head. "We can go broke
quicker 'n stupider than you think."

Thad joined the ringing laughter and waited patiently,
like a Mohawk in council, for the noise to die down.

"We will treat you right. Those of you who do not know
me, know my father, and you trust him."

"Where is that murderous father of yours?" roared one of
the brawny traders.

"Out in the woods, where else?" Thad asked. He knew
that he had answered the question with another one. The
expressions on their faces demanded more.

"He's got a new wife."

"Oh-ho!" they cried. "He ran away to the woods to escape her!" another shouted, and the rest sent a roar of
laughter through the open windows, which caught the ears
of nosy neighbors.

"No, she's with him. He swears he's not coming back to
town for at least another month. He says no man should be
without a woman as long as he was. He says he will die
before he ever lets it happen again."

More laughter. "Your father is a great man. I raise my
mug to him," said the runt, to the agreement of all. "She's a
young one, I hope."

"A young one," Thad said.

"I hope she doesn't kill him," the brawny trader declared.

With the help of Thad and a couple of men from Albany
whom Big Oak paid, the cabin had gone up quickly. It was
chinked tight, had a stone chimney at each end, two fire-
places, an upstairs sleeping area, and glass windows. It also
had a porch that looked east toward the Hudson River

valley. It was still a bit chilly to sit on the porch whittling in the red twilight, but Big Oak had dreamed of doing exactly that since they had started building, so there he sat, shivering in the cold wind, whetting his knife and remembering great hunts in the Genesee country around Tonowaugh.

"Sem!" came a voice through the open door. He turned and looked at her. He could smell the stew steaming hot in the fireplace, and thought about this wonderful young woman so determined to make a new future for herself. "Food," she said simply. He put down his stone, rose from his chair and walked into the hearth-warmed kitchen.

"I want to know what you are called," she had said to him not long after they had arrived in Albany. "Not Seneca name. English name."

"I am Sam Watley," he told her. To her that meant Semwadly, and he had to explain that Sam was all she needed. She had soaked up English like a hungry sponge, and if it came out of her with a rickety syntax, she made it melodic, and expressive.

"Sem," she said when they were seated at the table, "something there is to tell."

"What to tell?" he asked, slipping into her rhythm without a second thought.

"There be a papy coming." She smiled.

He nodded. "That be good. Soon back to Albany so Katherine can take care of you."

"And what you stay in the woods without me?"

He laughed. "Of course not. I will go too."

"What for you do in Albany?"

"Why, work on the business with Thad and Dieter."

The idea of business was something Cilla had still not quite grasped.

"I hear 'business.' I do not understand what is business.

You want to trade? You get the goods and go out and trade. What for need business?"

"You stay around it long enough, you will understand what is business."

"When for we come back out here?"

"After you have the baby."

"That is good. I need to fish. But wait. I cannot go. I must plant first."

"No plant this year, Cilla. Not until after the baby comes."

"How we get corn and squash to eat, then?"

"We will buy them in the marketplace."

Cilla had seen the marketplace. She laughed. "English women no work hard enough." She laughed again, like music, and refilled Sam's plate. "Sem, I want to be English woman."

"I don't blame you," he said. "We'll pack tomorrow, and leave the day after. I don't want you to get so big that you can't make the walk to Albany." It was more than forty miles.

"Ha, Sem! Tuscarora woman walk trail till she have baby. Have baby, cut cord, and walk again. We are strong women, Semwadly, you understand me?"

Sam pushed his chair back from the table, leaned it back on two legs and let his mind picture her strong rippling shoulders gleaming in the sunlight as she dug her canoe paddle into Lake Huron and made the water boil in deep eddies past their canoe, with Chippewa bullets skipping through the water all around them.

He looked across the table and smiled.

Strong woman indeed, he thought. Sweet woman too.

THE FIRST FRONTIER SERIES
by Mike Roarke

At the dawn of the 18th century, while the French and English are locked in a battle for the northeast territory, the ancient Indian tribes begin a savage brother-against-brother conflict—forced to take sides in the white man's war—pushed into an era of great heroism and greater loss. In the tradition of *The Last of the Mohicans, The First Frontier Series* is a stunningly realistic adventure saga set on America's earliest battleground. Follow Sam Watley and his son Thad in their struggle to survive in a bold new land.

THUNDER IN THE EAST (Book #1)
_____ 95192-2 $4.50 U.S./$5.50 Can.
SILENT DRUMS (Book #2)
_____ 95224-4 $4.99 U.S./$5.99 Can.

Coming Soon:
SHADOWS ON THE LONGHOUSE
(Book #3)